the
careful
undressing
of
love

corey ann haydu

DUTTON

To Frank

with all my love

Dutton Books
An imprint of Penguin Random House LLC
375 Hudson Street
New York, NY 10014

CIP is available

Printed in the United States of America

9780399186738

1 3 5 7 9 10 8 6 4 2

Design by Theresa Evangelista

Text set in Adobe Caslon Pro

I give you an onion.
It is a moon wrapped in brown paper.
It promises light
like the careful undressing of love.

—carol ann duffy, "valentine"

the careful undressing of love

prologue

When the Minute of Silence hits, I have a glass vase in my hands and I almost drop it.

We have been doing it for years, at 10:11 every Tuesday morning, but it takes me by surprise sometimes, still.

We pause, the dozen of us who woke up early to finish our Christmas shopping. We lower our heads. We purse our lips. We try to still our muscles and bones and heads and hearts.

I manage not to drop the vase. Mom, next to me, hangs on to the handle of a delicate teacup, her thumb and middle finger pressed together and lifting the thing to her lips, like she might take a sip.

The weekly Minute of Silence has an absurdity to it, if you raise your head and peek at the paused world.

The cashier is sneaking a look at his phone. The man in the ugly brown suit was lifting a bowl over his head to check the price and he's stuck there. He's sweating. On the street a mother is trying to keep her toddler still. I wonder at what age she'll explain what this is all about.

Someone's phone beeps. Someone in the stopped traffic on Fifth Avenue must sigh and inwardly rage at the interruption. They have places to go. The memory is inconvenient.

Traffic lights switch from red to green and back again.

I look back at Mom and the teacup. It's white with a gold rim and pink flowers. It's every bit as tiny and pretty and fragile as the ones she once threw against the wall. Her face today doesn't tell me much—I don't see despair or memories or a flicker of grief flash in her blue eyes or tighten her thin lips.

But I can hear her heart. I can always hear my mother's heart, and it's loud right now, in all this quiet. It's as loud and fast as it was that Tuesday six and a half years ago.

We didn't pick up the pieces of the shattered teacups for weeks. We're still picking up the pieces.

A month after Dad died, Angelika finally swept the collection of broken china into a plastic bag. She zipped it up and labeled the whole mess BROKEN BITS WE MUST ALWAYS REMEMBER, instead of throwing it away like anyone else would have.

All I've ever wanted is relief from the image of my mother, Dr. Emily Ryder, pajama-ed, her long hair knotted and alive, her face contorted in pain and confusion, flinging teacups at the wall, jagged pieces flying farther than I'd ever imagined they would, one nearly hitting me square in the nose.

I remember.

"Thank you," the store owner says, signifying the end of the silence and stillness. New York City comes back to life. The first few seconds after the silence are always uneasy. We clear our throats. We don't want to be the first ones to speak. We make gosh-this-is-hard grimaces and look up at the sky as if to say hello to the Victims. I shake my fingers and scrunch my toes like I always do when the Minute ends.

"Pretty," Mom says, putting down the teacup like the Minute never happened.

"Maybe for Angelika?" I ask. "She can probably never have enough teacups."

Mom smooths her long, slicked-back hair, and I run a finger through my just-as-long, just-as-fine locks. When we aren't on Devonairre Street, someone always comments on the silvery-white shade and the way it hangs all the way down the length of my spine.

"I was thinking of buying them for us," Mom says, not looking at me.

"No."

Mom blushes with the remembering.

Her heart skips a beat.

Conversations around us have lit up again, and the traffic on the street is noisy and raging. There's a line in front of the cashier now. I guess everyone took the Minute to decide what they wanted.

Mom nods slowly and puts down the cup.

Everyone else's Minute of remembering is over, but ours stretches on and on.

It doesn't end.

1.

Angelika grabs my face, stares into my eyes, and looks for signs of love.

Her hands are cool and stronger than I remember. It's not the first time she has pressed them against my cheeks. She leans in so close I can smell leathery Aramis cologne on her neck. She wears it every day—says it reminds her of her late husband. It is a Devonairre Street smell. Like freshly watered mint and basil that I planted in the garden or just-smoked cigarettes on Charlotte's stoop or my mother's chemical hairspray.

I keep my eyes open and on Angelika, but I'm aching to slide my sunglasses over my face and disappear.

I don't like the oversoft, worn texture of her hands or the way I can feel her wedding ring folded beneath her wrinkles.

She turns my face this way and that, like love might be hiding under my chin or behind my ear. She brings her fingers close to my eyes, pulling at them from below so they open a little wider. I shift my gaze skyward. Someone tied balloons to the rusting garden gate for the Shared Birthday, which comes every year at the beginning of April, and a few of them have freed themselves and are floating up, up, and away.

I think I wouldn't mind being a red balloon against a blue Brooklyn sky, looking down over Devonairre Street.

Angelika moves a hand to my forehead. Beside me, Delilah sighs. She's next. Angelika's eyes close and her lips purse and she tilts her ear to the ground like she's listening for an earthquake.

When her eyes open, she's beaming. From a certain angle she looks almost young, but most of the time she looks even older than her seventy-five years. That's what a lifetime on Devonairre Street does to a person, I guess.

I love it here in spite of Angelika and her minions and the crazy things they believe. Or maybe because of them.

She pats my cheek. It's almost a whack. There's power behind it. "Good girl," she says before looking over at my mother. "Lorna's not in love." Her Polish accent lilts on the word *love* so it sounds like *luhf*. The accent itself is a mystery—she was born on the street to a Polish mother and an American father, but her voice carries her mother's history instead of her father's or her own.

When we ask her about it, Angelika only shrugs.

"I am my mother's daughter," she says. "We are all our mothers' daughters, are we not?"

With Angelika, the only answer we are allowed is yes.

And it's true. Or it is for me. I look at my mother. She raises her eyebrows and lets her eyes laugh while the rest of her stays serious. I echo the look. I'm always a little bit scared and a little bit delighted during the Shared Birthday.

"There is not even the littlest bit of love on your daughter," Angelika says to my mother, who is across the garden, past the bench and the waterless fountain, by the opposite gate. My mother nods like it matters; Angelika nods back and pats the top of my head, telling me to step away so that the next girl can step forward.

• • •

Today is our birthday.

It is not anyone's birthday, but it's the date Angelika chose as the day Cruz, Charlotte, Delilah, Isla, and I would celebrate our birthdays. Our parents' generation goes without now. And the few kids younger than we are still have a couple more years of individual parties. Maybe the little kids look forward to them, but I barely remember my last real birthday, when I was nine. The Shared Birthday suits me. Devonairre Street suits me.

The Shared Birthday is one of dozens of things we do for Angelika. Like Christmas trees and Easter egg hunts and the block party on the last day of summer, we do things because traditions feel cozy and safe. But more than that, we do things like the Shared Birthday because Angelika is the person who fed us baked zitis and perfectly undercooked brownies when our dads died and our moms were too sad to get out of bed. Angelika played an ancient, faded version of *Life* at the coffee table with me every afternoon for a month. She fed Delilah from a bottle like she was her own. She took Charlotte to her piano recital and clapped so hard it was embarrassing. Angelika is the one who shouted "Leave the young ones alone, *dupki*," when reporters tried to take pictures of Cruz and Isla and me after the Bombing.

They didn't need to speak Polish to know she was calling them assholes.

That's why her scent—Aramis, lavender tea, celery breath, and the unidentifiable Something Else of getting old—makes me think of kindness and strength, safety and courage, all at once.

That's why I let her touch my face and determine my fate once a year in a garden full of my very best friends and the women who have watched me and warned me and asked me to be one of them.

It's easy to do ridiculous things for someone who bought you a stuffed rhino and a fairy-tale coloring book when your heart was breaking for the first time.

• • •

Isla misses her regular, on-her-own birthday. She's always asking when we can stop with all the Devonairre Street traditions. For now, though, she's wearing a tiara and eating an extra-large slice of honey cake. At fifteen, she's the youngest of us, Cruz's little sister, and we're not quite ready for her to grow up. But here she is, growing up anyway, in a blue dress the same color as mine, except hers shows the light brown skin of her shoulders and the tops of the breasts that I keep forgetting she now has.

"How's the cake?" I ask her. She was declared free of love right before me and looks happy to be on the food-and-mingling side of the garden, her knee resting on the bench.

She takes another huge bite of cake. Her fork is messy with lipstick and I try to pinpoint the day she went from little girl to something else, but I missed it, somehow.

"It's good, right?" I say, swooping in to take a bite from her fork.

And it is good. So good. It was my year to make the cake and I poured in an extra shot of whiskey from the bottle my father left behind when he died.

"We'll drink it at your wedding," he'd said.

"I'm not supposed to get married," I told him.

"Don't let them tell you that," Dad said. He gave Mom a look, and Mom gave him a look back. She grew up visiting her grandmother on the street every summer, and when her grandmother died and left the apartment to Mom, there was no question that we were moving here.

Mom used to say it was the only place she felt she belonged, and I feel the same. Even the worst things about Devonairre Street are better than the rest of the city. I like being tethered to people and rituals and bakeries with flaky chocolate croissants and fresh herbs next to cracked sidewalks, and old ladies who knew my father.

I like knowing how to make good honey cake.

Mom stopped making honey cake recently. Sometimes she talks about selling our building and moving to Paris or Canada or California.

"This cake is my best friend," Isla says now, licking crumbs from her fingers and lips. "You should make it every birthday. Charlotte's was gross last year."

"It's your turn next year," I say.

"Maybe I want to make chocolate cake instead," Isla says. She straightens her back. Pushes a waterfall of black curls behind her shoulders. "Maybe I want to make birthday cookies."

"Oh, come on, honey cake's not so bad. It's tradition."

"Couldn't there be a new tradition, where we eat things we actually like?"

"Don't be a brat," I say with a smile and a poke. Isla trills her lips but doesn't push it.

We look back across the garden to Angelika, who is still holding Delilah's brown face in her hands. They are opposites: young and old, dark and pale, a black cloud of an Afro growing high from Delilah's head, spools of bright white hair weighing Angelika down. Delilah could float away, she's so happy lately. Angelika's feet dig in and she stays right here.

"What's taking so long?" Mom whispers, her heart speeding up. "Angelika isn't letting her go." She makes a fist with one hand and flutters the fingers of the other. Her heart beats even faster, louder. "I wish she wouldn't put you girls through this. It puts everyone on edge. You know you can say no to her, right?" She looks at me hard, like the message isn't getting through. "We don't have to keep letting Angelika dictate all this craziness, if it's upsetting you."

I nod. Sometimes when I can't sleep I put on Frank Sinatra, because in the weeks after my father died, that's what Angelika played late at night. I'd be up in my lofted bedroom and she'd be downstairs, holding down the fort, sipping lavender tea in my kitchen, and waiting for our pain to ease.

"Why won't she let go of Delilah's face?" Mom asks. "Honestly, she's going to scare the girl."

I try to catch Delilah's gaze, to make sure she's okay, but she's not looking at this side of the garden. She's looking at her feet. Her shoulders slump forward in an unfamiliar shape and I wish I could get closer to her, so I could see the tiny details of her face that let me know exactly what she's feeling.

Angelika must tighten her grip on Delilah's face because she winces, shutting her eyes for longer than a blink. *It's almost over*, I try to telegraph to her across rosemary and dandelions and splintered picnic tables, from one side of the gated garden to the other.

"What's this, now?" Betty, one of the grandmother generation, calls out.

"Do we have a problem?" her sister Dolly says. They both cross their arms and straighten their backs, readying themselves for something.

"Why is she putting her through this?" Mom mumbles.

No one's smiling anymore. No one's eating honey cake. Another balloon has untied itself from the gate and is leaving us.

Delilah doesn't look up from her shoes, doesn't watch it escape.

Isla adjusts her tiara.

Mom clasps her hands in front of her. Nearby, Charlotte squeezes Cruz's arm.

It's warmer than it should be in April, warmer than it's ever been on our Shared Birthday, and even that starts to feel ominous.

All of Devonairre Street watches Angelika grab Delilah's shoulders. They're bare and sweating. I can see the shimmer from here. I like the way sweat can be ugly or beautiful, depending on the particular way it pools. It's beautiful on Delilah's skin right now.

"What have you done?" Angelika says. She drops her head, and Delilah finally raises hers. I take a step closer to her side, but it's not close enough to matter.

I stand back like a coward and protect myself instead of my best friend.

It's never gone this way before. Mom's heart is louder than ever, and the widows move in on Delilah and Angelika. Soon there are five of them breathing on Delilah, then five more. Delilah's hands find her face and she hides behind them.

For seconds that could be hours, I let it happen. Cruz and Charlotte and Isla let it happen.

Maybe we always knew this possibility was here—waiting for us. There's something fun about long hair and skeleton keys tied around our necks. We've liked being a little strange and a little untouchable. We've liked honey cake and Angelika's Polish accent and the way the street name sounds coming out of our mouths, like a secret or a bedtime story.

I'd forgotten about the hunch in my dad's back when we talked about the Curse or the way he always told me to be wary of Angelika and careful about getting too sucked into the ways of the street.

We haven't been careful.

Then I remember it is ridiculous, all of this. Devonairre Street and everything I love—everything that feels comfortable and familiar but also sometimes cruel. I remember that no one has died in two years and Curses aren't real and humoring Angelika isn't the same thing as believing her. I remember that Delilah is my best friend and that we are one entity—LornaCruzCharlotteDelilahIsla.

I look to Cruz and Charlotte and Isla. Old ladies hurl words at Delilah, but the four of us are fast and get to her side before too many of them hit her dead-on.

Irresponsible.

Selfish.

Hubris.

You know better.

I take Delilah's right arm and Cruz finds her left and we pull her out of there—me, Cruz, Charlotte, and Isla flocking around her like bodyguards—like she's ours, which she is. Delilah is nervous-laughing but also almost crying, and Isla loses her tiara and pauses for a moment like she might pick it up instead of continuing on with us. But we make our way out of the garden and down to the end of the street, to the place where the Devonairre meets the park. To the bit of sidewalk that means we are Devonairre Street Kids and the rest of Brooklyn isn't.

2.

"What was that?" Isla says. She's asking Cruz mostly, but the rest of us, too.

Charlotte with her epic braids and thick glasses lies back on the grass like the whole episode has worn her out. Delilah sits down and shakes her shoulders like she's a wet dog and Angelika is water.

"That was Angelika trying to scare me into celibacy," Delilah says. Her legs are shaking, but she's smiling and shrugging so maybe she's okay. "She can probably tell I cut my hair again last week. Public stoning seems like a fair punishment."

I lean back on my elbows in the grass and don't worry about the leaves that are going to attach themselves to my hair. Isla and I giggle. Isla and I giggle easily, and Delilah can make anything into a joke. Even today.

"What happens now?" Charlotte wrings her hands. She picks at the grass and looks at Delilah like maybe she sees something on her, too.

"Worst birthday ever," Cruz says. "Angelika's getting nuttier every year. What a mess."

"Good thing it's not really anyone's birthday," Delilah says. Isla and I laugh again.

It isn't funny, though. Not this time.

Cruz sits then, and so does Isla. All us girls are in blue dresses and Cruz is in a blue shirt and this is something that happens more often than coincidence would allow. LornaCruzCharlotteDelilah-Isla is a thing that used to be a joke but is the kind of joke that is real.

No one's followed us over here. There's nothing left for Angelika or any of the other old ladies to tell us. We know what they believe. We know what they want us to do.

But we can't stop ourselves from falling in love. And if we believed in the Curse at all, that's exactly what we'd be trying to do.

I remember the first time Angelika spelled it out for me, a year after we'd moved to the street. Cruz and I were on the sidewalk, drawing chalk stick figures, hearts, and monsters on the pavement. Angelika was watching from her stoop as usual, her dog barking up a storm.

"You two are spending a lot of time together, aren't you?" she asked. Cruz and I looked at each other. I liked his curls and that he let me choose what color chalk I wanted before he picked his chalk. I liked how the stick figures he drew had heads and legs but no torsos.

We shrugged.

"Be careful. Have you been told about the Curse?"

Cruz and I shook our heads. Angelika's accent made the word *Curse* sound even more dangerous.

"The Curse of Devonairre Street," she said, the same way she announced the titles of storybooks when she read to us. "Long ago, a generation of ungratefulness brought about a need for sacrifice. Any girl who lives on this street for more than one year shall forever be Cursed." Angelika paused to make sure she had our attention. She did. Her back was straight and her eyes unblinking. She spoke slowly, as if every word were more important than the one before. "If a Devonairre Street Girl falls in love with any boy, whether or not he loves her back, the boy will die. Devonairre Street Girls must not fall in love. That is the responsibility, that is the Curse, that is what is true." I could tell she had said it before, many times. It had a rhythm, a pace, a crescendo at the end that made me drop my chalk on the sidewalk, shattering it into purple dust. "You hear that, Lorna? I'll say it again, if you weren't listening."

Angelika always ends sentences that way. *I'll say it again, if you weren't listening.*

But I heard her the first time.

Cruz and I each took one step away from each other. All it did, though, was make me extra aware of the air between our hands. It felt electric.

My father died four years later in the Bombing. So did Cruz's.

The chalk hearts got washed away. I'd like to draw them again, though. To show her I'm not scared.

• • •

"I do love Jack, you know," Delilah says. She's cross-legged and making knots with blades of grass. Jack Abbound has an oceanic wave in his blond hair and hands fit for a piano player. He carries a flask and looks at Delilah like she's Niagara Falls.

"Oh, we know," Isla says. "Everyone knows."

We are LornaCruzCharlotteDelilahIsla and we aren't afraid of love, even if we're supposed to be.

"What's it feel like?" I ask, and Delilah tells me as best she can.

3.

"The A train is crap," Isla says, arms crossed, on the subway out to the airport.

"You didn't have to come," Delilah says.

Isla shrugs. It's always out there—the idea that we could go places alone, take the subway as far out as it goes, to Coney Island or the Bronx or the tip-top of Manhattan, and walk the streets by ourselves, one girl with long hair, one key around one neck.

It never happens.

Especially not today.

We travel in a pack everywhere we go—to school, on errands, to parties—like one being.

When we're together, everyone can all tell we are Different. The whole city of New York. New and old Brooklyn residents. The lonely Midwesterners who have made this city their home. The kids from the suburbs who like to pretend they belong. The constant barrage of tourists who want to head to Times Square and buy photographs of the way it used to look.

Isla swings around the subway pole. Charlotte keeps putting her hand on Isla's elbow in an effort to stop her, but Isla Rodriguez is an unstoppable force.

"What time does your mom get in?" I ask. Delilah scrolls through her phone. Mrs. James never tells us much about her monthly retreats, but they involve yoga and days of silence and nights of chanting and trying to heal.

Mrs. James loves the word *heal*, even though Angelika hates it.

"Our job is to remember, not forget," Angelika reminds Mrs. James every month when she leaves in the early morning for a flight to somewhere beautiful and quiet and decidedly Not Here.

Delilah never gets invited on the trips. She calls them New Age Bullshit Money Sucks but happily eats dinner at our house most nights her mom's gone and I don't think she misses being stuck in her apartment with her mother and her yoga chants and her craft projects. Still, we're diligent about going with her to meet Mrs. James at the airport after each and every trip.

I'm not sure if meeting people at the airport is an official Devonairre Street rule or simply something we *do*. Sometimes it's impossible to know the difference.

"Plane gets in at seven," Delilah says.

"The airport is crap," Isla says.

"You just said the A train is crap." Charlotte sighs.

"They're both crap," Isla says, her voice getting louder. People stare. People always stare.

"It's starting," I whisper to Delilah. She looks around. The man in the navy fleece is pretending to look at his phone but he's actually snapping a photograph of us. The woman in ripped jeans reading *Scorpio: The Year Ahead* keeps glancing up, then darting her eyes away. A few guys our age smirk and try out different disgusting things to say about Isla's body or our hair or Delilah's exquisite face.

I cling to the key around my neck and wish we weren't all in blue dresses today.

I take inventory of the passengers. Women with shoulder-length hair and bored eyes, men with scruffy beards and wives who love them fearlessly, kids with overalls and sticky fingers and fathers.

We are different.

Isla bends backward from the pole, her back arching like she's made of rubber. I swear I see her mouth the word *Devonairre* at navy-fleece guy.

The train shudders to a stop and I stumble, so Delilah, on instinct, grabs me from behind, her arms hugging me and pulling me close to her. Even when the stop is over, she holds on. It feels good to be close. Charlotte twirls one of her heavy braids around her wrist.

"Rapunzel!" a man who smells homeless and looks high calls out from across the car. "A whole group of Rapunzels!"

"Heard it before," Isla says, a little bit proud, I think, of the way we look like we have emerged from a fairy tale when everyone else looks like they're coming from a cubicle or a sweaty yoga class.

"Isla, there's a free seat over there. Don't you want to sit?" Charlotte says, tugging her braid even more tightly around her wrist.

Isla wraps one leg around the pole and slides her hands up as high as they reach. She shakes her dark mane. She's always treated the subway poles like playgrounds, and I think she doesn't know how it looks, now that she's turned from a little kid into one of us.

I don't want to tell her.

"You can sit," Isla says. Charlotte shoves her braids down the back of her shirt like hiding them will draw a line between her and us, but it doesn't make a difference. It is a long train ride.

• • •

We head to the gate. We have a ritual of picking up doughnuts and lemonades at an off-brand store right before security and watching the planes fly in after we pass through.

Today Delilah buys an extra doughnut for the youngest security guard.

"I got you a present!" she says, with a Delilah-flourish. He gives her a look like he wants to devour her and I step closer so that he can't.

It doesn't work. He gives me the look, too.

"What'd I do to deserve this?" he says. He thinks he's smiling, but it's a leer.

"Last time we were here you said you were jealous. We're just being good citizens," Delilah says. It isn't meant to be flirtatious, but that doesn't matter.

"What good girls," he says. His colleagues laugh. "No one ever talks about how nice you all are."

Delilah finally sees the thing I've been seeing all along. She shakes her head and digs in the doughnut bag to get one for herself. She takes a bite so big there's no room left for words, and we pass through security without another word.

I feel them watching us go.

"It'd be easier if you weren't so friendly," I say.

"It'd be easier if we weren't so cute," Delilah says, only a glimpse of unease flickering around the edges of her mouth.

"Pilots!" Isla says when we get to the gate and see a mini-parade of them.

Isla wants to be a pilot, but she's never flown anywhere.

"Hey!" she calls out to a few of the kinder-faced pilots. "Hey, which plane is yours?"

Most of the men and women ignore her, but a guy with a mustache and a streak of gray hair can't resist.

"Right over there," he says. "Flying to Miami."

"Can I see?" Isla says. "The inside, I mean? The cockpit?" It works every fourth time, but today the mustached pilot tenses at the word *cockpit* and shakes his head.

"Come on," Isla says, accidentally pouting and swaying and sticking out her chest. I want her to be seven again, or eleven, and able to be her exact self without anyone seeing something more into it.

The pilot doesn't reply.

"Today is crap," she says.

"I know, we get it," Charlotte says. Isla sighs so loud a few people turn to look.

Some of them don't turn away.

I don't even blame them. I like watching people here, too—especially the young couples going on honeymoons and the kids only a little older than I am going on volunteer missions to Africa and India and the Middle East. My heart flips at all the possibilities of the future.

"That'll be you girls soon," Isla says, nodding her head in the direction of a girl and a boy still wearing leis and dopey smiles from a Hawaiian honeymoon. They're holding hands and he's kissing her neck and she's shrugging—I bet with pleasure at the way the sensation zings from that one spot to the rest of her body. Their wedding bands glint in the crappy airport lights. Her hair is frizzy and his is braided and there are dozens of other couples just like them near our gate but I can't imagine myself on a honeymoon in two years, even if that's what Owen expects. I think Charlotte and Cruz might get married right out of high school, and a little bundle of nerves in my stomach tells me Delilah and Jack might, too.

"You think?" Delilah says, all stars in her eyes and shifting up on her tiptoes, a thing she always does when she's excited.

"You want that to be you?" I ask.

Charlotte wanders to the newsstand to read the article under the headline MAYOR AKBAR BACKS PREDICTIVE ARTS WORKERS UNION. She is the only one of us who has been to a psychic before and she insists on using the terminology they've given themselves. She says the word *psychic* is derogatory.

She wouldn't tell us what her future holds.

Charlotte wears me out.

"I want that to be me," Delilah says, putting her hands on her cheeks to feel how warm she's getting from the admission. The couple kisses on the lips, forgetting where they are.

"God, you really do love Jack, huh?" I say.

Delilah sighs. "He makes me want a lei and a gold ring and a veil and a different last name. I know it doesn't sound like me, so don't say it doesn't sound like me."

"Delilah Abbound." I try out the name because it is my job to be on her side and to hope for the same things she hopes for.

"Pretty, right?" she says. "I think he's talked to his dad about it."

I cover my heart with my hand. "Wow," I say, even though I know it's not so unusual anymore to get married as soon as it's legal.

I'm not uncomfortable with marriage, but I'm uneasy with the idea of Delilah wanting something different than I do. In two years our whole lives could be separate, in spite of the fact that we've lived practically identical ones until now.

"You'll be my maid of honor," Delilah says, so dreamy she's practically higher in the sky than the planes.

"Okay. But you'll have to come visit me in Ghana," I say.

"Okay. But when you come home you'll live next door and tell us everything about it." Delilah and I negotiate the future often. This is the first time Jack's been part of it.

I don't mind, as long as I'm still part of it, too.

"Yes," I say, thinking of a little place of my own in the same Devonairre Street building as Jack and Delilah and all the love between them. I've lived with people who love each other before. I slept better, being close to it. I wouldn't mind living in its shade again.

A plane comes in—maybe Mrs. James's—and we listen to the sound. It's not loud, exactly, but it's deep. It's a felt sound.

"You feel that, Lorna?" Delilah asks. She presses her nose against the window, next to Isla. Charlotte glances around to take note of who is noticing us. A few older women smile in our direction. A little kid fails at whispering *why do those girls look like that?* to his mom. A few men whistle at us, and a girl who looks to be about twelve watches us like she wants to memorize the way we speak and move so that she can try it on for herself later.

I try to see us the way they do. On our own, we'd look totally normal. Together, we're something else.

Together, we're special.

"Can I feel the planes coming in?" I ask. Of course I can feel them. Everyone can feel them. They make the floor vibrate and my ears ring. "Can't miss it," I say. "Nothing else like it."

"Yes. Exactly," Delilah says with her Delilah smile, turning away from the window for a split second. "It's that obvious. Love."

4.

It's Tuesday, so Owen's in my bed.

"I didn't know it was your birthday," he says. He overheard Charlotte saying something about the Shared Birthday at lunch this afternoon and he looked like he'd been hit. I've been waiting since lunch for him to say something about it, but Owen stews things over for a long time before letting them out. Even regular sentences—about the dentist or the way his father criticizes his haircut—take ages to get from beginning to end. When he speaks I think about a little boy kicking a stone on a long, winding road.

Owen gets up to put on his underwear. He is not someone who likes to be naked without a purpose.

"I mean Sunday," he says, and I try to take in what he's saying, but I'm more concerned with the long line of his torso and the unexpected flurry of hair below his waist. I like the way it all fits together—a collection of surfaces and textures that is only Owen's. I wish he wouldn't cover it up so quickly.

My hands are behind my head and I stay naked on top of the quilt someone made for our family after the Bombing. It's gray and blue and reminds me of my father's eyes but also the way he died in a puff of smoke.

"It wasn't my birthday Sunday, either," I say, and I know I'm being impossible but it's hard to explain the way things work to

Owen. Devonairre Street is a whole universe packed into three brownstone blocks with a deli on every corner and trees planted into the sidewalk, wishing they were somewhere else.

Owen waits for me to explain.

"It's a street thing," I say at last. I find my underwear hiding under the pillow. "We all share a birthday."

"You share everything," Owen says.

"I don't share this with anyone but you," I say, and wiggle my shoulders at him. It's not sexy, but it's silly and that's even better. He grabs my waist and climbs back on top of me, and I'm ready to slide his underwear off again, but instead we slow kiss and find our way onto our sides, our fronts pressing against each other until there's no space between.

"You could have invited me," he says, like the kissing never happened or the conversation was always floating right above us, waiting for us to come back in.

"You're not allowed."

"Angelika likes me," he says. I'm distracted by his boxers. They're covered in tropical flowers, a fact that I've loved since the first time I started seeing his boxer collection. They're never black or white or striped or serious. I pull at the waistband.

"Angelika tolerates the idea that you exist," I say.

"She likes me!" he says, sitting up so that I know he's not kidding. "She told me. Said I'm a good kid and good for you. Told me to stick around."

"That is literally impossible."

"I'm lovable," Owen says, but I want him to get how strange that sentence is coming from her.

"Exactly," I say. "That's why she'd hate you. She hates love."

Owen shrugs and pulls the quilt up to his chin despite how warm it is in my room. He gestures for me to slide underneath, too.

My mom won't be home for another hour. And I love taking naps with him.

"You said things were changing," Owen says. "Looks like Angelika's chilling out, too."

He knows about the street. He knows about it in the way I "know about" the Vietnam War or the Super Bowl.

I let it go.

Not because I'm going to stop thinking about it, but because I'd be better off telling Delilah and Cruz about it than talking anymore with Owen. We're okay at talking, but we're better at getting undressed in the afternoons and breathing in sync while we catnap.

Owen falls asleep first. He always falls asleep with his mouth open and his body curled like he's waiting for me to fit into the negative space between his chin and his toes.

I match my breathing to his and hope to find sleep in that rhythm but it doesn't come. I move closer to him. Usually the warmth of his body tires me out, but today it's too sweaty and my arm is at the wrong angle and the hairs on his arms tickle my skin. Sleep won't come.

I turn on my TV and mute it. My room is a lofted space above the kitchen. We have to climb a ladder to get up here and the ceilings are so low I have to hunch when I'm standing, but it's my favorite place to be anyway. It used to be my great-grandmother's sewing room. Mom says she used to make wedding dresses for the girls on the street, and I like picturing the room draped in white silk and lace.

We could move into the lower unit in our building. It's bigger— and no one has wanted to rent it since the Bombing. We've discovered that no one wants to live with the Affected. But I prefer my little loft, its history and its view. It's weird, but it's mine.

. . .

Owen talks in his sleep. It's another part of him I love, and I lean in close to hear him better. He's sleep-talking about the Mets.

I can't quite figure out the difference between loving someone and loving things about them, so I listen to him mumble half-familiar names of pitchers and catchers and something about sliding into third. Mostly, I'm happy to have someone around on Tuesdays. I wonder when enough time will have passed for us to give up the Minute of Silence, the constant worry about how and why and who. We got stuck on this one tragedy and we haven't quite moved on—not me and Mom, not Devonairre Street, not New York City, and not the rest of the country, either.

"It would be better if we knew why," Mom always says, and I'm never sure if she means better for us or better for the country. "It would be better if we knew who."

Mom's usually right about things like that.

Nothing's on TV, so I let the news play quietly. A lady with dark hair and thin eyebrows goes over the day's top stories. Crisis in Korea. Regulating predictive arts. Drought in California. New idea for what to do with the still-mostly-undone Times Square.

Owen keeps babbling away. "Lorna," he says, and I hold my breath. I want him to tell me sleepy secrets. I want to know what he really thinks about my thighs and the sounds I make when we're doing it and the smell of my hair.

"I love the moon and you and I don't have a chicken," he says, slurring and fuzzy and absolutely asleep.

His toes curl and I watch his body curve deeper, too, the word *love* hitting him in the belly. We've never said *I love you* to each other. I haven't exactly been waiting for the words. I'm not sure they're something I want. I love my mom and Delilah and the rest of the Devonairre Street Kids. I loved my father. I loved being in the presence of my mom and dad loving each other.

But I hate the way the world feels when love is gone. My mother changed after my father died. Not only in those first raw weeks, although I can't stop myself from thinking about that awful time, poking at it like a bruise, making sure it still hurts.

It does.

At 10:11 every Tuesday, the moment we became Affected, it aches even more.

I remember 10:11 the Tuesday morning of the Bombing. I was home sick from school. Mom screamed when she saw Times Square buildings exploding on the news. She knew he was inside one of them. She started throwing teacups at the wall. We had a set of eight. They were yellow and delicate and they made a deceptively sweet sound when they shattered. After four tiny crashes, I ran onto the street, looking for someone to fix her. Angelika was at our stoop already, like magic. She came in and held my mother under one arm and me under the other.

"Why did she break those teacups?" I asked Angelika after my mother fell asleep.

"Love." Of all the not-true things Angelika had said over the years, that one seemed true.

I don't believe in the Curse. But when Angelika sat with me on our living room couch and we stared down the bits and pieces of the teacups and listened to hours and hours of sirens screaming down every street in every part of the city, I wondered whether maybe I should start believing.

"You see what love does?" Angelika said.

I couldn't reply. I missed my father so much, so quickly, I wasn't sure the sun would rise the next day.

I nodded, because in the hours and days after my father died, I nodded at everything. Angelika rubbed my shoulder like my nod meant something, and an hour later we learned that Cruz and Isla's father had died in the Bombing, too.

"You see, you see?" Angelika said on her way out the door to check on the other destroyed families.

I nodded again.

I could see. If you love someone and they vanish, you are left nodding like a zombie and throwing teacups at a wall.

I never want to be a person who throws teacups at the wall.

• • •

Basically, sex is great and Owen is fun but I'm not sure love is for me. I like wearing sunglasses indoors and forgetting to bring books to school. I like sneaking red wine into the garden and eating rare steak at Bistro with my mother. I like rolling my eyes at Angelika. I like Owen's mouth on the back of my neck and being quiet in the after. I like being near love but not in it. I like having long Devonairre Street hair and a Shared Birthday and a red brick brownstone with a loft I can hide in and a shaky black fire escape out my window where I can sit and stare at the shapes the moon makes.

Sleeping Owen repeats himself.

"I love the moon and you and I don't have a chicken." It sticks to me this time, and I think it's the closest to love I've ever felt. I look over to the mirror leaning against the wall. I look for love on me. Is it there? Is this it? Is this the moment?

My face looks tired and my shoulders are so pale I wonder whether Owen can see right through them when I'm on top of him and the light from the window is coming in behind me.

Do I ever turn into a ghost?

I feel warm and tender. I want to kiss him awake. I want to let him sleep for a hundred years. That might be love, I guess. I try it out.

"I love you, too," I say in the softest whisper.

I wait to feel the Yes. That's what Delilah said love felt like. A big Yes blinking in your heart. An airplane touching down. Certain.

It doesn't come.

• • •

I can't sleep so I turn up the news. Something is happening.

". . . another attack," the reporter says, and I turn it right back down. Smoke and covered mouths and panicked eyes flash on the screen. They look so much like the images from the day of the Bombing that my heart stops beating and I think I die for a moment.

I must gasp or shake or scream because Owen wakes up in a start. He throws his arms around me before he even knows what's happening. Automatic, reflexive kindness. There's something to that. Not love, I guess, but something. I grab on to whatever it is.

"It's happening again," I say, and he knows what I mean without further explanation.

"Another Bombing," he says, which is what we have all been waiting for since the first one. Without a reason for the first one, Another Bombing has always seemed imminent.

Owen puts a hand on my cheek and turns up the volume. I close my eyes and cover my ears. My heart worms around inside me, looking for a safe space and finding none. It's stuck in my chest.

"It's Chicago," Owen says, lifting one of my hands from my ear. He uses a whisper I didn't know he had.

I wait for the phone to ring.

I don't know anyone in Chicago, but I have been to seventeen funerals in my life, and the first Bombing took my father, so it feels like the phone is going to ring.

"It's far away," Owen says, but it feels like it's here in the room with us. Times Square felt far away from Brooklyn, almost seven years ago. Death always feels far away from life, until it isn't. If I wanted to love Owen, these are the sorts of things I would explain to him.

"What if we know someone there?" I say, because once the worst thing has happened, anything could happen.

"I've never even been to Chicago," Owen says. He hugs me but I don't think he fully understands why he needs to.

It's been two years since anyone I know has died, so I'd need a new black dress. It would have to be wool, for Angelika. She likes us to wear wool. It protects your heart.

5.

"I feel like I'm supposed to do something," I say to Delilah and Jack the next afternoon after a long day off from school in honor of Chicago.

It's hard to see Delilah without Jack lately, but I don't mind. He knows when to be quiet and when to talk. I wonder whether Angelika would be able to see the love on him, too. I'm pretty sure I can see it—around his mouth and in the way he flips hair out of his eyes to get a better look at my best friend.

It calms me down, watching the way they love each other. It's like a patch of sunlight coming in through the windows. A perfect place for me to stay and warm up. He touches her shoulder and she covers his hand with her hand, to keep it there.

"Like, you want to send money to Chicago?" Delilah says. "It wasn't anywhere near as big an attack as Times Square. So, that's good."

"People died," I say. It's not an adequate statement.

"People are going to die," Delilah says. Her own father's been dead since before she could have known him. She misses him, but she doesn't know what exactly to miss. I miss my father's stash of cigarettes and when he swore under his breath. I miss how he talked about buildings like they were people with histories.

"They don't matter less because we didn't know them," I say.

"Well, they matter less to me," Delilah says. She isn't a cruel person, but Another Bombing has brought out a different side of her.

I guess that's what Bombings do: flip us around and shake us up so that hidden parts of us are exposed. I swear my elbows got pointier and my laugh got quieter after the first one. I look at my fingers and toes to see if I'm any different today.

"We deserve a break from funerals," Delilah goes on. "And, shit, I'll be honest, Angelika freaked me out the other day. I almost forgot that she's a total kook."

Jack blends into the wall.

He shouldn't be able to. He has a neon T-shirt and a battered blazer and somewhere beneath it, I'm sure, a flask. He has sloppy tattoos on his knuckles. They look painful and regrettable. I'd like to ask him about how he came to have them, and he's the kind of guy who would answer. But none of that matters. Delilah is big and Jack is small, in ways more meaningful than her little waist and his broad shoulders.

"How are you doing with it, Lorna? Dr. Ryder?" Jack says, finding his voice at last. "This must be especially—this must remind you of—this must be hard."

"We're just fine, Jack, how are you?" Mom says. Her back is straight and she looks like she's okay, but I know she isn't. Her hair is shiny and stiff, like she was trying to spray her whole self into place.

Like me, she must be thinking of the way the Times Square Bombing smelled like a campfire and fried hair and dust and the end of the world. It was a smell that carried. The smoke carried, too.

My eyes burn now, like they did then, and I wonder if the smoke traveled from Chicago to here.

But no. It's tears. They burn, too, sometimes.

In a few weeks, we'll be honoring the seventh anniversary of the

Bombing. I'm already dreading the way I'll feel and how poorly it will match up to the way the world will want me to feel.

"It's hard," I say. Mom startles. It's not like me to say exactly what I'm feeling, but the way Jack asked seemed like he wanted a real answer. There's something solid and focused about him that I like. It makes Delilah more solid and focused, and I like that, too.

Jack moves closer to me. I think of how certain Delilah seemed that they'd get married in a couple years. If I squint I can see Delilah's long white dress and Jack's neon tie and Angelika wringing her hands, ordering us to shower them with dried rosemary instead of confetti, begging us to wear wool instead of silk.

I can see them moving into the bottom floor of our building, me living on top of them. I'd like to know love is right beneath me, so that I can be near it but never have to have it for myself.

I'll be too busy taking off my sunglasses before diving into bed with someone new every few months, inviting my in-love best friends over for steaks afterward. I'll love the way Jack makes sure Delilah gets the best steak, with the least fat and the pinkest center.

I get a little lost in the wonder of the future, but Jack brings me back to the terrible now.

"I can't imagine what it's like," Jack says. I think more words want to come out of him, but he leaves it at that, punctuating the sentence with a nod and a long blink of his kind eyes.

"Aren't you sweet," Mom says, but she busies herself with packing her purse, then walks to the door. "Everyone be kind to yourselves today, okay? These things can be traumatic even when they're in another state. Lorna, you should take a bath later."

Baths are my mother's solution to everything.

I wonder if that's what she tells her patients, too.

Jack heads into our kitchen, which is the same room as the living room except there's a paisley couch creating an imaginary wall between the two areas and a change in flooring. In the kitchen there are black and white tiles and a fridge that looks fancy but sometimes leaks and glass canisters all over the counter—PASTA, FLOUR, SUGAR—with smaller canisters containing herbs from the garden and three kinds of cereal. In the living room there are creaky hardwood floors and a red-and-brown rug that Mom's grandmother hooked. It doesn't fit the rest of our apartment—which is all light and bright and patterned. It itches my feet. But it's nice, to have something from my mother's past. I don't know much else about her family or my father's. There's this rug and a black-and-white photograph of Dad's grandparents' wedding and my mother's mother's engagement ring, which Mom wears on her right hand, with her rings from Dad on the left. And my great-grandmother's sewing machine, which allegedly stitched hundreds of wedding gowns back when Devonairre Street was Blessed, not Cursed.

Delilah and I try to avoid the creaks in the floor on our way to the couch. It's a game we've played for years but have never actually mastered.

Jack watches us from the kitchen with a smile and makes me a mug of lavender tea. I didn't know Jack knew where anything was in my apartment, but I like that he feels comfortable taking over.

"He does that," Delilah says. "He sees a need and he fills it." She shrugs and grins. I catch her looking at herself in the large mirror we've hung in the place where the TV should be. We have a small TV in the corner, but the couch directly faces a mirror framed in delicate gold flowers and birds—the kind of thing that looks like it is either really expensive or was ten dollars at a flea market. Our mirror is the latter. I've noticed Delilah looking into it more and more lately, like she wants to see the love on herself, too.

"You like milk, Lorna? Or honey?"

"Both," I say. "Extra honey." That's a street tradition so far ingrained I couldn't say whether the preference for extra sweetness belongs to me at all.

Owen is kind but he doesn't know how to make tea and he doesn't ever ask my friends how they're doing. Delilah loving Jack makes sense. She is bubbly and flippant. She is bighearted and loud. He is calm and observant. She is fearless and fun. He has an almost-famous last name that he never talks about and he spends most of the time leaning against a wall or counter or the gate of the garden, dispensing small, perfect kindnesses. Delilah whirls and Jack leans and there's a perfect symmetry to that.

We watch him make tea and I tackle-hug my best friend.

"I'm happy for you," I say.

"I'm happy for me, too. Now put this mess in a ponytail. It's out of control." Then she does it for me. Combs my hair with her long fingers and slips an elastic from her wrist into my hair like she's done a billion times. It comes out bumpy and crooked. I keep it that way. "Lorna Ryder," Delilah says like she often does. "You are more wonderful than rain."

It's a thing she says, a saying that doesn't exist but Delilah says it as if generations of Brooklynites had said exactly that. She has a treasure trove of expressions that sound universal but are actually only hers. I hope Jack loves it the way I do. I think he might.

Jack brings me the tea and sits on the corduroy armchair, letting Delilah and me share the couch. I think he knows I need her more right now.

"Where'd you learn how to make tea?" I ask Jack, smirking. "Don't your maids do that for you at home?"

Jack takes my teasing like a champ, like I imagine a big brother might.

"You know how it is." I like that he doesn't tease me back.

"Let's turn off the news," he says, and again he is right and gentle.

"Yes," I say. "Thank you."

"Should I call the maid to do it for us?" he asks, grinning, and I kick his shin and it's a bad day out there, but it's a pretty okay day in here.

As soon as the news is off, I feel better. The great thing about something happening not to me is that I can shut it off. It's also the exact thing I hated about everyone who cried over the Times Square Bombing when they didn't know anyone who died in it. They were choosing to dip into the grief. I was being held underwater by it. I was drowning and they were wading and it made me hate the rest of the world.

Now I'm one of those people who feels a little sad and a little connected to the tragedy but isn't submerged.

Huh, I think, because it is both a good and terrible thing.

Delilah tells a long, convoluted story about why Mr. Manning, our bald English teacher, maybe has a crush on her, and Jack laughs only at the parts that are truly funny. I can't stop watching the way they seem to be touching even though they're not.

That's love, I think.

• • •

We call everyone else over when afternoon turns into evening. We've been on the world's most comfortable couch so long that we're a little surprised when we turn to the right and see the sun going down through our oversize windows, coloring the apartment pink and orange.

Owen comes first and he gives me a huge hug but he doesn't ask how I'm doing like Jack did. He tells me I look beautiful, though, and that's almost as good because I don't.

He and Jack guy-hug and Delilah giggles. We're still learning how to have boyfriends at the same time.

Cruz and Charlotte are next.

"You're lucky we made it over," Charlotte says. She gestures to the window, and we all look to see Angelika on her stoop. "She asked where we were going. When I told her, she said I had to bring this."

Charlotte has a folded-up piece of notebook paper in her hands, and I know what it is but Owen and Jack don't.

"The names?" Delilah asks.

"Of course it's the names," Charlotte says.

Owen takes the paper from Charlotte. "Chester Koza," he reads, "Adrian Sponak. Nestor Noon. Oliver Mundy. Jorge Ortiz—"

"That's enough," Charlotte says.

Owen snort-laughs and Cruz declares that he will be getting drunk. I can't stop looking at Angelika looking back at us. Delilah rips The List to shreds and I accidentally let Angelika's voice into my head. *Hubris*, she says, at the way we laugh it off.

The List is the one Devonairre Street ritual I hate.

"She's in rare form lately," I say.

"Is anyone else a little relieved it was in Chicago?" Charlotte says in her breathy voice, and no one answers, but Cruz and I look at each other and think the same thoughts.

But then Isla is at the door. Wearing a corset. She's wide hipped and starlet haired, and I wonder where she came from—in more ways than one. She looks right at me as she unveils two bottles of vodka and says, "We're going to party."

We could say no, but we don't.

I steal a bottle of my mother's wine because I have no interest in screwdrivers or the beer that Cruz unpacks from his backpack. I'm determined to be LornaCruzCharlotteDelilahIsla, to be Devonairre Street Kids. We'll do this together, the surviving, even if we don't know what that looks like yet. We stay in the living room to watch the tail end of the sunset, which always looks the best from our apartment, where the sunset meets a squint-or-you'll-miss-it view of the Statue of Liberty out the corner of the window. I like how the pink-orange-gold of the sunset dominates the sky, and how tiny the Statue of Liberty is in comparison, dwarfed by the colors and the mysterious way the clouds spread and shift. We're listening to an old Patti Smith song Jack likes and waiting for the alcohol to slide our feelings one way or another. I try to keep my eyes on the disappearing sun, because when my gaze drifts to the mirror and I see us all reflected back, I feel strange. We look lost and none of us are quite sure what to do with our hands so we keep trying to put them on each other.

What do you do in a tragedy where no one you know has died?

It's not a question we've had to ask ourselves before.

I wonder whether strangers drank to forget about my sadness when my father was killed.

Cruz takes a spot on the floor, offering Charlotte the chair. She pulls her knees to her chin and settles in—the chair might as well be hers, that's how often she's curled up in it. Jack's on the floor, too, but Owen joins me on the couch with Delilah and Isla.

I put my sunglasses on. They cover most of my face and turn my apartment sepia toned.

Owen makes a noise like a laugh, shakes his head, and kisses the place where my glasses wrap around my ears.

"She's too cool for you, man," Jack says, already refilling his glass with vodka and ice and no juice at all. Everyone else is drinking their screwdrivers slowly. Delilah and I share the bottle of wine, no glasses necessary.

Owen wraps an arm around me and raises his glass to Jack. Jack raises his glass back, and they toast the air. I smile at Delilah.

"See?" she says. "Things can be good here even when things in other places are bad."

I don't say I agree because it feels selfish to be cozy and comfortable with the people I love most in the world, but I don't disagree, either. It's at least a little true with the television off and the world shut out. We don't even crack a window, although the air is close and a little sweaty. It's worth the heat and the smell of skin to not hear Angelika monologuing about What It All Means on her stoop with Betty and Dolly and their endless yeses. We draw the curtains finally, too, so I can stop sneaking glances at her disapproving looks. I want to feel the good parts of being a Devonairre Street Kid for the rest of the night—the comfortable closeness, the swish of my long hair tickling my shoulder blades, the looks Owen and Jack give me and Delilah—open faced, starstruck—like we're something more than girls, which we are, because we are Devonairre Street Girls. I want to feel all that without the rest—without the List of dead men and the Curse and the always-there fact of Angelika reminding us how disappointing and dangerous we are.

Jack turns up the music and Cruz smiles and sways. He looks handsome, a fact that surprises me a little. His black hair curls with more control than his sister's and he has thick eyebrows and light brown skin from his Puerto Rican parents and shoulders that seem to have widened overnight. His nose is more delicate than the rest of his face, small and upturned, and that, too, looks good on him.

I look away. My mind is thinking all the wrong things since yesterday afternoon. I take the wine bottle back from Delilah and head to the kitchen to grab us glasses so that we can properly toast.

Cruz does the toasts. He always has.

He's so tall he could touch the ceiling.

He usually says something poetic or potent. He's good at toasts, the way he's good at practically everything. Basketball. Singing. Smiling with dimples.

"Cheers," he says, his voice cracking. That's it but it's somehow his best toast yet. He clinks only with me. We may all have dead fathers, but Cruz and I have something more. The weight of being symbols of a tragedy. The Affected title. The knowledge of what the people who lost family in Chicago are feeling. The pressure of the whole country mourning a person that only you really knew.

Isla should share that with us, too, but she says she doesn't remember their dad or the days after the Bombing or anything else from that time seven years ago. It's not true, it can't be true, but we pretend for her sake that it is. We are good, on Devonairre Street, at pretending to believe.

"Cheers," I say.

"Cheers," everyone else whispers.

• • •

We get blasted.

Mom will be pissed when she gets home around ten, after all her patients are gone and her paperwork is paperworked. But for now I don't care. The wine feels good going down and at some point Isla starts dancing and even the boys join in. The coffee table gets moved to the side of the room, by the windows, and Isla jumps on it, because the laws of physics say if there's a party, Isla will eventually end up dancing on a table.

If the curtains weren't drawn, Angelika and Betty and Dolly

would be able to see that, and they'd hate the way she looks carefree and proud. They'd lecture us about Our Terrible Generation and the Way Things Used to Be and What a Blessing It Is that no one we know died, and they'll wonder if dancing, too, is a sign of our awful hubris.

And if Another Bombing weren't the inaudible but unmistakable bass line underneath this dance party, there would be strangers on the street looking up at us, peering in through the windows like I've seen them do before, snapping pictures of Isla's hips and my hair and Charlotte's thick glasses and Delilah's smile and the way we drape ourselves over one another, the way we are carefree and wild on the saddest street in the world. They'd post pictures of us online, and I'd see what they see—irresponsible girls and the boys that love them anyway. They'd wring their hands over the bottles of wine and beer on the coffee table in the same breath that they'd discuss which of us is hottest.

On a dare, they'd ring the doorbell with the name RYDER next to it, to see what it's like to talk to someone who's Affected and Cursed and beautiful.

But no one can see us, for once.

• • •

The sun is long gone and so is the wine, but Charlotte's still sober. That's her way. She hands out water and snacks like a preschool teacher and we love her for it. When Isla's dancing gets too aerobic, Charlotte holds out her hands and takes Isla's wrists to steady her. Isla misunderstands and thinks Charlotte's joining in the dance, so she dances even harder while Charlotte's body stays still and her arms wave around, under Isla's control.

I point it out to Owen, but he doesn't get what's so funny about it.

When Isla lets her go, Charlotte moves next to Cruz on the floor. They aren't as cuddly as they sometimes are, but Jack and Delilah are so much more. Owen and I kiss every five minutes like there's a timer, and I like the reliable rhythm of our affection.

Delilah and Jack must have their own beat, and I wonder what it might feel like. My mind goes a little wild—wine tells me I'm allowed to think about anything at all—and I picture my best friend with her legs around Jack. I wonder whether she ever crosses her ankles over his spine. I like Owen's hands most of all, but Delilah might like something else about Jack and the things he does with her.

Delilah and Jack start making out by the ladder to my loft. I watch them a moment longer than I'd want anyone to see, hoping to catch sight of love in the way they kiss or the path that Jack's hands make from Delilah's neck to her butt. It's not like I believe Angelika, but I can't help looking for the thing she saw.

Owen snakes a hand around my waist and a little ways down my pants.

"Are we like that?" I ask, slurring and not totally sure what I'm asking.

"We're like us," Owen whispers, and for the second time in as many days I think I could love him.

"No one's like Jack and Delilah," Cruz butts in. Charlotte purses her lips. Isla screech-laughs and topples off the coffee table. We should all stop drinking.

Instead we send Jack out for more booze. It's easy for Jack to get alcohol. The guy at the closest bodega calls him the Prince of Brooklyn. I don't know about that, but I'm getting used to the easy way an

Abbound can navigate the city. We've seen Mets games from private boxes and cut in line to get pizza at Di Fara's and walked around the Museum of Natural History after hours. Jack is so unassuming I almost forget it's all because of where—or who—he's from.

"Whatever you guys need," Jack says tonight, and because it's Jack, I believe him. He runs a hand through his perfect one-wave hair and kisses Delilah so long and hard we all look away. When he's done, she has stars in her eyes. I can see them through my sunglasses, which I keep putting on and taking off. She sinks a little, like her legs are giving out.

"We love you, Jack," I say, wondering if he will officially become One of Us when they get married. LornaCruzCharlotteDelilahIslaJack. It's not the same, but it's pretty good. I don't mind it at all.

I didn't know that when your best friend falls in love, you do a little bit, too.

Delilah and I sit at my kitchen counter while Jack's gone. Owen comes over every few minutes to kiss me, but he's mostly playing quarters with Isla on the living room floor.

"Cruz keeps looking at us," Delilah says. "He's weird today, right?"

I look over at him and Charlotte on the couch. They're watching themselves in the mirror and probably wishing it were the TV instead. Isla leans against Cruz's shins and it's so distinct—the way a sister and brother touch versus the way the rest of us do. I could never brush against Cruz so casually. We catch sight of each other through the glass—his reflection meeting my gaze. It's a little easier to make eye contact this way—once removed.

Delilah waits for me to agree with her, but I shrug and flutter my feet because I'm a little weird today, too. I'm not annoyed exactly, but I'm feeling the little space between the things I've experienced and the things Delilah has. Her dad died of cancer when she was a baby. Charlotte's had a heart attack. Cruz's and my dads' deaths changed the world. Their dads' deaths changed only them. I envy them as much as you can envy someone whose father is also dead.

"You and Cruz," Delilah says. We're halfway through a second bottle of wine. She takes an extra-long sip of it. "You're like onions and butter, aren't you?"

I don't know what it means. It's another one of her sayings. But damn if I don't love the way onions smell, cooking in a pool of melting butter.

• • •

I'm thinking of butter and onions when we hear a screech and a yell and a crash out on the street outside our windows. The panes are thin, so we hear every bit of the sound.

There's no mistaking Jack's voice.

6.

Betty is the first one to bring a lemon for Delilah.

"She'll be back soon, no?" she says, approaching me, Isla, Cruz, and Charlotte on my stoop. The phrasing makes it hard to know whether to say *yes* or *no* so I don't say anything at all. "I'm sorry for your loss," she says, and I don't have anything to say to that, either, because the loss isn't quite mine.

Jack is dead.

I try the sentence out in my head over and over, which is what I've been doing since early this morning when Delilah called and whispered the words over the phone from the hospital. They sound like a joke, and the corners of my mouth turn up in response. I hide my smile behind my hands, but Isla catches it.

"It's fine. I laughed in the bathroom for twenty minutes," she says.

I cover my mouth anyway.

Jack is dead.

I smile again and lean over my knees to try to stop the laughter or turn it into something more appropriate.

We all stare at Angelika's house across the street because if we look anywhere else we'll see police officers and caution tape and the place where Jack's body was hit by a taxi. My mind pounds at the thought.

"We're not ready for this," I say. Charlotte, Cruz, and Isla nod even though I'm not sure what I mean. I think we're not ready to believe Jack is dead and we're not ready to be strong for Delilah and mostly we're not ready for tragedy to happen to someone our age. They've threatened us. They've said boys will die if we love them. But we didn't actually believe them.

I mean, we don't believe them.

Jack is dead.

It's an impossible sentence because he was so, so alive last night, kissing Delilah and pouring drinks and asking me what we could do to help the people in Chicago.

Owen comes back from ZeeZee Bakery with coffees and bagels. Jack would have known that for a morning like today we need laven-der tea and croissants. Cruz, Isla, and Charlotte thank him anyway, but I can't get the words out.

Owen kisses my hair and hands me a coffee. It's too hot but he snowed sugar all over it so it's sweet and made just for me. I give him a smile. It hurts my face. I'm in some alternate reality where grief makes me laugh but kindness makes me want to scowl. I close my eyes for a little longer than a blink, to steady myself.

Owen picks up a lemon with a bemused expression on his face. He rolls it between his hands.

"It's a lemon," I say, hating the way he finds Devonairre Street adorable, even now.

He puts it back down and shrinks a little.

"Oh, are you collecting them for Delilah? I have five from my mom," Charlotte says. She swings her tote bag onto her lap and hands me five more lemons. I start a pile next to me on the stoop.

It's hard to make them balance right, but I try until they're semi-stable. "She's not gonna want them."

Delilah doesn't do the lemon tradition.

Across the street, Angelika starts to open her windows. This is a tradition, too. The regular April chill has returned, but we're supposed to leave the windows open for a week after someone dies, so that their soul can escape. We watch, rapt and bored and miserable all at once, while each of her seven visible windows shudders open.

"Angelika's about to make her grand appearance, I'm sure," Cruz says.

"I don't want to see her," Isla says. "I don't want to see anyone but you guys. And Delilah. Jesus, where is Delilah?"

Jack is dead.

I give myself a shiver, an all-over-body shake that startles Owen, who is squeezed next to me on the steps.

"You need a sweatshirt or something?" he says. "I can run upstairs and—"

"No." I'm watching Angelika open her door, step out, close it behind her, and forget about locking it up. She's got a lemon in each hand. Isla turns her body sideways, like that will protect her from whatever Angelika is going to say or whatever look she's going to give us.

"You're all together," Angelika says when she reaches us. "That's nice." She looks at Cruz like she wants him to leave. She once asked him if he wanted to join the football team or maybe go off to military school. Cruz laughed but she wasn't joking. It's easier, usually, to pretend that she is.

Angelika hands the lemons to me, and I put them in my lap.

"She's going to need more than that," Angelika says. Owen starts to laugh, realizes no one else is, and stops. "I expect you will take care of finding more for her?"

We all shrug.

"I'll say it again if you weren't listening." Angelika's hands find her hips and she frowns.

"More lemons," Cruz says, but it doesn't sound like he means it and Angelika can tell.

"I'm sure more people will bring them by," Charlotte says. She knows how to talk to Angelika since she's lived on the top floor of Angelika's building forever. "It's early. You know Ambika and Iris like to sleep in. And my mom went to the store. I'm sure she'll clear them out. Don't worry."

"You say don't worry? I worry. I'm worrying right now. You think we shouldn't all be worrying?" Angelika's eyes are the lightest blue and they look right at me. Her hair is the silverest white. She wears it in a low bun like my mother wears hers, but without the sheen of hairspray. Her disappointment in us is not new but it's thicker today than it's ever been before.

"You are not meant to be"—she pauses, looking for the right word—"*wild*." Isla and I both have our hair out—loose and uncombed. Isla's hair curls and winds and tangles up in itself. Mine is thin and flat and too close to the color of Angelika's. "You girls have the long hair but the wrong hearts. It never used to be this way."

That is another favorite phrase of hers: *It never used to be this way.*

"The rules are simple, and in simpler times, we followed them," she continues, looking each of us in the eye. We don't remind her that even she didn't start following the rules until Chester died.

We don't talk about how Angelika is a Devonairre Street Girl, too.

When Angelika speaks, you get the impression she is speaking to the world, not only to you. She uses words carefully, as if they are being recorded, and gives a proud *hmph* after every few sentences.

We used to apologize, when we were littler.

We don't now.

"There is more for you to do than sit on the stoop and wish things were different from the way they are." For someone who spends most of her time on her own stoop, Angelika says this with surprising ease.

"Delilah's not into the lemon thing," I say, knowing it won't matter to Angelika.

"What did I say at the Shared Birthday?" Angelika digs her heels into the pavement, and I watch her weight shift back on to them. It's a slight movement, but imperative. She's angry. "So stubborn, all of you. I warned her, didn't I? I did." She *hmphs* again and looks at Owen, like she's only now realizing he's even here. "You don't listen, you children. I told you we'd be here, and here we are and you all seem so surprised."

It's cruel. Charlotte bows her head and Cruz's jaw tightens. Isla gets up from the stoop and pretends she has something very important to look for on the sidewalk.

"Please don't say that to Delilah, when you see her," I say. We never speak back to Angelika, even when she's at her most brutal. But there's a look of pride on her face—a sparkle in her eyes, a lift of her lips—that tells me she's not pleased exactly, but certainly a little smug that Jack is gone. I'm scared that if I say nothing she'll bask in that smugness, she'll pat herself on her back for *knowing this would happen* and she'll forget the way we're all broken and ruined by the fact that it did.

I don't want her to show up at Delilah's apartment with bowls of lemons and books of chants and Tupperware containers stuffed with lamb and rosemary and eggs and tell Delilah it's all her fault.

That Jack is dead.

Goddammit, my mouth twitches with a smile again at the ridiculous reality, and I don't catch it in time to hide it.

"How old was the Abbound boy?" Angelika says.

She says the words *boy* and *girl* in a particular manner that I've always noticed. *Boy* comes out sad, with the *oy* sound long and winding. *Girl* is said with a tiny growl in the middle. The kind of thing that could be her accent, but isn't.

We don't answer. It hurts too much. Everything hurts too much—sitting, talking, holding lemons in our hands, sipping at coffee, making eye contact, thinking about Jack. I start to giggle. I hold my sides and puff out my cheeks to make it stop but it won't.

"Jack Abbound." Angelika closes her eyes. I'm sure she's thinking about all the people who know his name, all the people who could possibly know about us. "Was he good?"

Charlotte starts to cry and Cruz holds her. I know it must feel great—I've been held by Cruz before while crying. His arms don't move. He doesn't give a back rub or a long squeeze or a hair brush. He stays perfectly still and solid.

"I've tried to protect you all. But you won't listen. Maybe now you'll listen." Angelika's chin shakes and I think we're about to see something new on her face, but she purses her lips, *hmphs*, and the moment is gone.

Jack is dead.

"Please," I say. And there's more I want to get out about how unimportant lemons and Curses and warnings are right now, but I can't say any of it because lemons are dropping from my lap and tumbling down the steps and onto the sidewalk and I am laughing and laughing and laughing and Isla is running after the lemons to pick them up and Cruz puts a hand on one of my shoulders and Owen gets up off the stoop like my breakdown is contagious and Charlotte's cries are throaty and powerful and two more women are approaching us with lemons in each hand and I am laughing so hard my nose is running and Jack is dead.

And then I am crying.

• • •

When the crying's over, Angelika gives me a pack of tissues. She always has them with her. It's a bit of the softness that balances out her sharp parts.

The lemons are next to me on the stoop again and Owen is rubbing my back and Cruz is looking at me like I am someone entirely new.

"Jack is *dead*," I say. Finally, it doesn't make me smile.

"You can keep some of the lemons for yourself," Angelika says.

"Do you . . . make something with them?" Owen asks. Everyone's speaking more quietly now, and I wonder whether we'll have to whisper around Delilah when she gets back. A selfish part of me doesn't want to see her—it's like watching footage of the Bombing or seeing open caskets or looking through Devonairre Street widows' photo albums. I don't like to look at the pain head-on.

"The lemons are for healing," Angelika says.

". . . How?" I like that Owen asks questions when the rest of us are so used to never being given explanations or reasons.

"When the Curse began," Angelika says, and all our shoulders move toward our ears at the word *Curse*, "my mother had a lemon tree. It only ever had one or two lemons at a time. She kept it in the apartment and not much sun got in and it was a silly thing. A silly pretty thing." She looks at us like we, too, are silly pretty things. "But when the first men died in the war, the tree blossomed. A dozen lemons. More. The branches sagged, there were so many lemons. There was no reason for them to appear, all of a sudden. My mother decided they appeared because we needed them. My mother was the kind of woman who believed—as we all should—that if something is provided, it's because a need has opened up. So she brought lemons to all the widows or girls who lost boys they loved. She did it the rest of her life. The tree gave for a long time, and when that tree died, the rest of the street carried on with the tradition anyway. Traditions don't come out of nowhere. They come from something sacred and strange. We hold on to them because we have to do everything we can to fight the Curse, don't we?"

We all hang our heads.

We have never believed in the Curse.

"Don't we?" Angelika says again. "I'll say it again, if you weren't listening." From the corner of my eye, I see Charlotte nod.

"Oh. Well," Owen says, a perplexed look crossing over his face. "I can get her some lemons, too, I guess."

Angelika puts a hand on his arm and gives him a tight, sad smile. She doesn't tell him to stay away. She doesn't tell me to let him be. She doesn't give us a stern warning about love.

She puts her hand on his cheek and lets it linger. She smiles.

• • •

By the time Delilah comes home, an hour later, we have two dozen lemons on the stoop. It is categorically too many lemons, I don't care what Angelika says.

Delilah is slumped over and I barely recognize her face. It's blotchy and her eyes are pink. Her T-shirt is stretched out, like she's been pulling at it all night, and one of her shoulders is exposed.

A couple walking their dog down our street straighten their backs when they see her. She brings them to attention. Even damp faced and messy, she is worth stopping everything for. I see them see her, and I see them see us. We are all in last night's clothes, twisting and tugging and trying to comb through our hair. Delilah's droops, mine tangles, Isla's grows, Charlotte's slips out of frizzy braids.

The dog barks at Delilah's grief or maybe her beauty.

The girl wraps a hand around her boyfriend's neck, trying to turn him to face her instead. She sulks. She squirms. She kisses his bottom lip.

They won't be coming back to this street.

"You're home," I say when the couple has passed and we can speak without the outside world looking in.

Owen, Cruz, Charlotte, and Isla move off the stoop. They know Delilah probably only has room in her brain to deal with one person and that one person is me. Her mom waits for her down the street, her arms crossed and her back straight, and I think Mrs. James will have to fall apart behind closed doors and I probably will, too.

"Not really," Delilah says, and I know what she means but it breaks my heart.

Angelika stands at her stoop across the street. She watches. She waits.

I don't say I'm sorry. I don't want to be a person that says the same things everyone else is saying. There's a grief handbook everyone's read and I don't want to talk from that. I want us to be Lorna and Delilah even if only for an instant.

I pull Delilah in for a hug and don't notice that Angelika has moved from her stoop to the sidewalk, to the very place we are standing. I smell her before I see her—Aramis hits me hard and I pull Delilah tighter.

"I remember the day my Chester died," Angelika says, and I hold Delilah closer still. Maybe if I squeeze her hard enough she won't be able to hear Angelika at all.

"The grief never quite ends," Angelika goes on, and I feel Delilah shift away from me a little. She pulls back and I let my arms loosen, against my better judgment.

"Not right now, please," I say. Angelika looks angry for a moment—she hates being told what to do. But she shakes it off with a shiver of her shoulders.

"Delilah needs someone who understands. I understand," Angelika says. "You remind me so much of myself, sweetheart."

Delilah steps out of my arms entirely. Her eyes are glazed over, her limbs limp. She turns and lets herself be held by Angelika instead of me. Through the dozens of open windows, the neighborhood watches. They should know to let the moment be private; they've been in this moment before. But the widows of Devonairre Street have their elbows on their windowsills, their chins cupped in their hands.

It's amazing what people forget, the moment tragedy has moved from their shoulders onto someone else's.

I hate what they're seeing. Angelika and Delilah in an embrace. I hate my empty arms.

"I should have listened," Delilah says, her whole body hiccupping, then slumping back down.

"It's not because of—" I try, but her face is in the swoop of Angelika's shoulder and I don't think she can hear me.

"I'm here for you," Angelika says, a little louder than is necessary. Loud enough so that everyone can hear. "I share in this tragedy with you. It is ours, together."

I think Delilah nods. The watching widows nod, too. I fight the impulse to pull Delilah off Angelika. To insist the tragedy is ours, not theirs.

Eventually Angelika lets her go, and Delilah stands between the two of us. I shuffle so that I am a little bit closer to Delilah than Angelika is.

"Help me with the lemons," Delilah says, speaking to both of us, I guess.

"Of course," Angelika says.

"I've got it," I say. I want a moment alone with my best friend. But Angelika's not having it. I see her glance at the women in the windows, smiling a little at the way they're watching her. I would think Angelika might not even be strong enough to carry an armful of lemons—her hands shake sometimes and her arms are weak. But she grabs five of them, cradling the fruit between the crooks of her elbows. Her back is straight and proud. I take as many as I can, and we carry them like that, in little awkward armfuls, from the stoop to Delilah's kitchen, where her mom has set up big fruit bowls on the counter.

It takes a few trips, but Angelika doesn't tire.

Lemons keep dropping out of my arms and rolling down the street. Angelika manages to keep all of hers from falling. Delilah holds each one like it's a fragile thing.

The thing is, Delilah hates lemons.

But when we're all done, she sits at the counter and stares at the bowls, at the neon cheeriness, like they mean something to her.

And she asks me to leave.

Only me.

7.

The next morning I open all the windows.

It's raining and soon there will be stains on the walls and the floor and water soaking through the sheer gold curtains but I don't care.

"You opened the windows," Mom says when she wakes up and sees me on the couch, wrapped in two sweaters, watching rain hit the screen and drip-drip-drip to the ground below.

"I brought lemons over, too, before you ask," I say.

"We don't usually do all this," Mom says. "We do the hair and the tea and the cake and the outside lights."

"And the Shared Birthday. And the keys around our necks." I play with mine, spin it around and around until it hits my clavicle and stops.

Mom slumps a little. "Well. When we move to California, we won't have to do any of that. We'll have so much freedom. And the ocean."

"Sure," I say. California is the place we talk about going when we are irritated with Angelika or our long hair or the taste of lamb. It's the place we talk about going when someone's stared too long at us on the street or at a restaurant or lying out in the park.

"We got approached again," Mom says, not seeing how desperately I want to be quiet and listen to the rain coming down.

"Some really serious buyers. Life-changing money, Lorna. California money. House-on-the-beach money."

I look at her like I've never seen her before. "What are you talking about?"

"I thought some good news on a terrible day might—"

"Jack is dead," I say, because it's the only refrain in my mind, and I think if she starts hearing it over and over, too, she'll understand how insane she sounds right now.

"I know."

"Delilah isn't going to be okay," I say.

"Eventually—"

"This isn't a California situation," I say. "This isn't a bad day. What's wrong with you?"

I've never told Mom that California's more her dream than mine. I've never told her about my idea of Future Lorna: making pasta for Delilah and Jack, buying new underwear for new guys, wearing sunglasses on gray days, and not noticing the looks people give us anymore.

Staying right here.

When Dad died, Mom would have punched anyone who suggested we move away from our home to heal. "The best thing about this street," she said one night when we'd been silently eating dinner for twenty minutes and I was wondering how pink was too pink for a chicken breast to be, "is that no one tells you to move on. No one's telling us to donate Dad's shirts to some Dress for Success charity. No one will ever tell me to try online dating or pick up knitting or yoga or to say good-bye. You know what a relief that is, Lorna?"

I shrugged. She slept with Dad's shirts most nights and that freaked me out. I didn't want her to be like Angelika—shrouded in a cloud of Dad's cologne, his wedding ring stuck around her finger, the house an unofficial shrine to the days behind us.

On Devonairre Street we don't throw away our memories. We hang on to them forever, as reminders of what we've done.

People on other streets let go of the past.

I have to let go of the future.

The picture of Future me, Jack, and Delilah fades, and there's nothing to replace it with. I miss their love already.

I keep staring at the spot where Jack stood the other night, wishing we could gate it off and preserve the air he breathed.

Mom clangs around the kitchen and stops talking about California or selling our home, and I work on pretending she never said it. "It's raining, sweetie," she says after a few minutes. "Do we really need the windows open?"

"Everyone else's windows are open and what if—"

"At least it sounds nice," Mom says, like she doesn't want me to finish the sentence. And it does sound nice—raindrops pinging on air-conditioning units and windows and rustling through the leaves of the tree outside our building. It smells nice, too—like fresh dirt and damp flowers and that something else that comes from a wet sidewalk. It's almost enough to make me forget about the sirens and honking cars and jackhammers on the street behind us, where Jack used to be.

• • •

We listen to the rain together in silence before Owen comes over. He's checking in on me a lot, which is nice, but I wouldn't have minded more hours alone with my mother and the open window.

We have a pot of lavender tea and matching headaches. Owen makes us eggs but we don't eat them, only in part because they're browned on the bottoms, overcooked, and cheese-less.

"Saad and Hiba," Mom says. "We never talk about Saad and Hiba. They're in love. They're fine. They're not—"

"*Mom*," I say. I can see her jaw clench on the word. Owen says nothing. I can hear the rain again. Whenever the word comes up in conversation, Owen looks at his feet and gets quiet. This time, I don't mind the silence.

Owen knew about Devonairre Street before he met us all, of course. People from neighboring streets have always known about our Curse, and now Cruz and Isla and I are known for our dead fathers. We are Affected. Kids learn our names in school. We get free coffee at most coffee shops and free pasta at seven different Italian restaurants.

I'd rather have my father.

"There's been too much focus on the mystery of who attacked," everyone heard the president say at the third anniversary. "This is our history now, something we have to teach our children. We can't teach them why it happened or who made it happen. We don't have those answers. But what we do know is who was affected. And we should care about those lives, too. Those lives are an important part of history. The History of the Affected."

Mom likes to joke that her generation had the "new math" but my generation has the "new history." The History of the Affected. It's more sprawling, harder to test, but maybe a little more beautiful, too. I know the names of individual Holocaust victims. I'm required to read about families of soldiers who died in the Gulf War, and families of Iraqi men and women who died, too. Last week, we memorized names of children who had been killed in school shootings—we know their ages, favorite colors, what they wanted to be when they grew up. We'll need to know about their families, too—we'll read stories of their grief and follow the years after the tragedy that Affected them.

The new textbooks don't say much about the people who did the shootings or why the wars took place. That's not as important anymore. It can't be, since we never were able to learn those facts about the Bombing.

"We were doing it backward," the president said, "giving fame to the perpetrators of violence and never knowing the brave souls who died or survived. We are fixing that now."

Mom says this new history is all wrong. "We don't need any more attention," she says. Being known has always been a problem for her. When she practiced in Brooklyn, no one wanted to go to a therapist from Devonairre Street. So she moved to Manhattan where fewer people had heard about our eccentric little community. Then the Bombing happened. Now no one wants a therapist who is also a Bombing widow.

We can't seem to escape ourselves.

• • •

"I didn't say you believe in the Curse." Mom finally blurts out the word. "I just wanted to talk about Saad and Hiba. It's been a hard week. It can't hurt to remember all the love in the world. And on the street. Those two love each other. It's a beautiful thing, the way they watch each other all day. That's all I'm saying."

Mom is practicing the History of the Unaffected.

We scrape our forks against our plates and eat tiny bites of crappy eggs.

"I like the name Saad," Owen says. Then we are quiet again. I remember this from when my father died, too. First there is noise and chaos and this choking sound in the back of your throat and muffled screams into your pillow. Then there is this awful quiet.

There's nothing to say except half-formed sadnesses: *fuck I can't believe* and *I miss* and *I feel like my heart is* and *I don't know how.* And after a while you can't say those things anymore, either, so you say nothing and wish there were a third option, in between sound and silence.

We can't find it, so we settle for silence.

I was in this kitchen not even two days ago, leaning against this counter, smiling at the way Delilah bops her head like a little kid when she dances.

"Cruz and Charlotte," I say. "They're in love, too." I thought I didn't want to play Mom's game of Reasons Not to Believe in the Curse, but apparently I do.

"Saad and Hiba have been married for fifteen years," Mom says. "Don't tell me they don't love each other. I mean honestly. Angelika can't just ignore the people on the street who are in love and completely fine. It's ridiculous and it's always been ridiculous and can we please shut the windows?"

"Leave one open?" I whisper, and she leaves the biggest one open like an act of love. The sound of the rain changes a little, with only the one window open. It's a more contained sound, more manageable.

"Esther and Aaron. They died at a nice old age. *Together*," Mom says.

We don't want to say Jack's name out loud, so we're saying these other names, like they can fill up that space.

My face tightens and my eyes fill. "Dammit," I say. "Funerals should be the day after—What are we supposed to do while we wait? This is awful. Isn't this awful? Are we supposed to talk about him all day? Or sit in silence? What do I do with my hands?"

"You should both be in school," Mom says. On top she's herself—a pale blue blouse hangs from her skinny frame and her tiny diamond studs are glinting. Her hair is in its low bun, but I think it's from yesterday's effort.

"We'll go back next week," I say. "I don't want to go back until Delilah goes back."

Owen sighs loud and hard like it's something he's been holding in for days.

"I can't even think about school," he says.

"Have you cried, Owen?" Mom says. "You should cry. I know boys don't always feel like they can, but it's an important part of grieving." The bottom half of Mom is not normal Dr. Emily Ryder. She has on huge red sweatpants that I didn't even know she owned and thick socks with holes in the toes. Grief and worry have literally split her in two.

"Yeah, Dr. Ryder," Owen says, never calling her Emily although she's asked him to over and over again. "I've cried."

I try not to react. Owen and I haven't cried around each other yet. And the mention of it is worse than people talking about sex when you're a virgin. It feels like this huge unspoken thing between us that we're being asked to be ready for. But I'm not ready.

I don't cry in front of people, except for Cruz and Delilah and even then I do it behind my sunglasses. And I don't watch other people cry.

It's another Devonairre Street tradition. We're supposed to look away from tears. Angelika says looking at them invites more pain.

"I've heard there's a girl named Anna in Bed-Stuy," Mom says at last. "She lived on Devonairre for a few years. And she's living with a young man now. People say—"

"The more you talk about how this Curse thing can't be real," Owen interrupts, "the more it feels real."

"Bad things happen," Mom says. "They happen without Curses."

"Tell me about Saad and Hiba." Owen wants to know he's safe. I want to know he's safe, too. I try to feel around inside me and see if there's love in there.

"They own the deli," I say. "The one that sells carnations and sketchy milk but really good sandwiches."

I've always liked Saad and Hiba. Dad did, too. He'd go out to grab a jar of pasta sauce and not come back for an hour, getting lost in conversation with the two of them at the counter.

Mom takes our mugs to the sink.

"Hiba loves Saad," Mom says a little too loudly. "She does. She smiles whenever I ask about him. As if the love is so deep down inside of her she is surprised that other people are even allowed to say his name. It's lovely. It's the loveliest look she gets on her face."

"I've seen them fight," I say.

"I've heard them fight," Mom says.

"People fight when they're in love," I explain to Owen. He and I have never had a fight before. What's there to fight about?

"It's true," Mom says. "Dad and I once fought about what we would name a dog neither of us wanted to get. I went hoarse from yelling. He left for three hours to cool down. That's love."

"Huh," Owen says, and I'm not sure it's really enough to quell whatever nightmare must be rolling through his head right now.

"What'd Dad want to the name the dog?" I ask.

"Horace," Mom says. "I liked King." I file the information away under Memories About My Father and think that if we got a dog I'd name him Horace for sure. "Not the worst fight we ever had," she says, looking out the window like the worst fight they ever had is out there somewhere, playing on a loop for only her, "but close."

"What was the worst one?" I ask, and I know she won't answer.

"I want to be clear about something," Mom says. "Jack was drunk. He was walking in the middle of the street. That's why he died. Anything else is magical thinking."

"Of course," Owen says, and I think maybe it's me that's needed convincing this whole time, not Owen. I don't want to stop talking about Saad and Hiba but I don't know them well enough to be able to think of anything else to say about them. Or about love. Right now I can only feel the ache of Jack being gone and Delilah not returning my calls and the vague worry about an eleven-year-old girl who is now fatherless somewhere in Chicago. Love might be underneath all that, the way the earth gets buried under snow every winter, flowers blooming when the ice is cleared away. You'd never know what's going to be in the garden in June when you're looking at it in January.

I stare out the open window, over the messy rooftops that people try and fail to make glamorous. Almost every roof on our street has a rusting lawn chair and a half garden and flimsy railing to keep people from falling off. Ours does, too—I miss having my own garden, my own roof to watch the rest of the world from. At some point everyone gave up on the rooftops and settled for the community garden. But the lawn chairs and cracked pots remain above the neighborhood. They're the kinds of things you don't notice until you do, and today I do.

I wonder if people stopped going to their rooftops because Angelika got nervous about boys falling off. Every once in a while a neighborhood tradition I didn't know about reveals itself, and I have a feeling this might be one.

I'm going to ask Mom about it, but she speaks first.

"I'm seeing someone." She says it fast, like she's been keeping it in for ages.

My mom hasn't dated since my father.

Devonairre Street widows don't date.

There's a hit of pain, picturing her looking at someone else the way she used to look at Dad. And relief, too, that I might catch sight of her smiling the way she used to. It's hard to know which feeling matters more.

"I've been meaning to tell you." The stools at the counter feel unusually hard. "I'm telling you so you don't worry. I'm telling you because I'm not scared and your father was never scared and we play the game and do the traditions and stay sweet with Angelika because she's been so, so good to us, but that doesn't mean we believe."

I hear her heartbeat. It's fast. It's getting faster, still.

First California, now this. My brain is crowded enough, trying to piece together how Jack is gone. Mom keeps adding new complications to the mix, and I can't keep up.

"Lorna. It's okay."

"Do you love him?" I look at my mother's face on Angelika's behalf. I see new wrinkles near her eyes and that her lips are an impossibly pale pink.

I don't see love or not-love. I see my mother exactly as she is— sad and strong, tense and trying.

Owen leans forward, like it means something, her answer.

"We can fall in love," Mom says, louder than is necessary given that we are all sharing a tiny space.

"Angelika says—" I stop myself. I know better than to begin a sentence that way. I can't let her get to me.

"I'm done with *Angelika says!*" Mom snaps, our thoughts intersecting as they often do. She goes to the kitchen drawer where we keep random shit. She's too worked up, though, and the drawer comes all the way out. Pencils and stamps and receipts and chopsticks and a red shoelace of my father's that we can't stand to throw away—it all goes flying. She doesn't care. She knows what she's looking for. And when she finds it, she stands right up in the chaos she's created.

She brings the scissors to her hair. We haven't cut it in years. But with trembling hands, my mother cuts her hair, right here in the kitchen, in big uneven chunks that fall to the ground like embers from a fire that have floated up and are flickering down.

Mom's hair—long and silver-blond like mine—shines all the way to the floor.

I listen to her heart beat and the scissors snap and Owen's fingertips play a tap-tap-tap song on his thigh.

She cuts her hair until it's all the way up to her chin. Anyone looking in on us would see something violent and unrestrained. They'd worry at the glint of the scissors and the look in Mom's eyes. Their eyes would grow wide at the way she stands still in a mess of her own making, at the strange new shape of her hair.

These things don't happen in other people's kitchens.

"See?" she says, and she has never been less like Dr. Emily Ryder. If this is love, I know for sure I don't have it and I don't want it. Love is insanity, apparently. There's a strip of sweat across her forehead and a rosy flush to her face. "See?" she says again, getting her voice back under her control. She clears her throat, returning to her usual self. Trying to. "Everything is fine. There's nothing to be scared of."

But staring at the silvery pile on the floor and the way my mother touches the new jagged edges of her hair, I'm sure the exact opposite is true.

8.

We aren't welcome at Jack's funeral.

We stand outside the church near Jack's brother, Michael, and when we wave hello he scowls.

"Ridiculous," we hear him tell someone else who believes they loved Jack as much as we did. I wish I could shield Delilah from the word.

We're all in black wool—Cruz and Owen in suits—me, Delilah, Isla, and Charlotte in ugly dresses. Delilah has three lemons in her purse and eyeliner to distract from the just-cried look of her eyes. I keep trying to hold her hand and she keeps pulling it away.

This is another awful truth of losing people you love: everyone needs something different. And the needs almost never match up. It's like a bundle of spare socks and none finding their mates.

"We shouldn't have come as a group," Delilah says. "You know how it looks."

"It looks like you have people who care about you," Charlotte says, but I see what Delilah's seeing. Scrunched noses. Pursed lips. Shaking heads. In this part of Brooklyn we are the Devonairre Street Girls, and we are as ridiculous as Jack's brother proclaimed us to be.

For a moment the six of us stay circled on the sidewalk in front of the church. I think that after our initial impact, we'll fade right back in. We are *other*, sure, but we're in black and we're being quiet. Smelling like lavender and lemons shouldn't alarm anyone.

Delilah keeps her head down and Isla glares at anyone who looks our way. The rest of us hold hands and focus on looking serious and small.

But Jack's brother won't leave it alone. Michael's always been more into the family name and all it means than Jack ever was. He has a straight back and straight teeth and a heavy brow and tattooless knuckles and a crisp suit. He isn't afraid of us at all.

"This isn't your kind of affair," he says, breaking into our tight circle. "We aren't looking for attention. Don't make a mockery of our Jack."

We're all a little stunned into silence, so no one replies.

"We don't want Jack's death to turn into one of your little urban myths. We aren't interested in being involved in all that." I wonder whether Michael has cried. I want to know what he did when he heard the news. I want to know what everyone in Chicago did, too.

I want to know if we are the same, in the moments when we're stripped bare.

It's hard to imagine Michael doing anything sloppy and unhinged.

It's hard to see Jack through Michael, and that makes me miss Jack even more.

"That's not why we're here," I say, finding my voice at last. "We don't believe in the whole Curse—"

"No, see? That's exactly what I'm talking about! You come to a serious event and start talking about magic and it's inappropriate. Go back to your neighborhood and do—whatever it is you do. We don't want you here. Today is about Jack and the people who loved him."

I don't think Michael has cried.

"We loved him," I say, surprising myself. "Delilah loved him." I put a hand on her back, and she shrinks away from my touch again. I look at her and see that she wants to disappear, not make a fuss. It's not like her.

"We'll go," a small voice from a sad part of her says. She does not look up. She doesn't meet Michael's gaze. Strong, vital, funny, brave Delilah has been replaced with someone nervous and fading, someone who believes it matters what Michael Abbound thinks. She takes a few steps outside our circle and runs right into Jack's mom. I assume it's Jack's mom. She has the same perfect wave in her dirty-blond hair, the same slouch in her shoulders, the same gentle voice.

"Delilah," she says. Her nose turns up the perfect amount. The world stops around her and her grief. This, *this* is a person who has cried. I think she'll see those same things in Delilah—their shared love, their shared horror at what's happened.

"Ms. Abbound," Delilah says, her voice strained and new. "I'm so sorry—" Then there's the silence again. The skin on Delilah's face is dry and her eyeliner looks all wrong, ringed around her sad eyes. I've never seen her look bad, but she looks bad. I watch Ms. Abbound's face and wait for it to fold into sympathy.

It doesn't.

"You're a nice girl, Delilah. We've welcomed you into our family even though we were surprised at you and Jack having anything, um, in common." Ms. Abbound clears her throat and Delilah finally raises her face. Nothing was said about the color of Delilah's skin or the pure white prestige of Jack's last name. But I think we all heard it anyway.

I'm shocked but Delilah doesn't look shocked.

"Jack would want me here," Delilah says. Her voice isn't much stronger, but her shoulders move back and she takes up a little more space.

"It has nothing to do with—" Ms. Abbound stops and clears her throat. Her eyes fill with tears. "You're a lovely girl, Delilah. But the hoopla around your street and all this silliness—we can't have that. We don't want a carnival. This is our loss. *Ours.* I'm sure you understand why we're going to ask you and your friends to leave."

The tears stay in Ms. Abbound's eyes, not falling. Maybe she never lets them fall in public.

I understand something new about Jack, which feels good for about a second before it feels awful—to know there is a finite amount of things I can learn about him now.

It's time to go into the church—the minister stands on the steps and gestures at people to head inside. Mostly they do, but a dozen head in our direction instead. They stand in between us and the church, forming a thick wall that tells us, again, that we are outsiders, that we are unwanted, that we are Devonairre Street Girls and they are something else.

I look to my friends—the ones who have been silent, who haven't been speaking up for Delilah or our right to be here. They don't say anything now, either. Maybe we believe the things they say— we're silly, sexed-up girls from a strange street who draw attention from the serious, real things in the world.

It is somehow extra-terrible that Cruz and Owen could stay if they wanted to. Cruz is a Devonairre Street Kid, but that is entirely different from being a Devonairre Street Girl. They don't even notice him. And it hits me hard, something I knew but didn't know. I'm jealous of Cruz and who he gets to be. On the street. In the world.

"You see how embarrassing this is?" Ms. Abbound says from behind the wall of men. "We're *grieving.*" She says the word like it's one we don't know. The rest of LornaCruzCharlotteDelilahIsla might be able to accept this, but I can't. I won't stand here and let this woman tell us we don't understand grief.

Next to me, Delilah stiffens. Something's hitting her, too.

"The Curse isn't a carnival," Delilah says. She wipes her eyes— I'd missed that she started crying. "I'm sorry. We'll go. We'll—I'm so sorry, Ms. Abbound."

I don't want to leave like this. I don't want Delilah to leave like this—thinking she's not good enough to say good-bye to the person she loved. We aren't who they think we are. We aren't who Angelika says we are. We're kids who live on a street. That's it.

Ms. Abbound turns away and Delilah does, too. Isla crosses her arms. Charlotte and Cruz go to Delilah. And Owen, of course, watches me.

"He was ours, too," I say, meaning he was ours and Delilah's, but also Future Lorna's. Everyone turns to face me. Sometimes words that I think are small come out big. Ms. Abbound, a woman with a beautiful last name and slight shoulders, cringes, inhales, and considers a scream.

The moment lasts forever.

When it's over, she heads to the church and almost everyone follows her.

"We can still go in," I say to Delilah, who looks angrier with me than she was with Michael or Ms. Abbound.

"We can't go in, Lorna." She gives my shoulder a little shove. It's not so gentle. "They don't want us there. And whatever—they're right. We shouldn't be in there."

"We're not jokes. We're not who they think we are."

"You're right," Delilah says. She pulls at a strand of her hair like she wishes it were longer. She closes her eyes and shakes her head. "We're so much worse."

. . .

The legend of Devonairre Street is something hipsters who've only recently discovered the brownstones of Brooklyn don't know about—they're concerned with fancy pickles, as if regular pickles weren't already perfection. New Brooklynites have beards and fluffy dogs and a way of walking past us on our stoops as if they don't see us at all.

But the rest of Brooklyn knows about us. Mostly it's a joke. A funny urban myth that gets dismissed or used as a punch line or referenced as part of the charm of the borough. People roll their eyes and ask why we would let some kook like Angelika have so much power. Then they ask if we've ever measured our hair. They reach for the keys around our necks and hold them in their hands, forgetting they are attached to actual people.

They talk about us when we're gone and call us quirky or charming or fame-whores or cult members or dangerous.

I don't tell them about the way Angelika sat next to me at my father's funeral or how she shielded me and Cruz and Isla from reporters trying to talk to the Families of the Victims. "Don't be a symbol for them," she said in a ferocious whisper. Cruz and Isla and I nodded seriously and held on to the words. "I'll say it again if you weren't listening."

But we were listening. Of course we were. We still are.

Then those same people called us Affected and put us in textbooks, so I'm not so sure who won.

Outsiders see the special way we say good-bye—grabbing each other's hands, weaving our fingers together, giving one squeeze, then releasing. They know old ladies talk about magic and that a few too many of us lost family in the Times Square Bombing and World War II. They know Angelika's name and something about lemons and they had a friend of a friend of a friend who died after marrying one of us, but it was all a big coincidence. They're pretty sure.

They don't know every widow has a closet full of her dead husband's clothes. They don't know about the way Angelika drops in to make sure photographs of the men we've lost are on our mantels, in our bedrooms, tucked into our wallets.

I don't tell them about the List of dead men we receive when we've let Angelika down, when we're not being good enough.

Days like today I am brimming with the desire to tell them all of it.

There's one man in a plain suit with big glasses left behind. He's not one of Jack's people, so he must work for the church. He has a pile of programs in one of his hands, as if he might pass them out to us, but he doesn't.

"It's time to go," he says. "You've had your fun."

Aside from funerals, I've never been to church. And it is not the first time someone religious has looked at me with disdain, but it's the first time someone's said something directly to me. I wonder whether a religious person is more or less likely to believe in Curses. I want to know whether he hates us because we are jokes or liars or Cursed girls.

"You think this is fun?" Isla says. I'm glad someone else has sparked to life, but I'm nervous that it's Isla. "Nothing about this is fun. Nothing about who we are has anything at all to do with fun."

"You're not cursed," the man says, smoothing out non-creases in his jacket. "You're reckless. You think you have an excuse for all your bad behavior. We don't put up with that here." I don't know if here means in church or in this fancier part of Brooklyn or just on the sidewalk, in the daylight. "You're dangerous girls. Just not for the reason you think you are."

"We don't think we're anything!" Isla says. It comes out as a whine—loud and high and a reminder of how Isla is closer to the age of tantrums.

The man sighs and rubs his hands together like he's heard it all before and maybe he has, but not from us. This is the most we've ever talked to a stranger about what it's like to be from Devonairre Street.

He thinks we're at fault, even if he doesn't think we're Cursed.

"She just wanted to say good-bye," Cruz says. "We all did."

"Please," Charlotte says, always softening Cruz's words with her sweeter ones.

"Can we go now?" Delilah asks. We're all somehow simultaneously focusing on her and forgetting she's here with us.

For the first time in our friendship, I can't tell how she feels or what she's thinking. Is her heart whirling or still? Is she sad or numb? Why is she carrying around lemons if she doesn't believe?

The man looks at Delilah and I think his heart breaks for her a little. He was in love at seventeen, I bet. But he looks for a moment too long and sees the key around her neck—Delilah's is shiny gold and hanging from a silver chain, like a cross might if we were different people entirely. The key reminds him, I think, of everything he hates about us.

Fine. It's strange that we wear the keys, that we grow our hair, that we drink the tea and eat the cake and switch the outside lights on when the sun goes down and armor ourselves in wool.

But Santa Claus is strange, too. And lucky pennies. And horoscopes in newspapers. And unbreakable mirrors.

These things are just as odd and useless; but they don't happen to be ours.

I bet this man in his shiny black shoes and perfectly parted hair blows out his birthday candles, knowing his wishes won't come true, but doing it anyway.

"If you didn't want to cause a commotion, you'd try to fit in," he says, but the good, remembering-young-love part of him hands over his pile of programs. "I can't let you in. But you can have these." I open one up. There's Jack's name. And the dates of his life.

It's awful. Final. I don't want Delilah to see.

"We're going," Delilah says, and this time her words are strong and sure and it's decided. We won't be saying good-bye to Jack. We're going to slink away and return to the only place we belong— our street.

The man, satisfied at last, joins the rest of Jack's family and friends inside.

Delilah watches the church and we don't make her move. Behind us cars honk and men wave sleazy hellos, a construction worker calls out to Isla, asking how she got that ass.

Cruz texts me, even though he's next to me. We do this. It's a secret thing between us that we never talk about. A conversation underneath the conversation.

You tried. And then: *I can't wait to change out of this suit.*

Wool's the worst, I text back. *You remember when I took off my tights at last year's memorial?*

Cruz pats the pocket where he held them for me.

I look up and we make eye contact, Cruz and I. We don't smile, but we something. We Something. It hurts, the way a deep connection to someone who isn't yours sometimes does.

We're all a little broken, on the sidewalk. On the street. In the city.

I reach for Delilah's hand. Again she pulls it away, shaking her head. She squints at the church and touches the key around her neck.

• • •

We go to the garden and Delilah sits in a patch of dandelions while the rest of us try to fill up the Jack-less space.

"Would Jack like violets in his honor?" I ask. "Or chives? Did he like chives?"

Everything I plant grows, and right now it feels like all I have to offer. I want to plant something that will have a smell, so when we smell it we will think of him. Delilah doesn't reply, and I don't ask again.

"Jack would have brought his flask," she says eventually.

"I can get you some beer or something," Owen says too quickly. He and Cruz are especially uncomfortable. I think they know that today was about us and not them. I think they know they could have stayed without us and said good-bye to our friend. They keep rearranging their bodies, moving their hands and feet into different positions. Charlotte and Isla sit on the picnic tables. I sit on the bench.

"Or vodka?" Cruz asks, looking to the rest of us for help. "What'd he have in there anyway? Whiskey?"

We've all drunk from Jack's flask a thousand times, but we never thought to ask what it was. Jack knew things we didn't know. And now we can't know those things. Delilah tears up.

"Oh my God, I'm not sure what was in there exactly," she says. "I hated it, whatever it was. It was gross. Like fire."

"We'll figure it out," I say. It's incredible how small the English language gets when you're trying to make it fix something. "Do you want to, like, say a few words?" I'm picturing some kind of makeshift funeral, which of course sounds terrible.

I miss him, too, I text Cruz. I watch him read it. He nods. *But there's no room for my missing him.*

I can make room for that, he texts back. Owen looks to see who I'm texting.

"My mom," I say, and hide my phone in my pocket.

Delilah fidgets in the dandelion patch. She'll never be able to wear that dress again—it will be covered in stains. I can see them even on the dark fabric, almost-invisible but still-yellow streaks.

Although I guess that will be the least ugly thing clinging to the fabric. Funeral dresses usually go in trash cans, too haunted by the things that hurt.

"Do you want me to toast Jack?" Cruz says. We don't have anything to toast with but it's clear that won't matter.

I think Delilah's going to tell him to go ahead, but she holds up a finger to quiet us.

"I want to say that I think we're all making huge mistakes." She's speaking slow, Owen-slow, and her essential Delilah-ness is missing. "I want to say that Angelika's right. I want to say that seeing you guys together—Cruz and Charlotte; Owen and Lorna—terrifies me. I'm seasick. I'm seasick from the things we've done. The things you're still doing."

She lies back so she's staring right up at the sky. The balloons from the other day are all gone except for one deflated blue one that hangs from a silver ribbon off the gate. I think we're all looking at that one balloon.

She'll feel differently tomorrow. If not tomorrow, then in a week or a month. She'll remember Saad and Hiba. I'll remind her to think about how very, very long Cruz and Charlotte have been in love. My mom will tell her about Esther and Aaron and alleged Anna in Bed-Stuy.

"Delilah," I say. "You know better than—"

"We didn't sacrifice." She interrupts me, all angry and unfamiliar. Isla shakes her head and bites her tongue. I do, too, but barely. "Hubris," Delilah spits, and I can hear Angelika's voice shoving in *I'll say it again if you weren't listening.*

Delilah makes fists with her hands and tells us without telling us that we need to shut up, that we can't touch her, that things are different now.

That she believes.

I feel stupid for thinking the future was going to be easy and simple and ours. I feel stupid for thinking nothing would ever have to change, even after knowing how quickly things can. I feel stupid for believing in Future Lorna and Future Delilah and Future Jack all living on Devonairre Street but no longer being Devonairre Street Kids.

I had this idea of the ways we could fall apart, of the ways LornaCruzCharlotteDelilahIsla might become Lorna, Cruz and Charlotte, Delilah and Jack, Isla.

This was not part of my list of fears and worries and imaginings.

This is the unimaginable.

"I have to go," Delilah says. She doesn't give us a reason or tell us what she has to do, but I can guess.

I miss her before she's even all the way out of the garden.

I miss her and the person she was supposed to become.

9.

The next morning I walk to the bakery to get breakfast for Mom and me, and I walk toward the garden on my way home. There's an old bench there and it's covered in hearts and initials and proclamations of love and curse words galore. I've always liked the romance of sitting on a bench that so many other people sat on before me.

Today I need it. It's been years since I've gotten to sit in a room with Mom and Dad's love, and I won't get to sit near Jack and Delilah's love either, now. The bench is the closest I can get. I'm desperate to sit on it with my coffee and a pastry and enjoy five minutes without thinking about Jack or Delilah or Chicago or the looming Seven-Year Anniversary of the Times Square Bombing.

It's sunny, finally, and little patches of pink are blossoming all over Brooklyn. It's strange, when nature conflicts with what's actually happening in the world. It should be a gray day in the dead of winter. The garden itself should be barren and flower-less and damp.

Instead it's downright beautiful.

Cruz is already at the gate to the garden, staring at the bench.

I stand next to him. Since yesterday, someone's painted the whole thing white and they've written LOVE WAS FOUND HERE on the back in shiny blue strokes.

It's actually sort of beautiful, and the carvings are all intact underneath the new coat of paint. You can't paint on top of shadows.

I put a hand on Cruz's arm and squeeze. He jumps a little.

"I didn't see you there," he says.

"You can't sense when I'm right next to you?"

I think he smiles.

"Who did this?" I ask. Cruz shrugs.

Delilah could have painted the bench, maybe, but as far as I know she hasn't been out since we were all in the garden yesterday. It actually seems like the kind of thing Owen would do—some grand romantic gesture I didn't ask for—but he didn't even want to kiss me last night when he walked me home.

"You remember us meeting here?" Cruz says.

I hadn't remembered, but I do now. My family moved to the street a few weeks before Cruz's. The day Cruz moved in, my dad took me to the garden to play while my mother painted my bedroom. Dad smoked a cigarette and told me not to come near him, so I had to stay on the bench while he hung out near the gate. Cruz and his dad were in the garden, too, kicking a soccer ball back and forth across the plants. Later, Angelika would come by and yell at us all—Dad for smoking, Cruz and his dad for disrespecting the plants, me for the unabashed way I was staring at Cruz.

"Hi!" I called out to him. I was different then. I liked other little kids and waving hello and the sun in my eyes, even.

"Hi," he said back, a little less enthusiastic, shading his eyes and wrinkling his nose.

"I like your curls!" I said, wishing I could run on over and pull one.

"I have a sister," he said. "You can play with her." He was seven and I was six. I didn't want to play with his sister. I wanted to play with him and his soccer ball and his springy curls.

"No thanks," I said. "I'll stay here and watch you."

I don't remember much about being six, but I remember that.

"That was a good day," I say, and want Cruz to agree.

I still want to pull on his curls.

Cruz swallows and moves closer to me. Our elbows touch and neither of us moves them away.

Love Was Found Here, the bench proclaims over and over, as loudly as if someone were yelling it.

"And we've been having some really bad days," Cruz says. I wince, Jack's face popping up in my head. That gasp of pain. I don't know how to get rid of it. Cruz covers his throat with his hand, like his heart has leapt up there.

"Right now's not so bad," I say, thinking that the bench is a little hopeful and being near Cruz is a little wonderful. When Dad died, Mom said to be sure to let myself have good moments. Even when everything hurts, even when other cities are exploding and people we love are disappearing, there's still space for sweet things. I let our elbows' resting against each other feel good, while everything else feels bad.

Cruz doesn't say anything. He keeps looking at that bench, so I do, too. And the bench looks right back at us.

10.

Mom allows me one more day off from school on Monday.

"Back to normal tomorrow," she says on our walk over to Delilah's place. I raise my eyebrows. Mom shakes her head at herself. "I sound like one of those people." We both know the people: the ones who have a timetable for how long grief should last. Probably the same people who came up with the idea of a Minute of Silence.

"You read the horoscopes this morning?" Mom asks.

"Mine was all about healing. I hate that word."

"They're predicting heartbreak for Aquarians," Mom says. "A long period of heartbreak." Mom's an Aquarius. She cracks her knuckles and I hear her heart speed up. Like most people, she never read horoscopes when they were hidden next to wedding announcements and crossword puzzles. Sometime after the Bombing, they started to grow. It's different now that they take up two whole pages in the front section, a collection of essays instead of a sentence about what your future might hold. It's hard to not read them now.

"Aren't we already in a period of extended heartbreak?" I ask. "All of us?"

"Oh, I think we can find our way out," Mom says, and she sounds sure but we don't believe in horoscopes anyway so none of it matters.

"Delilah's an Aquarius, too," I say.

Things aren't good at Delilah's apartment: Her mother is hiding out in the bedroom, and Delilah won't leave the stoop.

"It's where I need to be," she says when Mom and I arrive with tea and sunflowers in hand. She's in a new black skirt that goes past her knees. On top she's wearing a gray wool sweater that is too heavy for April. It's loose and close to her neck. I miss the delicate line of Delilah's clavicle. I miss her waist and her knees and floral rompers and skinny blue pants and T-shirts with lacy sleeves and faded lettering.

Delilah takes the tea and sips it hungrily. I've never seen her drink it before.

Angelika says lavender promotes longevity and healing, and that sweetened with generous amounts of honey it will keep our intentions pure. Personally it makes me sleepy. I have to hope it will do the same for Delilah. She looks like she needs a rest.

"Lorna thought she'd sleep over," Mom says. Delilah didn't take the sunflowers, so they're still in Mom's arms like she's a beauty queen at the end of a pageant. It's awkward and I've forgotten how to talk to my best friend. Delilah puts the tea down and focuses on her hands, which are weaving red and white threads together in her lap.

"Yes!" Delilah says, smiling for the first time in almost a week. "You can help!" Her eyes flicker between my mother and me, and she sees Mom's haircut for the first time.

Delilah's eyebrows dive into a deep V. "What'd you do?" Her voice is thick and grumbling, like the sound of the subway as it shudders beneath us once every five minutes. She starts shaking, and I don't know if it's from anger or exhaustion or if she's been forgetting to eat since Jack died. I reach out to take hold of her hands and make them still, but she shakes me off.

This is what we do now: I reach out for her and she shivers away from me.

Delilah can't seem to speak. She can't take her eyes off Mom's head. She brings a hand to her own hair and pulls at a few strands like she did the other day at the funeral, like she could make it longer right here and now.

"It's hair, honey," Mom says. "Don't change everything you've always known. Things are still the same."

It's the wrong thing to say. Delilah's eyes fire up and she shakes her head violently.

"Nothing's the same!" she shouts. She leaps up and touches the ends of my mother's hair. Mom lets her but it's tense.

"How could you do this?" Delilah's voice is rising, accelerating fast. "You don't care about me or Jack or anyone else? You only care about you?" She's yelling, and people are leaning out of their windows, which are still open out of respect for Jack.

Now it's Mom's turn to be speechless.

Delilah shakes her head and picks up a handful of bracelets, shoving them in Mom's face. "You need to wear these!" she says. "This isn't the time for hubris! I can't believe you would do this, after everything."

That's when Delilah finally cries. Mom takes the bracelets and puts them in her pockets and Delilah crumbles back onto the stoop, like she never should have stood up to begin with.

A few buildings down, Angelika's door opens. She and her dog stand on their stoop and watch. Angelika's arms cross over her chest and I get a flicker of fear.

"I'm too late to fix anything; I'm too late to listen to what I should have done," Delilah says, or I think she says, through the big heaves of her cries. "I shouldn't have cut my hair. I should have worn a dozen keys around my neck. I forgot about the lights all the time. I made fun of Angelika. And tea. I didn't drink the tea. I didn't make Jack drink the tea. Jack was supposed to drink the tea. I shouldn't have even looked at Jack." She's losing her breath but she says it again. "I should not have even looked his way. Not for one moment."

After a long while, Delilah starts weaving bracelets again and Mom can leave and I can stay and try to remember what we were like one week ago, before things fell apart.

"Hubris is planning a future when you're a Devonairre Street Girl," Delilah says a long while later, and I know she's been thinking it over and over for hours, days. "I planned a whole future."

I feel myself break a little more than before.

Angelika doesn't move from her place on the stoop. She watches us as we sit and try to be something that we aren't anymore.

I think I catch her smiling.

• • •

"Red is for protection," Delilah says. "White is for breaking curses."

She doesn't want to watch movies. She doesn't want to eat ice cream or drink wine or talk about Jack. She doesn't want to sleep or stay up or go for a walk. She only wants to make bracelets.

She shows me how to wind the threads around each other in a lazy not-braid.

"How many do you want to make?" I say. I'm careful not to let her know how much I hate this.

"We need a lot," Delilah says. "For the five of us, and you should hand them out at school, and obviously for your mom, too."

"So one for everyone we know?" I ask. I smile and wait for Delilah to smile back at me.

She doesn't smile. She rolls up the sleeves of her gray sweater. A red-and-white-striped pattern covers her forearms, and the effect frightens me.

I put a hand on her shoulder and this time she doesn't jerk away but she takes my wrist, and moves my arm in front of her. She ties on a bracelet, then one on the other wrist as well.

I hold up my arms to look at what she's done and attempt an encouraging smile. It comes out lopsided and wrong, I'm sure.

"Do you love him yet?" Delilah whispers. "Do you love Owen?" There has never been a more worried face, a bigger tremble in someone's voice.

"I don't know." I never got a chance to tell her about *I love the moon and you and I don't have a chicken.* I can't tell her now.

Delilah grins. It's a grin Angelika gives, too. Like she knows something extra about the world.

"If you loved him, you'd know." I half expect a Polish accent. "Love is something you have or don't have," she says. "Love is like a fever."

Just because Angelika says it, doesn't mean it's true.

"Angelika's teaching me how to see it. She's teaching me so much. I can't bring back Jack, but maybe I can save someone else."

Delilah squeezes my cheeks. Her mouth gets close to mine, her eyelashes practically fluttering against my own. I swear she smells like Aramis.

"Hmm," she says, but nothing more. Two more bracelets get tied around my wrists. Then another two. And another.

I want to ask her if she can see—if she knows whether or not I love him.

Not that it matters. It doesn't matter.

I don't believe.

I've never believed.

I weave a bracelet anyway. It doesn't hurt anything. And it makes Angelika, and now Delilah, feel better.

It takes me most of the evening to realize I feel a little better, too.

11.

I wake to the sound of Cruz's voice and I reach for him before remembering I'm on a cot in Delilah's room and Cruz and I have never shared a bed. I determine that his voice is coming from the hallway, which feels impossibly far away and dangerously close. I could go to him, but I decide to pretend to be asleep instead. I stay in Delilah's room and listen in.

I should be thinking of Owen and his romantic sleep-talking in the just-woken hours, when I'm horizontal and wanting and dreamy. I should be thinking of him when I talk to Delilah about love. I should be thinking of him all the time, really.

"It's early, Delilah." Cruz sounds exhausted and I'd guess between all of us on the street we've slept a combined ten hours in the last three days. "Why am I here?"

The clock says five. There's a clear bowl of lemons next to it.

"I had a dream," Delilah says. "I dreamt you and Lorna were together. So happy you were basically vibrating. Then we were all on the beach and you were writing your names in the sand like some stupid movie. And you kept kissing."

"All right," Cruz says.

I want Delilah to keep talking. I want to hear about the kissing and the vibrating. I want to feel the sand on my skin.

"I woke up sweating. I could barely get a full breath. My heart's still—well. Feel it."

I think she puts his hand over her heart. Their voices are low but the apartment is small and besides, I have extra-strong senses when it comes to Cruz and Delilah. I am attuned to the sounds of the people I know the best.

"It's gonna take a long time to feel okay again. I don't even know how long. You're going to have nightmares. Even normal dreams will feel like nightmares. And nightmares will feel real. And, Jesus, Delilah, it's awful. What you're going through—"

And then silence.

Cruz still has nightmares. He's in Times Square but the lights go off around him until he's in total darkness. Sometimes his father visits him in dreams. But he's made of dust and fire, not flesh and bone.

Cruz texts me the worst dreams, so some mornings I wake up to his recounted nightmares. On those days I buy him a bacon-egg-and-cheese sandwich from the best bodega, on the other side of the park. We don't talk about it. I just hand him the steaming, salty deliciousness wrapped in tinfoil, and he devours it and tells me it's going to be an okay day and we meet up with everyone else to walk to school. The dreams are secrets Cruz and I keep. People put too much stock in dreams lately, so they're best kept to ourselves.

Delilah moans and Cruz's weight shifts. I think he's hugging her.

"This isn't about me right now," Delilah says loudly. "You're not listening. I'm telling you to be careful."

"After my dad died, I basically thought the world was going to explode," Cruz says. "You feel like more terrible shit's gonna happen.

I get it. But, Delilah. This is it. This is the bad thing. It already happened. Don't make up more bad shit in your head, okay?"

"I don't think she loves Owen." Delilah's not listening. My mouth is dry and I can't clear it or cough or even risk swallowing. We're LornaCruzCharlotteDelilahIsla. We don't split into parts and tell one another's secrets. We all have the same secrets, the same histories, the same sadnesses.

"She doesn't need to love Owen," Cruz says.

"I don't think she loves Owen and I don't think Charlotte loves you." The floor creaks. Delilah must have stepped closer to him, for emphasis.

"I bet you need food," Cruz says. "I bet you could use some water and a sandwich and some sort of crappy TV. How's that sound?"

"Like bullshit. I didn't call you over for a snack. I called you over because I'm terrified about what might happen."

"Delilah."

"Cruz, she could fall in love with you. Everyone's always thought—"

My body contracts, waiting for the end of her sentence but it doesn't come.

"Don't be this person. Jack wouldn't want this."

"This is *exactly* what Jack would want." She's speaking more loudly, and soon I won't be able to pretend I'm asleep. Her bedroom feels small and the cot feels hard. I want to get out, but I can't.

"Even if Lorna did love me—" I squeeze the blanket harder. It doesn't help. I'm floating away, I'm flipping upside down. Where are my sunglasses?

"We can't lose you." Delilah hiccups on the last word and I know the tears are going to start again and I'll have to come out of the room and circle her with my arms.

"Hiba and Saad," Cruz snaps. "Remember them. And me and Charlotte. Remember us."

"Everyone's talking about you and Charlotte and Hiba and Saad. We need to be talking about the Curse. We need to talk about how much I loved Jack and how selfish that was and that Angelika knew this was coming. We need to talk about hubris. We need to talk about all the other stories, the books and books of notes Angelika has. The books and books of notes her mother had. All the things we've heard about the street and never talked about. We need to talk about the Curse."

Cruz doesn't answer.

"Angelika tell you about Emilio and Stacey ever?" Delilah says. Emilio and Stacey are one of those couples we've all heard about for years. Cruz must know the story, but Delilah goes on anyway. Sometimes it's a comfort to tell the same stories over and over. Sometimes it's torture. "Stacey had that husband who was fine and time was ticking and everyone was getting so nervous that the husband, what was his name?"

"Dominic." Cruz has thought about this story recently.

"Everyone's waiting for Dominic to die, slowing down their cars when he's on the road, feeding him apples and basil and everything they knew to try to save him and all this energy is going toward keeping him safe and worrying about him. Then *Emilio* gets hit by some woman in a Jeep. No one was worried about Emilio."

I get out of bed. I can't stand being in here for another minute. I'm burning with shame since I know where this story is going. Delilah is supposed to be my best friend. I can't stand her telling this story like it's a warning about me.

I hate her for believing something different than I do for the first time ever.

I hate Angelika for making her believe something new.

"Stacey was hysterical at the funeral. She absolutely lost it. She loved Emilio. She never loved Dominic. You can be married to someone and not really love them. You can even think you love them and not love them. No one ever had to worry about Dominic. He was fine all along!"

When Delilah and I first heard this story, I asked Angelika what Stacey should have done differently.

"I think that's clear," Angelika said. In her accent, *that's* sounds like *dat's* and the word *clear* comes out lighter, airier than the way Delilah and I say it. "Were you listening?"

"I was listening. But she married someone safe. And love happened anyway. What was she supposed to do? It sounds like love just sort of happens, whether you want it to or not, whether you're married or not."

"Like moons and tides," Delilah said. It was her saying for when something was inescapable, inevitable.

I wonder whether she thinks Cruz and I are like moons and tides. The thought paralyzes me.

"Did you forget all about them? Stacey and Emilio and Dominic?"

"I know the story. I know all the stories."

"What if you're Emilio? What if Owen is Dominic?" An awful noise follows. A cry. A heave. "There's not any part of you that's scared? Cruz. There has to be. Even a tiny part of you must be terrified of her."

I'm her.

I wait for his answer. I wait for a resounding no.

It doesn't come.

12.

Cruz leaves and I stay in bed until Delilah drops a pan on the floor in the kitchen, so I can pretend I woke up from that.

"Morning," I say. It's too early—school doesn't start for a while and I'm still full from last night's feast of sausage and lettuce and bread. Delilah gives me yogurt with almonds anyway, serving it up in a little bowl her mother made when that was a thing her mother was doing on a Healing Through the Arts retreat.

Mrs. James hid all the paintings and sculptures so that Angelika wouldn't see. But she hung on to everything functional—bowls and mugs and plates that fill up the cabinets of Delilah and Mrs. James's apartment. They're crooked and sloppy and I don't think they did much to help Mrs. James move on.

I hear Delilah's mother moving around down the hall and I'm glad for the noise because I don't know how to fill up the silence with words. I'm a bad liar, and I've never had to withhold anything from Delilah.

"School's going to be weird without you," I say at last.

"And without Jack." There's rage in her that I don't know what to do with. I nod. Delilah ties more bracelets around my wrists. I don't want them—the ones I have are leaving imprints on my skin from being tied too tight and they make me itch.

They feel more like shackles than thread. Delilah yawns.

"Sleepy?" I can feel her exhaustion. I can smell it—the raw, fuzzy smell of someone who hasn't slept or showered for a few days. Her eyes are dry from crying and lazy from not resting.

She rubs her eyes and walks to the love seat in the living room. She pulls her knees to her chin and falls asleep within five minutes, the total giving-out of a body against all the things keeping it awake.

Sleep comes, no matter how deep the sadness cuts. It's like a gift from the universe, and hearing Delilah's deep breaths relaxes me, too.

Everything else is changing, but the reality of sleep stays the same. It's there; it will find us.

Like moons and tides.

• • •

We walk to school in our straight line—me, Cruz, Isla, and Charlotte. Pedestrians hate us—in New York, people aren't meant to walk in horizontal lines. We're supposed to walk two in a row, like animals on Noah's ark.

But today we are four instead of five, so the sidewalk feels almost empty.

"That's a lot of bracelets," Cruz says, looking at my covered arms. The way he notices me gives me goose bumps. I've never given any thought at all to my arms, but with Cruz looking at them today, I can think of nothing else. I wonder what they look like when they move and if they're too pale.

I fumble for my sunglasses and my heart calms.

"Delilah's being sort of—Delilah's having a weird moment. We should keep Angelika away from her," I say. I think Cruz tries to look through my dark lenses but I know I'm well hidden here.

We're in striped shirts and jeans, all of us. The sameness makes me ache for old Delilah.

"Angelika's amazing in a crisis, though," Charlotte says.

"You saw her when Delilah came back from the hospital," I say. "It was not good."

"She was comforting her. She comforts us. It's what she does." Charlotte and I are disagreeing more than we ever have. I can't stand the idea of another divide in our group, so I nod and muster something like a smile.

"Angelika's insane," Isla says. Her striped shirt hits above her belly button. Her jeans are cuffed at the bottom and so tight I think they might pop. She looks about twenty-five and it makes me nervous.

"Be respectful," Charlotte snaps. Charlotte never snaps and even Cruz looks taken aback.

"We're always respectful," I say. "But the last thing Delilah needs is to feel guiltier. Or sadder. Or more confused."

We get to the school entrance. This is where we wait for Owen and Jack to meet us every morning. Owen always kisses my neck and Jack always kisses Delilah on the mouth for too long. Then Jack tells us some song we have to listen to that we've never heard of and he puts an earbud into Delilah's ear and we watch as they fade into a bubble and we walk behind them, not minding one bit.

I was never jealous, watching Delilah fall in love. I fell in love with how happy she was, and I was glad one of us could experience it.

Today it's only Owen meeting us, of course.

He kisses my neck. It's dry out, and we each get a zap of electricity between his lips and my skin.

"Ouch!" he says. "You stung me!"

I try to smile, but it fails. Everything is failing now. We don't move to the door—we don't have Jack and Delilah's love bubble to follow. We stand and watch other people living their normal lives. The school sits on a crowded intersection. Women with strollers sigh while they try to navigate around us, dog-walkers do their best to keep their five dogs from leaping and licking and wrapping their leashes around our legs. There's a crap playground across the street and adults eye us when we're walking by, ready to yell at us if we enter.

"Fucking teenagers," a girl not that far outside her teen years mutters, pushing my shoulder with hers.

I watch her leave and envy the way her life is exactly the same today as it was yesterday and the day before.

I did this a lot in the weeks after my father died. I watched people move from being shaken up and emotional right after the Bombing to being fine a few weeks later. It was astounding. They had the same wardrobes, the same slang, the same inside jokes as before. I was different. I was new.

People on the street are spilling coffee from walking too fast and they're rolling their eyes at us. They aren't looking for Jack or Delilah. They're not fretting about Chicago. They're absolutely fine. They're moving ahead.

"I don't know if I can go in," I say. "Can we really sit there all day talking about, like, Dickens or whatever? What about Jack's other friends? Are they here today? Does he have other friends? Aren't we supposed to know that?"

Isla shrugs.

"I don't have any friends in my grade," she says. "Maybe he didn't have any in his. He was new and then he met Delilah, so . . ."

I'm starting to panic at all the things we don't know about Jack. What was in his flask and who he was friends with and what he had for first period and whether he liked chocolate. I rush through my mind, looking for facts about him, things that we know for certain, so that he doesn't slip away too fast.

"What was that song he told us to listen to last week?" I ask. I can't go in there without a music recommendation from Jack. I can't give up everything all at once. That's what people don't get about the Devonairre Street traditions—we have to give up so many things when the people we love die. So we hang on to other familiar things. Maybe I keep my hair long in part because I no longer get to eat doughnuts with my father on Saturday mornings. Maybe Charlotte wears the key around her neck because her dad's not around to play Santa at their holiday party anymore.

"Something from that love song album," Isla says. "He was obsessed with that thing."

"*69 Love Songs*," Cruz says. He looks at me on the word *love*, like it's an accusation. My heart stops.

I look to Owen, but he's on his phone, probably looking up the album. He's so sweet and good and handsome, and I don't love him at all.

"Magnetic Fields' album, right, Lorna?" Cruz says, and I'm forced to look at him again. I nod.

"'I Don't Want to Get Over You,'" I say.

Cruz's eyebrows jump. He jumps. Charlotte notices and gives us both a look. I shake my head and pull my lips in.

"The song," I say, but I'm blushing and Cruz is blushing and Charlotte or anyone with eyes can see it all. "The song Jack told us to listen to last week was 'I Don't Want to Get Over You.' Magnetic Fields from the *69 Love Songs* album. It's good. It's great."

"Right." Cruz is blushing, too.

I need the moment to end. The song is playing in my head now, and I need that to stop, too.

"Hey. What do we do during the Minute of Silence today?" I grope for a new subject.

"Whatever you usually do," Charlotte says. It's not as nice as she's supposed to sound when she's talking about my dad's death. "I mean, whatever feels right for you."

"Will they have it, though?" I ask.

Owen tilts his head and everyone else is looking at me like I've lost it, like the weekly Minute of Silence is a pillar of our world, like nothing could ever change our need for it.

Maybe they've forgotten that seven years ago it didn't exist. I hate that we pretend it's been this way forever.

"Well, there was Chicago. Won't we need a Minute of Silence for Chicago? That was a Tuesday, too. How much silence can we really take every Tuesday for the rest of our lives?" I'm getting a little loud. Until now, Cruz was the only person who even knew that I'm bothered by the silences at all. I sent him a text during one a few months ago. We aren't supposed to do anything like that—the silences are meant to be still, too—but it felt good. *I'm not so silent on the inside,* I wrote. *We're some of the only ppl in the world who could be loud during the moment of silence and actually get away with it. What would they say?*

When I saw him in the hall later that day, he smirked and I felt the deepest kind of gratitude for Cruz and I being in it together.

"Huh," Owen says, which isn't a response at all.

"You think we'll do one for Chicago?" Charlotte asks. It seems like everyone but me and Cruz has almost forgotten about Chicago already. Jack's death was so enormous and close, and Chicago is so far away and there's only so much that can fit into one single week. Chicago's hung on to me, though. It's hard to grieve so many things at once.

When I was little, my dad and I liked to bake together, and one day when I was measuring out the sugar and the flour in perfect copper measuring cups, I stopped mid-pour in a panic, the practice of measuring things suddenly disturbing me.

"You've got your worry-wrinkle, Lorna," Dad said, pointing to the place between my eyes where I hold everything that frightens me.

"You say you love me more every day," I said. Dad smiled and nodded and took the chocolate chips out of the cabinet. "But what about when you run out of room? Will you have to start loving me less?"

Dad laughed and gave me a huge hug, lifting me a little so my legs were left to wiggle in the air. "How much love-room do you have left?" I asked into his shoulder. "A tablespoon? Or a cup?" Once I had that one question, I had a million other questions, popping like popcorn in my brain. I wanted to know the exact size and shape of love. Its volume, its density, how much it weighed, how much space it inhabited, whether it was a solid or a liquid or something else entirely.

"You are so much like me, little one," Dad said, giving me an extra squeeze before letting me back on the ground. "I'm still learning, but what I can tell you for sure is that hearts expand to fit more love in them over time. You think there can't possibly be any more room, but there always is."

Now I'm not so sure about that. It feels like our hearts are so stuffed with sadnesses that they're collapsing, getting too crowded to fit any more feelings into. I don't have room to love Owen or forgive Angelika or properly mourn Chicago.

Dad liked big questions about love and hearts and the ways of the world, but when he died I wasn't old enough to ask him the most important ones.

I got to ask him so few huge, worthwhile, complicated questions, and this week I have a new one every hour.

"If there's another Minute of Silence, we can think about Jack," Owen says. The valley between what I'm feeling and what he understands is growing so wide I sometimes think we can't even see each other across the divide.

"What was it Jack liked to say before we went inside?" Isla asks.

I close my eyes and picture Jack as I saw him every morning all these months—the exact way I let myself believe I would see him every morning, even after high school and into real life. He used to squeeze Delilah close, turn his head to face the rest of us, and say something before breaking away from the group. It's unspeakably sad that the thing he said every morning is already hard to remember.

I promise to pay attention to the details of my friends from here on out. I'll remember their funny sayings and verbal tics and whether they say *what's up* or *how are you* or *how's it going* when we run into one another in the hallways. I'll remember every one of Delilah's made-up sayings. Moons and tides and onions and butter and whatever else she comes up with when she shifts back into being Delilah again.

I scrunch my eyes, keeping them closed tight. I can see Jack's face and his earbuds and his beat-up blazer and his messy hair. I can see his hands in his pockets and remember he always had his hands there, if they weren't on Delilah.

"'Let's do this thing, kids,'" I say. "That's what he said every morning."

It's such a small thing to remember, but I'm relieved to have grasped on to something that was slipping away.

We don't move for a minute, missing him saying it. Missing something we didn't know mattered at the time. Missing it in the now, and also the promise of it in the future.

"Let's do this thing, kids," Cruz says.

And like that, we have a new ritual. It's Cruz's job now, to usher us into the day.

• • •

At 10:11, we have our Minute of Silence.

In the room across the hall, I can hear Cruz sigh.

13.

When school's out, I want to see something pretty. Mom and I tried to do it every day after Dad died. "Every day we'll find one thing that's beautiful," she said, bringing home a Renoir postcard from one of the knockoff stands outside the Met. Those were the worst days, the ones when she brought home postcards, like we had to reach back a century to find something not awful in the world. On the best days we'd find something pretty inside our own apartment or out on the street. On the best days we'd be able to see beauty in a world without my father.

I go on a long walk and end up in the garden. It seems unlikely I can find beauty there today—places that Jack has been will be ugly for a long time, I think.

But I see it. My beautiful thing for the day.

Cruz on the bench.

My face must change. I can feel it blushing, but it does even more than that, shifts in some stark, recognizable way. I put on my sunglasses as fast as I can, but it's not fast enough, because instead of saying hello, Cruz says, "You heard us talking this morning."

I'm warm and shaky. I'm fluttery and hollow. Of course he can tell what I'm thinking about, what I'm trying not to think about.

After the Minute of Silence this morning, the principal came over the loudspeakers. "Thank you," she said, as always, followed by, "There will be a second Minute of Silence to commemorate the Chicago Bombings at 4:36 this afternoon. We expect you to take it just as seriously as you take the one in the morning. We stand by our Chicago brothers and sisters. We wait for answers with them. We will learn the names of the Affected. We will know their stories and the stories of their families. Thank you."

We're not far from 4:36 now, and the five new names we learned are stuck in my head, which I guess they're supposed to be. Next Tuesday we will learn five more, and five more the week after, and by next year they will be on our History of the Affected tests; they will be words on flash cards.

I used to think that people learning my name made me more real, made my grief more solid. After Jack's funeral, I'm starting to doubt. We're vocabulary words, we're concepts, we're like the state capitals or the pledge of allegiance or the Lord's Prayer—words people can say without meaning anything at all.

I sit next to Cruz. Closer than I have to. He makes me feel real.

I look to make sure Angelika isn't lurking, but I think I know deep down that she's with Delilah. That she is always going to be with Delilah now.

"I didn't hear much," I say finally, and Cruz pushes my sunglasses from my face into my hair.

"What'd you think, about what Delilah said?" he whispers.

"I'm with . . . Owen." I pause before his name because I forget it for a second. "I don't think about you like that." But even when I say it I'm thinking of the size of his arms and the shape of his curls and that we're both quiet and strange when we're sad or worried.

I think about how he knows me in an impossible way that no one else will ever know me.

I think about the moon—that it is always there but waxing and waning. That it is both predictable and shifting. I think love is something like that.

Like moons and tides.

Cruz moves closer to me.

"My mom has a boyfriend," I say. "And she cut her hair."

He nods.

"You and I don't believe in the Curse," I say. It did not used to be something we had to clarify. It was as obvious as not believing in the Easter Bunny. "Our dads didn't believe in the Curse." I pull my sunglasses back down. It's a little like taking a shot from Jack's flask—the volume of the world gets turned down, the edges seem less harsh.

Thinking the Curse is ridiculous was easier when Jack was alive.

Cruz looks at the bench. His dad's name is on there somewhere. So is my dad's.

"We can be sad about Jack without being terrified of everything?" I wanted to say it as a statement but it slips out as a question. I hate not being sure about things anymore. I look at my phone and it's four thirty and we are moments away from the newest ritual, the next thing that's supposed to make us feel stable and in control, but there's chaos happening beneath the surface of my skin.

Nothing's certain. I reach for my hair, then for my key, then for the edge of the bench. None of it steadies me. I am officially unsteady.

Cruz reaches for my glasses and pulls them right off my face. The sun is strong in a way it wasn't a few minutes ago. It moved in the sky, and now we're in sunlight instead of shade, without moving an inch.

The world is too bright and too harsh, and I have to squint.

Cruz kisses me.

When Owen kisses me, I know exactly how I feel. I feel good, in the simplest, best way. I feel sexy and eager; I always want more. I can get lost in it.

This kiss with Cruz is a hard and true kiss. Lips. Tongues. My hands in the softness of his hair, his hands on my shoulders, the bench holding us up. I am alert. I am not lost at all. I am right here in the garden, desperate and awkward and unsure.

I can't breathe.

We keep kissing and I think I might pass out from the endlessness of it. I thought kissing was an escape, but I'm still right here, aware of honking cars and my hair slipping into my eyes, getting caught between our lips, aware of Cruz's nose hitting mine and the creak of the bench when we try to move closer together.

When he finally pulls away, I leap up from the bench like the kiss was gravity. My knees buckle and I stumble a little. I don't have balance or breath or any of the things a person needs.

I grab my glasses back from him and throw them over my face so that I can breathe again.

I look at the time. It is 4:36. It is the first second Minute of Silence. It is the beginning of a new time.

"We should—" Cruz starts, but I put my finger to the lips he just kissed. I can't not do the thing I'm supposed to do. This is a part of our life now, whether we like it or not.

The street goes quiet. Cars pull over. Someone who didn't get the memo honks, a long sustained note, then they screech to a stop, too, the sound of remembering.

Someone's TV is on, and someone's water is running, I'm sure of it. When everything's quiet, you can hear more clearly. Cruz and I are breathing hard.

In Chicago someone has been in bed for a week and is starting to smell like they're rotting a little. In Chicago someone is calculating the number of seconds they've been without the person they love. In Chicago someone is capturing bits of bone and flesh in test tubes, trying to name victims that everyone already knows are dead. In Chicago they are at the very beginning of the things I know so well.

We're at the beginning, too, I think, standing in the shadow of the thing we shouldn't have done.

"I'm sorry" is the first thing I say at 4:37, when we are allowed to move on from the tragedy half a country away. In Chicago they are still stuck, of course, and I feel guilty for the moving forward.

Cruz touches my hair and I think maybe he's not so sorry.

"Mom says people do crazy things after a big loss," I say.

"So this is about Jack," Cruz says.

"I'm with Owen," I say again, but it's even less convincing now.

"Are you afraid of being with someone you love?" My heart stops in the garden. All I can think of is lemons and lamb and The List of names. I don't want to look at Cruz. I look at my bracelet-covered wrists.

I want to be Lorna who says, "No, I'm not afraid of anything!" but I am not that Lorna. I am Lorna who already lost the idea of one beautiful future. I don't want to take the risk to imagine another.

"Owen's wonderful," I say.

I'm not afraid of the Curse. But I am maybe a little afraid of love and the way it changes everything.

"So is Charlotte." Cruz sounds defeated, though, like he doesn't want it to be true.

We're supposed to talk about it more, the thing that happened, the things that are happening. But I'm trying hard to decide kissing Cruz doesn't mean anything. That's the easier choice, and I am desperate for ease.

Dolly and Betty appear at the entrance to the garden. Betty clears her throat and there's no more room for Cruz and me to talk about anything. I take one big step away from him. The space feels easier.

I've always been LornaCruzCharlotteDelilahIsla, and I liked the way the future looked, all of us staying that way forever. I imagined texting Cruz the kinds of secrets someone in their twenties or forties or seventies might have. I imagined a Shared Birthday at twenty-one with big bottles of champagne and at thirty with Delilah and Jack's kids hanging on to them, eating honey cake for the first time. But that's already gone. We're all these brand-new people, and on a street filled with tradition and old widows and long histories, that seems impossible. I've never been brand-new.

"You know, you'd look good with short hair, too, I bet," Cruz says like he lives inside my mind. I reach for my hair. I'm scared kissing him has made it vanish. It's still there. Long and fine and silvery and tangled at the ends.

Betty and Dolly wave hello like it's a warning. They pick basil leaves and mint leaves and they water the whole lot. It smells fresh and foreboding.

Cruz and I say good-bye the Devonairre Street way, with our hands clasped for one second.

Grab, grasp, gone.

14.

There's a café that turns into a bar in the evenings. It's called Julia's and it's in Prospect Heights, straddling two distinct Brooklyns— one that is settled in with families and histories and old men who stand on the sidewalk and talk in loud voices over the sound of traffic, another that is shiny and new, filled with just-married couples who drink expensive cocktails and go to cafés with their laptops and are pursuing master's degrees in predictive arts or the History of the Affected. They bump up against each other, these two Brooklyns, and Jack took us to Julia's once to watch them move around each other, avoiding eye contact, both sides scowling at the other but never actually speaking.

Julia's was his favorite because everyone went to it, each group huddling into its own corner, but necessarily waiting together in the bathroom line. Plus, since Jack was an Abbound, they didn't ID us.

I go there now, wanting Jack but also wanting to be far, far away from Devonairre Street and Angelika and Cruz and the way I am starting to feel. It's a long walk, down streets that I know so well I notice the smallest changes—one bank chain morphing into another, a bodega with a new awning, a sad city tree planted at a corner where there used to be a newspaper dispenser.

Each change feels like another tiny loss, a bit of the future that was promised to me and taken away. The last two blocks I get nervous that Julia's won't be there anymore. Maybe it's become a boutique or an Olive Garden or a parking lot. When I catch sight of the white lettering on the huge windows at the front, I can finally breathe.

No one knows where I am.

I step inside and it's not the usual mix of old and new residents. Everyone inside is young and dressed up and a little bit too drunk for the time of day. There's a white girl in a white dress with flowers in her hair and a black guy in a fancy suit is kissing her earlobe.

It's a wedding party.

I bundle my hair on the top of my head, a silvery bun, and hang my sunglasses from the top of my shirt. I wish I were wearing something satiny and sequined, but I'm stuck in tights and a shirt that barely covers my ass.

I decide not to care.

I take a flute of champagne from a waiter who doesn't look at my face to guess my age and I finish it off in three epic swigs. It sparkles in my throat and it gives me permission to move closer to the bride and groom, who are now holding hands while they talk to different groups of friends. I like the way love lets everyone in—if it's around, everyone can feel it. It makes some people uncomfortable or wistful or jealous, but it warms me up and helps me relax. I like how we dress up to celebrate love, and that no one in this room is afraid of what happens next.

The groom rubs the bride's hand with his thumb. The bride turns to look at the groom every third sentence. They move around their party and I follow close behind, making sure to keep love in my line of vision.

"I didn't get the cocktail-attire memo either." There's a guy behind me. He's my height, pale skinned and rosy cheeked. He's wearing jeans and an untucked plaid shirt that's frayed around the sleeves. He is staring at my ass.

"Who says this isn't cocktail attire?" I polish off my second glass of champagne. It bubbles in my nose, an uncomfortable feeling that makes me squirm and giggle.

"Bride or groom?" the guy says.

"I'm not either." I feel like Isla, not myself, and I swing out one of my hips so that my body takes a new, un-Lorna-like shape.

"Bride," the guy says, smiling at himself. "Bride's friend, I mean. Denver."

"Like the city."

"Denver like the city. You?"

"Lorna."

"Not a city, then." He is moving closer to me, this guy who might be seventeen or twenty-two or someone else's boyfriend or a terrible person.

"It means *forsaken*." I shrug, like it's not a name with weight and form and fate. I shrug like I am not a Devonairre Street Girl or an Affected person or the littlest bit famous, sometimes. I shrug like I have been to more weddings than funerals, like being around love is no big deal for me.

"That's one of those words that I know I should know what it means, but I don't really," Denver says.

The word *love* is like that for me, but I don't say that. "I have a secret," I say. "I don't know the bride or the groom. Or anyone else in this room."

Denver grabs us two more glasses of champagne and lifts his up to toast. I get a spark of guilt. "To showing up unannounced," Denver says.

"To being in the company of love," I say.

We clink. We drink. Julia's looks good, covered in champagne and white balloons and confetti. I decide on a new Future Lorna. She'll change her name and seek out weddings across the country. She'll sneak into them, soak them in, and disappear. She'll kiss a new boy at each one, but she won't love any of them. She'll have a collection of cocktail dresses and a stomach for champagne and cake.

The bride and groom's song is "Unchained Melody" and they don't dance to it so much as melt into it. They sway, but only slightly. Some of the guests look away, like the embrace is too much, too intimate to watch. They refill their drinks and pile cheese onto crackers. Denver takes my hand and we watch like it's a movie, like it's for us.

I explore the shape of his hand. It's rougher than Owen's, smaller than Cruz's. He has an unworried face and a hard grasp on my hand. Other friends of his wave hello and I beg them all not to notice me, not to recognize me. I'm terrified someone will pull him aside and explain who I am. When he's grabbing us cupcakes, I tuck the key around my neck down my shirt and make sure no strands are coming loose from my bun.

I watch him weave his way back from the cupcakes. It takes much longer than the few feet between us would suggest. He hugs pretty girls in short dresses and they laugh at jokes that probably aren't funny. A guy friend of his steals his cupcake and stuffs it in his mouth and Denver takes the guy's beer and polishes it off, the both of them looking like they're in a dance they've performed a hundred times before.

They look the way LornaCruzCharlotteDelilahIsla does when we're eating honey cake or sneaking wine in the garden. Practiced. Familiar. Like nothing will ever change.

I stop waiting for him to return to me and I go get him. I don't care who he's talking to or what normal-person ritual he's enacting.

I kiss him.

I kiss him so hard he stumbles back before recovering and kissing me too. I can hear his friends snickering and whooping, but it's not embarrassing, it's glorious, it's what they would do if he was kissing any girl from any street, and it makes me kiss him harder, letting more of him in through my lips, wrapping my arms more tightly around his neck. It feels good, it lights up my senses. It's not a world-altering kiss. It's nothing like kissing Cruz or Owen.

I don't care.

I pull him through the music and the candlelight and the tipsy trays of champagne into a bathroom. I press against him.

"Is this okay?" he asks, which makes me laugh because I'm making it happen so of course it is.

"This is great."

I reach down his pants and he pulls my tights down too and the touching is frantic and exciting. The bottom of my back is pressed against a sink and someone could walk in at any moment, but I don't let that stop me. I move against him and it's not sex but it's all the movements of sex, all the back-arching and grinding and heavy breathing of it.

One of his hands pulses between my legs and the other travels up into my hair.

I tense, and he feels it because he slows the hand between my legs, but the hand in my hair is the one I'm worried about. My hair loosens and his breath quickens and—

"Your hair's amazing—"

"I should go," I snap, pulling up my tights and shifting my hips around, trying to get them back in place. I'm all crooked and wet.

"What's wrong? I thought you wanted—did I do something wrong?" Denver looks a little brokenhearted, and I thought he was maybe older but now that I'm really seeing him in the harsh bathroom light, I think he's probably my age. They're all about my age—eighteen and getting married and seeing a vision of the future that is clear and lovely and romantic and safe.

I hope this is the worst thing that happens to Denver this year.

"I don't belong here," I say, touching my hair, feeling for fallen strands, clues of who I am.

"We can sit and talk. We don't have to—I didn't expect any—"

He's sweet, this Denver, but he's also a huge mistake and a secret I'll have to keep forever.

I leave the bathroom and the synthetic lemon smell of cleaner. I push aside balloons and weave around tables with white floral arrangements and discarded unfrosted ends of cupcakes, half-full champagne flutes, lipsticked napkins.

I let myself walk by the bride and groom, taking a last look at the way their elbows keep them connected. She doesn't notice that the bottom of her dress is picking up crumbs and spilled beer and dust; he doesn't notice the bad music that no one's dancing to or that another couple is having a fight in the corner.

Love is maybe about not noticing, and that's a problem, because now I notice everything.

I leave behind Julia's and the taste of champagne and an hour of being a normal girl and the biggest mistake I've made that no one will ever, ever know about.

It's a long walk home, each step of it trying to forget the taste of Denver's mouth, the feel of his hand desperate for me, and the idea that I could be someone else, UnAffected and UnCursed and reckless and free.

15.

I'm hungover the next morning. I'm glad that Denver's face was indistinct and that I never got his last name. He was an impossibility and a terrible thing I did and that's it. I will leave him there, at Julia's with a flushed face and unzipped pants and the memory of a mysterious girl.

Downstairs, Mom's left the paper open to the horoscope section. Every single horoscope says some version of Be Careful or Live Your Life to the Fullest or All We Have Is Each Other. I flip through the rest of the paper, and the news is even worse. There might be Yet Another Bombing, we need answers for the Chicago Bombing, some say a psychic in Milwaukee knew it was coming. There are studies on how the History of the Affected is working in schools, and the results are inconclusive but compelling, an impossible combination. Politicians are advocating a daily Minute of Silence. If my father were around, he'd ask why we think silence helps anything. That would be one of those complications he loved. I think he'd be fascinated by the way things are today, and I miss him even more, wishing he could question it all.

"Things will calm down," Mom says when she comes into the kitchen after a shower. She makes tea. It's vanilla. I've never had vanilla tea. Even the smallest things are changing. The tea smells like something I'd wear on my skin but I'm not sure I want to drink it.

"The paper says nothing is calming down," I say.

We stopped getting the paper for two years after the Bombing. Almost every article was about the Victims, the mysterious suspects, the beauty of a country in recovery, the fear of it happening again, and profiles of people who were moving on, the way that human connection perseveres after tragedy. It was strange to read about the biggest thing that had ever happened to me through the eyes of someone else. Mom used to crumple the whole thing up and stomp on it when she got especially frustrated.

We read a lot of books at breakfast over those two years.

"Should we stop getting this thing again?" I ask.

"When we move to California, we'll stop," she says. "We won't even let them know where we live. Won't that be sort of great?" I wonder if Mom's picturing California a little like Mars.

"We'd have to worry about earthquakes out there," I say, trying to make it a joke even though she sounds a little serious.

"We can survive an earthquake, Lorna."

I pretend not to hear. We could never leave the street. We *are* the street.

Further into the paper there's a long article on Jack Abbound and the Abbound family and their grief. There's a picture of his mother and Michael and I suppose someone who is his father—pale and powerful.

In the article they call Jack "*a promising youth from one of Brooklyn's most prominent families*" and "*a boy on the verge of something great, only to be taken down by wayward partying and a penchant for the wrong crowd.*"

I turn the page to where the article continues.

There's a photo, but it's not of Jack and it's not of his well-heeled family. It's of us. Our backs are to the camera. Four girls in black wool dresses, three of us with hair all the way down our backs, Delilah in the middle, her hair making her taller. We stand in a straight line looking at the church.

I see us, for a moment, the way other people see us. We look unusual and frightening. We look old-fashioned and misplaced. We look like outsiders in a city we've lived in our whole lives. We look all wrong.

No wonder they hated us.

For decades, the residents of Devonairre Street have experienced an unusual number of tragedies. The historical street is known for its public mourning and the storied rumors of a curse. The names of the street's best-known residents are now recorded in the History of the Affected. The Ryder family, the Rodriguez family, the Partona family, the Chen family, and the Joneron family all are Affected families of the Times Square Bombing. According to demographer Dr. John Ganderton, the number of Affected families on one single street is statistically unlikely. "Often we see streets with high levels of firefighters or police officers Affected in a tragedy like the Bombing. Neighborhoods that house a great deal of municipal workers often experience disproportionate loss. The numbers in those cases can be more easily explained."

But Devonairre Street is no such neighborhood. "These numbers in this neighborhood are highly improbable," Dr. Ganderton explained. "I would consider this a statistical anomaly."

Others, however, consider it concrete evidence of a curse. "We avoid those women," a man on neighboring Belleford

Street, who asked to remain unnamed, says. "Good thing they keep that long hair. Lets us know what we're dealing with. That rich kid? I'd have told him to stay away, too. It's a shame."

All the residents speak of Jack Abbound and the warnings they wish they'd issued him upon learning of the socialite son's death.

"We want the focus to be on my brother. We won't be commenting on the curse," Michael Abbound, brother of the deceased, said in a comment made the day after Jack Abbound's untimely death.

"We wish our son had made better choices," Bert Abbound, the deceased's father, said after the funeral. "We had high hopes for his future, for him finding his place in the city we love. He would have done the Abbound name proud. We aren't interested in commenting on the unusual company he kept in the last few months of his life."

"Of course he died; she loved him," Devonairre Street resident Angelika Koza said. She explained the logistics of the curse, saying the deaths always happen in the first five years of a girl loving a boy. "If a boy or a man hasn't died within five years, I know he wasn't ever truly loved," she said. "I tried to stop it. I always try, whether the boy has a fancy name or not."

This boy did have a fancy name, though, and according to many friends and family, a bright future. His death occurred only a few hours after the Chicago Attacks, a fact that believers in the curse say is further proof of its legitimacy.

"Too much coincidence for one street," a waiter at the street's famed Bistro said. And on that, at least, local Brooklynites and mathematicians can agree.

The Abbound family asks that their privacy be respected during this difficult time.

• • •

I shut the paper when I finish reading and look to Mom to see if she read it before her shower.

"I know, Lorna," she says. "I don't know how they even reached Angelika. Probably wandered the street looking for someone who would give them something juicy. You know how these reporters are."

My mother and I have appeared in three different major feature articles about Families of the Victims, and every time they captured us in some way that felt decidedly wrong. It's what we hate about the History of the Affected. We have been "Lorna and Emily: Strong Survivors with Unusual Beliefs," "Lorna and Emily: Struggling to Move Forward," and "Lorna and Emily: Focused on Community in Their Time of Need."

We are not those Lornas and Emilys.

Often we are Lorna and Emily: Not Doing the Dishes and Not Really Talking Much Either, or Lorna and Emily: Skeptical and Scared, or Lorna and Emily: Pissed at the World.

Today we are Lorna and Emily: Trying New Tea and Wondering What Love Even Is.

Jack Abbound wasn't the Jack Abbound in the article. They didn't mention his tattoos or his flask or how often he kissed Delilah or the lyrics to his favorite songs. They didn't talk about the way he would have put his feet up on the chairs in my future kitchen, or how I would have grown to know the difference between his tired yawn and his bored yawn and his just-because yawn. It mentioned his bright future, but forgot to describe how he might have looked in a tux or what flavor cake he and Delilah would have had at their wedding.

How he would have looked silly and too young.

That they would have had honey cake.

The article assumed he would have lived in one of his family's angular buildings by the water, but I know he would have lived on our street, proving everyone wrong—his family, Angelika, maybe even me.

"Hopefully Roger won't see this," Mom says.

"That's the name of the . . . person?" I don't want to talk about the guy in Mom's life.

Then I get a flash from last night at Julia's. A champagne hiccup. My hip bone hitting a ceramic sink. A bride with flowers in her hair. I swallow it back.

"He's from Queens." Being from Queens is shorthand for *Roger might not know about the Curse.*

"They get the paper in Queens, I think," I say. Mom's face falls a little.

"He's not the kind of guy who would buy into this stuff." She's trying to convince herself more than me so I don't bother saying anything. "He throws away the horoscope section. He thinks the unbreakable mirrors are a joke."

The mirror in our living room is decidedly breakable.

I don't want to know too much about Roger or the things he likes or doesn't like or believes in or doesn't believe in.

"He says it's important we all try to remember the way things were before. Too much changed in the way we all view the world, he says."

"I remember the way things were before." I'm thinking of Dad's wide hands and coffee breath and method of cutting sandwiches into strips instead of in halves.

Mom tucks the paper into her purse, finishes her tea, and kisses my forehead.

"I'll be home late," she says.

I didn't get a chance to say anything about my picture in the paper, or the way the image looked: stark and strange and like we are who they say we are.

• • •

We don't linger quite so long outside the doors before Cruz brings us into school today. It helps that two army recruiters are unashamedly staring at Isla while they finish their cigarettes. Or maybe they've read the paper and they're staring at all of us. I'm too tired to worry about it or Isla or anything at all. I feel a little bad for them, anyway. They look downright bored. It's a thankless job, these days, getting kids to join up. Recruiters spend most of their time trying to talk seventeen-year-olds out of engagements and into enlistment. Mom's always saying, "You can't get anyone to join an army when you don't know who you'd be protecting the country from." I try to imagine one of us joining the army, but I'm finding it impossible to conjure up any future at all.

I look them right in the eyes before we get all the way inside. I don't hate them, but I want them to know I see them seeing us.

• • •

I hang on to Owen at lunch. I wrap my arms around his neck and kiss the space where his T-shirt meets his skin. I do not think about Denver. I do not think about Cruz. I do not think.

"You smell good," I say. "You coming over later? My mom's going to be out with the guy."

"Of course," Owen says, and I try to look for worry under the words. *Are you scared of me?* I ask in my head, but I can't find an answer on the surface of his skin. I shake off the kiss with Cruz and the things we said and felt in the garden; I lock away the moments in the bathroom at Julia's and focus on Owen, who is a great kisser and a good boyfriend and a person who is safe and easy and uncomplicated. I kiss his mouth, which isn't allowed in the cafeteria, and guys start whooping and Charlotte and Cruz are across the table from us and fidgeting with discomfort.

"You're having a good day, huh?" Owen says, which is so far from how I feel but I kiss him again to see if I could kiss it true.

"That's one brave man," a guy behind us, Anton, says. He has the sad beginnings of a beard and wears the same shirt almost every day.

"Who knew you read the paper, Anton?" Cruz says. He is straight backed and frowning. Charlotte nudges him to shut up.

"It's all fucked up, bro. I didn't know that Jack guy but it's pretty fucked up."

"Step back, man," Cruz says. He's leaning forward like he might stand up, but Charlotte's pressing down on his knee. I put a leg over Owen's thigh and feed him a French fry from my plate, like that proves something. I try not to look at Cruz.

"I'm just saying." We don't know what it is Anton's saying, exactly. But my heart's pounding from the way things change slowly and all at once. We mostly keep to ourselves at school. And mostly people don't look at us except right after the Minute of Silence, like they want to catch sight of something sad crossing our faces. Otherwise they've grown used to us and the way we exist as a single organism.

That's gone now, too.

Anton turns around and more people might be whispering, but I don't hear them because all I can hear is Isla entering the room.

She has tall boots that make loud noises on the floor and her tangle of hair is swishing so wildly I swear it sounds like an ocean. She's wearing an extra-short blue dress and a collection of five keys around her neck and dozens of Delilah's bracelets. Her boobs are pushed up and out, and she smells like musk and the end of the day.

Cruz looks uncomfortable but doesn't say anything; he knows better. None of us say anything, but a lot of people are looking at the way she swings her hips—unpracticed, a little awkward, demanding attention.

"What'd I miss?" Isla asks, grabbing Cruz's sandwich from his plate and taking a hungry bite.

"What'd *we* miss?" Charlotte says. For girls who look so different, we've always looked a little bit the same. But today Isla is Something Else. She rolls her eyes at Charlotte and touches her own hips like she's making sure they're there.

They are.

"Exactly what you'd expect," I say. We don't talk about the Jack article or the picture of the four of us girls. It goes unsaid.

"It's gonna be okay," Owen says.

"That sounds nice," Isla says, "but it's not actually going to be okay."

Charlotte pats the seat next to her. If we can get Isla to sit down, maybe we can stop them from looking at us. I try to imagine what it would be like to be Anton and his friends, watching our lives instead of living them.

Isla doesn't sit. She stands up straighter. She pulls her hair from behind her back to over her shoulder. "I'm not going to be some sad, untouchable girl." She scans the cafeteria and I wonder what it is she's looking for. She isn't being quiet. I want to fade away, but she's making it impossible. I hear giggles and a hush. "I can still have fun."

I put my hand high up on Owen's thigh.

Charlotte clings to Cruz.

We all pretend we are not being watched.

Except Isla. Isla smiles at everyone watching her. She watches them right back.

16.

On Saturday, Delilah starts knocking on doors.

She comes to ours first, still decked out in gray wool, her hair covered in a red scarf I'd seen Jack wear around his neck. Her clothes are getting looser, her mouth tighter.

"Looks good," I say, but what she really looks is strange and unkempt and worried.

"Come over at noon," she says. I squint and try to really see her. I can't.

I nod.

"I think we need to all come together," Delilah says. "It's an emergency."

"Emergency?"

"You'll be there?" Her face doesn't change expressions and she's not quite meeting my gaze. She's lost weight, I'm sure of it. Her face looks slimmer than it did a week ago; the bones are more prominent, the angles of it all new.

"Are you okay?" I ask, begging her to look at me full-on. "You don't seem great. What can I do?"

"I need everyone to come over at noon to talk," she says. I want to shake new words out of her, different expressions. The night Jack died I saw her face shift a hundred times, and imagined her body in all new shapes, wrapped around Jack. Now she's frozen in this one expression, and I'm having trouble remembering the way she looked when she kissed Jack or drank wine or rolled her eyes at honey cake. "You can help me tell everyone."

"Everyone like Isla, Cruz, and Charlotte?"

"I'll tell Cruz myself." Delilah gives me a heavy look. "Your mom here? Maybe she'd help get the word out, too? I need to set up."

"Set up what?"

"My place. Angelika's over there already but I'm sure she needs help. She's told all her ladies. But we haven't gotten to the families at the end of the block. Maybe you can do that for me?"

"Delilah," I say, hoping that somehow hearing her name will turn her into Delilah again.

It doesn't.

So I knock on doors. Because I don't know what else to do.

• • •

No one is late. I wonder whether it was Delilah's gaunt, serious face that scared people into punctuality or if Jack's death and the Chicago Bombing and maybe even the looming seven-year anniversary are making people too nervous to relax into things like tardiness or dismissiveness. Everyone I talked to comes with tea and lemons. They pile the lemons on the coffee table in Delilah's little living room.

Delilah's mother sits in an armchair and watches the fruits roll around, drop to the floor, light up the room with their insistent sunniness.

Mrs. James has a wrinkle between her eyes and I can't tell what she's thinking but she looks older. She's wool covered, too, and puffy faced. Everything that has always been in this room has vanished—books about healing after tragedy, prayer rugs, a yoga mat, a framed meditation that has to do with the power of letting go. All the things Angelika hates.

Those artifacts have been replaced with photographs of Mr. James. I haven't seen his face in years—Mrs. James and Delilah never listened to the rules about keeping the men's memories alive by papering our homes with their images. But today he is everywhere—bald headed and squinty eyed with Delilah's exact shade of dark brown skin and the smile she used to have.

"I forgot what he looked like!" I say, and Mrs. James glares at me like I've cursed in a holy space.

"Exactly," Angelika says. She is busying herself by lighting little red candles all over the room. It's an eclectic collection of tall dining candles and short tea candles and stumpy smelly candles. The scent is overpowering—a mix of different red-themed scents—Apple Orchard and Christmas Holly and Velvet Rose and Strawberry Pie.

At least fifty people are crowding the room, spilling into the hallway, sitting all the way up the staircase, drifting into the almost kitchen that is really only a counter, two cabinets, and an old yellow fridge that Mrs. James refuses to replace even though it's ancient and barely cold enough to keep milk from going sour.

Cruz and Charlotte and Isla sit on the ground near Delilah. Mom and I stand by the bookcases and we both cover our noses with our hands, trying to escape the smells of scented candles and old lady perfume and days of overcooked eggs and undercooked lamb. Even Mom's hairspray isn't enough to cover all the other scents. She's using more of it today than usual—her short hair is somehow harder to contain than her long hair, and wisps keep falling out of the tiny bun she's fashioned at the back of her neck.

"Thanks," Delilah says, her voice so small that it can't compete with the din of the whole street asking one another why we're here and shaking their heads at the Abbound family's cruelty or Isla's dress that might be a slip and her tights that are ripped all the way up her thighs.

They're always more concerned with Isla's outfits than mine. The other night at Julia's I was wearing less than Isla is now, but it didn't incite the same kind of outrage when I walked down the street. I think Isla must notice it, too, the way her body is a particularly tense battleground compared to the rest of ours. I think of the way Ms. Abbound looked at Delilah, too. It's uncomfortable to think of us as anything but a single organism, but of course it's easier to be a white Devonairre Street Girl.

Isla has red and white bracelets from her wrists to her elbows.

I cut mine off. They were itchy and got ratty and gray as soon as I showered in them.

"Thank you for coming," Delilah says. Angelika puts a finger to her lips and hushes everyone who hasn't stopped chattering.

I text Cruz. I can't help it. I should be texting Owen, telling him where and when we can meet up later, who will be bringing beer or ice cream or a condom. But I don't need to text Owen. I've been pawing at him all week, resting my head on his shoulder while watching movies, straddling him most nights in my loft and once in the garden when it was late and I couldn't sleep and I persuaded him to sneak out.

In the three a.m. blackness, I felt good that Cruz was no longer the last person I'd kissed there.

By sunrise, I was miserable.

Everything's all wrong, I text Cruz now. I watch him feel the buzz of his phone; I watch him check it; I watch him tell Isla it's someone else entirely, probably.

You're scared, he texts back. *I'm not.*

Isla's scared, I write. *Delilah's scared. Even Charlotte seems scared.*

I watch him read my list and he scratches Charlotte's back but I think it's by accident, a gesture so familiar it doesn't have meaning anymore. If he were scratching my back, it would be something to notice.

Cruz doesn't reply. He doesn't stop looking at me, either.

I look away first.

"We have to do something," Delilah says, like we are in the middle of a conversation already. "Something must be done."

"Delilah came to me," Angelika says, weaving her way around the bodies sitting on the floor and nearly tripping on a few dropped lemons until she reaches Delilah's side and squeezes her shoulder. "Too late, she came to me. But now we have to look forward. It's too late to fix everything. Delilah knows now. She understands. She's one of us. And finally it's time to do more."

I cringe at the words *one of us.*

"Delilah's one of *us,*" I say, even though I know better than to talk back to Angelika.

Angelika looks my way. Her gaze shifts between me and my mother. Her nose wrinkles. Mom's heart flutters. Mine gets close to stopping.

"*Us* is a funny word, is it not?" Angelika says, after decades have passed in this small room that is in desperate need of an open window. "It never used to be this way. We used to all be women of Devonairre Street. In it together. There was one Us. You young kids . . ." She drifts off, lighting another candle. "Well. It never used to be this way."

Charlotte looks at the floor. Delilah and Cruz look at the floor. Isla, even, looks at the floor.

I don't know where to look.

"Are you one of us, Lorna?" she asks.

"I—"

"Don't answer now," she says. She doesn't tell me when to answer. "*Naiwny*," she mumbles, a Polish word I don't know.

There is so much space between Angelika and me and the things we understand.

There is a space growing between what Delilah and I understand, too.

I can't stay and watch this new future unfold. My heart squeezes, thinking that Delilah might never fall in love again.

"I made a mistake," Delilah says, lowering her head. She shakes it, swallows, and tries again. "No. More than that. I killed someone. I killed—I didn't listen—I—"

Angelika nods. I hate her for nodding.

"Okay, all right, that's enough," Mom says. I'd forgotten she was beside me. She tucks the rogue strands of hair behind her ears. She captures my shoulder in her hand.

"It's not enough," Angelika says, staring Mom down. I watch the two of them wait each other out, and it's Mom who gives up first, her chin dropping to her chest, her head moving back and forth in a tiny, silent *no*.

I choose to look out the window instead. There's an older couple walking by the building and I wish Delilah had thought to draw the curtains, because I see them seeing us. I'm positive they're tourists from their slow gait and their running shoes. They came by to see the Cursed street from the paper before heading off to the site of the Times Square Bombing and a tour of Ellis Island.

I know what we look like to them: sad, hunched women cramped into a small living room, all long haired and wool clad. I wonder if they can smell the lavender or if they notice how we all shrink in Angelika's presence. The woman smiles like she's seen exactly what she came here to see. The man blushes and wipes his forehead.

She says something and snaps a picture.

I hate whatever it is she's seeing in us.

Angelika—standing up straight, shoulders back, face relaxed and almost young looking—scans the room, looking at every girl and woman with a critical, careful eye.

The couple on the street light up at the sight of her. They whisper something, shake their heads, and finally move on.

"Charlotte," Angelika says, stopping on Charlotte's braids and blue eyes and nervous, twitching mouth. "No key?" Charlotte touches her collarbone, the place her key usually rests. It's not there. She turns a deep red, as red as some of the candles. It's not like her to forget anything and it's not like her to get embarrassed.

"I took it off," she says. "A couple hours ago. I forgot to put it back on."

"You shouldn't be taking it off at all," Delilah says, which I thought was Angelika's line.

"Right," Charlotte says. And then again, "Right."

Isla runs her fingers through her collection of keys and they clatter, a metallic chime. She smirks. Angelika looks her way, too, but doesn't praise her for her keys. Even Angelika must know that they're not enough.

The one around my neck has done nothing at all to keep me from being terrible.

"I wanted to meet you all because it's been an awful ten days and I don't know what else to do but reach out to my community," Delilah starts. She rolls her shoulders back and she looks like the Delilah I know again. I want to be near that Delilah; I want to take her away from here so we can sit close and spill secrets and laugh at the things that hurt the most, like we've always tried to do.

She's not looking at me, though. She's not looking at anyone in particular. She's not part of LornaCruzCharlotteDelilahIsla. I feel it as certainly as I feel that I don't love Owen, that I miss my father, that I wish the anniversary weren't looming, that I can't believe Jack is gone.

"I asked Angelika for help," Delilah goes on. Her breathing changes and she hunches over. She speaks like she's at confession, rattling off her sins, all the ways she's disappointed Angelika, all the things she should have done differently. Her hands shake, her knees shake, her voice gets louder, and her hands grip the sides of her neck like she's holding herself together. Then she's crying, my Delilah, tears rushing down her face so fast I couldn't catch them if I tried.

Older women nod and fold their hands in front of them like prayers of having known better. Isla on the floor deflates, pulling her knees to her chest and resting her forehead on top of them. I wonder if she feels hidden, sitting like that.

Charlotte keeps her hand where her key should be, but Cruz just looks at me. I'm not positive, but I think his head shakes a little *no*, like my mother's did before. No, we're not going to believe. No, Delilah's not right just because she's sad. No, whatever's coming next isn't for us. No, we can't let Angelika steal this power, take advantage, make Jack's death her own imperative.

I can't locate that certainty. I can't really locate myself.

Angelika takes Delilah's hand in hers. I know Angelika's hand so well I can imagine it in my own palm, the gold wedding band hard on my finger, the texture of her palm surprisingly soft. A hint of a smile is on Angelika's face and I watch her thumb rub a spot on Delilah's hand.

Mrs. James gets choked up and leaves the room.

With Delilah crying and the rest of us stunned and saddened and subdued, Angelika is in charge.

"We used to have rules," she says. Her voice rumbles and I wonder what the Polish word for *rules* is. "They were good rules. They made us good." The word *good* sounds like a fist on a table, the way Angelika says it. Delilah keeps crumbling under the words. A candle near her goes out. Delilah gasps and shakily relights it, then loses herself in the flicker while Angelika carries on.

If the tourist couple were still on the street, I think they would be scared of the way Angelika watches Delilah's every move; they'd talk later about how we nod in sync, fold our hands in time with one another like we're in church. They'd notice the intimidating lean of Angelika's body as she starts her new list of rules. They'd see what makes the rules impossible to ignore.

"We will light red candles every night. Keep them in the windows so we can see them. So we can know they are lit. We will be looking for the keys around your neck, for your growing hair, for the lavender tea and the things you are eating. We will tend to the garden." Angelika is listing things we already do, aside from the red candles, which seem a small price to pay if they'll help Delilah calm down. "Your skirts will be below the knee. Your shirts will be above the collarbone. There will also be a curfew. Ten o'clock at night, all women and girls need to be home, without men or boys around." The older ladies stay still. I think a few of them even smile their thin-lipped smiles. Saad and Hiba lower their heads. They are used to being ignored and forgotten about in these moments. They don't count because Angelika has decided their love isn't real.

My insides and my outsides start to shiver with a cold fear. "We can't control the world out there," Angelika says, lifting an arm like it weighs a great deal and gesturing to the window and the world beyond. "But we can control our world." She pauses, considering. She looks at me. "Us."

Mom tenses up beside me. She's about to say something, but doesn't. I look to Cruz again, and he's looking at me still, for longer than anyone has ever looked at anyone else, I think. I can't read his face. I can't read Charlotte's face, and Isla's is still hidden. I am the temperature of winter, of ice, of the things that scare us most of all. I am that exact temperature.

Delilah is the only person I can read, and all that's there is grief and fear, a combination so familiar I can barely name it. It's the look of the widows of Devonairre Street; it's the look our mothers have had and fought off; it's the look Angelika and Dolly and Betty and the rest of them wear like a badge.

Maybe I have that look, too, now, but without the shadow of belief hanging over it all. Belief turns fear and grief into something simpler. I get that now.

Belief makes grief seem solvable. But it isn't.

"Love happens at night," Angelika says, whispering like it's a secret some of us might not know. "So we'll take away the night."

A few throats are cleared. A few feet are shuffled.

I'm faint from the smell of apples and cinnamon and melting wax. Fifty people is too many to be in this tiny space and ten o'clock is too early to be locked into my home and even what I'm wearing today—a wool skirt that hits above my knees and a pink shirt that dips low—is suddenly in violation of the Devonairre Street rules. Angelika and the other widows look at me and Isla and Charlotte like we should have already found a way to cover ourselves up and make ourselves invisible and acceptable and unwantable.

I'm frightened by Angelika saying *we'll take away the night*, as if night were a thing that is up for grabs, something that is hers to distribute, the way love has always been.

I wait for someone to laugh it off. When that doesn't happen, I wait for someone to tell Angelika she's not in charge. Instead, a room full of people chew on their lips and wipe their eyes. My mother's hands make tight fists at her sides.

I think I see Charlotte and Isla nod, and that tiny maybe-movement forces words out of my mouth.

The night is ours, I think, but I am too scared to say. *Love is our right, and so is the night.*

"You can't—" I try to stand up to her a little, even if not with the words I wish I could say.

"I'll say it again, if you weren't listening," Angelika says.

"I was listening," I say, and that's it; the discussion, somehow, is over. All that's left is a table of Curse-fighting food no one wants to eat but apparently everyone will.

• • •

When the first few people are readying themselves to leave, Angelika stands again, gripping the back of one of the folding chairs Delilah put out. If she leans too hard against it, it will topple over, and I think I want that, a little.

I hush that thought and remember Frank Sinatra and jigsaw puzzles and crying into the crook of Angelika's neck when my mother had locked herself in her room and asked me to stop bothering her.

I think of Aramis, the smell of someone who is solid and comforting and there.

"The article," Angelika says. "I know we've all seen it. I've given it thought. After the war, people knew about us. They avoided us. There were fewer temptations, fewer deaths. Fewer accidental loves."

When Angelika says *the war*, she means World War II. She was a little kid at the time, but it's when her father died and it's when the Curse allegedly began. None of the married men from Devonairre Street came back; none of the boyfriends returned.

According to Angelika, Devonairre Street was Blessed, first. Everyone on the street was falling in love. It was said that if you lived on Devonairre Street you would find true love and remain happy forever. Single women and men moved into the brownstones, hoping to find husbands and wives. Bridal shops, florists, chocolatiers all moved to the street. "The commerce of love," Angelika always calls it with a sour look on her face. "They called it a love epidemic, but it was only hubris," she always says right after. "They took that love for granted. They thought it would always be there. You must pay for hubris."

The Curse happened when too many people were taking the Blessings of Devonairre Street Love for granted.

The day Angelika was born, a dozen men from the street were shipped off to war.

"My parents were part of it. My mother moved to the street to find someone. Rented an apartment and waited for love to come to her. Like she was owed it. Well. She learned. We all learn, eventually." The things Angelika says when she is talking about the Blessing of Devonairre Street are frightening. If anyone from off the street heard her, there'd be even more stories about us.

"My grandparents always lived here," my mother always reminds everyone with a shrug, like that makes us better than those whose ancestors moved here to fall in love.

"I think the article was a good thing," Angelika says after a long pause. No one moves, like we're having a Minute of Silence here and now, even though it's not a Tuesday morning or Tuesday afternoon. "Delilah has been contacted to comment on Jack Abbound's death."

Delilah winces at the word *death*. It takes ages for it not to be a surprise. My stomach dropped for an entire year, every time someone mentioned what had happened to my father.

"The city wants to know more about our street. About the Curse. There's interest. I think it will be wise for us to tell them everything we can." She looks to me, to Charlotte, to Isla, to Delilah. "For you girls to tell them what you've done and who you are."

I don't want her to say it again, but she will.

17.

We are on display at Bistro the next night.

Mom's wearing her short hair down instead of in a bun, and I'm housing an order of French fries and mayo. I don't know the official street stance on mayo, but I know the stance on me and Mom.

We are bad.

Mom's knees are showing, and I found out I don't own a shirt that covers my collarbone.

It's nine. Curfew is looming and Roger hasn't arrived yet, but we're waiting for him. I think we're waiting for him and we're waiting for ten o'clock and we're waiting to see what will be done about us when we break more rules.

"You'll love him," Mom says, but I have no intention of feeling anything toward him at all.

Owen's here, too. He's nervous—playing with his napkin and picking at my fries and looking at his watch like he, too, wants us to be home on time. He has a hand on my thigh and I try to remember how good that used to feel. On our first date we went to the movies, and halfway through his hand found its way to that same spot and I could swear my leg was burning from the thrill of it. Even after he took his palm away I could still feel it there, for hours after.

But I'm already forgetting the way I thought I could feel about

Owen on that dreamy Tuesday afternoon. That's the difference, I guess, between love and wishing something was love: how long the remembering is.

"Couldn't we have gone somewhere else?" I ask. Mom shrugs like she can't imagine why I'd want to be anywhere else, but the answer is obvious. Angelika has walked by Bistro once already, and it doesn't feel coincidental.

"This is our favorite place." Mom says the words *favorite place* like she's staking her claim.

"I'm starving," Owen says.

"We'll order the second Roger gets here," Mom says.

Last night she removed the key from around her neck and told me it was about time I met the man she loves. She threw out her hairspray. "My hair's short, I don't need this," she said to me or to no one. Now she smells like soap and cotton. We didn't turn on our outside light before we walked to Bistro.

That is untrue: I turned on our outside light, like we do every evening as the sun starts to set—Angelika says lights help us find the right path. She says we have to combat the night. But on our way out Mom looked at the light—at the dusty glass of the fixture, at the row of lights all the way down the street, predictable, symmetrical, safe—and she flipped the switch to off.

"Waste of energy," she said.

It's dark now; everyone will notice.

We have been home at ten the last two nights, since the meeting, but tonight will be different.

Mom and I are about to be the first ones to break the curfew.

Reporters are coming by next weekend to talk to me, Delilah, Isla, and Charlotte. It has been decided the way everything is decided now: swiftly and without our input.

I haven't told Owen about the photographers. His hand goes from resting on my thigh to gripping it. He needs to cut his nails; I can feel them digging into me.

I love the moon and you and I don't have a chicken, I think, and try again to remember what it felt like to hear the sleepy sweetness of those words. Now it sounds like gibberish. Maybe he wasn't even saying those things to me. Maybe in his dream he was in a rowboat with a supermodel or on a rain cloud with his mother.

"Your hand is sweaty," I say, and move my thigh so that his palm slips right off. "I want to go home."

"You're scared," Mom says. It sounds like an accusation.

"Delilah wants us to do the curfew thing. If you don't want to do it, fine. But I want to do it for her." A waiter comes by and fills our glasses, and we shut up for a minute.

"Well, this is important to me," Mom hisses when he's gone. "Roger's important to me."

"Lorna's not scared," Owen says. He turns to me and I see that he's scared. It's like a disease, a very contagious disease moving its way through the people on our street. "You said you're not scared. That there's no reason to be—right, Dr. Ryder? No one's scared?"

This is what it will be like now, trying to have boyfriends. There will be sweat and fast-talking and checking the obituaries. There won't be easy, romantic nights; there won't be passionate lapses in judgment like at Julia's. There will be measured decisions and risk assessments and Jack's ghost hovering around like a warning.

Mom sighs, not exactly answering but proclaiming, "This is why we have to move to California. I'm not kidding. I can't listen to this stuff anymore."

I ignore her and grab on to Owen's hand. I need Owen to stay. I'm pushing him away but what I need is for him to stay firmly in place, to be a sort of brick wall between me and actually falling in love with anyone. I think about our first kiss and the first time we did it and the party we went to in the fall where we slow-danced to even the fastest songs, driving everyone crazy. I dig and dig, looking for those feelings.

But.

I keep thinking about Cruz's lips and the shrug of his shoulders and the chalk monsters we drew on the sidewalk so many years ago.

If I can forget Cruz and Mom can forget California and the whole world can forget about us, it will be okay. I try to see it—things working out. It's hard to picture.

Bistro's door opens, and he's here. Roger. He stands tall and skinny at the entrance and scans the place. He's gray haired and droopy eyed and carrying a bouquet of pink tulips.

The tulips are a mistake. It's all a mistake. Angelika appears at the window with a scowl, peering in at Roger and my mom and the hug he gives her and the tulips he hands over to me and the slow, easy way he pulls out a chair and sits down in it—legs spread wide, smile growing, like he has all the time in the world.

Angelika sees it all. I get the unsettling sensation of being in a movie of my life. That's what being watched does to you.

"The famous Lorna Ryder," the man who is Roger says, extending his hand.

It's the worst possible thing he could have said.

"Right." I put the tulips on the table and some of the petals get dipped in whipped butter and I don't care enough to move them. "And you're Roger."

He shakes Owen's hand, too, and that is another kind of injustice. I wonder what Dad would have done, meeting my boyfriends.

He would have asked if they like the Mets, I think, and would have teased them if they were too formal. He would have asked me later, over homemade sundaes and big glasses of ice water, whether I was in love with them, because Dad liked to talk to me about things that fathers and daughters don't always talk about.

Roger is making small talk about subway delays with my mother and Owen is nodding like it matters, but it doesn't.

My dad liked to talk about love—how big it was and how small. How strong and how delicate. How I should be on the lookout for it. How I shouldn't listen to anyone else's opinions about it but his and e. e. cummings's and Shakespeare's.

These are the details that they don't write about in the papers. These are the facts that aren't part of the History of the Affected. These are things that Angelika herself doesn't care about. They're mine, and I'm keeping them.

"Your father and his talk of Love," Betty said once when I asked her what she remembered about him most of all. I ask the widows that question on his birthday every year. Sometimes their answers change, and that fascinates me. Why do they remember him one way one year, and another way the next?

"He loved love?" I asked. It's what Mom always says about him, with a roll of her eyes and this faraway smile that I would like to capture in a bottle.

"He was fascinated by it," Betty said.

"He loved it, too," Dolly said, interrupting as always, to put her stamp on the conversation.

"Well, sure. But he was . . . well. He was a little like Angelika. He wanted to put words to it. He liked trying to find the right way to describe it. That's why they got along so well."

"My father and Angelika?" I asked.

"Oh yes," Dolly said.

"Oh yes, yes," Betty said. "They had long conversations the rest of us couldn't follow."

"Or we got bored!" Dolly said. "I would get so bored, once the two of them got going."

"But your father, he was never bored," Betty said.

"Not when it came to love," Dolly said, and they both sighed the saddest, longest sighs.

"I don't remember any of that," I said. Sometimes I got nervous that they were inventing my father, that he was becoming part of the story of the street and not my father at all, anymore.

"That's okay," Betty said. "We remember him for you."

"What's good here?" Roger asks. Mom's watching me meet him, this man she might love, and I think she's looking for something but I'm not sure what. I haven't been at a table with my mother and a man since my father was alive and I didn't actually realize that until this exact moment.

Seven years is an eternity and it is also an instant, and both things are true right now, looking at Roger's ironed blue shirt and fading blue eyes.

"The steak is delicious, but please don't get it," I say, thinking of my father and his love for Bistro's rare steak.

Roger nods like it makes sense, and maybe that's why my mother might love him.

I look to the window for Angelika, but Delilah has taken her place. It hurts, to see her watching me.

"Mom," I say, and jut my chin toward the window. Mom follows the gesture and takes a deep breath.

"It's okay, Lorna," she says, playing with the ends of her hair like she holds a secret power there. "She'll leave if we ignore her."

"I don't want to ignore her." Delilah crosses her arms and stares at me. "She's my best friend."

"She's also involved in something we don't want to be involved with." Mom is using her therapist voice. I know because it's lower and slower and more formal. Owen shifts in his seat but Roger stays very still.

"We could just make them happy and go home. For tonight. Give them tonight." It feels simple in my head. We've always given a little, we've always surrendered bits and pieces of ourselves to Angelika and the street and I don't know why tonight we have to take a stand. We could take a stand tomorrow or the next day. We could do the curfew for a week or a month. I'll happily do the article, if it will keep Delilah calm, if it will give us all a chance to regroup and find one another again.

I'll do almost anything, I'm realizing, for the chance to stay LornaCruzCharlotteDelilahIsla.

"I think maybe I should go," Owen says. I don't know whether it's the tension between me and Mom or the threat of Delilah and Angelika outside Bistro or whether the tiniest bit of belief has seeped into him, but he stands up and sticks his hand out for Roger to shake again and barely looks my way.

"I'll walk you out," I say, but Owen only shrugs.

I kiss him at the door in front of Delilah, in front of my mom and Angelika and Roger, who still has the slump and stillness of a person who isn't scared. I kiss him like I might find something new and startling in his mouth. I kiss him and lean into him and scrunch my eyes and beg my body to get lost in the kissing.

He kisses back, but lightly.

All the while, Delilah watches and I feel her watching us.

"I gotta go, Lorna," he says.

"Are we okay?" I ask.

It's almost ten. I'm at the door and could leave with Owen, could walk home with Delilah, could run away from my mother and Roger and the things we believe in.

Except: the things we believe in—love and not being afraid and that Curses are silly—are the things my father believed in. I can't run away from those things of his.

Bistro is the place my father loved most. It's an older building with crown moldings and tin ceilings and huge steaks. Some afternoons Dad and I would come here after school. He'd order steak frites and I'd eat the fries and do homework and he'd look over building plans and blueprints or architecture magazines and we'd spend hours like that in the dim lighting. We'd come home smelling like butter and beef.

I don't remember much, but I remember that. I don't have to ask Betty and Dolly for those memories; I don't have to hope their retelling of him is right. Bistro and cappuccinos and rare steak and blueprints are the things about my father that I know for sure, which means that they are the best things about him.

I kiss Owen again but there's nothing there. Even the spark of wanting is gone, because I don't love him and I never will. Because I love someone else.

I stand at the door, halfway in, halfway out, three minutes to curfew and watch Owen walk away.

Delilah grabs my hand. She notices the way I pull back from her.

"Lorna," she says. Inside my name there's disappointment and a plea and all the love in the world. I've missed my name in her mouth. I wish she'd say it again, but she is silent, waiting.

"We don't believe," I say, taking care to look her right in the eyes.

Delilah shakes her head hard, not hearing me. She grabs my wrist, looking for the bracelets, and when she finds none, she throws my arm back to me, harder than either of us expected. I open my palms and pull my shoulders up to my ears.

She makes fists at her sides.

On Devonairre Street, you're either in it together or you're not. We are girls without fathers and wives without husbands and people who have seen the worst of what life has to offer. And we stand in it—in the mud and grief and fury and rubble and ash and burning buildings. We stand in it together.

That's what we have always done, even when it seems silly or strange. Even when it is exhausting or annoying. We have stood in it together.

Angelika and Betty are striding down the street now, too.

"Curfew!" they call, Betty's Brooklyn accent seeming to harmonize with Angelika's Polish one. I want to do what they want me to do. But I can't.

"What about Jack?" Delilah says. She whispers his name. I think saying it too loudly would make it hurt even more.

"What about us?" I ask.

Angelika and Betty push into Bistro, Delilah and I stay on the street, ten o'clock happens, and it rips us apart.

18.

Roger isn't living with us or anything but his socks are on the bathroom floor, and the living room smells like men's deodorant and bacon, which he has made for us every morning.

This morning is different.

This morning I hear him before I smell bacon or see his socks.

There is a groan. It is an awful, bass sound that travels from my toes to my throat where it stays. I close my eyes, and hope that somehow shuts out the sound, but it only makes it louder. I can hear my mother's heartbeat, too, hard beats that speed up and skip around. She sighs.

I turn over in bed and wish myself anywhere else in the world.

Her sigh is high and airy. It is filled with all the things I don't want to know about her.

I curl into a ball and put my pillow over my head.

Roger lets out another groan—a loud, crumbly, final one that I think I will spend the rest of my life trying to forget.

I am stuck between weeping and laughing, between blushing and screaming.

I consider staying in bed for the rest of the day or at least until Roger leaves, but it's not an option today.

• • •

"A morning's not a morning without bacon," Roger says when I come downstairs ten minutes after the sounds that shook the apartment. It's something my dad would have said.

I think.

I try to separate Roger's voice from the sound I heard coming from my mother's bedroom. I try to imagine them as coming from different beings.

I blush at the bacon and at Roger's bare forearms and at the way his thin hair is messy in the back.

The deep discomfort is not eased by the extra batch of bacon and a whole pot of Mom's new vanilla tea and a dozen slices of cinnamon toast, soppy with butter and dipping in the middle from the weight of his special cinnamon sugar mix.

"Thanks," I mumble.

"It's a good morning," Roger says, and my head squeezes in an effort to unhear the last hour of my life. "I know you've had a tough week. Wanted to make things a little better for you and your mom."

I can't even fake a smile.

He's right, the week has been tense. Delilah isn't speaking to me, Angelika is stopping by daily to have it out with my mother, and we've all grown quieter at school. We talk about pizza and Dickens and the sad state of the girls' bathroom at lunch, but almost nothing else.

Owen has still been sitting next to me and kisses me when I kiss him, but he hasn't been over and he keeps looking at me with that Angelika look—searching for hints of love on me.

I don't think he finds anything.

You ready for this? Cruz texts me when I'm polishing off the last of the bacon. We've texted every day this week, but I've been avoiding the garden. The smell of mint and basil and soil feels dangerous now. The bench itself feels like a warning—a bright white sign of the ways things have changed since Chicago exploded and Jack died.

I don't even know what this is, I write back. All I've ever been told about reporters is to avoid them, so meeting up with them on purpose feels all wrong.

We are going to the bench today.

The people in charge of the photographs and the article fell in love with the bench, I guess.

"You don't have to do this," Mom says when the doorbell rings. She emerged from her room so rosy cheeked and chipper that I had to hide my face behind my hair.

We peek outside. There are five women on our stoop ready to do my hair and makeup and talk to me about what it's been like to be a Devonairre Street Girl.

"It's okay," I say, but I don't think it is.

"This is the last thing we're doing for her," Mom says. Angelika is pacing the street, patrolling again. Not alone anymore, either. She is gaining followers. It makes Mom shiver. It makes my throat go dry. "This is why we can't stay here," Mom says.

I pretend not to hear her. Roger hums the chorus of "California Dreaming." He has on one of her old flowered aprons and a pair of flannel pajama pants.

"I'm doing it for Delilah," I say.

"I can't believe Angelika got into her head," Mom says. "I always thought Delilah was the strongest of you all."

If Delilah was the strongest, who was I? And who am I now?

"Those reporters should take pictures of those batty ladies, if they want a real story," Roger says, always making light of the things that feel heaviest to me and Mom.

We don't laugh.

They leave my hair long. They line my eyes in black and it's stark against my too-pale skin. They make my lips pinker and an hour later I'm me but not-me. The stylist flips through my closet and picks out my heart sweater and my gray leggings and asks me if I have "a few of those keys, like the other girls."

I slip on the one I always wear, and they exchange a look that tells me we are living up to expectations.

"You're all so pretty," the makeup artist says. She has a streak of pink in her hair and bronze eyeshadow. "Must make it even harder."

"I usually wear sunglasses," I say, showing her mine. They are large and dark and rimmed in blue. I put them on. She puts a finger to her chin.

"Mysterious," she says. "I like it."

When I look at myself in the mirror, I wish the sunglasses hid more of me. The shape of my face and my long hair and the way my lips part are all too distinct.

"Are you an Aquarius?" the stylist asks. Each of her fingers has at least two rings on it and the way she moves her hands makes me think the rings are heavy. I wonder if it's a choice she made so long ago that she can't get out of it now. I wonder if she's happy with the choice to be this girl versus that girl.

I guess that's the question Mom's been asking in her head. Who would we be if we lived on the beach, if it were seventy degrees every day, if no one knew who we were.

"Nope," I say. "Leo."

"Thank God," the stylist says. "Aquarians are supposed to have an awful month. And you all have been through enough."

"The bad things happen anyway," I say. I'm quoting my father but she doesn't know that. She nods seriously. This is another funny thing about being Affected. Strangers think your grief makes you understand something bigger, more profound.

The reporter, a Puerto Rican woman with shiny hair and tailored clothes, writes down my words.

"Good stuff, Lorna," she says.

I don't want to be quoted in the magazine saying my father's words. I don't want to be anyone's oracle. But it's too late. The words are out there and I'm looking like someone's idea of a Devonairre Street Girl and soon we're all at the garden, crowded around the bench, the lot of us prettier and bigger eyed than usual.

Delilah doesn't wave hello.

She removes herself from the rest of us, standing under the tree where Angelika declared her In Love. It's something the reporters would eat right up, but none of us say anything about that afternoon. Angelika's getting her picture taken, too, over on her stoop, holding a candle and a lemon, surrounded by her adoring followers.

"Didn't she have a great look?" the photographer asks the man positioning the lights.

"Absolutely perfect," the man with the lights says.

We all rub our foreheads and wish the day away.

• • •

Cruz stands by the gate of the garden. He's not meant to be part of the shoot, but he's here, maybe for Charlotte, maybe for me, maybe for the faded idea of LornaCruzCharlotteDelilahIsla. He has a bagel and sad eyes that won't stop looking at me.

I'd like a bagel, but it wouldn't fit with the image of Devonairre Street Girl.

146

"No one wants to see you eating or laughing or doing home-work," the reporter says when I ask if we can do something aside from sit here. "That's what regular people do. We're here to capture something special."

"You, with the braids?" the photographer says, pointing at Charlotte. "You sit on the right side of the bench." Charlotte nods. They've let her keep her braids but they've painted her lips a dangerous red and she's wearing one of her mother's hippie dresses—it's low in the back and lacy in the front and too big around her middle. They've cinched it onto her with a leather belt that she would never wear. She looks the least like herself. I think maybe they didn't like Charlotte's conservative collared shirts or thin lips or worn-out sneakers. Those things don't fit in with the idea of romantic, dangerous, untouchable, sad, sad girls.

Isla is in her blue dress and she has a dozen keys clatter-ing around her neck. The photographer keeps telling her to stop fidgeting.

Delilah is all in black. Her Afro has grown and they stuck a sprig of lavender near her ear.

We don't quite fit into the new dress code. My collarbone is showing and so are Isla's knees. Charlotte's exposed, too. Only Del-ilah is covered up the way we're supposed to be now. I can feel her eyes on my neck; I watch her swallow hard at the bit of Isla's thighs that are on display.

They seat Isla on the left side of the bench and ask me to sit in the middle. My heart sweater itches. So does my made-up face.

They let Delilah stay a little separate, standing a foot to the right of us all. Her back is straight and her gaze is, too. She stares right into the camera, like a challenge.

"Make sure you get the back of the bench," the reporter calls out, and we're asked to turn around and face the camera as it moves behind us, our faces now framing the proclamation *Love Was Found Here*.

I'm sweating.

Cruz won't move and more of the ladies are gathering by the gates to watch. Whenever I shift I elbow Charlotte and when Isla's legs cross, her heel kicks my shin and we're already bruised enough.

"I can't do this," I say when the sun's in our eyes.

"Wide eyes, wide eyes," the camerawoman says, her voice high and persistent and terrible.

"It's really sunny," I say because the rest of the girls are zombies and everyone watching has forgotten we're people, I think.

"Blink in between shots, okay? We'll get it. Wide eyes, wide eyes." I squint under my glasses. I look to Charlotte and Isla and Delilah, but none of them will look at me. I don't recognize any of them anyway. We're not ourselves. We're someone's idea of what the Devonairre Street Girls might look like.

"Can we get a break?" I ask.

"Just be yourselves," the photographer says, but what she really means is the opposite.

I float up high and watch us from the one tree in the garden. We don't look anything like ourselves. We look exactly the way someone might picture us—exaggerated ideas of what girls might be. Delilah's face won't move from a frown and every part of her is stiff, every muscle tensed like if her left pinkie relaxes she will fall apart. The rest of us are slump shouldered and slippery with makeup and sweat and something else—submission.

I'm aware of my skinny legs and powdered skin and the curve of my back and the hearts on my sweater, so loud and ridiculous I can't believe I let them order me into it.

No one seeing us now would know the way Delilah smells when she's crying or how Charlotte wrinkles her nose when she kisses

Cruz or what noises Isla's boots make when they hit the Devonairre Street sidewalk. They don't even know that underneath my sunglasses I am looking only at Cruz.

It's amazing, what they'd see if they really looked.

19.

I don't take off my heart sweater and I stay in the garden long after the reporters and photographers and the hungry, cruel ladies who have watched me all day have left. My hair is tangled and in my face so I tie it back, and Isla and Charlotte and Cruz hug me before they eventually go, but the gesture feels ghostly.

Delilah lingers, like maybe she has something to say now that the others are gone. But she stays quiet and heads to the gate. When I ask where she's going, she tells me she has work to do.

"You remember what Jack said about leaving early?" I ask, thinking of the smirk he used to get when we'd break up a party to get sleep or do homework.

Delilah looks at me funny, like I'm not supposed to say his name.

"Jack used to say leaving early was the saddest thing a person could do. That leaving a good time was a tragedy. Then you'd always say it was as sad as a butterfly in a net." I keep my voice quiet, because memories are quiet things. My throat closes a little around Jack's old words, but I'm happy to have remembered one more thing about him. I think maybe Delilah will soften, too. She looks up at the sky like she often does.

"When I said that, I didn't even know the meanings of words like *sad* and *tragedy*," Delilah says. "A butterfly in a net. God.

I was . . ." She pauses, looking for the word. *Brilliant,* I think. *Lovely. Charming. Perfect.* "Silly," she says with a sigh.

"You know now," I say, because we're best friends and best friends say the truest things. For the most brilliant moment, I think Delilah sees me again. The thing between us—the crazy bond that comes from having dead fathers and magical rituals and tiny apartments and a Shared Birthday—appears and we're a yard apart but we might as well be pressed right up against each other. We might as well be one again.

Then my phone buzzes and I glance at Cruz's name and a text from him and the answer to the question *who's texting?* is all over my face, and like that, the moment's over.

"I miss the hell out of you," I say when she turns to leave.

She turns back in my direction. She drinks me in but I don't know what it is she's seeing.

"Don't you want to stop terrible things from happening?" she says after what could be a minute or an hour. Her eyes are shiny and her bottom lip has a little-girl quiver. We aren't being watched, we aren't being photographed, we aren't being seen as Those Girls.

"I wish terrible things would stop happening. Of course I do. I mean. Of course. But we're not the answer. We can't stop the world from happening."

Delilah shakes her head. "Jack was here. Then I loved him. Now he's gone."

"You know that's not—" I don't finish my sentence. I get distracted by a flicker of a feeling in my chest. A tiny pulse of something I've been avoiding.

Doubt.

I am so close to positive that Angelika is absurd, that Delilah is heartbroken, that people are desperate but not right. I am close to positive that a Curse is an impossible thing.

But I am not quite all the way positive.

I have the smallest little drop of doubt.

"We love Cruz. We all do. We don't want to lose him, too." Delilah speaks in a ferocious murmur.

"What does Cruz have to do with—" My stomach turns. My eyelashes feel heavy from all the makeup and the exhaustion and something else, too. My face is melting—daylong foundation and shimmery blush and too-pink lipstick sliding down under the Devonairre Street sun.

Delilah's melting, too, the two of us shifting from who they think we are to who we actually are.

"We all love you with Owen. Angelika thinks Owen's perfect. Safe. Make that work, okay? For me?"

"I don't love Owen," I say, and Delilah laughs. I have missed her laugh the way I miss water when I'm thirsty.

"Of course you don't," she says.

Delilah was the first person I told when Owen kissed me at the fall dance. She's who I told when I decided to have sex. I told her about the shape of his calves and the funny lilt in his voice when he talks to his mom on the phone. I like Owen. I *like* like him. I do.

But Delilah knows and I know and Angelika knows that I will never love him.

According to Angelika, you can only really love one person at a time. "Real, true love is singular in focus," she says. "Real, true love is so big there's not room for anything else." I asked Dad if this was true and he handed me a book of Neruda and told me even poets don't have the answers, let alone Angelika.

"But you and Mom only love each other," I said. "You have Angelika's version of real, true love."

Dad paused.

He squeezed one hand with the other.

He didn't answer. Instead he kissed my forehead and went onto the fire escape for a cigarette. The memory hits me hard, something I hadn't remembered at all until now, when I remember it perfectly.

It feels out of tune with the rest of the things I've been told to remember.

I want to tell Delilah, but she's looking at me for an answer, for a promise to stay with Owen, and she doesn't want to talk about anything but that.

I give a half smile and a half shrug. "I'll try," I say. It's an empty sentence, and the second I say it, I want to do the opposite. I don't want to try at all; I want to give up.

• • •

The sun starts to set and still I'm in the garden looking like Devonairre Street Lorna instead of Actual Lorna. It's weird how they used to be the same person.

There are a few plants that need to be set in the ground, so I start digging. I don't talk about my green thumb to Angelika or any of the widows. I'm afraid it would somehow be another thing that means more than it is. I want it to be mine, not theirs.

I dig with my hands. I like to get a feel for it—damp, dry, clumped, dusty—if I can feel it in my fingers I know what plants to put where and how deep to dig and how to care for them. One of the lemon trees—the one with the biggest lemons and greenest leaves—is mine. So is the patch of spinach and a pot of pansies.

It's good to have secrets, my dad used to say when I'd catch him sneaking a smoke on our fire escape. *Everyone has them.* I've kept mine close, and I've come to hate my father's. The problem with keeping secrets is that once you're gone the secrets are gone, too. I can ask the widows for stories about my father every day until the sun goes down, but they'll never be able to tell me the deepest-down most important things about him.

I think he'd like my secret gardening, at least. I think he'd like how hard I'm working not to believe and the smile I get when I think about Cruz. He'd like all the things about me that Angelika hates.

I've heard the ladies talk about different flowers appearing in the garden, and they make their own list of reasons for it. Magical reasons.

It's only ever been me.

There's a noise by the garden gate and I look up. Nothing. I'm expecting Delilah to come back. We have more to say to each other, and she's always said her favorite thing is to watch me garden.

"I love the secret side of you that no one else sees," she said once and it sounded almost romantic. It was maybe more romantic than anything Owen or any other guy had ever said to me. There's a romance to a real best friend.

I liked being seen, too. I liked Delilah knowing my secrets, and maybe if she came back to the garden, I'd tell her some of my newest ones. She'd hate them, but I don't think that matters anymore. I think it's more important for her to know me than it is for her to approve of me.

With dirt under my nails. I place peonies in the hole I've dug. Peonies are fussy. If they're planted too far down, they refuse to flower. They are easy to care for, but they can't be rooted too deep in the ground. And even in the best of circumstances they don't bloom for very long.

I like peonies for those same reasons that they drive other people crazy. I like that they want to be in the garden but not too firmly embedded. I like that they can only flourish if they're given a little space, a little room to move. I like that they won't flower year round, but when they're at their best they're truly spectacular.

When I plant them, I let them know they can leave this place. I dig shallow holes and don't pat the dirt tightly around them.

I thought I was deeply rooted at Devonairre Street, but now I'm not so sure. I want to be here, but not too far in. I don't want to go to California, but I don't want to be only a Devonairre Street Girl either. I remember the people in the airport a few weeks ago, with their futures and their choices and their firmly rooted love and their lives that mattered to them but no one else.

I try to imagine myself on some other street in some other state. I don't fit in there, either. I'm not fitting in anywhere anymore.

Soon I know Cruz is there, all the way across the garden, without looking up.

"You're there," I say, patting the last of the peonies in place.

"Your mom's looking for you."

"I forgot to tell her I was staying out." I stand up and try to brush some of the soil off, but it mostly sticks to my knees, my elbows, my wrists.

I can hear Angelika not far away, walking the streets, telling and retelling the story of how the day went. She's so close she could hear us, too, if she were listening.

But I have a feeling she's not listening.

"I figured you were here," Cruz says. He's caught me planting in the garden before, but we've never spoken of it. He's nodded hello and gone on his way. Cruz and Delilah are different in that way.

"Do you think I'm like a peony?" I ask instead of a greeting.

"These things here?" he asks, stepping farther into the garden, closer to me. I nod. He leans down and inspects the pink petals. I like that he's seriously considering the question even though it's a nonsensical one. He's always been that way—jumping on board with the frantic way my mind sometimes works, the strange connections it makes.

"They're my favorite flower," I say. There's dirt on my neck. I can feel it. Gardening is messy business. My heart sweater is probably ruined forever, but that's fine by me.

"I don't think you're like anything," Cruz says. He stands back up and steps closer to me.

I should step away but I don't. I already forget what I promised Delilah. I forget the little spark of fear or doubt I feel when I think too hard about Jack or Bombings or Angelika. I forget how clearly I can hear the rest of the neighborhood, Delilah's serious voice rising up occasionally to ask if someone wants another bracelet. I forget everything as the toes of our shoes meet up.

I don't know who leans, but one of us leans and the other follows and we're kissing.

A Devonairre Street Girl wouldn't kiss Cruz like this, not now, but I kiss him even harder because I don't know that I ever signed on to be a Devonairre Street Girl.

I am Lorna Who Kisses the Boy Next Door and I am Lorna Who Looks Like Shit in Makeup and I am Lorna Who Gardens Without Worrying About How Messy It Can Get.

I am Lorna Who Doesn't Care That the Street Is Busy, That We Will Get Caught, That Someone Could See Us.

Cruz's hands are on my face. I wonder if I taste a little like peonies or garden ground or sticky all-wrong lipstick.

I forget to breathe, so we have to break apart for me to finally inhale.

I wipe my mouth with the back of my hand. I'd never do that with Owen; it would feel rude or gross or something. But with Cruz it's fine. It was a messy kiss and we both know it and it was a great kiss, and we both know that, too.

It was a secret kiss, and Delilah loves secrets. Maybe she can sniff them out, the way I have an extra-strong sense for my mother's heartbeat.

"I knew it."

It's Delilah's voice at the gate of the garden. Cruz and I leap apart from each other but it doesn't matter, she's already seen.

They've both seen.

Angelika and Delilah are shoulder to shoulder at the gate. They are holding lavender and lemons and I can tell from the looks on their faces they've seen everything.

Delilah said she knew it, and I think I knew it, too. Knew that she'd catch me, knew that she didn't trust me, knew that we needed to stop pretending things could be okay.

Delilah stays back but Angelika rushes forward, her hands finding my face, her nails digging in. As always they are cool, they are worn, her ring hits my cheekbone. It hurts.

"It's not anything," Cruz says. "Whatever you think—whatever you saw—we're tired. This isn't—"

"You're tired?" Delilah screeches like something has come loose inside her throat.

"You shouldn't have made them do the pictures and interviews—" Cruz keeps stepping farther away from me. And I don't know what Angelika's finding on me, but I know what I see on him.

Fear. Actual fear.

He covers his face with his hands. Delilah covers her face, too, all of us hiding from the things that are happening.

"Secrets are only bad when they're not secrets anymore," Dad said once, not long before he died. He seemed sad and sure. He hadn't shaved and I remember thinking that he sounded like he was talking about something specific, but I didn't ask him what.

I should have asked him what secret was making him so sad.

"Not there yet," Angelika declares, giving my face one last squeeze before letting it go. She reaches into the bag she is always carrying and takes out a gray scarf. She wraps it around me, and I let her. I am so used to letting her tell me what to do, I don't know another way.

"I'm sorry," Cruz says, and they all look at me like I'm supposed to apologize, too, but I'm in too much shock from hearing Cruz apologize to say anything at all. "I love Charlotte," he goes on. "This was—I'm sorry. I'm so sorry. I'm with Charlotte."

Her name is a slice on my skin, a thing that shocks and hurts and burns.

"You're not sorry, Lorna?" Angelika says. She drops the lavender and steps on two of the newly planted peonies. "You're too good for us? You think you're above all of this? You forget your father? You forget the pictures of my Chester, or Dolly's Harold, or Betty's Richard? You forget them all? You think I don't know what your mother's doing, trying to tear this community apart? You think you can leave here and leave us and have some happy life?" Angelika is shaking and growling. Her finger is darting around, pointing at me, at Cruz, in the direction of our building, at the peonies, at the sky.

"We haven't—I didn't—I did what you asked today. I did what you wanted." I am speaking so quietly it's a wonder she can hear me.

"You've forgotten everything that's ever happened, everything we've ever taught you. You and your mother."

"I haven't forgotten anything," I say. Angelika must have soaked herself in Aramis, must have bathed in the stuff. It's all I can smell. It's choking me.

"Do what's right!" Angelika says, her voice rising, hitting the trees and the metal of the gates and the cloudy beginnings of a moon in the sky. "Do what's right! You have a dead father and a dead friend and still, *still* you insist on being Lorna Ryder, Above It All! Still you do! You want to be some other person from some other street. But you are this person, from this street."

This last part hurts the most, because it's true. It's the only part of what she said that I know for sure is entirely the truth—plain and ugly and terrible and mine.

Right now, right this instant, I would get in the car with my mother and drive across the country with Roger. I would take that money for our building and hope that memories of my father traveled well. I would let Devonairre Street become something different, and hope that I would become something different, too.

"I see your thoughts," Angelika says. "Hubris. It is believing you can escape what is. You can't escape what is."

The gates of the garden feel like prison bars.

I am always going to be Lorna Ryder, one of the Affected, a Devonairre Street Girl.

I look at the peonies. Angelika has stepped on two more. They won't recover. They're not that strong.

20.

They title the article "The Ones You Shouldn't Love."

The title hurts, but it's also wrong. The Curse says that they can love us, we just can't love them back. It's somehow sadder. I wonder if the reporters think it sounds more romantic to be unlovable, and more depressing to be told not to love.

Reporters, I've learned, only like the romantic kind of tragedy. That's why they were so happy we were pretty. That's why they were so eager to dress us in heart sweaters and lace dresses and dark eyeliner, and that's why they wanted our hair loose and windblown.

I am Affected. I am a Cursed Devonairre Street Girl. And now I am the One You Shouldn't Love.

I try to imagine Future Lorna again, all free and easy and not anyone's symbol of anything. But I can't see her.

In the same pit of my stomach where I have fear about the Curse, there is a new question, something that has popped up and won't quiet.

Is this how it will be forever?

Is this it?

I think of the wedding party at Julia's. The bride in her flowing gown and the girls leaning against their boyfriends, not thinking of what anyone thought of their love. They were my age, on a street not far from mine, in the city that has always been mine, but they were another species. I thought I could be one of them, one day.

I can't see it.

Looking at the article, I understand now that the rest of the world can't see it, either. No one sees that future for us.

Mom and I sit in front of the computer and watch comments roll in on the story of our life. It is exactly what the stylist told us not to do. "People say crazy things," she said, tying a scarf around my neck, then taking it off. "Don't read the comments. Don't engage."

We engage anyway. Mom pours herself a huge glass of wine and asks if I want a few sips. I don't want to drink in front of her. I want to be little again, too young for things like drinking and love.

We scroll by a comment from BronxBomber1978 who wants to know when "the one with the tits" is turning eighteen and by all the women who ask "who's parenting these girls?" and try to decipher whether they believe. They think we're hot; they think we're fame-whores; they think we're stupid; they think we're mentally ill; they think we caused the Bombings; they're angry with us; they think we should control ourselves; they pity us for being Affected, they wish the reporter would cover Serious News and not Frivolous Stories; they think New York City is a cesspool; they think we are privileged and entitled; they think we are what's wrong with the world; they wonder if we're in a cult; they want to know more.

"They'll forget all about this in a week," Mom says, but she doesn't sound so sure.

Roger is in the kitchen making us stew. The apartment is filling with smells that remind me of cold days and cozy nights. Roger is a comfort although I don't quite want him to be.

One window is open, letting the heat from the stew and the overwhelming smell of pepper escape. The kitchen is a little smoky, which means the living room is a little smoky, and up in my loft I'm sure it's a little smoky, too.

I'd never want to live in a big house with my mother. Even if we sell our building and move to California, I hope we live somewhere small and contained. I like that we live identical lives because of the tininess of our apartment. We can't escape each other. If she smells onions and garlic and sizzling meat, so do I. If she hears car alarms or police sirens or street musicians, I do, too.

"You okay, babe?" Roger asks. I shiver at their intimacy and hear, for the hundredth time, the echo of his groan. We can't escape those hidden parts of each other, either, in our tiny home. I can't un-know that they have sex most mornings. I can't ever pretend my mother is only Mom.

"We're fine," Mom says. She sighs a different sigh from the ones I try not to hear.

A noise floats in from outside. I strain to hear, and I'm pretty sure it's Angelika because it's always Angelika. I'm not sure who she's talking to, but I can imagine what they're talking about. She must be tired of talking about us. She must be desperate to talk about dress patterns or roast chicken recipes or new soil to plant in the garden.

But right now she can only talk about us. Our shame. Our disappointment. Our rebellion. Our hubris.

Always our hubris.

More voices join Angelika. Three, five, eight, and it's about time to close the windows.

"What now?" Mom says. She sighs. She's been taking cabs to and from work. They come to the front door of our apartment and deliver her to the front door of her office building. She asks me to bring home groceries after school, get coffee from ZeeZee, pick up a takeout order from Bistro.

She doesn't say that she's afraid to walk down the street, but she's stopped doing it.

She doesn't know that I'm the one who should be scared; I'm the one who's been caught with Cruz, like I think they've always known I would be.

There are at least a dozen voices outside the window, but the words are indistinct. The quality of light changes, too. It's mostly dark outside, but a warm light is reflecting through the window.

An orange-y light.

Candlelight.

"Almost ready, girls," Roger says from his station at the stove. He has sauce on his mouth, and the counters are covered with herbs and vegetable juices and dirty utensils.

Dad used to cook, too. He liked to wear a chef's hat he had from a Halloween costume and he'd slice his finger from trying to show off fancy knife moves that he wasn't actually very good at. I liked his cooking—it was surprising and weird. I'd think I was eating meat loaf and it would taste like curry. I'd twirl a bite of spaghetti onto my fork and it would be lemony and oily and almost too spicy to swallow.

Roger cooks plain and tasty, but never shocking.

Mom goes to the window and I join her. Our entire neighborhood is on the sidewalk below our window. Angelika, Betty, Dolly, Maria, Mrs. James, Charlotte's mother, the Jonerons, the Chens, a few of the little girls whose birthdays are about to disappear and become one Shared Birthday.

Delilah is there, of course.

So is Isla, in her wicked boots and her always-longer hair. I've heard she's meeting boys in the park late at night. It's a thing being whispered in the halls at school, being talked about online. It's also a thing I can see on her skin, which looks irritated around her chin and mouth. Her lips look puffy from too much kissing.

"It's not love" is all she said when Charlotte asked her about what she was doing every night in the park.

We live in a world where it's better to fuck a hundred boys you don't love than kiss one boy you do. It's all topsy-turvy, and I want Isla to have both—the sex and the love. I want her to wear her short skirts and tight tops because she likes them, not because she's trying to be Someone Else. I want her to show her clavicle when she's in the mood, and to cover up her knees when it's cold or she's forgotten to shave and for no other reason. I don't want gross men and mean girls to look at her and talk about her beauty like it's something exciting and terrible, like she's desirable and Cursed in some magnificent way.

Most of the comments on the article were about her, but they don't know her. I notice the way they talk about us, using different words depending on the color of our skin, the size of our breasts, the shortness of our skirts. I get off easy, with my blond hair and white skin and B cups. It doesn't matter that I'm the most dangerous one. They can't see that. They don't know any of us.

There are at least twenty-five people on the sidewalk and more pouring out from their buildings. They all have red candles in their hands. Angelika travels around striking matches and lighting the flames. Her shoulders are back and she looks younger every day that passes. The things that have happened in the past weeks have made the rest of us tired, our eyes are pink with dark circles hanging underneath. Our hair is stringy, our backs hunched, our faces gaunt and pale. Grief is supposed to ravage you. But Angelika is rosy cheeked and bright eyed.

She might be smiling.

The crowd falls into silence, seeing us in the window.

We haven't been lighting red candles. We haven't been obeying curfew.

"What's going on out there?" Roger says. The din of voices has stopped but the light is brighter and Mom and I are stuck to the window.

"Street thing," Mom says. She opens the window wider.

"That's enough," she calls down. Angelika looks up, her face alight from the candles, a red glow over all our neighbors.

"Now, that's exactly what I was going to say to you, Emily," she says.

I see Delilah making fists and scowls. I see Isla. The keys around her neck look heavy. I wonder where Charlotte and Cruz are, and get distracted by the idea of them somewhere together—wrapped up in each other on Cruz's bed, under his ugly orange blanket, staring at his collection of comic books, the sad plastic basketball net affixed to his door.

Does he kiss her the way he kisses me? An unexpected pattern of open and closed lips, hands moving from hair to back to hips to neck in a frantic search for the right place to hold on to?

"It's too late anyway, Angelika," Mom says. I kick her. It's time to close the window, eat stew, let the candles burn down, let the ladies lose interest in their tiny protest. I listen for her heartbeat. It's steady and loud. It's ready. "We're getting out of here," she announces to the crowd, but mostly to Angelika. "We're selling. Other people will sell. This place won't be around forever. Don't you see that?" She pauses, like she's not sure if she should say the other thing in her mouth. "*You* won't be around forever, Angelika."

There is an awful moment where I wonder what Angelika will

say, but she doesn't say anything. She glares at Mom and at our building and at the betrayal of our candle-less existence.

"We're trying to keep everyone safe," Delilah says, "That's it. It's our responsibility."

"Moving solves nothing," Betty says, her voice craggly and late-night. "You can't leave the Curse behind. We're in it together."

"We're in it together," Dolly echoes. It makes my stomach turn.

I hear Roger turn on the news. Maybe it's to drown us out, or maybe it's simply a part of his routine, a thing he does on autopilot.

". . . we mourn with the victims," a reporter says in a too-chipper voice. "None of us will forget."

I know the words well, the things people say to feel part of a tragedy. Not forgetting and actually remembering are two different things, though.

"Please turn that off," I say to Roger, and he's kind and easy so he does.

"Let me look at you," Angelika calls up. "Let me see your face, Emily. Let me look for love."

I look at my mother's face. She has a pointy chin and small eyes. Her eyelashes are long, and since candlelight exaggerates every-thing, they are longer still.

I think I see it.

Love, near her lips, around her eyes, hiding under her chin, twitching her nose as she smells rosemary and thyme and effort. Love, in her short hair and how far out the window she leans. Love, in the way she talks to Angelika.

Roger comes to the window and stands behind us. Delilah looks away, like even seeing a man is too much.

"Yes, okay. I love him," Mom says.

Roger tenses up, then reaches for Mom's hip. He squeezes three times and smiles.

I feel myself get cloudy eyed. It's hard to breathe.

"No," Delilah says.

"Emily," Angelika says.

"I do," Mom says, louder than the rest of them, louder than she needs to be. "I'm not scared."

And even though I don't believe in the Curse, even though I've never believed and I'm not planning on believing, I want her to take the words back, swallow them down, never speak them again.

Roger whispers into her ear, not loud enough for the people on the street to hear, but loud enough for me to hear and feel in my veins. "I love you, too."

I shiver.

On the computer, the article about us is still up, "The Ones You Shouldn't Love," in bold black script across the screen. It looks like a sentence—a life sentence where we have to be lonely and scared and not-quite-real people forever.

"It's too late," Angelika says, her voice breaking, her face old again immediately.

"No," Delilah says again. "No."

Mom turns away from the window and Roger follows her, but I stay.

I only have eyes for Delilah.

My Delilah who isn't mine anymore.

Mom and Roger eat stew but I stay at the window. I watch Delilah and Delilah watches me. I am not as fearless as Mom and I am not as fearful as Delilah. I don't know what I am.

"I see it on you, too," Delilah says, right before curfew hits and she has to hide away from the possibility of love. I catch sight of Isla, scowling at me. Delilah's told her about me and Cruz, for sure. Wondrous Isla Rodriguez is also a scared little girl who doesn't want to lose her big brother. "I see it all over you, Lorna."

21.

I walk to school alone. It is something I've never done before, and the streets look different when I'm by myself. They're wider, for one, and I notice things like broken windows and purple-painted doors and missing bricks on the surface of brownstones. One lawn has a statue of the Virgin Mary I'd never noticed, which seems impossible because it's practically life-size. There's a new bar that looks seedier than things in this neighborhood usually do.

Cruz, Charlotte, Isla, and Owen are at the door when I get there. They are standing not exactly together and not exactly apart.

"It's bad," Isla says. Her lips are colored red and her eyelashes are so long I think they must be fake.

"What's bad?" I ask, assuming she might mean me. Charlotte's hands are wrapped around Cruz's bicep and she's pressed against him so tightly not a breath of air could get in between them.

Cruz isn't looking at me.

"They're talking about us," Isla says. "They've seen."

"Maybe I should go," Owen says. He forgot to kiss me hello, or maybe I forgot to kiss him.

"Hey," I say, and everyone's watching us too closely. "Your shirt's all messed up. You missed a button somewhere along the way." I let myself touch his chest, at the place where the button-missing occurred. I have the feeling—dreadful, certain, sinking—that it is the last time I'll be touching him there. He looks surprised at my finger and at his shirt and at being in the morning sun in front of school. He looks surprised at the way the world has been, lately.

"I'll fix it," he says. "I'll catch you guys later, okay?" He leans toward me and then away from me, like a tree in the wind, trying to decide whether to kiss me. It is the moment. If he leans one way it means we are together; if he leans the other, it changes everything. It's funny, the way one missed kiss can matter so much.

He steps away, and I'm left unkissed.

My friends give me a breath to recover before pointing to the door of the school. It's our picture from the article.

We all look caught by surprise in the image, which is funny considering how much time we spent readying ourselves for it, how made-up and overly styled and hyperaware we all were that day. But there it is: me, Isla, and Charlotte sitting down, our bodies mostly covered by the back of the bench, our necks craned as we all look over our shoulders, the words *Love Was Found Here* on display below us. Isla's mouth looks like a doll's—all red and surprised, and Charlotte's lips form a tight line. But in the photograph I have the shadow of a smile—it's hanging on my lips, which are almost all anyone can see of my face, with my sunglasses taking up the rest of me. Delilah stands behind us, looking up at the sky, at Jack, but when you look closer, her eyes are actually closed, like she is tilting her head to feel the heat of the sun.

We are us but not-us in the photograph.

We are us but not-us here on the sidewalk in front of the school, waiting an impossibly long time to go inside.

Over our faces, written in red Sharpie, the words AT YOUR OWN RISK.

It is worse inside.

Cruz and Charlotte veer left to their first period of class while Isla and I veer right. Isla has a strut. Her hips wag and she keeps flipping her long Devonairre Street hair. I wonder how she does it, how she manages to stay strong while they all watch us.

Then I find out.

"Hide me?" she says, turning to face the wall. She slips a flask out of her pocket. It's smaller than Jack's, and probably filled with something sweeter. She drops her head back and takes a shot. "You need some?" she asks, and it's so early in the morning I still remember a few of my dreams, but I almost take a sip, too. I shake my head and Isla grins.

"You'll be begging me for some later," she says.

Isla heads into her homeroom and I reach the door of mine.

Mr. Manning's lumbering frame blocks the door. He has a stain on his tie and hair in his ears but he's a good teacher. That's what I told Delilah when she told her story about the crush she thought he had on her the night Jack died. "You think everyone has a crush on you," I said. "You think this chair has a crush on you. You think Angelika's dog has a crush on you." Delilah shrugged like *yeah maybe*, and Jack didn't laugh but he smiled.

I have Mr. Manning for English second period, and I like the way he talks about characters in books like they're real people. He's always asking us how we feel about them, instead of what we think about them. It's a small difference, but it matters to me.

"Ms. Ryder," he says. "How are you holding up?"

"Oh. Okay. Thank you. Thanks." I'm surprised by the gentleness of his voice.

"I lost a friend very young, too. I know you and Jack were close." He is half whispering, like death is a secret.

"What was his name?" I ask, some part of me wanting to know everything there is to know about Mr. Manning's dead friend.

Mr. Manning takes a step backward, a small shuffle of a step that I wouldn't normally notice, but he sort of trips when he does it so it's hard to miss.

"Alan," he says. I nod, like that makes sense. I have more questions—when and how and why—but Mr. Manning's eyes keep drifting to something behind my head and his neck is turning pink. I glance behind me, to see whatever it is he's seeing.

It's the photograph. I can see more details now—the glint of the keys around Isla's neck, the over-the-top brightness of the hearts on my top, the way Charlotte's braids are uneven, the clench of Delilah's fists.

Mr. Manning clears his throat. "I remember when Alan passed away, school was just awful. Hard to focus. All I wanted was some time alone."

"Sure," I say. The bell rings but Mr. Manning isn't letting me in the door.

"I bet you're feeling that way, about Jack. He was a good kid. Had him in my AP class with Delilah. Saw them fall in love right before my eyes. Figured they'd be getting married right after graduation."

"Sure. I thought that, too." I try to look around Mr. Manning to see my classmates but he takes up so much of the doorframe that I can only catch sight of a few curious faces. I take a step, to remind him it's time for class to start, but he shifts and braces his elbows against the frame.

"Anyway, Ms. Ryder, I was thinking you might like a free period. A few free periods even. We were all thinking . . . Some of us thought that might be good. For you. The room next door is open. Maybe you'd like to go there?"

Mr. Manning has stopped looking me in the eye.

"I'm okay being in class," I say. Mr. Manning wipes his brow. He looks at the photograph behind my head again.

"Delilah and Jack. I never would have put them together. We teachers don't always know what's going on with our students." He stuffs his hands in his pockets and behind him the class is being rowdy. Still he doesn't move from his place at the door. "I'd never have thought Delilah would fall in love with Jack, but there you go, right?"

"Love works in mysterious ways?" I want the conversation to stop, or shift, or turn into something else entirely.

"Exactly," Mr. Manning says. "Anyone could fall in love with anyone."

There's a siren somewhere outside the building. We listen to it build in volume, then recede. I think of Cruz, even though I shouldn't. I think of the Bombing. I think of Jack. And we're both quiet for longer than is comfortable. "I don't really need a free period," I say. "I'm okay for class."

Mr. Manning doesn't move. His elbows stay pinned to the frame. His feet move a little farther apart so that his legs help create a wall, too. He clears his throat again. And again.

I'm dizzy.

Mr. Manning looks at that photograph one last time, shuffles back into his classroom, and shuts the door.

"Don't ever be ashamed," my father told me when I was little and Angelika was trying to talk to me about the Curse. "The second you start to feel shame, you get rid of it." Even in these last few days I've felt nervousness and doubt; I've felt sadness and fear. But I haven't felt shame.

Now I feel a wet, itchy feeling.

Shame.

I go to the empty classroom, and I wait for the moment of silence to come.

It does, of course. It always does.

. . .

In the moment of silence, all I can think of is Cruz.

I think my father wouldn't mind. This is what he wanted for me. To be in love. To feel like my organs are weightless, like they've left my body, even. Like I am hollow except for thoughts of Cruz, which are filling me all the way up. My father wanted me to be in love.

I don't know that this is love.

Except I do.

I touch the key around my neck, for protection that I don't believe in. My father used to roll his eyes at that reflex. "That key is just a key," he'd say. "Nothing magic about it. It doesn't even open anything." He always sounded so certain, I'd drop the thing right away. Today I hang on, my mind finally asking the question *What if the Curse is real after all?*

I try to hear my father's voice again. A forgotten memory blossoms—my father holding my chin in his hand for the first and only time. "Whatever happens," he said as we sat on the stoop finishing ice-cream cones and watching the sun go down, "don't listen to Angelika. Don't let her persuade you to be afraid. Ignore her. No matter what."

"Okay," I said. I was eight and it sounded fine. Easy. "Can I have another cone?"

He gave me another cone, like the extra ice cream sealed the promise.

Some promises are hard to keep.

The Minute of Silence stretches on forever when you're by yourself, quarantined. The rest of the city, the nation, gets to move on. But I'm stuck in an ugly Spanish classroom, looking at a list of basic verbs, remembering my father and the promises I made, and trying to figure out if they mean more or less now that he's gone.

It is 10:11 on another Tuesday morning, and my father has been gone for almost seven years, and maybe, *maybe* I'm in love like I promised him I would be.

I put my head on my desk and listen to the silence ending, the world moving on. I don't move on, though. I never do.

They won't let me.

22.

Charlotte joins me during second period, and Isla during third.

None of the male teachers are letting us into their classrooms. Some of the male students protest us, too.

Charlotte says, "Ms. MacQuinn was fine, but the boys said it was either them or me. What is that even? They can't do that!"

"Plus you're with my brother," Isla says.

"Right. Yes, I mean, of course." Charlotte blushes and plays with the key around her neck and a ring around her finger I hadn't noticed before. It must be new. It's copper and thread thin and pretty on her hand. "I have a boyfriend," she whispers, and I swear she looks at me from the corner of her eye.

We've never been close on our own, Charlotte and I. She's always been skeptical of me and I've always been judgmental of her. It's never mattered, because we were LornaCruzCharlotte-DelilahIsla and those ugly feelings were one tiny part of it.

Now it feels like it matters.

All this time I've been thinking that Delilah is the one floating away from us. But Isla and Charlotte are sitting close together and they exchange a series of secret looks and I think of Isla on the sidewalk in front of my house last night and the fact that I keep kissing Charlotte's boyfriend, and it hits me.

I'm the one who's different.

I'm the one who's floating away.

Isla's lipstick is smudged and a button on her shirt is undone. Angelika would go crazy at how much of her is exposed.

I bet her flask is empty now.

"What happened with you?" I ask, but I already know.

"I'm not going to be a nun just because I can't be in love," Isla says. Her shoulders betray her. They shiver and shake and I think she likes whatever it is she's doing in the Latin room and under the stairwell and in the basement, but she'd like love, too.

She has a scarf from Angelika with her, I think all the girls do but me, and she pulls it from her backpack, wraps it tight across her chest so that she's covered the way Angelika wants us to be. Her head drops a little, a telltale sign that she's drunk. It's strange—what rules Isla follows perfectly and what she rebels against.

"You can—" I start, wanting to tell her she doesn't have to listen to Angelika.

She shakes her head. "This is what I'm doing. I don't want to talk about it. You obviously don't get it."

"I don't get it," I agree.

"I don't get you, either," she says.

"I saw you outside my building last night," I say. I want her to apologize or tell me it didn't mean anything or laugh it off. She doesn't.

"I know," she says, and that's that.

And even though she said she didn't want to talk about it, Isla starts talking about it.

"I'm not going to fall in love," she says, "I'll be the girl they can be with and not worry about love." She shrugs and I'm positive there's a hickey on her neck. "Love's not worth it. I'm not made for all that."

"What does that mean?" I ask.

"I don't believe. But I don't not believe. I'm not like you or like Charlotte or like Delilah used to be." Isla says it all like a challenge, and I wonder whether the things I've always loved—being part of a whole, being attached in this complicated and unbreakable way, the street itself—are things Isla has always hated. "I'm doing this my way. I'm not going to be the girl they're telling me I am—all sad and alone or brokenhearted and in love and fated to destroy everything. You all can be those girls. I want to be . . . I'm a different kind of girl."

When we were younger, Isla looked up to us, I think. She borrowed Charlotte's glasses and my dresses and Delilah's turns of phrases and practiced being some combination of the three of us.

Now she only looks and talks and acts like Isla Rodriguez.

"Isla," Charlotte says. But the way she says it tells me she doesn't have anything else to say.

"Like I said, I don't want to talk about it," Isla says. "What happened to Jack—I can't let that happen to someone that I—no. I don't need love. I don't even know what it is. I'm starting to think no one actually knows what it is."

"Angelika says it's a leap. It's a fever. It's a certain thing that shows up on your skin," Charlotte says, like a good student.

"What do you say?" Isla asks.

No one is asking me.

I'm not ready to answer anyway. Angelika and Delilah say love is knowable and clear, but I disagree. It's blurry. It's shaky. It's not math or a fever at all. Not for me.

"I don't know that there's a moment when you're in and when you're out," Charlotte says, all careful and whispering, and I wonder whether she's hearing my own thoughts. "I know that's what Angelika says; I know that's what we're supposed to think about it.

But I think it's more like a shadow. It follows you around. And you don't know when it's there or not, until you catch sight of it, attached to you, stretching and showing some strange new part of you."

We sit in the poetry of the way Charlotte's speaking.

I hate that she's talking about Cruz. I hate how beautifully she's able to talk about loving him. I hate how real those words make it.

"Maybe you never know if you're in love or not," I say. "Maybe no one knows, and we all wander around talking about it like it's something tangible and knowable, but actually we're all full of it. Maybe even the people who say they're in love are wondering *is this what they meant?*"

I can see that the idea bothers Charlotte and Isla, but I like it. I like the idea that there aren't answers, no matter how many goddamn questions we ask.

Maybe that's what my dad liked, too—the quest for answers, but not the answers themselves. Only the asking.

The minutes pass, and so do hours.

The principal comes in at lunchtime with her assistant, bringing lunch trays to our desks. Lasagna, a sad iceberg salad, a chocolate chip cookie, a soft dinner roll, a too-hard pat of butter.

"Room service!" the principal says, her glasses thick like Charlotte's, her nose a beak, her voice too enthusiastic for the occasion.

"When are we getting out of here?" I ask when it's clear Isla and Charlotte aren't going to say anything at all.

"We're working out what our plan is," she says, an implied enthusiastic exclamation point at the end of the sentence. It hurts my ears, how hard she's trying to make this seem normal.

"You can't keep us in here," I say. Isla and Charlotte are still quiet, looking out the windows, at their feet, at the lunch trays, anywhere but our principal's eyes.

"We've never had a situation quite like this," the principal says. "The media attention is a bit of a new thing for our school, and we haven't ironed out a great plan yet to make sure the student body and the three of you are all comfortable and safe and able to do your best jobs learning."

"It's fine," Charlotte mumbles.

Isla's silent and still.

"Are you going to kick us out?" I ask.

"Of course not," the principal says, but her eyes move to the left and to the right and I know it's a possibility. "It's been a very troubling few weeks. The attack in Chicago and Jack Abbound's death and of course we're coming up on the seven-year anniversary and the papers have been—well. It's a hard time. It's a hard time to feel safe and comfortable. But we're going to make it work for everyone, I can promise you that much. And we won't hold this all against any of you. We're not mad at you."

She wipes her hands against each other, all *great, that's done*, and looks at her assistant, who keeps biting her lip. The assistant has a tattoo of scales on her wrist. Gemini. It's popular these days, to get a tattoo of your astrological sign on your wrist.

It makes me dislike her a little. Distrust her.

They leave and we eat our lasagna and try to think of something to talk about.

"What would Delilah do about this?" Charlotte asks. Her glasses look a little foggy and her face is drawn. I wonder what Cruz likes about her face. Maybe her green eyes or the straight line of her nose or the way she puts the perfect puff of blush on each cheek.

"New Delilah or Old Delilah?" I ask.

"Our Delilah," Charlotte says, and we all know what that means.

"She wouldn't sit here and let it happen," I say. "She'd, I don't know, protest. Petition. She'd laugh it off and bust into her classes anyway. She'd fix it."

If she saw us right now, she'd say "don't sit around and let the earth do all the spinning." And we'd laugh at the way Delilah says the perfect things in the perfect moments.

But Delilah's not here so we sit until two thirty, when Cruz comes by and releases us from the classroom.

"I should have come earlier," he says. I nod. Charlotte kisses his mouth like it's fine that he ignored us all day and let us take the fall once again. He walks us through the hallways like a bodyguard. His arm is around Charlotte.

Owen's outside the building, and the sight of him makes my heart jump. Not with the happiness of being around him, but because I'd forgotten about him all day long, so his face is a surprise. I'm not much of a girlfriend, it turns out.

"They locked me up," I say.

"Yeah." Owen's hands are in his pockets and my friends don't leave us alone but they give us some space.

"You didn't come save me."

"I didn't know I was supposed to."

He keeps looking at my shoulder instead of my face.

"You're not the same with me," I say at last, because Owen's not saying much else. "You knew about the street and the Curse and stuff. You knew and it didn't matter, I thought. But now it does?"

Owen looks at my other shoulder.

"You didn't even look like you in that picture," he says. "What'd they do to your face?"

"Makeup."

"Oh."

I know Owen's slow way of moving and thinking and speaking,

so I take a deep breath, still my busy hands, and try to quiet my heart while I wait for him to speak.

"Every single person who was married to a Devonairre Street Girl during World War Two died in battle," he says at last.

He read the article. Thoroughly.

"Yes."

"It's weird how little I thought about that. But I don't know any other widows except for your mom and Charlotte's mom and Cruz and Isla's mom and Delilah's mom. Your moms are all widows. The only widows I know in the whole world all live on one single street."

"You're starting to believe," I say. Out of the corner of my eye I watch Isla flirt with a nervous boy. I see Charlotte and Cruz hold hands and avert their eyes from everyone staring at them.

Owen is extra slow with his words. He's barely even blinking.

"I've never felt about anyone the way I feel about you," he says when I think we're going to stay in silence for the rest of our lives. I can sense a *but* to his sentence, and I think maybe this is it, we're breaking up, he's letting me go because I'm too scary and dangerous and wrong.

Then I'll be left alone with thoughts of Cruz, whom I don't want to be thinking about at all. I want to think about Owen. I want Owen to stay. I want to hook up in my bed, all angles and gasps and perfect fits and dream-filled naps. I feel powerful in bed with Owen and vulnerable in the garden with Cruz and I want that power back. I want to drink in the garden with our friends and not worry about things like love, and only worry about Owen's blue eyes and big hands and sweet snores.

It feels like we had built something with blocks—Lorna-CruzCharlotteDelilahIsla. It feels like we had a delicate castle of blocks on our living room table and Jack's Death and the Chicago

Bombing swooped in and knocked the whole thing over—and then mocked us for believing blocks were anything real. All I want is to build it back, exactly the way it was.

But I can't put it back together without Owen.

"You told me you loved me once, in your sleep," I say. Love is the last thing I want to be thinking about, the last word I want to be saying, but there it is. Love. Always popping up when you least expect it. Always invading perfectly safe and sweet things like affection and tenderness and sex.

"I did?"

"'I love the moon and you and I don't have a chicken,'" I say, smiling at the words although so much has happened in between the time when he said them and this moment right now.

"Huh?" Owen says. He doesn't smile back. Whatever magic is in those words for me isn't there for him. They might as well have been said by someone else.

"It's what you said a while ago. When you were dreaming." I'm fluttery inside and I want him to think I'm beautiful. Those things aren't love but they're something even better. Safer. Easier. What I feel for Cruz is thick and inescapable and heavy. What I feel for Owen is light and lovely. I want to keep it. I want to hold on to it.

"Well. Sounds like it was quite a dream," Owen says. And I think, yeah, yeah, it was.

We are maybe about to end or we are maybe about to kiss but instead someone spits on me.

At first I think it's a drop of rain, so I look up to find storm clouds. There aren't any. It's a sunny day. But Henry Pollan is a foot away, ugly-scowling and wiping off his lips.

"Get away from us," he says, his voice deeper than I remember from sophomore year math class. He asked me to a dance once and

I said no, because I knew Charlotte and Cruz and Delilah and Isla weren't going to the dance and I couldn't see myself there without them; I couldn't picture my arms around Henry's thick neck.

Now he's waving his arms and doing a menacing dance with his feet like he's ready to fight.

"What the fuck?" I say, hitting the spit off my skin, slapping my arm over and over in the hopes that I will somehow feel the sting of the hit and not the wetness of his spit. I gag.

Owen rushes at Henry, all instinct, and in that moment, too, I love his body and the easy way it moves. He shoves one of Henry's shoulders, jerks his head.

Cruz sees and comes at Henry, too. He raises his shoulders, like that will make him wider, stronger, scarier.

"Fuck you!" Cruz hits Henry's other shoulder. Owen and Cruz flank Henry, making menacing moves with their chins, their elbows, their shoulders.

There's a scuffle—Cruz, Owen, Henry, and a few others get into it—but it doesn't last because Henry and his friends end up running away, scared, I think, not of the boys, but of the Devonairre Street Girls.

"Jack would have fully kicked their asses," Cruz says when it's just us on the sidewalk.

I nod and Owen nods and Charlotte tears up and Isla juts her hip out and pretends not to care.

"They believe," I say. "Every single person we see on the street believes. At least a little bit. They wonder."

"They're scared of us," Isla says, and for the first time in weeks I see little girl Isla again, sad eyed and wishing the world were different.

23.

We follow Isla's lead and get drunk after school.

"Finally," she says, like she's been waiting for us to join her since early this morning, which I guess she has.

"To Chicago," Cruz says, but it's not a very good toast, and we don't want to think about Chicago. I've heard most of the city hasn't gone back to work and kids haven't gone back to school—things have paused for even longer than they did here after the Bombing. Chicago doesn't want to rebuild, the news says. It wants to dedicate all the shattered space to gardens, with the ashes of the lost men and women buried underneath the ground.

"To Chicago," we repeat back to him, downing peach vodka out of plastic cups. It's a terrible taste but I'm thirsty for the way I'll feel after a few more sips.

Owen is here, but quiet. We aren't touching or speaking or even looking at each other. But at least he's here.

We get drunk in the sad way, not the fun way.

"We should get Delilah," Charlotte says. "She'd do this with us, I bet."

"She's busy with Angelika tonight," Isla says. "We're making a tribute. To everyone we've lost."

"How do you know that?" I ask with a laugh, like we're back in the old days, where no one would ever know more about Delilah than I do.

Isla doesn't answer. She waits for me to figure out the answer myself.

My spine sweats and I know, for sure, that I'm the outsider, not Delilah. That everything I've thought was true isn't, that I don't understand the street I live on or the people that I love.

Isla braids a few pieces of grass together and Charlotte leans against Cruz and takes bigger sips of vodka than usual. I survey the plants. Someone has been overwatering them and they're drooping.

People think they're helping, but they're actually hurting things.

The second Minute of Silence hits at 4:36.

"We have to be quiet," Owen says. Cruz and I roll our eyes.

"I don't have to be quiet," Isla says, but she is. We all are. Cars stop. Devonairre Street pauses. I'm thinking again about the afternoon in bed with Owen and I look to him to see whether he's remembering the same thing, but he's misty eyed looking at the bench.

"I gotta go," he says when the minute is over.

"We didn't finish our talk earlier," I say. My voice shakes and everyone's listening but pretending not to. Owen sighs.

"What do you think about during the Minute of Silence?" he asks. I get the feeling there's a right answer and a wrong answer.

"You," I say. "I think about you." At least this one time, it's true. "What do you think about?"

Owen pauses. He looks a little sick. He looks a little sad. He doesn't look so much like Owen. "I think about Jack," he says.

The way he says Jack's name, I know it's over.

He takes a lemon on his way out. Plucks it from the tree like it's a thing he's always done.

. . .

We get drunker.

Then we get drunker still.

We are angry-drinking, we are lonely-drinking, we are grief-drinking, we are fear-drinking. Isla is somehow our leader.

When we are bleary eyed and it's six thirty in the evening, Cruz brings out his phone to look again at the article. He reads it aloud, in his most ridiculous voice; and if we were even the littlest bit sober I don't think it would be funny, but we're blitzed, all of us, even Charlotte, so it is downright hysterical.

"That's about *us*," I say. "They're talking about us! How crazy is that!"

"So crazy!" Isla says.

"How many people in the world are talking about us right this minute?" Charlotte asks. She lies down on the bench, her legs swinging off the edge, her head at an awkward angle that can't be comfortable.

"A hundred," Isla says.

"Hopefully none," I say.

"They don't know the first thing about us," Cruz says. He says it right to me.

"One hundred percent incorrect," I say. "They know everything about us. Wait. Wait. Okay. Look." I pull out my phone and bring up HistoryoftheAffected.gov and find my way to my own page, the one that people can look at if they want to put themselves in my shoes or something.

"The History of the Affected will build compassion and understanding. It will help us remember the tragedies, and build a better world," the president said when the program was first being introduced. It was an impassioned speech that people say will go down in history like the Gettysburg Address. The words are written in fancy calligraphy across the header of the web page.

"See? They know me," I say, staring at a picture of myself on the screen.

There's me at eleven, cross-legged at the one-year anniversary in Prospect Park, lost in the grass while everyone else sat on chairs. My hair was uncombed, a key was around my neck, and at the edge of the frame it's clear I'm holding someone's hand.

Cruz's.

Isla's haunting the background of my photograph as well—I can see her little-girl dress as a blur behind me. But it's Cruz's hand that I can't take my eyes off.

"God," Cruz says, leaning in to take a look with everyone else. "You look sadder than I ever remember either of us being."

"I hate the memorials," I say.

What's most clear in the photo, more than my sadness or Cruz's hand or the fact of the photo existing at all—the person who captured it wanted, I guess, to get a vision of what tragedy looks like—is the pile of lemons in my lap.

I feel a wave of anger on behalf of eleven-year-old me, looking to a pile of fruit to make me feel better. When the lemons didn't work, it felt like something was wrong with me. I didn't understand those first two years why the pain kept coming, like a flood.

"Angelika's always there," I say. "Lurking." I think of the way she's tied herself to Delilah. Their afternoons braiding bracelets on the stoop. Their identical mugs of tea. The way Angelika now has a framed picture of Jack in her kitchen window, stealing a bit of him for herself.

"You're telling me," says Charlotte. It's an unexpected joke from someone who never makes jokes. I throw my arms around her, and for an instant we are best friends.

Charlotte gets woozy, and it disappears, the thing between us. She moves toward Cruz, grabs on to his shoulders to steady her, and I'm back to resenting the hell out of her button-up shirt and pressed cardigan and sensible shoes.

Isla doesn't say anything about Angelika or lemons until a few minutes later, when she says, simply, "Nothing helps."

The sun's starting to come down and we're due home soon and I'm not any closer to understanding anything except that being near Cruz makes me want to be near Cruz more and thinking of Angelika makes my palms sweat and my heart race and I'm sad for the little girl with a lap full of lemons.

"How do you think they're doing in Chicago?" I ask. "I keep forgetting about them. Isn't that disgusting? We should go to Chicago. We should write letters to people in Chicago. We should be . . . doing something."

And in an instant, I understand the lemons. I want to bring them to Chicago, hoping that they'll help.

"Let Chicago do Chicago," Isla says, her voice a little slurry. I wonder if Isla should have friends her own age, if we've done something terrible to her by treating her exactly as one of us. "They don't need us worrying about them. They want space."

I remember after the Bombing we hated the people who wanted to crowd our space with their vague grief. They cried at candle lightings and spoke about being a mile away or upstate or across the country.

And now here I am, wanting to take a bit of the Chicago Attacks for myself. Trying to grieve for someone I didn't lose, for people I never loved, for a place I've never known.

"I feel like we're connected to them," I say, trying to defend myself but I know I'm wrong. "We're the same."

Charlotte dozes off in Cruz's arms. Isla gets a call and lets us know she's meeting someone in Prospect Heights.

"Who?" I ask, because no one else remembers to ask.

"Doesn't matter," Isla says.

"It matters to me."

Cruz shifts. "You'll call me if you need me?" he says, an all-wrong response. We have to keep Isla here. We have to keep her safe and away from whatever it is she's trying to do. She's trying to be Someone Else and we can't let that happen. She's ours. She'll always be ours.

"I won't need you," Isla says. She doesn't turn back to look at us when she goes. She looks straight ahead, her hair flapping behind her like a cape, giving her superpowers.

Then it's me and Cruz and sleeping Charlotte in the garden.

It is always me and Cruz alone in the garden, with all the things we cannot say.

We don't speak, we don't stare, we don't text. But minutes pass and we don't move, either. Cruz hands me his phone. He's still on the History of the Affected database and he's pulled up his page. There is a picture of Cruz, suited and sad. He is staring at someone nearby. A girl in a familiar gray dress with my silvery hair.

He is smiling the smallest bit at the way she holds a lemon.

I'm seeing a different history in these old pictures. The story of me and Cruz.

I finally, finally look at him. Something in my heart bursts and there it is. The feeling. The Yes. Love.

Then we see a flash. Cameras. The garden is no longer ours.

24.

"I brought doughnuts," Delilah says Saturday morning. She is on my stoop at five in the morning the day of the Seven-Year Anniversary, just as she's been every other year since my father died.

Five a.m. on the day of the Bombing was the last time I saw my father. He used to kiss me every morning before he left for the gym and work, and I'd whine at him for rubbing his stubbly face against my smooth one before the sun was even up.

"But I love you!" he'd always say with a big, toothy grin and a mean tickle.

"It's too early for love!" I'd say.

"Never," he'd say. It was a script said every single morning for so many years, but he always sounded serious on that final word.

Now Delilah's on my stoop, like she is every year at this time, and she's got maple-bacon doughnuts from the place off the G train that my father told us had to be a secret we kept forever so they didn't get too famous.

"This is what life's all about," he'd say when he bit into one.

These are some of my favorite memories, because they're all mine. My mom hates doughnuts, so Dad would only take me and Delilah. No one else from the street knew anything about the place.

"We should bring one home for Angelika," I said once, and my father laughed, wrinkled his nose, and winked. The doughnuts were only for us.

The memory is only for us, too, so there's no one around to twist it up or turn it upside down or rewrite it as a cautionary tale. Angelika and Betty and Dolly don't know about twenty-four-hour doughnuts. The History of the Affected won't ever know. On the website, my father's favorite food is listed as steak, but Delilah and I know it was doughnuts and we'll never tell.

"You're here," I say now, taking the doughnut from Delilah, who has already taken a huge bite of hers.

"I couldn't wait," she says, like she does every year. "It was calling to me. It told me I had to take a bite."

I throw myself on her. My arms fit around her neck and I feel hers go around my middle and we both hold on so tight there's no space between us. I'm ecstatic to have this Delilah—the one who knows the one secret memory I have of my father, the one who will buy me a doughnut in the middle of the night if it will help ease the pain of the world's worst anniversary. That's the Delilah I squeeze. That's the Delilah whose shoulder I cry on.

"I didn't think you'd be here," I say, "but I came downstairs any-way." She doesn't say anything, but she rubs my back and lets me stay pressed against her until I've cried enough tears and squeezed her enough times.

"I always forget how delicious these things are," she says. I finally take a bite and it makes me smile. Salty and sweet and indulgent and ridiculous, everything my father was.

"I thought you'd maybe forgotten about them altogether," I say. She takes another bite of doughnut.

The sidewalk is empty. I fall back in love with Devonairre Street, standing there with my best friend in the universe, looking at the lit-up lamps leading a path to the garden, where the yellow lemons hanging from the lemon tree are almost bright enough to light up the night, too.

This is my home.

"To be honest, Lorna," Delilah says, and the peace is broken because her voice is New Delilah voice, and she looks up at the sky, which is where she now looks whenever she is thinking of Jack and Curses. "I thought maybe you'd forgotten. About today. About your dad. About the things that have happened."

I look left and right like Angelika must be somewhere nearby, for her words to be making their way out of Delilah's mouth. She's not here, though.

Sometimes my nose fills with the scent of the dusty, ruined air, even though there's no other smell like it and it's been gone for years. Sometimes the Minute of Silence feels like it may never end and my throat closes halfway through and I watch the clock, wondering whether I'll breathe again.

I haven't forgotten the day of the Bombing.

And if Delilah were Delilah, she'd know that.

"I remember everything terrible." I am trying not to fight with her because I can't fight with Delilah on the Seven-Year Anniversary. "I remember every terrible thing. Don't worry. I only forget the good days and the best memories."

I still have most of my doughnut left but I couldn't eat now. I feel ill. I can't stop smelling the remembered soot smell. It won't leave my nose. My eyes burn, and that, too, is a remembered feeling. My eyes hurt for days after the Bombing—all of us walked around pink eyed and teary. Something in the air infected us—like we were all allergic to tragedy.

Delilah puts her hand on my hand. "I don't want to upset you. I want to save you."

"I don't need saving."

Delilah's eyes fill and her head drops. Soon the sun will come up and the day will begin in earnest, and what I hoped had changed between us will go back to normal, and we'll be stuck in our new roles again. It's a miserable kind of destiny.

"You'll see," she says. "You'll see and it will be too late and then you'll be just like me."

She's shaking a little and I rub her back.

"Do you want to be like me?" she asks.

"I—"

"No. Trust me. You don't."

Delilah moves off the stoop. On a regular anniversary day she'd come in for tea and to give my mother a hug. She'd walk us to the vigil in the park; she and Mrs. James would make us dinner while we were gone and leave it covered in foil on the counter, ready to be heated and consumed in front of something silly on TV.

"Are you coming up?" I ask. "Please come up." Delilah shakes her head. Her hair is hidden under a scarf again, her body draped in a long, loose gray dress. Her face is the only truly visible part of her anymore, but even her face is unfamiliar—hidden under unreadable expressions and a new kind of exhaustion.

"He'll die," she says, "and you'll live your whole life knowing you could have stopped it."

Delilah leans in to me. She smells like lavender and rosemary and sweat. Her breath is sweet from the doughnut but still a little raw from the morning. I'm sure mine is, too.

"It gets worse every day." She pauses, and in that pause is everything about our friendship—honesty and saying things that are awful and true and trusting each other and sharing a history and a street and a whole identity. "You'll see," she says before walking away.

25.

We are wearing black wool for the Seven-Year Memorial. We are in long skirts and tops with high necklines, like Angelika demanded.

"Covering it up doesn't mean it doesn't exist," Mom says.

"What?"

"Sex. Love. Bodies. It's all still there, under the layers of wool and keys. Whether Angelika wants it to be or not."

My mother had sex last night, past midnight, and Roger snuck out after it was over. I wish I hadn't heard, but I did.

"I'm doing it for Delilah," I say. I am doing it a little bit for me, too. That's the secret I'm keeping from my mother.

"It doesn't mean we believe in anything," she says on our way out the door.

Mom holds her head high and I don't have to ask—not today, not ever—if she thinks there's even a tiny chance it could have been her fault. Dad insisted that everyone had secrets, but I don't think Mom has them. She is solid and consistent and I can hear her every gasp and cry and grunt and heartbeat. There's nothing to hide.

I imitate her certainty and pull my shoulders back.

The street is empty but there are faces in every window, watching us walk from the neighborhood to Prospect Park, calculating how many rituals we have upheld (not enough), how many failures we have enacted (too many). I wonder if Delilah has gone back to bed or if she's watching us from her window, too. If she's monitoring my face and my gait to see if she's affected me at all, if she's changed my mind.

I pull my shoulders back harder, lift my chin more.

"Is Roger meeting us there?" I ask. It's the first time in a week I've been with my mother alone.

"Not today," Mom says. "I don't want him to be part of all this."

"Part of what?" I ask. "This is our life." We both exhale as soon as we turn the corner off Devonairre Street. We're still being watched on other streets, I think, but less harshly.

"I told Angelika to prepare herself. Once I sell, pressure will be on for the others. We'll live a nice, calm life. And we can have an enormous house on the water. We'll be able to afford—well. Things will be great."

"Then what? You'll leave Roger? You'll leave your practice? I'll do senior year somewhere else? None of it makes any sense."

"Roger's talking to work about transferring to their West Coast office." She doesn't answer any other questions or give me any other solutions. "See? Easy. You like him. You'll like him even more without all this pressure."

I wonder if she sees herself getting married, having a California tan, growing an avocado tree in the front yard.

"I'm not going to California."

"God, Lorna, what do we have here? You can't even go to school. Your best friend is . . . everyone is . . . We can't leave the house. We can't cut our hair. We can't date. I don't know why I didn't listen to your father in the first place. It's not a place for us. For anyone. What do you even love about living here, at this point?"

I pretend it's a rhetorical question so I don't say anything about

Cruz and Future Lorna and the view of the faraway Statue of Liberty and the smell of basil after it rains and Delilah with her doughnuts and the simplicity of turning the lights on at sunset to keep terrible things at bay.

I hold my tongue so that I don't say anything about the way it feels to know someone forever and realize you love them in spite of a million reasons not to.

And I don't say anything about rare Bistro steaks and the hope, the persistent hope that I have every day, that Betty or Dolly or someone else will remember something new about my father.

Four months ago Betty recalled a day that he sat on the stoop and played a harmonica. She laughed, telling the story, because a few nonlocals stood and listened and dropped change at his feet, thinking he was a busker.

I didn't even know he played any instruments. I don't remember him loving music and I don't remember ever seeing a harmonica.

But there it was, out of nowhere, a new fact about him, all these years later.

I'll stay here forever for the hope to get one bit of treasure every few years.

One little secret.

• • •

Cruz, Mrs. Rodriguez, Maria, Ashley and her boys, and the Chens are standing by the trees that we always stand by. Isla never comes to the Memorials. Cruz and I aren't given the choice, but the world is different for Isla Rodriguez. She's at home watching daytime television and waiting to have her Minute of Silence in absolute peace.

Cruz is wearing a suit that doesn't fit.

"I see your ankles," I say, expecting him to laugh. We can make each other laugh even on days like today. He goes grim.

"It was my dad's suit."

I squint, trying to remember Alejandro Rodriguez in those pants, that jacket. I can almost imagine him. He was shorter than Cruz is now, and stouter, but with the same handsome jawline, the same alive eyes, the same dark curly hair. "I'm not doing it to be weird," he says. "I don't have another suit. And Mom freaked out at my jeans. So."

"So. Here we are," I say, thinking it's strange when someone is beautiful and sad all at once.

I tell my mind to shut up about the things Delilah said.

"It's ten eleven," someone says over the speakers, like they do at every Anniversary. No flowery speeches. No call for silence and thought. Just the announcement of the time and a crowd's immediate response.

We all hang our heads.

It's a little terrifying, a crowd of hundreds of people doing the same movement at the same time. It gives me a shiver.

On the anniversaries, the Minute of Silence magically turns into ten minutes instead of one. It seems arbitrary. How much destruction happened in one minute, in ten, in twenty? Are we meant to stay silent for the length of time it took for everyone to die? I think we'd have to be silent all day, all week, in that case.

It's a long ten minutes and I let myself think of my dad for the whole time. I think about how every birthday he'd give me a book of poetry and said I'd understand it when I was older. I'm starting to understand some of the poems now, the ones about sex and love and the ways they are sometimes the same and sometimes not.

I think about when he taught me to play basketball and how he lifted me into the air to dunk the ball whenever I got discouraged. I think about when he gave Mom a necklace with a tiny ruby heart hanging off the end, and that he got embarrassed when she gushed to everyone in the neighborhood about it.

We've never been allowed much joy on our street. Angelika thinks we don't deserve it, and maybe sometimes we believe her.

My mom always wore the ruby, but she tucked it under her shirts to be safe.

I peek at her. She's not wearing it today, and I don't know what that means.

"Thank you," the speaker says when ten minutes are up. We raise our heads in unison.

The park is crowded with family members of people who died. Every year Cruz and I try to recognize them. We know some of their names from the History of the Affected and we know some of their stories from the speeches they give at the different memorials, and some we recognize simply by the particular black dress they wear every year.

There are reporters everywhere, and I don't want them to recognize me so I slide my sunglasses on, forgetting that will make me more recognizable.

Cruz and I grab hands the Devonairre Street way and look over our shoulders to see who's watching us.

Mrs. Chen and Ashley tilt their chins and cross their arms. The covered-up clothing isn't enough apparently. What they really want is for me to be locked up in a tower, unable to get to anyone at all.

The school wants the same thing "for now." They have provided us with online learning material, and it's so dry and stale it is the educational equivalent of a cracker.

Maria inserts herself between Cruz and me, pretending to talk to me but it's clear what her real goal is.

"How are you doing today, Lorna?" Maria asks, but she's not even looking at my face for an answer. Which is good, because I'm wondering whether Cruz and I are going to kiss again, and when.

Ashley and Mrs. Chen circle Cruz, chattering full force at him. His mother joins in, too, putting her strong hands on his even stronger shoulders.

"You missing your father?" they say. "Has school been hard? Have you heard they're planting a tree in Jack's honor? Did you hear Scorpios are meant to spend time alone this month? How's Charlotte, is she coming today? Are you going to help us plant more lemon trees? Have you noticed all the photographers lurking around the street? Are you eating rosemary every day?"

A violinist plays a funereal song they play every year and I miss having Cruz next to me. We do the Memorials together. It is the time every year when we are closest. I try to scoot past Maria and the other ladies, but they shift and maneuver around me, making it impossible. I look to my mother, but she's in her own world. She's stepped away from the Devonairre Street crowd. She has her eyes closed, and she nods along with the melody like she's memorizing the exact way it sounds and feels.

I think she's hanging on to the memory of this, preparing herself to never come to a Memorial again.

We stand in a straight line, listening to the music, me on one end and Cruz at the other and both of us leaning back and forth to find each other's gaze.

Angelika said, "Love is a thing that is or isn't."

She also said, "Love is a permanent state; there is no going back."

And, "Love is falling because there is a moment before you touch the ground, when there is still hope."

She has a lot to say about love, about *luf*, but she's never told us what we're meant to do in that moment before we've fully fallen. She calls it permanent and unstoppable but asks us to stop it. She calls it true or false, but finds us when we're caught in between.

I can't get the image out of my head of me hovering above the ground, wanting to stop myself but unable to fight gravity.

Falling in love sounds violent, when you get right down to it.

The song ends and I start to feel sick, picturing my father in that same moment. The falling. Seven years ago. Right before he hit the ground, wondering what he could do to stop it.

Nothing, I think. He couldn't do anything at all.

• • •

They've made the park pretty for us. There's that, at least. Along with the lone sad violin, they've brought in bunches of flowers and rows and rows of wooden chairs for us to sit in. The mayor is here and a stage and a large screen with the names of our loved ones projected across its surface.

We wait for my father's eyes. They call out the names of the Victims, and I could practically recite them myself, they are that familiar. My mother finally moves toward me and Cruz sneaks closer to me as well. We avoid the cheap wooden seats. We stand tall with our arms crossed over our chests in case the wool doesn't offer us the protection Angelika promises it will.

We fade into the sea of mourners, and for a moment I feel almost cozy in our shared pain.

I survey the field of the Affected. There are men in suits carrying framed photos of their dead wives. There are seven-year-old kids grinning and missing the point because they've never known life with their mother or father. There are ancient mothers with puffy eyes and gruff men with shiny, new wedding rings. There are kids our age—looking at their phones, in groups, with wrinkled suits, crying, wishing they were somewhere else.

I'm looking at them.

Until I find that they are looking at me.

I wish away my silvery hair and my height. I wish away my mother's sharp, recognizable features and Cruz's handsome face. I wish away the article most of all.

A girl with short blue hair and big brown eyes smiles and waves at me, as if she knows me. I wave back as a reflex.

She takes a few steps in our direction, so that we're in earshot.

"I love you guys," she says. "So badass."

"Oh," I say. I guess she means me and Isla and Delilah and Charlotte. But I don't know what it is she likes about us—our long hair or my sunglasses or the way we answered the reporters in short, surly statements, leaving Angelika to fill out the article with elaborate descriptions of the Curse, of the old days of Devonairre, of her dead husband and our responsibility. I have no idea what about us could possibly be badass. I'm practically dressed as a pioneer woman today—wool itching my calves and my neck. Mom's right, though. Underneath there's wanting and feeling and the length of my legs and the ways they could wrap around Cruz.

They can hide it, but they can't make it disappear.

"No comment," I say like a person on TV. The girl with blue hair scrunches her nose and rolls her eyes. She walks away but not before snapping a picture of me and Cruz.

A few men in their forties overheard the blue-haired girl

point me out, and their eyes light up with that same recognition. More men's and women's faces flash on the screen, more names boom over the speakers, but even here, even now, we are more compelling.

"Bitch," one of them mumbles under his breath.

It makes my knees ache. It makes my throat close.

"This new generation. So entitled," his friend says.

"What the hell is she wearing?" a woman behind them says. It's the same question women ask when we're in short skirts or tights. We are wrong, always, no matter what.

There are other whispers around us now, growing like rolls of thunder, the beginning of a storm.

Fame-whores.

Sluts.

Selfish.

Attention-grabbing.

Careless.

Hilarious.

Feminist.

So fake.

The sanctity of the event.

Rubbing our face in the—

Not caring about who they—

The real victims—

That street—

Those girls—

"Okay, all right, we gotta get out of here," Cruz says. I'm dizzy from the way people are looking at me. It brings me back to Jack's funeral and the awful way they looked at us then. We aren't allowed at sacred events anymore. We aren't permitted to mourn the people we've lost.

Maria and Mrs. Chen and Ashley are busy pulling Mrs. Rodriguez into an embrace as Alejandro Rodriguez's picture hits the enormous screen. I want to take a moment and look at his face, but it's our moment to leave. Even my mother has stopped listening to the things people are saying about me as the alphabet moves toward my father's name. She's so busy waiting to hear *Patrick Ryder* she doesn't notice Cruz taking my hand and moving me away from the crowd, away from the Memorial.

We slip past the people who don't know me but hate me anyway, or admire me, or pity me. We move quickly so that by the time the Devonairre Street ladies remember to keep their eyes on us, it will be too late.

It takes time getting out of the park. The field is crowded and even with my head down, my long hair is a giveaway. I try to tune out the words they're whispering about me.

I pause only when I hear my father's name. We are almost out of earshot, but not quite. We turn around, and there he is on the screen. Smiling. He had big front teeth and a scar on his chin. He had my pale skin but dark hair. I can't breathe.

"I know," Cruz says. "He'd want you to get out of here, though."

And that much I know is true.

Cruz and I make it to the edge of the crowd, then to the edge of the park, then to the sidewalk. There's police tape everywhere, keeping people out of the park. It's like a quarantine.

"Are we who people think we are?" I ask. He laughs.

We haven't laughed in a while. We're still holding hands. We grip harder, our palms going numb from the pressure.

"We've never been who they think we are, right?"

I search the sky for an answer. Then my hands. I look at them like they might be able to tell me who I am. I pull at the key around my neck.

I shrug. "They used to say I was brave, but all I felt was sad. I never match up with the thing they say I am. Seven years ago I was only allowed to be Lorna Whose Father Was Killed in the Bombing and nothing else. And now I'm this other thing. And I can't be anything else but that girl in the picture."

"The Falling Girl," Cruz says. He nods at the mess of things I've said, and I think he is the only person in the world who understands every word.

"The Falling Girl," I say, except I think I already fell.

The Fallen Girl, I think, and shiver at how right it sounds.

26.

We go into the city, Cruz and I. We don't talk about it, we just hop on the A train and get off at Times Square, like our fathers have been calling us there.

"We can stay down here," Cruz says before we emerge onto the street, when we're still on the subway platform. It's the nicest platform in the city—glossy black tiles on the ground and a mural of the Affected on the walls. It had to get renovated after the Bombing, and they made it a strange combination of sleek and crafty.

The muralist painted thousands of Affecteds' faces onto the long walls of every line of the Times Square subway system. He didn't paint the Victims, only the families.

I forgot all about it.

"Are we somewhere on here?" I ask. We came to get away from being seen, but if we wanted to truly escape being known as Affected, Times Square probably wasn't the place to come.

"We're by the One train."

"You've looked?"

"It felt weird, thinking there was some picture of me somewhere that I'd never seen. It was keeping me up at night." Cruz looks embarrassed. He shouldn't be. I'm surprised, though, that he has secrets from me.

Everyone has them, I hear my dad say again.

"I try to pretend it's not happening," I say. "Like, I heard about the mural and decided he'd probably never get around to painting my face, so it was no big deal."

Cruz puts his hand on the back of my neck and we don't discuss going to look at ourselves. We don't need to see a painting of the way we look—we're right here.

I don't take in the other Affected on the walls either. I want them to have their privacy.

When we get out of the subway and onto the street I remember why I never come here. I have memories of the old Times Square— neon and flashing and crowded with gawking tourists. I remember the tall buildings caging us in, and the constant stream of yellow cabs honking on the street, and the cartoon character mascots asking you in their smokers' voices if you wanted to take a picture for a few bucks.

I pretend that no one is noticing me, but some people on the subway definitely did and someone will here, too. There's no hiding. Especially not today.

"Devonairre Street feels far away," Cruz says, stretching his arms high above his head like the real problem with our street is lack of space or something.

The streets are crowded with people with candles.

"Not that far," I say.

Next I notice the buildings, the ones that aren't there anymore. The rebuilding has been slow. In the immediate few blocks there aren't any buildings that reach higher than a few stories, and there are dozens of empty lots, places where skyscrapers used to be. Places where people used to be.

"This was a bad idea," Cruz says.

"It was a joint effort. I didn't want to be in Brooklyn. But . . ."

Cruz and I look at the same things—a few storefronts with psychics, a bunch of wreaths and flowers and photographs strewn about as mini-shrines to the people we've lost, and street artists selling photographs and paintings of the old Times Square.

Remember, remember, remember, the whole place seems to be calling, which is really only an awful reminder to me that other people are allowed to forget.

"You want a picture? You want to remember?" an old man with an accent like Angelika's calls out to us. We shake our heads no and try not to make eye contact with him. A crowd of white-candled kids our age push by us. They don't look at us, and the man doesn't recognize us, and we're grateful for the moment to take it all in alone, without being observed.

"I want them to rebuild it," Cruz says, looking around. It's not in shambles anymore. The rubble is gone, the dust and ash are gone, but he's right—it needs to be taken off pause. It needs to become whatever it will be in the After.

"My dad would have loved a project like that," I say, thinking of his blueprints and the stories he told about how the Brooklyn Bridge was built, why Penn Station was rebuilt, the wonder of Grand Central Station, the glory of the Twin Towers, which I still look at hearing his voice in my head.

"I can picture your dad rebuilding the city," Cruz says, and I can picture it, too. I smile at him. It hurts, but it also helps, sometimes, to picture the what-might-have-been, the lives they could have had.

The lives we could have had.

"That's her!" one of the other artists calls out. She's a middle-aged woman with very white sneakers and a nasal voice.

"Hey! You shouldn't be here!" someone else says. "You're that girl! That Cursed girl!"

"That shit's a joke," a guy our age says. "Pretentious Brooklyn assholes."

"This is a sacred space," the woman who saw us first says.

I laugh. I don't mean to, but calling the place where five thousand people died *sacred* is so wrong. Sacred implies beautiful and clean and healing, and this place is the opposite.

"She's laughing!" someone says.

"Of course she's laughing; didn't you read about her and her friends?"

"Where's your respect? How dare you come here? And today of all days!"

Candles extinguish from the spit that comes out of their mouths while they yell. Some people move away from us, like we're toxic. Others move closer to us and I'm nervous they might touch us or hit us or forcibly remove us. Tons of people take pictures with their phones. I can already see them up on the internet with captions declaring who I am, when I'm not even so sure.

"Who'd you lose in the Bombing?" I ask no one and everyone. I look from person to person. Most of them look at the ground. One woman in ripped jeans pulls her shoulders back.

"We've lost so many New Yorkers," she says, indignant. "There are so many Affected. So many. And you being here is a slap in the face. This isn't for you."

"But who'd you *know*?" I'm surprised at my own voice. It's deeper than I thought; it carries farther. Many of the candle-holders have stopped walking. All the painting-sellers have stopped shouting at passersby.

"I'm sorry?" The woman rolls her eyes, looks at the other candle-holders, licks her lips.

"Did you know anyone who died in the Bombing? Did you lose a single person?"

"I can list all of their names," the woman says, but I can see her getting flustered, looking for words. She starts listing them in alphabetical order, the way some people have memorized them. "Aaron Abromowitz, Alice Akerson, Arthur—"

"I'm asking who *you* lost. Who you miss. *Specifically.*" I feel strong. The woman doesn't have anything to say. She chooses to be sad today, but doesn't have to be other days. She has a thin nose and too much blush. She's awful.

"We all share the pain of—"

"This is where my father was killed. This is *my* place." I point to Cruz. "This is *his* place. You're all—you're borrowing our feelings. Our fathers. You're borrowing them to feel something of your own. But this place isn't yours. This day isn't yours. This heartbreak"—I get a pain in my chest, quick and hard and brutal—"this heartbreak isn't yours."

The woman doesn't stand back, but people around her do. A few of them blow out their candles, and that feels good. Cruz takes my hand. That feels good, too.

For an instant it is ours, this terrible, ravaged place. The artists nearby don't call out for tragedy-tourists to buy their paintings and photographs. The candle-holders lower their lights and make room for us to walk by them. The lady in the ripped jeans with the terrible voice and the list of five thousand names of dead people on the tip of her tongue keeps her legs planted but she shifts her shoulders a little so that she's no longer facing us, and that, too is a victory.

She lowers her head as we cross 42nd Street.

• • •

By evening our photograph is all over the internet.

AFFECTED BOY AND CURSED GIRL REMEMBER THEIR FATHERS AMID CONTROVERSY.

I don't read the article. But I save the picture and keep it with me, to remind me of something, I'm not sure what.

27.

"This party looks a lot like the other party," Cruz whispers to me that evening at the Anniversary Party. We have one every year. It's only ever been us. LornaCruzCharlotteDelilahIsla. But this year the party has multiplied.

People I've never seen before arrive unannounced with six-packs and snarls. Guys with thick arms and girls with long hair give us hugs and look at my home like it's a museum.

One of them picks up a saltshaker and another stands extra close to a photograph of our family on the wall, staring at our faces as if there were something to learn there.

"This reminds you of last year's party?" I say. I'm distracted watching Isla dance on the coffee table and Delilah sit on the kitchen counter, starting a new round of red-and-white bracelets. Every girl here is already wearing one of them. Three girls have Charlotte's braids. I can feel my picture getting taken and it makes my head hurt.

"The other party."

It takes me too long to realize he's talking about the night Jack died.

I look around. Isla on the coffee table, her hair piled up on her head, her shirt inching up past her belly button; Charlotte eyeing her like she might fall over, nursing a beer; Delilah in the kitchen; me and Cruz talking to each other from separate chairs while the couch stays empty.

Chairs seem safer.

I guess it's the same but it's different, too.

Delilah is alone.

Jack is gone.

Owen is gone, too, of course. Owen is gone like he was never here at all. I'm embarrassed by how little he actually meant to me. How far I was from love with him. I feel the absence of Jack and the shift in Delilah, but I can't even feel the missing piece of Owen.

The place is crowded with wall-to-wall people. I didn't invite them. Delilah and Charlotte and Cruz didn't invite them. One of them asks for lavender tea. Another asks if there's honey cake. They have done their research. The boys look like they want to be tough—they have pink hair or Brooklyn accents or black boots or flasks of their own. They have smirks and eyeliner or football jerseys and cigarettes. The girls have loose tops and key necklaces and zodiac tattoos and tarot cards on our kitchen counter, and one of them is wearing a heart sweater.

There is only one person on Devonairre Street who would want to turn a LornaCruzCharlotteDelilahIsla party into an all-school party of posers and hangers-on. And that someone is licking the side of her bottle of beer after some of it splashed out. She is smiling at a sophomore boy with a small nose and enormous jeans. She is wiggling her fingers at someone who just came in the door.

"It's not that much like that night," I say. I wonder whether Cruz is somehow blind to the people taking over my apartment, to the disaster his sister has created. To the way we are museum pieces and objects of interest but not actual people.

Or maybe Cruz is only looking at me.

"I can't remember the sound of the crash," Cruz says.

"That's probably a good thing," I say. "You don't want to remember that sound."

"You remember," Cruz doesn't ask but proclaims. I wish we were on the couch. We should be on the couch, legs touching. But instead Charlotte is on the couch with a long-legged, tattooed Indian girl I don't recognize and she hasn't looked over at Cruz and me for a while. Delilah won't stop looking at us.

I was foolish to imagine her splitting a bottle of wine with me, toasting my father, cheering up me and Cruz and Isla with her favorite memories of our dads.

She's here to convert people.

Kids have to pass by her to get to the booze. They can't seem to decide whether they want to rub against her or avoid her altogether.

"You're so beautiful," a drunk girl whispers in my ear.

"Can you feel the Curse in your veins?" a drunk boy asks. His breath smells like beer and he leans away from me after he's asked the question.

"It's not real," I say. He nods but his eyes shift around and I don't think he believes me.

"Are you like Isla?" He wiggles his eyebrows. I want to say yes, because I can see he's too scared of me to fool around with me, but I turn away from him without answering at all.

I float around my own apartment, from one grotesque encounter to the next, for what might be minutes or might be an hour.

"We should get out of here," Cruz says when we finally cross paths again.

"There's nowhere to go." We tried once today and failed. We're trapped. Cruz sinks back into his chair. I put on my sunglasses.

Delilah keeps tying bracelets onto hands of drunk girls and sleazy guys and she's answering questions about us. I can hear her explaining things like lemons and Angelika and hubris and our dads. It's terrible.

"Hey! Come drink with us!" I call out when I can't stand any of it anymore.

Someone is asleep on our floor. A few couples are making out in the corner. I think beer's been spilled on the couch because the smell of it won't leave me alone. We're going to have to kick people out soon.

"I'm not drinking," Delilah says.

I pat the couch and wave my hands around. I want to get her away from the vultures and freaks. From the vampires and tragedy-lovers and fame-whores. I want to make her ours again.

"Your father wouldn't approve of what you're doing," Delilah says, eyeing me and Cruz, threatening to finally, finally talk about what she saw us doing in the garden. But she's wrong. If there's anything he would approve of, it would be the way Cruz looks at me and the way my heart feels when he's nearby.

"My dad wouldn't approve of what *you're* doing," I say.

Delilah's admirers listen with interest.

"I'm showing my respect for him. I'm saving lives. Angelika says—"

I get up; I have to get away from this person who used to be Delilah. Cruz follows.

"Cruz," Delilah says, "I need your help over here."

"With what?"

Delilah pauses. She's about to start speaking in Polish, that's how Angelika-like she's becoming.

"I'll be right back," Cruz says, and he follows me up the ladder to my loft. It's a place he never goes—my lofted room is where I disappear with Owen, and it's where Delilah and I used to spend late nights, and it's where Mom and I lie on the bed and she tells me secrets about her patients that I have to cross my heart and hope to die not to tell anyone. It's the place where my great-grandmother stitched satin into gowns, draped lace into veils.

We won't do anything. We'll steal away for five minutes to not have to be Devonairre Street Kids or Affected or Cursed.

Still, I'm shaky climbing up the ladder, unable to stop thoughts of what else we could do up here, what I want to do up here. I am certain I can feel him shaking, too, the thing between us so strong it could knock us right off the ladder. I turn to smile at him—a secret, closed-mouth smile—but something stops me as I reach the last rung.

There is someone in my bed.

I see her long braids first, then her naked shoulder, her glasses left behind on my nightstand, her socks still pulled up her calves. And next to her glasses on the nightstand are the keys that should be around her neck, the ones Angelika scolded her for not wearing.

I'm so distracted by the discarded keys, it takes me a moment to register who is next to her: the girl from downstairs. Brown skin and messy black hair, flower tattoos blooming across her arms and her stomach. She has a bra on, and nothing else.

Charlotte and this girl. In my bed. Mostly naked. Touching.

And Cruz and me, trapped at the top of the ladder with no place to go.

28.

Charlotte and the girl leap away from each other, but there's nothing left to hide.

Cruz covers his face with his hands. I do the opposite. My eyes stay so wide-open they start to ache in the corners.

"Charlotte!" Her name comes out strangled and like I've never said it before.

"It's okay," she says, but it isn't. The girl finds her shirt and pulls it on. She hands Charlotte a shirt as well, and Charlotte shifts so her back is toward me while she puts it on. I think she wants to start the moment over and hopes when she turns back around we can press reset.

We can't.

Cruz uncovers his face. He is blinking fast.

My mind leaves my body. My heart leaves, too. I am body and nothing else.

"This is Nisha," Charlotte says. I stick out my hand because I don't know what else to do, and Nisha does the same. We shake. It is ridiculous and too polite and it's strange how in the craziest moments you reach for normal things like handshakes and formal introductions. Nisha's hand is bony and strong. Her fingers are long.

"I'm Lorna."

Nisha smiles like this is the funniest thing in the world. Meanwhile, I'm not sure my face is working at all. I touch the corners of my mouth, my chin, my eyebrows. All in place.

"I know who you are," she says, that barely contained smile not shifting. "Everyone knows who you are. You've met me, too. But you Devonairre Street people—you're all in your own world, aren't you?" She shakes her head. I either think she's fantastic or awful. I'm not sure. "We all know you, but you don't need to know us."

"I think I'd recognize you—" I try, but Nisha's not having it.

"I've always been around," she says, and I can feel the world shifting under me.

"I know you," Cruz says. He looks less stunned than he did only a few seconds before, like he's piecing something together. I'm not there yet. I'm waiting for Charlotte to apologize and tell me why she's in bed with a girl, why she's in bed with someone who isn't Cruz, why she's in my bed at all.

Her braids are frizzing and she reaches for her glasses. Once they're on, she's still a different Charlotte. She isn't flustered, which doesn't make sense. She isn't drunk, either. I'm waiting for Charlotte to be Charlotte again, the way I've been waiting for the return of Delilah.

"We've been together a long time," Nisha says. Charlotte looks down, but she doesn't deny it.

"You can't be together," I say. "Charlotte and Cruz are together." I look back and forth between the two of them, the golden couple of Devonairre Street, one of the main reasons I know the Curse isn't real, the people I've built a whole sense of the world on.

Charlotte loves Cruz so we are all safe. Charlotte loves Cruz so I can love Cruz, too.

I don't see much between them right now.

Charlotte is starry-eyed looking at Nisha. She touches her earlobe and the side of her neck. She's saying *I love you* with her fingers.

I've never seen her touch those exact places on Cruz.

"Cruz doesn't love me," Charlotte says, but I think what she really means is *I don't love Cruz.*

He sits so his feet hang on top of the ladder and shakes his head. I think he might climb down and leave me here alone. There's a clatter downstairs and Isla's laughter rings out followed by Delilah's voice trying to quiet everyone down. I won't remember anything about the party except for this, right now.

"I should go," Nisha says. "You don't need me here for this." She wiggles into pants under the sheets and runs fingers through her hair. "You guys have never needed the rest of us, huh?" She shakes her head at me again. I want to remember her. I want to say I can recall shaking her hand before. I want to believe I pay attention to more than what is happening with the street. That I am better and more complicated and more normal than Angelika. But it wouldn't be true. There's a garden tattooed on her skin, and in a different life I'd ask what each bloom is, I'd search for peonies, I'd wonder at the way we both love flowers. In a different life, I'd know her and care about her and see the things that other people do on other streets.

But nothing else matters, when you're a Devonairre Street Girl.

Nisha kisses Charlotte and Charlotte kisses her back. It's the sweet kiss of people who have kissed a hundred times before. Cruz and I both look away. Somehow—even though we have all been part of one being for years, even though Cruz is supposed to be Charlotte's boyfriend and Nisha is supposed to be a stranger—we're the outsiders.

It is one of those impossible things.

Cruz has to get up for Nisha to get out, and I think he can't decide whether to commit to the room or climb downstairs. He eventually lifts himself into the loft and Nisha lowers herself down and Charlotte watches her go.

I am seeing Charlotte in love for the first time.

"I did my best," she says when Nisha's all the way gone and Cruz is all the way in and I'm wondering what kind of math I have to do to recalculate the world around me.

"Your best to what? Be with me? Keep that girl a secret? Lie?" Cruz is finally getting mad. He isn't raising his voice, that isn't his way, but his ears are red and his body's stiff.

"I did my best to protect you," Charlotte says.

She doesn't look nervous. She looks downright relieved that we know.

"Protect me?" Cruz says. "What the hell does that mean, *protect me*?" He is flushed and shaking.

For the first time, I think California sounds nice. Warm and breezy, palm-treed and bright. I let myself imagine being there for a breath. I imagine a Future Lorna with a suntan and a yoga mat and a loose, easy way of talking. Maybe that Lorna would play guitar or marry a struggling actor. It's the only escape I have right now.

"You think we can't all see the two of you?" Charlotte asks. She's getting mad now, too, unhinged in some particular way that is also unfamiliar. "The way you look at each other? The way you think no one else could possibly understand you? You're like a brother to me, Cruz. I didn't know what else to do. Angelika didn't know what else to do. We thought maybe if you were with me the two of you wouldn't—"

I'm stuck on the idea that everyone notices the way we look at each other.

The way we've always looked at each other.

"We don't believe in this shit. I mean, Jesus Christ, what have you been doing? What are you thinking?" I say, almost laughing but heroically managing to keep it in. The room spins a little, and I'm wishing I'd drunk less or more. I drank the exact wrong amount for this situation.

"*You* don't believe," Charlotte says. I squint, but it doesn't help. Everything's still all wrong. "I believe. I've always believed."

Her eyes are steady. Her voice is steady. I want her to stumble and fumble and trip all over her words. I want there to be something uncertain about what she's saying.

"We don't believe," I say again.

"*You*," Charlotte repeats. "You don't believe. And Cruz doesn't believe. But I believe. Have my whole life. Isla believes. Delilah believes now, too."

"Who are you?" Cruz explodes. They'll be able to hear us downstairs but I'm glad he can yell. I can't find my voice at all.

"I'm the person who's been saving your life." Charlotte stands up straighter, adjusts her glasses, making sure they're squarely on her nose. "You should be thanking me. I did this for you. Nisha did this for you. I'm lucky to love a girl, I'm lucky to love Nisha, but you're lucky, too. To have had me looking out for you. I knew I'd never love you. I knew you'd be safe with me."

I try to remember the last time I saw them really kiss. I try to remember if Charlotte ever said they slept together. I try to unwind everything I thought I knew.

"Angelika." I don't need to say anything else. My wallpapered walls—faded blue paisley from the days of a different Devonairre Street—are closing in on us. The whole building might collapse.

Charlotte shrugs.

"She asked me to make a sacrifice. So I made it," Charlotte says. "Someday the Curse will end, and it will be because we've finally sacrificed enough." This, too, is an Angelika sentence. The promise that if we do enough, if we sacrifice enough of ourselves, if we listen to every word she says, we'll be free of the Curse.

I didn't know anyone really believed it.

• • •

Eventually Charlotte goes downstairs and my apartment empties out and Cruz and I stay upstairs in silence, listening to the way the party escalates right before the ending and then zooms into silence and stillness.

Finally, we can hear only three voices: Delilah's, Isla's, and Charlotte's.

That's when we climb back down the ladder. The room smells like pine cleaning product and beer. It doesn't smell like Devonairre Street at all.

The girls are quiet.

Delilah is still on the counter. Isla is curled up on the couch. Charlotte is lying on the floor.

"You all knew," I say, because it can't go unsaid for a moment longer.

They don't agree or disagree.

"You all believe." The words scratch my throat coming out, like they have claws.

Cruz takes my hand like he did on the street in Times Square. We are the photograph they took of us earlier today—holding hands alone on the street, walking through the things that hurt the most.

"We don't believe," he says. He looks at me to agree, to nod, to kiss his lips or squeeze his hand.

I don't do any of that.

I can't.

29.

Mom doesn't come home from Roger's, so the girls sleep in my loft with me, even Delilah smushed against me in bed and breathing on my shoulder like it's the old days and we are young and hopeful about the next morning.

Roger's not feeling well, I'm going to stay here, Mom texts when I am not sleeping at two in the morning.

I know you probably don't mind. Be safe. Don't let anyone walk home drunk, Mom texts at two thirty in the morning when I am still not sleeping.

Did today make you want to leave the street? Mom texts at three a.m. when I'm not sleeping and she's not sleeping either, I guess.

Charlotte snores and Isla is so still I half wonder whether she's dead and Cruz is in his own room, probably not sleeping either. I almost text him. I don't text him.

I have to do something, though, so I get out of bed and say good-bye to dreaming Delilah and the rest of the girls. All this time I've been wanting to be close to them and now, at our very closest moment where we are sharing air and breath and beds and truth, I want to get away.

From the living room I look out over the street. The lamps are all lit up, including ours. Without Mom here to turn it off, it burns all night.

I wonder why we aren't in more trouble, all of us, for the party, for missing curfew, for the assortment of random people walking our street, staring at our brownstones, wanting to know everything about us. I've felt free of the widows today, at least, as trapped as I've been by everything else. I guess if there's anything they understand it's Anniversaries. At three in the morning, though, the Anniversary is over. It's the day after.

I don't move from the window and it doesn't take me long to spot Angelika. She isn't on her stoop, but her face is in the window, in the crack between her ugly floral curtains. She's watching. She's probably been watching all night.

Or maybe she's been waiting.

Maybe she's been waiting for me to finally, finally go to her.

So I do.

• • •

She meets me on the stoop in her nightgown.

"Here you are," she says with a smile like she's known this would happen.

"I can't sleep," I say.

Angelika invites me in and it's been a while since I've been in her kitchen but not an inch of it has changed. There's an enormous portrait of her husband on one wall and a cat clock on another, a gift from Charlotte when she was little. There are remnants of all of us—photographs on her refrigerator, a few messy crayon drawings of her that she must have framed and hung years ago, a lopsided green mug Delilah made her in art class that can't hold water so holds pennies instead, a card I wrote her for her birthday a few years ago, still perched on the counter like it arrived in the mail yesterday.

"Tea?" she says, and I nod because I'm aching too much to speak. There is love in this room.

"Who drew this one?" I point to a framed piece of construction paper on the wall—a stick figure drawing of a long white-haired Angelika sitting on a cloud.

"Cruz."

I smile. I can't help it.

"Cruz's pictures were always the sweetest. The most fantastical. Clouds and rainbows and starlight and the world the way he must wish it is. Poor boy."

"Maybe that's the way the world seems to him." Cruz's optimism is something I love about him. To Angelika, it's something to pity.

"He's going to die."

I lose my breath in a moment of belief. I recover and tell my heart to slow down. Angelika pours tea into teacups that look exactly like the ones Mom broke seven years ago. Delicate. Pretty. Too easy to destroy.

"You must be happy with Mom. She wants us to move. You'll get rid of us and all our trouble."

"That solves nothing. You can't run away from the Curse. Moving? You can't move. You'll only love him more, being away. No. There won't be any moving."

"Mom's pretty set on it." I didn't come here to talk to Angelika about California. She loads the tea with honey, so much I will barely be able to drink it, but I don't say anything. I didn't come here to talk about tea.

"And you?" Angelika asks. "What are you set on?"

"I don't want to leave."

"Good girl."

"Sometimes I want to leave."

Angelika nods, and I wonder whether she ever wants to leave. Whether she has dreams of a different life where she doesn't have to be so diligent, where she doesn't have to worry about love and teenagers and young men dying and how many lemon trees or rosemary sprigs are in the garden. Maybe there is a Future Angelika, too. Maybe she has a book club and three more dogs and a pasta-cooking second husband.

"Leaving is easy." Angelika takes her entire cup of tea in one long sip, like it's medicine. "Sacrifice is hard."

"Haven't we already sacrificed? Hasn't Charlotte?" I watch Angelika's face to see what happens at the sound of Charlotte's name. Nothing changes, though. Angelika stays steady.

I've always thought Charlotte and Cruz were one reason the Curse couldn't be real. But Angelika has shrugged them off, year after year, insisting she's never once caught love on Charlotte during the Shared Birthday.

"Charlotte did sacrifice to protect Cruz. And it didn't work, I see. Although you still have time. A tiny, tiny bit of time. You are on the cusp of love, not there yet."

"I think I'm in love."

"When you are in love, you know, you don't think. Trust me. You have time."

"I don't know if I can stop it."

Angelika twists her hair around itself until it's a bun at the nape of her neck. She looks at the crayon drawing Cruz made of her. We both do.

"Sacrifice." She pulls the word out long and slow. "The Curse came because we weren't grateful for all the love on the street. My parents weren't grateful. They moved to Devonairre to meet someone to love and they did, and they shrugged like it was owed to them. We can't shrug, Lorna. We took without thinking, and now we have to give." I try to sip at the tea but it's so sweet it makes my mouth fold into itself.

"What are we supposed to give? You say it like it's so easy, but obviously you haven't figured it out, either. You didn't sacrifice enough. You and Dolly and Betty and everyone else—you never figured out what it was you had to give up. And when you try to give up love—well. That doesn't work."

Angelika looks at me so full-on I feel like her eyes are flashlights and she's found me. "I don't suppose we'll ever know. You never tried to make that sacrifice. You all decided to love anyway." She shrugs, but I'm pretty sure that what she feels is the exact opposite of a shrug.

"Angelika—"

"I'll say it again if you weren't listening."

"I'm listening! I'm here. I'm ready to listen. I'm scared, okay? I am finally scared out of my mind. I thought Charlotte and Cruz were the reason that—but they're not. I see. I get it. But if love is a fever, how are we supposed to stop it? If love is a decision, why do you act like it's an involuntary action? Is it something we can stop or something that happens to us? Is it falling or choosing to jump? I honestly don't know anymore. I don't think *you* know."

Maybe it's the time—almost four in the morning—or the sweetness of the tea, or the smell of Aramis haunting the air, or the way Angelika covers her kitchen in thoughts of us, her Devonairre Street Kids, but I start to believe she might actually have the answers. I start to believe a lot of things I never thought I could.

"Sacrifice," Angelika says again, like it's the only word she knows, like it's the only word that matters, and maybe it is.

We sit for hours and watch the sun come up, and when it's up and the girls wake up and walk out of my building, looking for me, they find me on the stoop with Angelika, braiding bracelets and trying to think of how to stop the Curse.

30.

By nine we are all braiding and Cruz hasn't been out of the house yet. He said he doesn't believe so I wonder whether Mrs. Rodriguez is keeping him locked in there, or whether maybe he was lying and there's a part of him that knows I'm dangerous.

I have braided fifty bracelets. Angelika has added ten keys to my chain. I will my hair to grow faster and my heart to grow more slowly.

Delilah is sitting so close to me she's practically on my lap. "You needed to see," she says. "You needed to understand. And now you see. Now you understand."

I am scared enough to braid until my fingers hurt. I am scared enough to leap off the stoop when I see Mom a few blocks away, coming home from Roger's. Her hair is sticking this way and that and she doesn't have on makeup or stockings. She's in a blue button-down that must be Roger's and she's in a rush.

I meet her a few buildings before ours and Angelika's, in front of Bistro, which is opening up for the day, waiters tying their ties and reorganizing chairs and filling up saltshakers.

"Charlotte doesn't love Cruz," I say, because that is the only place to start. Mom looks past me, to our building.

"Honey, I don't have time. I'm picking up some stuff and heading back to Roger's. He's really having a tough morning."

"Mom. Charlotte doesn't love Cruz." I want her to have the same moment I had last night—the zap and the panic and the need to be by Angelika's side and the sureness that we Have to Do Something. The belief.

Instead she pats my head, smoothing some of the flyaways.

"I hate seeing you like this," she whispers, like people are listening, which they probably are. Behind her there's a group of outsiders, snapping pictures of buildings and wearing keys around their necks.

More tragedy-tourists.

"Charlotte's in love with a girl named Nisha. And I'm falling in love with Cruz. And what's wrong with Roger, Mom? He's sick? How sick?" I feel a little like Delilah and I try to breathe deeply. I find a breath big enough to fill my throat and chest and I try again. "What if we've spent so much time not believing we've forgotten to look and see if there actually might be reason to believe?"

Mom gets a look on her face that has never been directed toward me. Something hard and cold and indignant. She runs a hand through her messy short hair. Before she has a chance to speak, the group of tourists approaches us.

"You're Lorna!" one says. They have matching white T-shirts and matching wide eyes.

"And you're her mother, right?" another says. That one's wearing sunglasses and I want to believe it's because of the sun, not me, but it's a gray day.

Mom and I nod and try to look at each other instead of the group, but that doesn't seem to stop them.

"Can we have a picture?" the first girl asks.

"Are you in love?" an older woman asks. There are two men and they look sleazy and sneering. I cover my chest and cross my ankles on instinct. I look over at Isla and want her to do the same, but she's eyeing the group of strangers with interest, with intent.

"No pictures," Mom says. She puts a protective arm around me, but the group doesn't shy away.

"Where's the old lady who runs everything?" one of them asks.

"Where's the Isla girl?" a man says. His friend snickers next to him, and I feel ill and overtired. Behind us, in Bistro, are more strangers who look at the menu like it's an ancient artifact and stare out the window like they're on the top of the Empire State Building.

When we don't answer, the group moves on, but not before snapping a few more photos of our dumbstruck faces and the way grief has imprinted itself along our jaws, in our pupils, inside our fisted hands.

We watch them approach the girls on the stoop. Delilah gives them bracelets and Charlotte avoids eye contact. I wonder if she's thinking of Nisha and a way to escape all this. Charlotte could get out. Charlotte could leave this all behind and live a normal life with love and happiness and no threat of misery around every corner.

Her braids are frizzy and uneven, bumpy on top. Her nose is too serious and her bracelets are braided as sloppily as her hair. She has to keep shoving her glasses back onto the bridge of her nose and she can't carry a tune or run fast or be much fun at a party. There are so very many things that Charlotte Pravin isn't. But she is a girl who can love without fear, and nothing else really matters.

"I have to go, Lorna. I don't want to leave Roger alone for long," Mom says. She kisses my cheek. "Don't get caught up with this. Go for a walk. Or a museum. Go with Cruz. Live your life, honey."

"This is our life." I gesture at the street, but Mom is already rushing to the apartment to pick up who knows what for her boyfriend; and I don't have time to ask her again what's wrong with him, how sick he is, how much more worried I should be.

Meanwhile Isla poses for the tourists. She stands on the stoop with one hip jutted all the way out and her arms up in the air, reaching toward nothing. They look disappointed. I think they want her to look sadder, more serious, more romantic. They turn toward Delilah and snap her picture, too, and seem more pleased with the effect.

Isla sees the way they fall in love with Delilah's serious face and busy hands, and she mirrors her. She sits next to Delilah and furrows her brow and separates her lips the tiniest bit and hunches her shoulders and braids.

The visitors grin.

"You're exactly like we thought you'd be," one of them says.

"Isla Rodriguez," one of the men says, and my heart worries for her, "can I get your autograph?"

Isla beams.

"Of course," she says, and the man brings out a pen and a copy of our photograph on the bench, and Isla signs below her face before Angelika shoos them all away, telling them it's not safe.

For who? I wonder.

• • •

"They love me," Isla says hours later in the garden. I am on high alert for Cruz, who still hasn't left his house. Charlotte and Delilah are on the stoop, but Isla and I needed a walk and a moment away from red and white threads and huge thermoses of tea.

"We love you," I say, because I want her to know that's the more important thing.

Isla hums a non-response and stretches her legs.

"They'll love me, but I'll never be allowed to love them," she says.

When Cruz comes to get her, the sun's going down and I can't believe we've spent the whole day being Angelika's Devonairre Street Girls.

"Mom's looking for you," he says.

"I'm right here," Isla says, and she looks so sad it vibrates off of her. "I'll always be exactly right here."

"Head home. I'm going to talk to Lorna for a minute," Cruz says, but Isla doesn't move. She shakes her head the tiniest bit. She plants her feet. Cruz plants his feet. I look at the peonies because I'm scared that if I look at Cruz for even one minute more, the falling in love will be complete.

Eventually he gives up and Isla leads him out of the garden, away from me, and I'm all alone with the peonies and the question *what now?*

31.

I stay in the garden long past the sun going down. There's no one waiting for me at home and I can't spend another second on the stoop and Bistro is, I'm sure, crowded with people who want to know my favorite color and whether I'll ever get married and whether I blame my mother for my father's death.

I plant seeds all along the perimeter of the garden, not thinking about whether the soil is right for the particular plant, not worrying about how deep to put each one in, or whether they need to get watered often or who will trample them. I just plant until the garden gate opens and Angelika arrives.

Betty and Dolly and Delilah aren't far behind.

Isla and Charlotte and their mothers are next.

Maria. Mrs. Chen.

I wonder about Saad and Hiba and what they think of all this. But their store has been closed for the last three days and I haven't seen them walking down the sidewalk and turning the corner to go to the mosque a few streets away. They have vanished.

"Of course you're here," Angelika says.

"We're making a sacrifice," Delilah says. She has lit-up eyes, the way she used to look at Jack, and no matter how much I believe, I won't ever believe like that. Her arms are loaded down with white tulle and silk. Widows are carrying wedding albums and veils and branches from the park.

I laugh.

I laugh so I can leave my body and see us from just above the garden. It is a ridiculous sight, long-haired ladies weighed down with the keys around their necks, preparing a bonfire sacrifice to fix a Curse that we all of a sudden believe.

My father would have laughed, too, I think.

"We'll live in this wacky place," he used to say, "but we all have to promise not to get wacky ourselves."

We are getting wacky.

Soon there is a fire, and we are throwing wedding gowns and wedding albums and wedding rings that will melt into little pools of gold into the fire.

"Sacrifice," Angelika says.

Delilah is holding an old flannel shirt of Jack's and a dried-out corsage from the fall dance.

"You'll want those," I say.

"Exactly." There's a shiver in her voice that tells me she's already cried about it, and she's determined to do it anyway.

"I thought we were supposed to remember them." I try to piece together the growing list of rules. "I thought we were supposed to hang on to everything and not move on or whatever." I am thinking of mother's bedroom closet, of the framed portrait of my father behind shoes that don't really fit and purses that are too worn-out to use but too expensive to throw away. Angelika gave us the portrait.

I wouldn't mind burning it. It's not a memory of him, exactly, but a memory of how he's not here anymore.

Delilah pauses, and I think she's considering the same contradictions.

She drops the flannel into the fire and it flares a little. "We have to remember and sacrifice." She scratches her arm like the inconsistency is irritating the skin there. "We're trying to figure it out. This is different from moving on. This is sacrificing. For Cruz." She lets the corsage go, and we watch the petals turn to smoke. My heart thumps with the knowledge of what these women are willing to do for the person I love.

And like that I want to have something to give up, something to throw in the fire. In our apartment there is the drawer of my father's things—shoelaces and old receipts with his handwriting on them and a birthday card he gave me the last year he was alive even though I wasn't supposed to celebrate my individual birthday by then. In my mother's closet there's her wedding dress—a lacy, casual thing I loved to try on when I was little. And my father's suit, the one he wore to every wedding, the one that we never dry-cleaned. The one we wrapped in plastic, hoping it would preserve the smell, "if we ever really need it," Mom said, packing it up. There's also a shoebox of love letters Mom has never let me read.

I watch Mrs. Rodriguez hold her gown close to her chest before letting it fall into the flames. The rhinestones around the bodice glint and the lace smolders. It will take a long time for it to fully turn to ash. She catches my eye and she's crying. We both know a little about the way things turn to ash.

I run to the apartment.

"Mom?" I call out, hoping she's snuck in, that Roger's back, too, that they've simply been too busy looking up California homes to find me. But the apartment is empty. I'm hoping, I guess, that she'll stop me from what I'm going to do.

I open the drawer and put my father's things in my pockets, to see how it feels. It feels awful, like I'm robbing us. Sacrifice. I go to my mother's closet. Roger's clothes are hanging in one section, and it shocks me. They hang next to the few things we have left of my father's—his suit, a Christmas sweater, his favorite pair of jeans.

I take the suit and my mother's wedding gown. I lay them over my arms and imagine burning them. I think of my mother's face and what it will do when she sees these things are missing. I can't do it.

My phone buzzes.

It's a text from Cruz.

I think I love you and I think you love me and I think I'm finally scared.

I can barely breathe. I find the shoebox of letters. I will burn them, too.

I open the box—it's green and worn and stuffed to the brim.

I almost don't read them. "People are allowed their secrets," Dad said. But I am missing his words, his poems, his way of looking at the world like it is lighter and easier and better than it feels right now.

I open one up. It's a Hallmark Valentine's Day card dated a year before Dad died. I'm surprised at the image on the front. A huge heart with a bow around its middle. It doesn't remind me of my father, who liked to make his own cards with portraits of me and Mom sketched on the front. The words inside don't sound like Dad's, either. They are simpler, without poetry. *I love you*, the note reads. *I will always love you. I'll always be happy I met you. It will always be worth it.*

I try to imagine Dad sitting at our kitchen counter, penning a boring note to Mom in a store-bought card. I can't see it.

Happy Valentine's Day. All my love, R.

I start to shake.

I sweat.

I pick out another note. This one is on a folded sheet of hotel stationery.

It's a dirty one. About Mom's legs and her breasts and the way she feels inside. My blood is cool and I'm dizzy.

All my love, R.

I take a breath and hold it until I almost pass out. I want to leave my body. I want to leave the moment and the street and my mother and my mind. I want to rewind and never have opened these letters. I want to have opened these letters years ago.

I want to hate Roger and I want to hate my mother.

I want to talk to my father. I want to talk to my father more than I have ever wanted anything. I close my eyes and try to summon him, but I don't believe in ghosts or afterlives or his presence watching us from heaven. I have no room for that belief.

A dozen memories flicker in my brain—my father's talk of secrets and his search for the understanding of love. My mother's late nights at work when Dad was alive and how certain she's been that the Curse didn't exist.

Everything looks brand-new.

A few months before he died, I caught Dad crying in the garden. He was on the bench. His face was in his hands. I remember the glint of his wedding ring, newly polished, in the sun. I sat next to him and waited for him to talk to me. Whenever I cried, Dad never told me not to. So I didn't tell him not to then.

I can't believe this memory waited for so long to resurface. I wonder how many other memories are hiding out inside me, how many will visit me when I need them most.

"Love's not one thing," Dad said, after a long, long while.

I didn't know what he meant, but we sat on the bench and he repeated those words two more times, and eventually they made him stop crying, they made him put his arm around me and pull me close. They made him pick up a bottle of wine and a cupcake for Mom on the way home.

It wasn't the sacrifice Angelika demanded of him. But it was sacrifice all the same.

"Love isn't what you know," Dad said before we opened the door and reentered the apartment. He squeezed my arm. He sounded sure. "Love is what you don't know."

It's the last thing Dad ever told me about love.

I don't read any more of Roger's old letters. I bring them with me, though. I bring it all with me. The letters. The suit. The gown. The eleven slim books of poetry. The memories of my father. The ones I've always known and the ones that are new, aching, uncomfortable, imperfect.

Sacrifice. It's the one thing Dad and Angelika agreed on.

The fire has grown in the brief time I've been gone. So has the crowd. I push past them to the sound of my name being called over and over, *Lorna, Lorna, Lorna.* I don't turn toward any of them. I keep my eyes on the fire, on Delilah, and on Angelika.

Delilah's head is bowed like she can't bear to look at the flame.

Angelika stares right into the fire.

When I approach, Angelika looks at me.

"Good girl," she says.

"At last," she says.

There is an ocean of feeling in my stomach and my heart feels overlarge, explosive, dangerous. I am all sweat and hollowness—in my stomach, my head, my limbs. I thought I would be dreamy and free; I thought I would be sexy and brave. I thought I would be loose and wise.

I didn't understand how the past and the future are intertwined.

I didn't understand that one came from the other. The present keeps changing. Even the past is changing. So the future won't stay still, either.

I throw everything in my arms and everything in my pockets into the fire. It hurts, like the fire is burning me and not the things I've hung on to for seven years. I buckle over.

"It's meant to hurt." Angelika is next to me. "If it didn't hurt, it wouldn't be sacrifice." Her hand finds its way to my shoulder and holds me steady but the pain is unbearable.

"Is that enough?" I ask her or anyone or whatever God there might be. "Is that enough?" No one answers.

• • •

I don't help the bench come down. They don't need me. The masses have entered the garden, and they help dismantle it alongside the widows with hammers and screwdrivers and eager bare hands.

Delilah, Isla, Charlotte, and I watch.

"I loved that bench," I say, unable to shake the memory of Dad sitting on it, crying over everything he learned about love.

"All their names were on it." Charlotte's hands are white from holding on hard to memories that she eventually threw in the fire, too.

"Jack and I wrote our names on it. In a heart." Delilah's voice is going hoarse from the smoke, and she sort of laughs but it turns into a cough. "Hubris," she concludes. I wonder whether Mom might have written Roger's name on it, too. Maybe hidden on the bottom, far from where she and Dad declared their love.

A stranger throws the first slab of initialed wood into the fire. She hoots and hollers at the crackling noise it makes catching flame.

"We have to dismantle everything?" I say, knowing the answer. I am living the answer.

"Of course," Delilah says, so serious it scares me. "We have to sacrifice everything."

Isla doesn't say a word. She sways and I see her take out her flask.

What is left when everything has come undone?

Silence and sacrifice and a flask of something that will make you forget everything you've lost. And the smell of ash. Always, always the smell of ash.

I can see the fire from here, Cruz texts me from his locked-away room.

By midnight, everything is burnt and gone. The garden, too. The peonies. The basil. The rosemary. The air smells like herbs and smoke and burning plastic.

Strangers walk the scorched ground.

It is no longer ours.

32.

Roger is sicker.

Mom brings him home the next morning, and he is pale and sunken in. I can barely look at him.

"He'll get better," Mom says. "He needs rest. And water. I thought he'd be more comfortable here." She has her floaty voice, the one she used after Dad died when people asked how we were. "Oh, just fine," she'd say. "It takes time, but we'll be okay, Lorna and I." It would have scared me less if she'd talked about the long hours she slept and the empty fridge and the fact of her not showering for days on end.

It scares me now, the way she has her hand on Roger's forehead like he has a little flu.

It scares me how easily Mom hides things, how many secrets she has. I thought living in a small space meant we shared everything. But so much can be hidden even in the most cramped apartment on one of the shortest streets in Brooklyn.

Even love.

I do not tell her about what I burned last night, but she smells smoke in the air. "That smell." She shivers, not finishing her sentence.

I wonder whether she will go looking for her love letters or her wedding gown. I wonder when she'll find out what I've done, and realize what I now know.

Roger has a house-shaking cough and watery eyes and dry skin. I don't want him in my home but I don't want him to die, either.

"You want tea, Roger?" I ask, and he nods. I pull lavender from the back of the cabinet, behind Mom's collection of vanilla, and make him a pot. Mom smells that, too, her nose twitching and wrinkling.

"He doesn't need that," she says while I squeeze in honey, watching it skim the surface and plunk to the bottom of the mug.

"Maybe he does," I say.

Mom runs her fingers through her hair. She sighs and we can both hear chatter from the street below. I think I can pick out Angelika's voice and Charlotte's on top of it, the two of them probably holding down the stoop.

"The building is sold," Mom says.

"Angelika says even if you move off the street—" I say, and Mom looks like she's about to explode.

"I won't listen to any more of this! You know what you're saying when you believe? You're saying I killed your father. You're saying that you will have a life filled with lovelessness or grief. You're saying you're giving up on your future before it's even begun. Your father was right about living here, I'll tell you that much. He was fucking right about it. We never should have moved to this street."

"Because we lost him."

Mom looks at me like I'm no longer her daughter, like I'm someone else entirely. "Because we're losing you," she says.

Roger coughs on the couch and asks for a blanket. I deliver him his tea and a wool blanket. I turn off the news, which is playing a loop of the Chicago Bombing clips.

"With none of our questions answered, the country works to accept the unacceptable," a newswoman in red says. "Senator Lee urges us to turn our attention to our lives and let the government search for answers about the Bombings." Roger coughs harder.

"What does that even mean?" Mom says, mostly to herself.

Roger is turning red, then blue.

"Mom!" I lift Roger's head and it's the first time I've touched him—his skin is warm and sticky; he smells like a father, just not mine.

"What's going on? What's wrong?" Mom says, shaking her fingers and doing nothing. For a doctor, she's terrible in certain emergencies. I broke my leg when I was six and she sat on the playground and wept while my dad brought me to the hospital. "I love that about your mother," Dad said when I asked him how mad he must have been.

I wonder if he was able to love all the worst things about her.

"Water, Mom!" I say, but change my mind when Roger starts to shake. "No. Nine-one-one. Call nine-one-one."

Roger catches his breath but the coughing doesn't stop and he closes his eyes and his skin gets sweatier and warmer.

I move my hands off him. I am a selfish girl who doesn't want to hold someone as he dies.

• • •

"I'll call you," Mom says on her way out the door, following Roger, still coughing, on a stretcher. Men in uniforms speak loudly and efficiently to each other in terms I can't quite understand. "Devonairre Street," I hear one of them say and I know what they're thinking. I see them see me. I see them try not to think about the fact that if I took a liking to the bend of their arm or the sweep of their hair I could kill them too.

I want to leave my skin.

I want to go back to the day in the airport where it felt like there were options for how things would go.

Those futures have all vanished.

There's just this reality: I will try to not fall in love but I will fall in love anyway. And I will lose it all, again and again, while the world watches. I will always be Affected. I will always be Cursed. I will always be a Devonairre Street Girl, and nothing else.

Even my mother, Dr. Emily Ryder, with short hair and vanilla tea and shoebox of terrible secrets and fancy office on the Upper East Side, will only ever be Affected and Cursed and a Devonairre Street Girl.

That's all we are.

That's all we'll ever be.

Now it's me who is on the couch, unable to breathe.

33.

We are in my loft.

It is hot and sweaty and we are trying.

We are trying but it's not working.

"Hold on, hold on," Cruz says, holding his soft penis in his hand.

"I want you," I say. I've said it before and it's made boys crazy, simple words turning illicit when we're naked. This is the easy part— sex. This is the part that doesn't scare me.

I push against him, grind a little.

"I can do this," Cruz says, and it sounds like a pep talk. I stop the movement of my hips. I stop licking his neck.

"I want you." I don't know what else to say. It's never not worked before.

The curtains are drawn and I am not wearing anything but bracelets on my wrists and keys around my neck.

I have always been enough.

I want the easiness of Owen and the passion of Denver. Instead there's an awkward pause, nakedness that feels more terrifying than beautiful, Cruz's voice shaking as he tells me, again, to hold on.

He moves his hand between my legs, like that might help him, but I'm dry there and I can tell from the way his fingers don't know what to do that he can tell. I want to want this. I have always wanted this. But my body won't respond and his body won't respond and one more thing that felt certain and solid—sex—is gone now, too.

"You okay?" he says.

I nod. "Are you?"

He nods, too. We try kissing, but we don't get lost in it. I keep hearing Roger's coughs in my head, a warning of everything that will come.

"It's okay," I say eventually, but it isn't.

I put my clothes back on. The dressing feels like it takes hours longer than the undressing did, and it's depressing, buttoning buttons, zippering pants, covering up everything I wanted him to see.

"That's never—" Cruz starts a sentence I don't want him to finish. There's a waver in his voice and, when I look at him, there are tears in the corner of his eyes.

I look away. "I shouldn't have called you. I don't know why I called you. I wanted to do the opposite of calling you." I look at my phone like the answer's there, but it's not. There's not any news from my mother, either, no updates on Roger, which I try to believe is a good thing. If he were gone, she'd call right away.

"I shouldn't have come over." Cruz looks at the messy bed that we failed to do much of anything in. "Obviously."

In the after with Owen we catnapped and cuddled and made sandwiches downstairs and ate them over the sink or back in bed. Mustard tastes better after sex. Cheese, too. I don't know what to do in an after where there was no during. My skin is ill fitting and my toes are tingling.

"I guess we aren't—I guess it isn't—this is all—this is usually easier." They aren't the right words, but they're the only ones I have. I almost ask him how it's been with Charlotte, but I stop myself.

I'm jealous of how comfortable she looked naked with Nisha. I want that with Cruz. I want not this. "Maybe it means there's not love here? So you're okay?"

Even Mom and Roger have love in the way they sound in the early mornings.

We don't have that. I don't know what we have.

"You've got it all turned around, Lorna." He touches my waist, over my shirt. When we were naked his hand felt cool and sticky. Now that tiny touch warms me up.

My knees shake.

Something slips into place.

Cruz still has tears in his eyes. I don't wipe them. I let them roll.

"Will you take care of Isla?"

"Take care of her?" I don't think anyone would know how to take care of Isla Rodriguez. Not anymore. She's stopped being a little girl and has become a legend.

"When I'm gone," Cruz says. "And my mom. Will you spend time with my mom? She says she likes to be alone, when she's sad, but she actually really wants to be around people."

"You're not going anywhere," I say. I check my phone again. Still nothing from my mother.

"I could have five years. I guess I could do a lot in five years. Something meaningful. What could I do that's meaningful?"

"Cruz."

"My dad wanted to become a teacher. He was going to go back to school. Mom told me that. He was sick of the office job and wanted to do something that mattered and he was really going to do it and then he didn't and I'm not going to be like that." Cruz is talking so fast he's slipping and sliding over the words and all I want is to hold him and kiss him and tell him everything's going to be okay, except he won't believe me because I don't believe me.

His phone starts ringing.

"You'd be a good teacher," I say. He shrugs. His phone keeps ringing. They've probably figured out we're alone together, the neighborhood. They've probably realized they're too late.

Love isn't one thing, Dad said, and it was the truest thing he ever said. I've been waiting for one thing, but love can be anything.

I try to count everything I was wrong about: sex and love and my parents' marriage and the Curse and lavender and my future. I lose track . . . I can't add it all up.

I am terrible. I am selfish and small-minded and reckless and filled with hubris.

Cruz is thinking about something. He paces. "What do you think causes the Bombings? What's the reason?"

"I—I mean, no one knows," I say.

"It's the question no one's really asking," Cruz says. "Who did it? Who killed our fathers?"

I stay still and silent. There's no answer. I try to peek out the window, to see how much trouble we might be in, but Cruz blocks my view.

"Not enough rosemary? Too many mangoes? A cotton shirt instead of a wool one? I mean honestly, Lorna, what did it? A broken mirror or this fucking street or our mothers or the way we think love is safe and we deserve it or someone in another country or an act of God or some Curse from seventy-five years ago? And what will kill me? One of those things, too?" Cruz's voice booms and he throws his arms in the air at the unfairness of it all, of love, and his angry elbows hit my dresser and knock over photographs of LornaCruzCharlotteDelilahIsla together at seven and nine and thirteen—and last year when we thought we knew everything.

I look at it all, broken on the ground, unfixable.

He makes a growling noise, a sound beyond words that I never want to hear again.

He climbs down the ladder and his phone keeps ringing and mine keeps not-ringing and I follow him and see outside the living room window that people are gathered on the sidewalk outside our building because this is now the way things are.

"It's like my funeral's already begun out there," Cruz says.

The word *funeral* latches on to my skin, makes me ache.

"They think we—" But it doesn't matter. I am good at sex. If we'd been able to have sex, maybe it would mean the thing between us was just that.

If we'd been able to have sex, it would mean we weren't so afraid.

Cruz shakes his head.

"I love you," he says. "But please don't say it back."

His phone starts ringing again. I look at mine. My mother's texted:

Roger's not doing well.

34.

We sleep in the garden. There is red wine from my mother's stash and a six-pack of beer from Charlotte's mom's fridge and a bottle of vodka that Isla has gotten her hands on and no bench to sit on or gather around.

I don't sleep, but I watch Charlotte drift off and Delilah, too, and Isla and I sit cross-legged, knee to knee, and take shots. We make our way through her flask first, then tackle everything else. I think she was already a little buzzed when she arrived. I think she has been a little buzzed for days or weeks.

I'm jealous.

I notice scratches on Delilah's wrists. They are long and fresh and they frighten me and also make sense to me.

I don't mention them.

I open a bottle of red wine.

I wonder whether they'd take a picture of us now, the reporters and tourists, whether they'd want to see us like this. Unshowered in accidentally matching jean shorts and black long-sleeved shirts. Our eyes are puffy; our skin is blemished. Even the garden is a wasteland. There are nails and screws where the bench used to be and not a flower to be found.

"I can't do this forever," Isla says in the thick of the night.

Her voice is sloppy and overloud. My heart won't stop pounding, thinking of things that could happen to Cruz, wondering what's happening with Roger.

Forever is starting to sound awful. It is too long. Even the night is too long. I take another shot of vodka.

• • •

When Delilah wakes up from her dream, she shakes Charlotte awake, too.

"Sacrifice," Delilah says. Her eyes are a little crazed, but all our eyes are a little crazed. "Angelika keeps telling us to sacrifice and it keeps not working but that's because we're the ones who have to be sacrificed."

There is a quietness that is quieter than other silences. There is a line between what feels crazy and what feels acceptable, and when it's blurry, the world is a scarier place. There is a time of night when you haven't slept and anything seems possible. There is a kind of sadness that feels so heavy and tight that you would do absolutely anything to not carry it anymore.

We are in that quietness, on that blurry line, at that particular time of night, stuck in that exact feeling.

We are woozy and wild from drinking and grieving.

We are Devonairre Street Girls. We are finding out what that really means.

"I tried that," Charlotte says. "I gave up myself to save Cruz and it didn't—well." They look at me and I burn red.

"That's not what I'm talking about," Delilah says.

"I know what you're talking about," Isla says. She is stony and the spark of Isla Rodriguez seems to have flickered out.

I know what she's talking about, too. I've seen it on her wrists. Charlotte looks confused still.

"What are you most scared of in the world?" Delilah asks. "It used to be drowning, for me, until Jack died."

"And now?" I ask, but I know the answer because it's what I'm most scared of, too.

"Living this life. Losing everyone I love forever, over and over."

I see Charlotte swallow and Isla sit up straighter.

"We could save them," Delilah says.

"Delilah," Charlotte says.

"Angelika has been trying to tell me," Delilah says. "She's been trying to make it clear. And I've been stuck on all the simple things. Following the little, easy rules and missing the bigger picture."

Charlotte shakes her head and I know how much she's given up, but I also have to hate her for the ways she's lucky, for loving Nisha, for not having to live the life the rest of us would live.

If we live.

Isla's fingers twitch. I think I will see those twitching fingers for the rest of my life, however long it is, in my head. Isla's fingers twitch and Devonairre Street starts to wake up and I realize it's a Tuesday and we will have to make it through another Minute of Silence and another and another. All those minutes of silence that do nothing at all.

Charlotte clears her throat. She doesn't like how hard we're thinking, how drunk we are, how unslept and wide-eyed and sorrowful we've become.

"You can't sacrifice your whole future," she says, like a graduation speaker who doesn't know that we've been asked not to return to school, who doesn't know that at best we'll be graduating in our kitchens or in this no-longer-a-garden garden.

"What future?" Isla says. She gestures at the street, at the burnt ground, at our long hair and vanished dreams. She gestures at Angelika's building, standing tall like a threat of who we will someday become, of the very best the world has to offer a Devonairre Street Girl.

I let myself see Future Lorna one more time—pouring wine and making spaghetti in a kitchen in California, Cruz rubbing my shoulders, the windows wide-open because that's how we like them, not because anyone has died. Future Lorna with her short hair and white linen dress and unmade bed and anonymous smile.

I watch her. I linger on her. I let her go.

Grab, grasp, gone.

35.

They found out about Roger so more reporters and photographers are taking over the street. I swear they look pleased at the turn of events.

ANOTHER CURSED TRAGEDY IMMINENT, one headline online reads.

CURSE UNDENIABLE? another asks.

THE MOST DANGEROUS LOVE.

DEVONAIRRE STREET: FROM URBAN MYTH TO FRIGHTENING REALITY.

We continue our drinking at my apartment and shut the curtains. We can hear the street below. I peek out the window at the Minute of Silence to watch everyone go still. Angelika lowers her head. She is stuck on her stoop, waiting for us to do something to save everyone.

And save ourselves.

Every hour I text my mother, but the texting gets harder the more I drink. Soon my messages to her are mostly gibberish. But she only ever responds with two words. *No mprovement. No improvement. No improvement.*

"My mother won't survive losing him," I say.

Isla ravages our apartment and finds new liquors. One whiskey is dark and stranger than the others. Stronger. Uglier. We know the taste.

"That's it," Delilah says. She smiles and I remember for a minute how beautiful she used to be, before. How alive. "That's Jack's drink."

We all relax, like we have solved the last great mystery of the world just in time.

. . .

"Should we leave behind notes?" Isla asks. I am so drunk my head is rolling from one side to the other.

"I have to leave a note," Charlotte says. It's the first time Charlotte has said anything but *no*. She's drunk, too, beyond drunk. She keeps mumbling Nisha's name over and over like it might conjure her up. Her eyelids flutter, but she doesn't pass out.

"This!" I say. I have a million thoughts in my head but it's so hard to get them out. I blow air through my lips and they trill and I try again. "This is how an idea becomes something more. Than an idea. This is how something ugly is beautiful."

It was good in my head, but muddled coming out. Some of the words were too wobbly. Others were too slurry. I don't think anyone got all of it.

"Okay, Lorna," Delilah says. She is not as drunk as the rest of us. I look at her forearms again, and I think maybe she doesn't have to be.

"No!" I say. I want her to get it. If this is it, I want to see the look on Delilah's face again, the one where she understands me and I understand her and we are LornaCruzCharlotteDelilahIsla.

Cruz Cruz Cruz, my mind says. *Mom Mom Mom. Roger Roger. Jack. Dad.* The names are keeping a beat in my head so strong I forget that I was saying something until I remember again. "No," I try. "What I'm saying? I'm saying is this. This is how it feels. This is how you get to the end of the world." My head rolls and I feel an almost-lightness at the idea of the world ending. I have felt so small and trapped for so many weeks, and for the last few hours I have felt something else. Large and magical. Strong and powerful and free.

"I don't need to write a note," Isla says. She used to do everything we did, our Isla, but not anymore.

Charlotte and I get paper and write sloppy drunk notes to Nisha and Cruz.

Delilah pours more of Jack's whiskey in each of our glasses, and it goes down harsh and warm and mean.

• • •

We leave the apartment and it's hard to walk so I slide down the stairs of our stoop like I used to do when I was little. Charlotte cracks up and Isla doesn't. Delilah leads the way because that is what Delilah does now.

They snap our photograph, the people on the street, and the rest of them hand us red candles, already lit, and shake their heads at how much we've ruined. We hold the candles and hope we can keep them upright. We march past them all—the people who want to be us and the people who want to destroy us and the people who want to judge us and condemn us and make symbols of us. We follow Delilah past them all. Some of them I've known my whole life but today they are blurs, everything is a blur, and we find ourselves at the building at the far end of Devonairre Street where it stops being Devonairre Street. There's a rooftop my father loved, and from up there you can see the whole street and so much of Brooklyn and parts of the city and maybe even farther on a clear day.

We make it to the top, past hotel guests who must think we are drunk, which we are, and dirty, which we are.

And desperate. We are so desperate.

We make it to the top and look out at everything we are ready to leave behind.

This is what we were always meant to do, we Devonairre Street Girls. This is what sacrifice meant; this is why the Curse hasn't been broken.

My father is the one who told me love is the only thing worth living for.

"That's why you can't believe those kooks," he said.

But I believe them now and, if love is the only thing worth living for, I shouldn't be living. I open my mouth to say these things to Charlotte and Isla and Delilah, to tell them I am sure now, I get it, I see what we are doing, and I just need one or two more shots of Jack's whiskey and then I can jump, we can all jump, we can end this thing, like Delilah said we could.

I feel a surge of love for them all, for Charlotte's braids and her unlucky luck and Delilah's sayings and the way grief changed the shape of her face and the tone of her voice, and for Isla and her sureness and the way she grew up to be so much stronger than the rest of us. I love them all so much, and that, at least, is a safe kind of love.

My heart twists.

I need more to drink.

The sun's bright and it's waking me up and so is the way I love them but I have to do this because I have another text from Mom saying *ICU* and I have the image of Cruz's shoulders and sad, scared eyes in my head, realizing what my loving him was going to do to him.

I'm still embarrassed by the way he folded over himself when we couldn't make our bodies fit together right. Love is too uncomfortable, too vulnerable, too dangerous in every way.

I think back to the day our fathers died: It was a day a lot like today, just over seven years ago, and we met on the sidewalk and held each other and I liked it so much I felt a little guilty.

I remember wanting to pull him closer and I remember a feeling I couldn't quite identify at the time but I can now.

A feeling of Yes.

I loved him then, I think, and I smile a sad sort of smile.

Delilah's handing the bottle to Charlotte, and Isla is eyeing the edge of the building. I don't want to look; I only want to leap. One more shot, I think. Or two. Then I'll be able to do it.

I really did love Cruz in that moment, I think, in that embrace and the shared pain and the way I wanted to kiss him even though it had never occurred to me before and the way I felt a sureness in the midst of so much doubt. I loved him then like I do now.

Love is a fever, and I was feverish. Love is a certainty, and I was certain.

Isla inches closer to the edge.

I've loved him a long time.

My mind is slow, but starting to shift around itself. It is looking for something.

I felt the Yes over five years ago.

I fell in love over five years ago.

My mind is so slow, and I have loved Cruz for more than five years and he isn't dead, he is right on the street, locked in his room, waiting for something awful to happen, but nothing awful has happened.

And then something has.

Isla jumps.

Isla, who has always been last in line, who has always watched us and imitated us and waited for us to decide how to be Devonairre Street Girls, jumps. Without waiting. Without letting us decide it's time. Without watching us do it first.

Isla jumps.

I must scream, "No." We must all scream and fall to the ground.

We don't jump after her. Even Delilah is grounded, trying to grab on to the roof as if it might catapult her off for thinking of this terrible plan. We reach for the ground first, for our knees second, and for each other third.

LornaCruzCharlotteDelilah—

And then a new moment of silence.

epilogue

Our new California home is the first one completed in a subdivision that could be any subdivision. Mom has told me the name a dozen times, but I can't hold on to the words, they are so vague and nondescript.

I am having trouble holding on to much of anything.

There are white walls and white countertops and no furniture at all, save for a long white table that Mom bought yesterday along with two white chairs to sit at either end.

She stands at the shiny white counter and chops avocados and tomatoes and cucumbers, which she has done every night for two weeks. There are no groceries in the fridge. We don't order takeout. We don't use the stove. We eat the food she makes—fresh and clean and new—and when we are done we throw the garbage down a chute and it vanishes and we are unburdened.

That is Mom's word for what we are. *Unburdened.*

"These avocados," Mom says when we sit down to eat. "Glorious."

I think the salad might be good with a squirt of lemon, but I know better than to suggest it.

"What do you think of the name Diana?" Mom asks, a smile on her face. She threw our licenses away.

I don't respond. My back hurts since we haven't bought beds yet. We sleep on the floor and look up at the stars through the skylights in our bedrooms.

They are bright, here. They are plentiful.

We'll never want for stars or avocados again.

I have a new wardrobe of sundresses and tops that billow. Loose shorts. Bright-colored cardigans. Skirts that reach all the way to my ankles. None of it feels quite right, but it doesn't feel wrong, either.

"Don't bring anything," Mom said. "We'll buy new." She took me out of my funeral wool before I could make it to the church for my nineteenth funeral. She dressed me in a light blue sundress with polka dots around the bottom. She tore the tag off with her teeth before I'd even tried it on. It didn't quite fit.

I barely noticed.

We left behind our suitcases, our dishes, our lemons, our loves, our street.

It was cold on the plane, but I didn't care. I let my arms goose-bump and by the time we landed in California it was warm and sunny and I was supposed to forget all about things like wool and winter and Isla and Cruz.

"Sometimes there's nothing to salvage," Mom said when I begged her not to take us away. She took my shoulders and looked me right in the eyes when she whispered, "When there's nothing left to salvage, we have to save ourselves."

No one else has moved into the subdivision yet. Most of the homes aren't finished, so for this one moment in time we are on our own. Mom told me the history of the land, but I chose to forget it. The soil is sandy and full of rocks. I have no instinct for what grows here.

I don't want to know what this place used to be. I will pretend it didn't exist until the moment we stepped foot on the California pavement.

I will pretend I didn't exist until that step, too.

There are no neighbors on stoops, no ice-cream trucks, no screeching sirens. There's only the sound of the ocean, which we can see from the living room windows, washing away the shores, cleaning away the remnants of each and every day.

We watch it for hours at a time.

I sometimes forget where we are and strain for a glimpse of the Statue of Liberty. When it's not there I feel sad for a second, before getting lost, too, in the predictable rhythm, the unexpected color, the mysterious and new green-blue of it.

We eat off paper plates with plastic forks and knives and drink clear Solo cups of cool water.

"We could have a glass of wine on the porch when we're done eating," Mom says. She has one bottle of Chardonnay from a local Monterey vineyard in the fridge—a gift from the realtor I think—and she hasn't touched it yet. I didn't think it was for us to share.

"I'm not thirsty," I say, although thirst was never the reason for the drinking.

It's been two weeks and I swear I'm still jet-lagged, but Mom says that's impossible. She adjusted to the time change right away, like she'd thrown away Brooklyn time the way she threw away everything else.

I can't shake the image of her, my phone in one of her hands, hers in the other, dropping them like pennies in a fountain in the trash can outside the airport.

I made a wish on the phones, like I would have on a penny.

"How will Roger get in touch?" I asked, when what I really meant was how will Cruz.

"There is no Roger in California," Mom said, and my heart shook at what that meant about LornaCruzCharlotteDelilah.

Isla.

"What do you think of your middle name?" Mom asks, slipping the last delicate bite of avocado into her mouth, smiling at the fresh green taste. She keeps looking at me in a way I don't recognize, but I think it might be love.

"I don't mind Lorna," I say.

"I'm not sure it fits anymore," Mom says. In her sentence is hope for a future, one where I am not lonely, not forsaken, not Affected or Cursed. A future where I am Something Else. "Give it some thought. You can be anyone. I don't mind."

Elizabeth, I think. *Samantha. Isabelle. Madison. Caroline. Lily.*

We drink white wine on the porch like we are friends instead of mother and daughter. I've never cared about the taste of the wine, but the label of this one promised "bright notes of tart citrus." I stare at the ocean and hold the wine in my mouth, waiting for the familiar taste.

It doesn't come.

I am a little in awe of the ocean and the way things can be one way forever, then wholly different so quickly your head spins. Nothing is the same. Time is different here. Water is different here. And stars. And love.

"I love you," Mom says, something she never said much in Brooklyn. She sounds sure of it, like the word finally, after all this time, makes sense to her.

Her certainty makes me think the way she dragged me from the street was an act of love. That love isn't always something made by building things up, but also by stripping things down. That love is what's there when you've left everything else behind.

It was love that took Mom from Roger's bedside.

It was love that put me on a plane.

It is love in the California air that rushes through the windows, neat and dry and smelling of absolutely nothing but salt.

• • •

Early the next morning we shop for beds and sheets and sandals and dishes. Mom wants white everything and clear everything. White cotton sheets. White wooden beds. White strappy sandals. Clear dishes. Clear bowls. Clear teacups.

She buys them without thinking about anything else but the way they are pure and simple and unburdened with history.

They will gleam in the too-bright sun.

We will try not to stain them.

It's Tuesday, and I'd forgotten it was Tuesday. If Mom could have dropped Tuesdays in the trash can, too, she would have. The only thing I have held on to is my hair, which I'm leaving long.

Today it's in a high ponytail, a way I've never worn it, and I like the way it swings as I step. Mom's is under a big straw hat.

She seems to think love is an act of forgetting, and she wants me to think the same thing.

An hour in, our rented car is so full of new objects to put in our new home that I don't think we have room for anything else. But we linger over a set of delicate wineglasses, long stems, breakable tops. I lift one up, to see if it fits our brand-new life.

The store stills. Heads drop. Cars pull over.
It is 10:11. The Minute of Silence hits.
The world pauses.
We go on.

acknowledgments

The first thank you goes to my agent, Victoria Marini, whose support, belief, creativity, friendship, wisdom, resilience, clarity, and enthusiasm made this book a reality. I am a lucky writer to get to go on this journey with you. Thank you for being there for me when I need it the most.

A huge thank you to my editor, Andrew Karre. Your guidance, curiosity, sharp mind, and collaborative spirit made an idea into a story, a series of scenes into a whole world. I'm incredibly grateful for the care you took with this book and the places you helped me discover. I could not have written this book without you.

Thank you, Brandy Colbert, for your invaluable insight and for doing this whole being a writer thing with me. I'm lucky to have you. Thank you, Amy Ewing, for pushing me on early drafts, and Alyson Gerber, Caela Carter, and Jess Verdi for support, love, celebration, and commiseration. And wine and cheese.

This book idea started years ago, and along the way so many people have talked me through ideas, read scenes, encouraged me to grow, and given valuable feedback. Thank you to Anica Rissi, Alex Arnold, Katherine Tegen, Andrea Hannah, and Bethany Jones.

Thank you to the amazing team at Dutton. I am so thrilled this book found its home with you. I am especially grateful to Julie Strauss-Gabel, Natalie Vielkind, Melissa Faulner, Rosanne Lauer, and Theresa Evangelista. Thank you also to Anne Heausler for your thoughtful copyedits and Antonio Rodrigues Jr. for the magnificent cover art.

Thank you, Mom, Dad, Andy, Jenn, Ellen, Amy, Mrs. Scallon, Nivia, Ian, Shane, Brennan, and the rest of my family for all the love and encouragement a person needs to write a book, which is a lot. I am grateful to have you in my life.

Thank you, Julia and Honora, who did those first few weeks of New York City with me just over over fifteen years ago. The great ones, and the impossibly terrible ones. This book is for you, and for those first weeks, too.

And thank you to Frank, who sees every bit of joy and fear and discouragement and excitement that goes into writing a book, and keeps me smiling through all of it.

MARGARET MEAD

A Portrait

Also By Edward Rice

THE PROPHETIC GENERATION

THE MAN IN THE SYCAMORE TREE

MOTHER INDIA'S CHILDREN

TEMPLE OF THE PHALLIC KING

THE FIVE GREAT RELIGIONS

JOHN FRUM HE COME

THE GANGES

JOURNEY TO UPOLU

MARX, ENGELS AND THE WORKERS OF THE WORLD

TEN RELIGIONS OF THE EAST

EASTERN DEFINITIONS

BABYLON, NEXT TO NINEVEH

CITIES OF THE SACRED UNICORN

MARGARET MEAD

A Portrait

by Edward Rice

HARPER & ROW, PUBLISHERS

NEW YORK

Cambridge
Hagerstown
Philadelphia
San Francisco

1817

London
Mexico City
Sao Paolo
Sydney

Library of Congress Cataloging in Publication Data
Rice, Edward.
Margaret Mead

Bibliography: p.
Includes index.
SUMMARY: A biography of Margaret Mead as seen
through her work.
1. Mead, Margaret, 1901–1978—Juvenile literature.
2. Anthropologists—United States—Biography—Juvenile
literature. [1. Mead, Margaret, 1901–1978.
2. Anthropologists] I. Title.
GN21.M36R5 1979   301.2'092'4 [B] [92]   76-3827
ISBN 0-06-025001-1
ISBN 0-06-025002-X lib. bdg.

ACKNOWLEDGMENTS

The author gratefully acknowledges permission to excerpt from the following works:
Columbia University Press for *Omaha Secret Societies* by Reo F. Fortune. Copyright 1932.
Reprinted by permission of Columbia University Press.
Doubleday & Company, Inc. for *The Complete Short Stories of Somerset Maugham* and *A
Writer's Notebook* by Somerset Maugham. Reprinted courtesy of Doubleday & Company, Inc.
E. P. Dutton and Routledge & Kegan Paul Ltd. for *Sorcerers of Dobu* by Reo F. Fortune.
Copyright 1932 by E. P. Dutton, renewal 1960 by Reo F. Fortune. Reprinted by permission of
the publishers.
Harper & Row, Publishers, Inc. for scattered excerpts from *Letters from the Field 1925–1975*
by Margaret Mead. Volume Fifty-two of the World Perspective Series edited by Ruth Nanda
Anshen. Copyright © 1977 by Margaret Mead. Reprinted by permission of Harper & Row,
Publishers, Inc.
William Morrow & Company, Inc. for *Blackberry Winter: My Earlier Years* by Margaret Mead.
Copyright © 1972 by Margaret Mead. *Coming of Age in Samoa* by Margaret Mead. Copyright
1928, 1955, 1961 by Margaret Mead. *Growing Up in New Guinea* by Margaret Mead. Copyright
1930, 1958, 1962 by Margaret Mead. *A Way of Seeing* by Margaret Mead and Rhoda Métraux.
Copyright © 1970 by Margaret Mead and Rhoda Métraux. All by permission of William Morrow
& Company, Inc.
The New York Times Company for an article on Margaret Mead by Laurie Johnston, December
16, 1976. Copyright © 1976 by The New York Times Company. Reprinted by permission.
Stanford University Press for *Naven* (2nd ed., 1958) by Gregory Bateson. Reprinted by permis-
sion of Stanford University Press.

Frontispiece: Margaret Mead in Tambunam, New Guinea, 1938. Photo by Gregory Bateson.

To Beth and Cathy

Contents

PART ONE

PART TWO

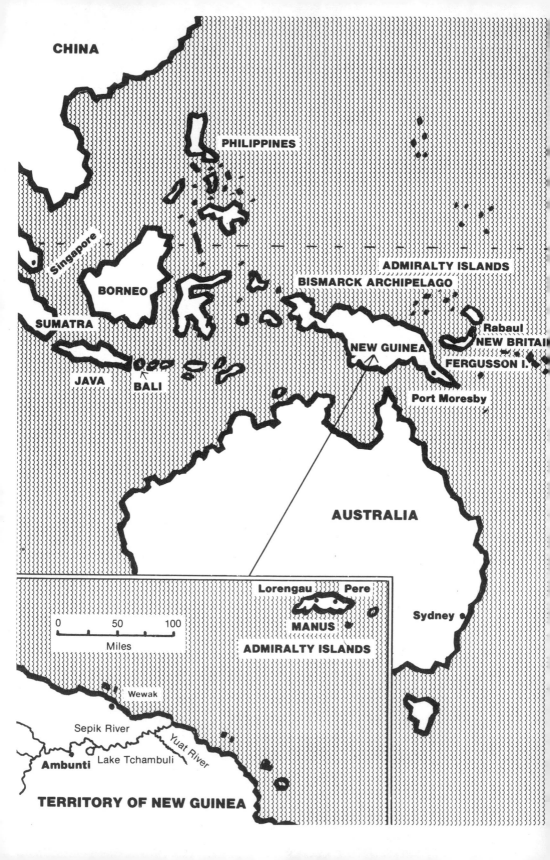

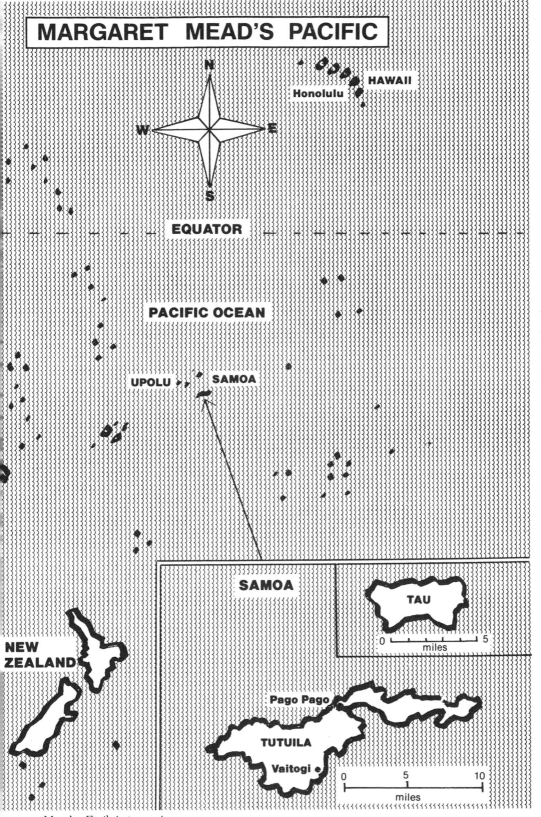

MARGARET MEAD'S PACIFIC

N
W E
S

HAWAII
Honolulu

EQUATOR

PACIFIC OCEAN

UPOLU · · SAMOA

SAMOA

TAU

0   5
miles

NEW
ZEALAND

Pago Pago

TUTUILA

Vaitogi ·

0   5   10
miles

Map by Emil Antonucci

MARGARET MEAD

A Portrait

Introduction

"THE WAY IN WHICH each human infant is transformed into the finished adult, into the complicated individual version of his city and his century is one of the most fascinating studies open to the curious minded." So wrote young Margaret Mead after her first field trip to the Manus island people. The date was 1929.

The same statement might have been applied to Margaret Mead herself, for her own life—an unusual and exciting one—was an example of how an infant developed not only into a "finished adult" but, moreover, into one of the legends of our age, for she stood bigger than life on our anthropological, sociological and cultural horizons.

Even if Margaret Mead had not gone into professional life but had remained within the boundaries of her own milieu— that of the intelligent, well-educated, literate, verbal middle-class American—she would have been a good example herself for study by an objective observer of Western culture. Suppose, for example, that one of the so-called "primitive," Stone Age headhunters of New Guinea, where she had done so much research, had possessed the same type of anthropological "tools" that she had used in her own studies. Suppose he had been able to apply her own methods to an analysis of

Margaret Mead. What would he have found? What would he have made of this slight, self-possessed, energetic woman, who could arrive out of the unknown, find a house and work area in a jungle village, quickly learn a foreign tongue and the customs and traditions of another culture and assert herself as a human being? What kind of soul-force guided this tiny woman? What was her myth-dreaming? What ghosts did she answer to? What was her totem and her clan? Who was her brother? Did she bring a dowry or was there a bride-purchase price? How many dogs' teeth or pigs was she worth?

What follows is a reply of sorts to the New Guinea islander, the biography of an unusual woman, half of whose life had been spent in faraway places, whose mind could absorb unfamiliar themes and connect the daily life of primitive cultures—religion, methods of child care, rites of initiation, marriage and death—directly to the most complex American way, with its thousands of variations in living, rural, urban and suburban, and its many ethnic and cultural strains.

Whatever she had studied, obscure cannibal tribes, a declining Indian reservation, a simple Balinese village, the rituals, customs, traditions and rebellions of her own people, Margaret Mead had been able to relate them all into a global unity. Even in the most primitive society she had often discovered amazing parallels to the American way. She could compare the easygoing, simply structured adolescence of Samoan girls with the complex, often contradictory choices presented to the teenage American of the same period. And she had been able to establish direct comparisons between the Manus, a canoe-culture, trading people of the South Pacific, who worried incessantly about business and their neighbors' opinions, and the upwardly mobile, automobile-loving Americans of the new suburbs of the 1920's.

The Manus were a central theme in Margaret Mead's life. In 1928 the Manus were a scattered tribal society of some

13,000 people living in offshore stilt houses on a remote island off the northern New Guinea coast. When she left their coral lagoons after six months of study, she had thought she would never see them again.

She had expected that the Manus would become a depressed proletariat. Instead, quite unexpectedly, they joined her in the twentieth century, compressing five thousand years of human development into fifty, the same half century of adult life that Margaret Mead enjoyed after meeting them. In a way they were partners with the people of America in working their way through the twentieth century.

The lives of the Manus and Margaret Mead, a tribe and an individual who had met by chance, became interwoven by historical forces outside everyone's control. Both parties, these Melanesian islanders and the young anthropologist, seized the historical moment.

It is this unifying thread, of Margaret Mead and the Manus, that ties together the diverse themes of this biography, for the Manus became more important to her than her work in any other area, and more significant than the many other important tasks she was to accomplish and the numerous honors she was to gain.

PART ONE

Coming of Age

ONE TORRID DAY IN AUGUST 1925, a slightly built young woman in a cotton dress steps ashore on an island in the South Pacific. It is Margaret Mead, twenty-four, thin, perceptive, aggressive, student of the much neglected science of anthropology. "Travel lightly" several people have advised her. In her scanty baggage she has five more cotton dresses and some simple tools for her work—notebooks, a camera, a portable typewriter. She intends to study a previously ignored field: the ways in which girls in a primitive society—in this case Samoa—grow up. She hopes—expects—that her projected study will shed some light on how this segment of Pacific island culture relatively unaffected by modernization attains maturity. She has already been warned that what has been written about Samoan culture is anything but fresh and uncontaminated by Westernization. But the growing up of young women in Samoa has so far been ignored.

Mead is one of a small group of anthropologists in the United States, a few professionals—who also teach, argue and theorize and engage from time to time in field trips—and some students; there are probably not many more in Europe, and a number of the U.S. anthropologists were born abroad. Anthropology—the study of peoples and their physical, social

3

and cultural characteristics—is, in 1925, a relatively minor subject, almost unrecognized in the academic community. But the anthropologists, like warriors holding some embattled post, are concerned that the ancient, archaic and primitive societies that still exist will disappear soon under the pressures of modernization. Already the metal ax, the nail, the outboard motor and the Gramophone have replaced the stone knife, the peg dowel, the canoe paddle and the tribal chant in many cultures. Plywood and plastic threaten. From one end of the globe to the other the societies that had so interested and intrigued early explorers, traders and missionaries are changing, giving way to the more powerful forces of the industrial nations.

The journey to Samoa was not easy to embark upon. Young Mead had to battle her elders to get started. She had been given permission to undertake the project with some reluctance by her teacher, the noted anthropologist Franz Boas. He worried that she lacked the stamina to endure a harsh life in the tropics remote from Western amenities. "I myself am not very pleased with this idea of her going to the tropics for a long stay," Papa Franz (as he was familiarly called by his students) had written to Ruth Benedict, his assistant, and also a close friend of hers. "Margaret is high-strung and emotional." Yet Boas feared that if Mead didn't make the trip she would become depressed. One of Boas's colleagues, the anthropologist and linguist Edward Sapir (like Boas, German-born), had been quite blunt with her. He told her that she was not strong enough to survive in the field—that she would do better to stay at home and have children as a woman should than to study adolescent girls in the South Pacific.

But subtly defiant and skillfully manipulative, Margaret Mead worked her way around her teachers' fears, and now she is in Pago Pago, Samoa, about to prove herself far more resilient than her elders had imagined.

En route to Samoa Mead stops briefly in Honolulu, still an undeveloped Pacific outpost, a scandalous port of bars, brothels, shops, warehouses, slums and factories. Fortified by numerous letters of introduction, she visits friends of friends, who smooth paths for her. Through them she reaches the inner circle of the famed Bishop Museum, repository of a hundred disappearing Pacific cultures, and is able to begin a study of Marquesan, a tongue related to Samoan. A friend of a new friend presents her with a hundred small squares of old torn muslin "to wipe the children's noses." Someone else recommends always carrying a little pillow and "you can lie on anything." Practical advice.

Mead meets a part-Samoan family who give her the names of relatives still at home. It is a felicitous beginning, and extremely pleasant, she notes. After two enjoyable weeks ashore, happy in the anticipation of her coming work, and weighed down with flowered leis of farewell, she boards the boat for Pago Pago, capital of the Samoan island of Tutuila.

After an uneventful week at sea, the ship glides past the fragrant shores of Tutuila, and into the great circular bay at Pago Pago. It is a wonderful, even awesome sight, a thin strip of silver beach crowded by the encroaching brush. The bay, second in size and importance as a naval base only to Pearl Harbor at Honolulu, is large enough to hold a fleet. Towering over Pago Pago is Mount Matafao, 2,141 feet high, almost purple in the heat. Here and there Mead can see the thatched tops of the Samoan houses, and among the lush tropical greenery the simple accents of the white mission churches. But the effect is spoiled by the constant roar of airplanes overhead and warships dripping oil into the calm waters.

She is not particularly interested in Pago Pago, but she must stay there while arrangements are made to go to a less developed island for her studies. The heat is oppressive; in fact the entire Samoan archipelago is moist and often unbearably uncomfortable. The rainy season runs from October to March, and coincides with her stay in the islands. The English novelist Somerset Maugham, who had visited Samoa a few years earlier, wrote in his journal, "There is not a breath of air in Pago Pago. It is terribly hot and very rainy. From out of a blue sky you will see heavy grey clouds come floating over the mouth of the harbour, and then the rains fall in torrents." It is the ever-present rain that forms the background of Maugham's famous story about a woman named Sadie Thompson, which was later made into a play (and a movie) called *Rain.*

Mead takes a room in a hotel overlooking the harbor. It is the same hotel in which Maugham had sat for two weeks waiting out a small epidemic of chicken pox that prevented his boat from continuing to another island. Maugham described it in some detail.

> The lodging house. It is a two-storey frame house with verandas on both floors, and it is about five minutes walk from the dock, on the Broad Road, and faces the sea. Below is a store in which are sold canned goods, pork and beans, beef, hamburger steak, canned asparagus, peaches and apricots; and cotton goods, lava-lavas [a kind of sarong], hats, rain-coats and such like. The owner is a half caste with a native wife surrounded by little brown children. The rooms are almost bare of furniture, a poor iron bed with a ragged mosquito-curtain, a rickety chair and a washstand. The rain

rattles down on the corrugated iron roof. No meals are provided.

Such is the setting for her introduction to anthropological work. Because she is a woman, the National Research Council, which is helping to underwrite the costs of her research, has decided she cannot be trusted with her entire grant in advance, and so has insisted on sending it in monthly portions. The mails are slow, get lost. Her first check—for $150—has temporarily disappeared in the languor of Samoa. The hotel costs $28 per week; until she receives her allotment she cannot leave. She must spend six weeks in the lodging house, at times the only occupant, without money to pay her bill. Six "laborious and frustrating weeks" in a kind of tropical house arrest. But she begins to learn Samoan.

The lodging house has added a cook-boy after Maugham's time, a young man called Misfortune—in Samoan, Fa'alavelave. Mead has mixed reactions to Samoan food. "Dreadful" is her first verdict. "Papaya and coconut oil and taro, that tasteless yet individual carbohydrate, serve for taste and the frangipani blossoms with their heavy oppressive odor for smell, mixed on the warm breeze with the odor of slightly fermented overripe bananas" is how she describes her introduction to Samoan cuisine in a letter home. Later she learns to eat and "enjoy" Samoan food, but even after that she can add it was "painfully learned." (And even fifty years after her first field trip she can remark that "Learning to eat the food is harder than learning the language.")

Her letters of introduction get her, through the navy medical department, a Samoan tutor, Pepe, who speaks excellent English. She has an hour a day with Pepe and seven hours a day trying out her accumulating knowledge of Samoan on the children she encounters in her walks.

Another letter of introduction. She meets the governor, "an elderly and disgruntled man."

"I have not learned the language and you will not too," he remarks.

"It is harder to learn languages after one is twenty-seven," she replies.

An incautious remark is her afterthought.

Her money arrives at last, and she is freed from the lodging house and Misfortune's dreadful meals.

A Samoan woman, a member of the family she had met in Honolulu, arranges for her to spend ten days at Vaitogi, a village near Pago Pago. Here Mead stays with the family of a chief. The daughter, Fa'amotu, teaches her Samoan etiquette, the proper things to do and say in various situations according to the circumstances. She learns how to sit on the floor—painful at first, and her legs ache—how to sleep on mats, and how to act during the rituals of meals and ceremonies. She puts away her cotton dresses and wears a lava-lava, the all-purpose unisex garment worn from East Africa to the Pacific. When she bathes under the village shower, in the full sight of staring children, she learns how to slip off the wet lava-lava and put on a dry one without feeling clumsy.

In Vaitogi the food is "wonderful." Two chickens every day for herself, with breadfruit, mangoes, limes, papaya, pineapple, tea, coffee, American-style bread, and fish.

She takes up Samoan dancing, which, she writes home, is not practiced "in a puritan fashion." She probably does not know that Maugham's missionaries—the actual people upon whom he based his story—were "very bitter about the dancing." The natives were crazy about dancing, the missionaries had found. "We made up our minds the first thing to do was to put down the dancing."

On her first field trip—to Samoa—Margaret Mead often
goes barefoot and wears a Samoan lavalava. Her companion here is Fa'amotu, who teaches Mead Samoan customs
and helps her with the language.

Mead will dance many nights throughout her stay.

Pains in the legs from sitting on the floor and from too much dancing go away. She is rapidly becoming acclimatized. Samoanized. The food in Vaitogi is better. The lessons in Samoan etiquette produce results. Samoan society is highly structured, and rank is important. One behaves a certain way for this person in the hierarchy, that way for another. One must use the correct phrases.

A chief from the neighboring island of Upolu visits the family. After a while he makes an offer which Margaret attempts to put into perspective. But she is able to affirm in her broken Samoan, "marriage" between them would not be fitting due to the difference in their respective ranks. She hopes her Samoan is adequate to the occasion.

Regrets. But the chief adds: "White women have such nice fat legs."

Returning to Pago Pago, with its veneer of Westernization gained from the naval base, Mead hears from her friends that she should do her research in a more "old-fashioned," that is, unspoiled, area. She is offered quarters at the medical post at Tau, an island in Samoa's Manu'a group.

Chief Pharmacist's Mate Edward R. Holt and his wife Ruth give her living space on a verandah at the rear of the dispensary. From here she can see the village. Nearby is a small Samoan house she is to use as a center and office, and where she can talk in private to the Samoan girls. She is in an ideal situation for her work: She has the authority of the government behind her, and can thus maintain the privilege of rank; had she lived with a Samoan family, etiquette would have kept her from talking to the village children. Now, with a Samoan girl as her companion and teacher, she can wander about the village and talk to anyone. Equally important, as she writes home, "I can be in and out of the native homes from early in the morning until late at night and still have a bed to sleep on and wholesome food. . . . The Navy people have canteen privileges."

She goes to work. But immediately she wonders if she is approaching her work properly. She has complained on several occasions that anthropological students learn theory but not practice; no one in the field for the first time truly knows what to do. (One anthropologist's first impression was that "the feet of the natives are large.")

"The truth was," she states, "that I had no idea whether I was using the right methods. What were the right methods? There were no precedents to fall back upon."

In graduate school at Columbia University there had been little information about how to proceed in the field. The student was sent out with very vague notions of what to do once he or she had landed among "his" or "her" people. Mead's teachers had been two of the greats of anthropology, Franz Boas and Ruth Benedict, but sometimes even they had emphasized abstractions more than how to proceed face to face with primitive people of far distant cultures, customs and languages.

With her head crammed full of the highest levels of anthropological concepts but blank about working procedures, Mead takes a commonsense approach. She is in Samoa to learn, and she goes about learning much as her aged grandmother, Martha Adaline Mead, had taught her when she was growing up in small towns in rural New Jersey and Pennsylvania—to go out and observe, listen, ask questions, analyze and write it all down in her notebooks.

Fieldwork, Mead notes about her first trip, is very difficult. One must clear one's head of misconceptions and presuppositions about other cultures and open it up to the flood of new and unexpected information that comes pouring in. A practical approach seems to be the solution.

Accompanied by an ever-changing group of young Samoan

girls, she wanders about, asking questions and checking the questions with other questions. She analyzes each household in three neighboring villages of Manu'a, noting down location, relationship and closeness to other households, rank, wealth, and the age, sex, social standing and marital status of each person in the household. Each child is studied in the context of her own particular environment.

"In the field nothing can be taken for granted," she remarks. Even the fact that people live in houses should be seen as if for the first time. She notes that Samoan houses are round, with a pagodalike roof and open sides—no enclosing wall shuts out the view of the entire village. The floor is made of pebbles, and rolled-up mats are kept for the arrival of visitors. At night a bark-cloth curtain is all that separates the guest from the family. This openness of the Samoan house helps her get a picture of the daily comings and goings of the young people she is working with. Details build up the great picture, and she misses nothing, not even the slightest nuances of gesture and language.

Mead works as long as there are light and people awake to talk to or watch or overhear. But she has other methods, too, of establishing the character of each girl's life. Sometimes she tries standard Western tests in interviews, among them color-naming, completing drawings, interpreting pictures, rote memory of numbers and digit symbol substitution, and word tests. In some of them, especially those involving numbers, the girls do poorly or have no interest; but they excel at words, and often with drawings. She also draws up charts of standard activities, such as gardening, fishing, weaving, making bark cloth, athletics, to learn the girls' understanding of their own culture and its numerous codes and taboos, and fills them in casually as she gathers information about each person.

Her self-taught methods of fieldwork are to produce one of

the most unusual books of anthropological history. Nuances of Samoan life are captured, slight events others might have overlooked. In her hands they show a novelist's touch.

The life of the day begins at dawn, or if the moon has shown until daylight, the shouts of the young men may be heard before dawn from the hillside. Uneasy in the night, populous with ghosts, they shout lustily to one another as they hasten with their work. As the dawn begins to fall among the soft brown roofs and the slender palm trees stand out against a colourless, gleaming sea, lovers slip home from trysts beneath the palm trees or in the shadow of beached canoes, that the light may find each sleeper in his appointed place. Cocks crow, negligently, and a shrill-voiced bird cries from the breadfruit trees. The insistent roar of the reef seems muted to an undertone for the sounds of a waking village. Babies cry, a few short wails before sleepy mothers give them the breast. Restless little children roll out of their sheets and wander drowsily down to the beach to freshen their faces in the sea. Boys, bent upon an early fishing, start collecting their tackle and go to rouse their more laggard companions. Fires are lit, here and there, the white smoke hardly visible against the paleness of the dawn. The whole village, sheeted and frowsy, stirs, rubs its eyes, and stumbles towards the beach. "Talofa!" "Talofa!" "Will the journey start today?" "Is it bonito fishing your lordship is going?" Girls stop to giggle over some ne'er-do-well who escaped during the night from an angry father's pursuit and to venture a shrewd guess that the daughter knew more about his presence than she told. The boy who is taunted by another, who has succeeded him in his sweetheart's favour, grapples with his rival, his foot slipping in the wet sand. From the other

end of the village comes a long drawn-out, piercing wail.
A messenger has just brought word of the death of some
relative in another village. Half-clad, unhurried women,
with babies at their breasts, or astride their hips, pause
in their tale of Losa's outraged departure from her father's house to the greater kindness in the home of her
uncle, to wonder who is dead. Poor relatives whisper
their requests to rich relatives, men make plans to set a
fish trap together, a woman begs a bit of yellow dye from
a kinswoman, and through the village sounds the rhyth-
mic tattoo which calls the young men together. They
gather from all parts of the village, digging sticks in
hand, ready to start inland to the plantation. The older
men set off upon their more lonely occupations, and
each household, reassembled under its peaked roof, settles down to the routine of the morning. Little children,
too hungry to wait for the late breakfast, beg lumps of
cold taro which they munch greedily. Women carry piles
of washing to the sea or to the spring at the far end of
the village, or set off inland after weaving materials. The
older girls go fishing on the reef, or perhaps set themselves to weaving a new set of Venetian blinds.

We are immediately at home in the thatched, circular
houses, at peace under the lazy, swaying palms, engrossed in
the amatory intrigues of the young girls and boys. We see a
life of simplicity and ease that is beyond our experience, yet
the ideal of our dreams. Swimming, fishing, living in the
open, dancing, storytelling, ceremonies, an economy without
the need for money, sexual experimentation—in the 1920's
this is far beyond the hopes of the ordinary Westerner, even
among the young.

But along with this idyll, Mead is careful to point out (but
a point that many readers will ignore), come social responsi-

Margaret Mead begins her Samoan fieldwork in the village of
Vaitogi. She stays with a chief named Ufuti, who formally makes
her a member of his family. The little boy with Mead is Paulo,
also part of the chief's household.

bility and social integration. In her Samoa even the five- and six-year-olds have definite and understood responsibilities, caring for the younger children, learning to plait palm or pandanus leaves, to climb coconut palms, to open coconuts skillfully, and attending to numerous other minor but necessary chores. Boys go through the child-caring stage and then move on to their assigned tasks, helping with the fishing and preparing boats for sea. In their teens the girls will learn the ways of cooking with primitive equipment (stones, bamboo leaves, coconut shells, plaited baskets and carved bowls), and the boys will pick up the techniques of canoe handling, of tending taro roots and coconut trees, transplanting and harvesting. Each boy must take part in communal activities, not slacking or showing too much precocity. He must fit into the larger structure, for individuality is discouraged.

High-strung and frail her professors had thought she might be in the field, yet Mead has accomplished an amazing job. She has worked with sixty-eight girls mainly in the three neighboring villages of one coast of Tau. From time to time she visited four other villages in the Tau archipelago, and she talked to numerous children, young men and adults. Her broad observations about ceremonial usages surrounding birth, adolescence, marriage and death are collected from the entire group, but it is the teenage girl's psychological development that is crucial to her work.

In *Coming of Age in Samoa*, the book that resulted from her trip, her most important discovery is that the storms and tensions of adolescent life in the Western world are not necessarily shared by other peoples. Unlike adolescence in America and Europe, she discovers, Samoan "adolescence represented no period of crisis or stress, but was instead an orderly developing of a set of slowly maturing interests and activities. The girls' minds were perplexed by no conflicts, troubled by no philosophical queries, beset by no remote ambitions. To live as a girl with as many lovers as long as possible and then to marry in one's own village, near one's own relatives, and to have many children, these were uniform and satisfying ambitions."

The idea seems to appeal to a lot of her readers, and her frankness in speaking so plainly about sex and love in Samoa soon make her famous.

Everyone's Favorite

SHE IS A PRECOCIOUS, EAGER, inquisitive child. "There's no one like Margaret," the family says, half in admiration, but at times with a touch of annoyance. Nevertheless, among all the children of Edward and Emily Fogg Mead, Margaret is everyone's favorite.

She is a Sagittarian. An Archer: "someone who goes as far as anyone else and shoots a little farther" is her definition. But as a scientist astrology means nothing to her.

The Meads have five children: Margaret, born in 1901, is the eldest; Richard, the only boy, is two years younger; Katherine dies in infancy in 1906; after her come Elizabeth, born in 1910, and Priscilla, born in 1911.

Edward Mead is a professor at the Wharton School of Finance and Commerce, part of the University of Pennsylvania. He is the author of a number of books about business subjects, and edits a railroad magazine.

Emily Fogg Mead, three years older than her husband, is working on her master's degree in sociology at the time of Margaret's birth. In 1901 it is still unusual for a woman to attend and be graduated from college—at best, many young women go to what is called a finishing school to learn social graces before marriage—and postgraduate education is even

Emily Fogg Mead, 34, and young Margaret, age four. This is the period when Emily Mead is studying Italian-American families in Hammonton, New Jersey. She often takes Margaret on her field trips.

rarer. However, Emily Mead is hard at work on an unusual subject for her master's thesis: Italian immigrant families in the then-rural town of Hammonton in southern New Jersey, not far from Philadelphia.

As a child of three, Margaret accompanies her mother on visits to the immigrants. They are mostly former agricultural workers and slum dwellers who have come to America along with tens of thousands of others in search of opportunities they cannot find in their homelands. The Italian families are warm and open, and they serve as the first introduction in Margaret's education as an anthropologist. She sees that there are other ways of life, other languages, other forms of relationships between families, husbands, wives, children, cousins, uncles and aunts from what she is experiencing in her own academically centered home. One form of living is not necessarily better or worse than another, merely "different." Each way of life, with its unique history, thoughts, culture, customs and religious beliefs, might be strange—"foreign"— to the casual observer, but is nevertheless normal in its own context. A basic lesson that is imprinted early on young Margaret's mind.

Her mother's thesis receives little recognition, Mead notes. It is eventually published as a pamphlet by the United States Government Printing Office. Its value lies in another field: It helps young Margaret in learning how to see other people. Two decades later it will serve as the basis for some of her own studies.

For a while these researches into the lives of the immigrants dominate the Mead household. The family had moved to Hammonton in 1904 in order to be closer to Emily Mead's subjects. The town is an ideal place for raising children. Here the Meads live in an old farmhouse on five acres of land, with blueberry thickets, woods with secret pathways, trees to climb, a barn and an abandoned dinghy planted with flowers.

Part of each year the family returns to Philadelphia so that Professor Mead can be closer to his job. For two winters the Meads live in the city itself, and then in different outlying suburbs, usually among other members of the academic community.

During this period of moving from one home to another, from country to city or suburb, Margaret has but one full term of formal schooling; this on a half-day basis only, much to the envy of her other classmates and the annoyance of teachers. It is an age when truancy laws are not readily observed. Her other terms in school are fragmentary. Most of Margaret's schooling comes from her own family members. But by the time she is nine, young Margaret is led to the mature decision that this hopping about has its disadvantages, for in her first month of fourth grade, she fails at arithmetic—"dismally" is the word she uses. However, by the third month of the term she has made a great discovery: School is a system. From near failure, she rises to a 90 percent grade in arithmetic.

She carries the step further. Not only school but life itself is a system is the conclusion she reaches in later years: A home, a town, a school, a classroom subject, a primitive society—all are "systems" with their parts and pieces to be studied, analyzed and mastered. Life at Hammonton, superficially chaotic, is a system. Most children would have found little in the Meads' moves but a memory of pleasant disorganization. An analytical mind like young Margaret's is needed to see the basis of a lifetime of ordered discipline out of what passes as daily living and learning in the Mead household.

An interesting, powerful figure dominates young Margaret's education: her father's mother, Grandma Martha Adaline Mead, who, more than her mother and father, influences Margaret's life. She lives with the family, a tiny, strong figure with flashing dark eyes and an endless fund of information. As a girl in her mid-teens (she had been born in 1845), she had become a teacher in a local school in Winchester, Ohio, though it was uncommon for so young a woman to teach. When the Civil War ended in 1865, she married a young ex-soldier, Giles Mead, who had just been demobilized. Together, the young couple went to college. Giles Mead became a school superintendent, expert in reorganizing problem schools, and Martha left teaching. But Giles died young, only thirty-nine, leaving Martha Mead with a six-year-old boy, Edward Mead—Margaret's father—to bring up. Martha Mead taught in various schools, or served as principal, until 1900, when Edward Mead, now twenty-six, and Emily Fogg married. Martha then came to live with them. By that time she was fifty-five.

Clearly Grandma Mead, active, decisive, loving, and intelligent—the young Margaret's model and favorite adult—gains both obedience and devotion, not by acting dictatorial but by the simple graciousness of her being. Grandma Mead, says Mead of her grandmother almost seventy years later, "was the most decisive influence of my life. She became my model, when, in later life, I tried to formulate a role for the modern parent."

Easily but effectively Grandma Mead teaches the four Mead children the ways of running a country house. They learn how to tend gardens, raise chickens, cook and can. It is a frontier-type life, close to the land, working with what one grows, finds, makes, not with what one buys.

Grandma Mead is also Margaret's first and most important tutor. She supplies what the school fails to supply: She teaches algebra (in preference to arithmetic, which she curiously believes is injurious to young minds) and botany. She is a moralist in her approach: Every lesson is accompanied by anecdotes meant to illustrate some virtue or positive quality.

"She taught me until I went to high school and even then helped me with my lessons when my teachers were woefully inadequate, as they often were," says Mead. And after each day's formal work, Grandma Mead sends Margaret to the woods and meadows to learn about plants, and explains how to analyze and catalog each specimen. Much of what Margaret learns is to be of value in her approach to fieldwork in later years as an anthropologist and scientist.

Grandma Mead leads Margaret to one of her most important discoveries: "I was always glad I was a girl," she writes in her autobiography, *Blackberry Winter.* Grandma Mead "had no sense at all of having been handicapped by being a woman." In another passage: "I think it was my grandmother who gave me my ease in being a woman." Grandma Mead's stories are liberally sprinkled with accounts of "a fair number of no-account men in each generation and, appropriately, a fair number of women who married the same kind of men."

Mead's other grandmother, her mother's mother, Grandma Elizabeth Bogart Fogg, gets short shrift. A small handsome woman with snapping black eyes, "dutiful but lacklustre with children." A sharp tongue: She calls Margaret "tiresome." No love is lost in Margaret's later memories. At sixteen she gives Grandma Fogg a volume of Guy de Maupassant stories inscribed, "To my wicked little grandmother." "A quality of inconsequential triviality" is her summing up, a verdict which, in *Blackberry Winter,* she stretches to include her own mother and her sister Priscilla. But there must have been some special spirit in Grandma Fogg: In her nineties she ran away from the old age home in which her children had deposited her. Wicked woman!

Margaret's mother Emily is not so broad and open as Grandma Mead. As a young woman, Emily Fogg had been determined and earnest, and at the same time careful and humorless, characteristics she retains in adult life. In growing up, Margaret can see that her mother is not happy about Grandma Mead's favored position in the household ("Mother never ceased to resent the fact that Grandma lived with us"), yet Emily Mead always makes sure that her mother-in-law has the best room in the house.

Emily Mead is altruistic in public causes. She vehemently fights the local political machine, protests the slaughter of birds for decorating hats, opposes the telephone company, Standard Oil and sweat shops. Battles that have not yet been won. But for the people she meets personally, Emily Mead has only gentleness and a radiant welcome.

Emily Mead could be comfortable about life, her daughter remembers: The Mead home is filled with books and papers, and the children are encouraged to participate in the household, not forbidden because they might disarrange things. Margaret's views about her mother are thus mixed with pleasant memories and some criticism.

Blue eyes, golden hair, slight. An old photograph shows Emily Mead as a fine-boned, beautifully vibrant woman with a Mona Lisa smile and bright, intense eyes. Professor Mead, who is a good six feet tall, calls five-foot Emily Mead "Tiny Wife," a name the child Margaret also uses in addressing her mother.

Years later Mead observes that her mother believed life was too serious for little pleasures—she disdained pretty clothes and elaborately dressed hair, since more serious things demanded her time and energy, not only for running the house and raising a family but for various causes and for righting the wrongs done to the downtrodden. Was she too efficient, too committed? In the luxury of the quiet of her last years, after a stroke, Emily Mead confides to her son-in-law Leo Rosten (Priscilla's husband), "Margaret always wanted a little rose-bud mother." At death she is dressed in pale blue and given a bouquet of sweetheart roses.

Margaret's father, Edward Sherwood Mead, occupies an even more ambiguous place on her horizon. The passing of time may have mellowed the harsh views she seems to have held during her growing years. She is never clear whether Dada (who calls her "Punk") is one of those no-account men in the family, for he had too high a position in the university to be slighted, or whether he was a major figure diminished by the fact that he was never so important as he might have been. Or at least, as important as she thought he wanted to be. Nevertheless he stands as a commanding figure, tall, strong, well organized and in control of his universe, with a voice that makes known his wants.

Sixty and seventy years afterward, Margaret Mead can make some biting remarks about her father. One suspects the battles between them were even fiercer than she admits to in public. In her own old age we can see that she resented some of his characteristics—"He thought he could buy anything with money," Mead remarked shortly before her death—and she hints that he was unfaithful to her mother, and that he was far from honest in his dealings with Mead on the question of her going to college. Yet in the end she tries to be fair and objective about him, and makes allowances for the problems he experienced. But—"I resented furiously what I regarded as his entirely arbitrary intrusions into our lives . . . represented by his very occasional acts of discipline. . . . In general, however, he left the supervision of his daughters to my mother and concentrated, instead, on worrying about and overprotecting his son."

It is through her father that she learns about the world of academia, the university world where men jockey over intellectual standing and scholarly credit quite as ruthlessly as

Margaret Mead's father, Edward Sherwood Mead, as a young professor at the Wharton School, where he teaches economics. He also edits a railroad magazine and experiments with various business projects.

men in business do for power, adopting ruses and stratagems to ensure their own positions. Such knowledge is to be helpful when she enters university life herself and has to learn how to steer a course between conflicting demands and to maintain her own interests in the face of pressures to conform to others.

Professor Mead teaches economics and his business courses are among the best at Wharton Graduate School, but practical business interests him too. He is an editor of *Railway World* (at a time when American railroads were a major economic force). He is also the author of several books, among them *The Ebb and Flow of Investment Values*, *The Careful Investor*, *Corporation Finance*, *Trust Finance*, and *The Story of Gold*. The latter work seems to have been his daughter's favorite, for of all his books it is the only one she describes in detail in her autobiography. She notes how he began with an abstract interest in the economy of gold, and then, as he became more absorbed in his subject, the book developed into an account of the entire use of the metal, from mining to its practical possibilities.

Professor Mead is an inveterate tinkerer with the business process, attempting to turn abstract theories into economic realities. On one occasion he becomes deeply involved in an experiment to use molasses to bind coal dust into briquettes. The attempt fails. Coal dust everywhere in the Mead home; smoke all over. The Meads give up molasses.

The Professor's successes and failures are a great example in practical learning for young Margaret, for she is absorbing the untaught lessons of melding abstraction with reality through "his knowledge both of the concrete sequences of activities necessary to carry out any process and of the men involved—the workmen, for example, who alternately cursed and made the sign of the cross over the recalcitrant machinery." And: "Father's vivid accounts of how a street railway in

Massachusetts had failed and of the fate of a pretzel factory also gave me a sense of the way theory and practice must be related." Her father's insistence on getting the facts is also an important lesson: "You either had the facts or you did not, and the facts—not any abstract theory—dictated the conclusions."

But this man, who is so skilled in the theory and practices of the business world, is almost helpless with his own children. Mead complains that her father had virtually no body skills—he could not put his children's shoes on them without occasionally mixing left and right feet, nor brush their hair without bearing down too vigorously. However, he is a loving father, perhaps too loving, for in his concern he fears for the children's physical safety, endlessly warning them against taking chances while playing, forbidding them to climb trees or to risk danger.

But he has many appealing characteristics. One is his ability to listen to his children, to concentrate on their problems and to give them a fair hearing and sensible criticism. From the time Margaret is a small child, he teaches her how to speak in public, giving her the confidence and the techniques to reach out to an audience. She will become a skilled, relaxed speaker, at home, in a university class, at a council in a remote village, in an auditorium before thousands.

Because the Meads are educators, they are always dissatisfied with the schools available for their own children. They adopt a casual attitude about attendance in schools and classes, following a method which allows their children to learn much more than what they would get from formal classes. Some years the Mead children stay at home, others they attend local schools, depending on where they happen to live.

"From the time I was six," Mead has remarked, "the question was not when does school open, but what, if anything, is to be done about school." So, between the ages of five and seventeen, Margaret spends two years in kindergarten, one year on a half-day basis in fourth grade, and six years in high schools, having been forced to repeat some courses because of her family's moves. Elizabeth and Priscilla do not go to any kind of school until 1918, when they enter the Homquist School at New Hope, Pennsylvania, a very special private institution.

She remarks casually that in a family of educators, her parents' views about schooling were "paradoxical." Some of the moves are made to obtain a certain type of educational experience—but not necessarily in a school. The Meads disapprove of any kind of school that keeps children chained to their desks for long hours indoors. So, in place of classroom work, Emily Mead sends her children to special teachers, to learn skills they otherwise would never have. Consequently over the years young Margaret is taught drawing, painting, modelling, basketry and music; she learns how to construct a small loom, and takes woodworking lessons from a local carpenter. She believes later that this kind of education, seemingly so haphazard, actually gave her the model for the ways in which she was to organize work as an adult, with assistants, researchers or the informants in a native village, making the most of each person's talents and fitting each into an effective, productive team.

One of Margaret's most important lessons, as often, comes from Grandma Mead, who sets her to work taking notes on the behavior of her sisters and brother. Grandma Mead points out that each sister is different in temperament and has different interests. Notebooks about the children are a tradition begun by Emily Mead, who filled thirteen about Margaret, four about Richard, one about Elizabeth and none about Priscilla, for she had lost interest in this simple anthropological study. It is a task Margaret takes to "with love," for she sees the babies as "her" children (much as an anthropologist has "his" or "her" own tribe of people to study) whom she can watch, teach and raise.

Emily Mead runs into difficulties in handling this large family and her tall, somewhat erratic husband; perhaps the moves have affected her more than she expected. Whatever it is, after the birth of Priscilla in 1911, Emily Mead falls into a deep depression, and must go away for a few months, to be cared for by a medical friend of the family.

The Meads, motherless, live in a rented house in Swarthmore, near Philadelphia; the house is so cold in the winter that water freezes in the bedrooms at night. Margaret, only ten, assumes care of the children, especially the two girls, and takes her notes about Elizabeth and Priscilla, writing down how one mimics the servants, or another defies authority, commenting on the differences between Elizabeth (enthusiastic, loving and devoted) and Priscilla (self-centered but unrelentingly honest about herself). "I was fascinated by the contrasts between my sisters," she remarks.

As she grows up, she attempts to formulate the differences between each of the three girls in the family and the one boy. The differences between the girls, she decides, could not be attributed to sex. She tackles the problem more formally years afterward in one of her most famous books, *Sex and Temperament*, when she concludes that the differences between sexes and persons of each sex come from subtle interactions of heredity and environment.

Despite her parents' wide range of interests and their intellectual curiosity, they think that only a small amount of reading is good for a growing child; too much harms the eyes, and they try to limit the amount of reading engaged in by their children. For Margaret, who is an inveterate reader, books become a secret pleasure, almost a vice, indulged in at night when she is believed to be asleep, or during the day when the Meads think she is in the woods searching for botanical specimens. Aside from the rules against too many books, the children are usually allowed to do quite what they want, with broad parental direction but not too much close supervision and guidance in their odd byways.

This freedom and the intellectual curiosity that develops from it encourages young Margaret, though only eleven, to seek out some kind of religious way—"anchorage" she calls it later. Grandma Mead was once a devout Methodist; Professor Mead followed no church; Emily Mead had for a while been a Unitarian but gave up religion, apparently out of a lack of intellectual challenge. When Margaret had shown some religious yearnings at the age of seven, Emily Mead gave her the story of the Nativity of Christ in German, hoping that the events of the Incarnation would seem "crude." "All it did," remarks Mead, "was to make me regard credibility as irrelevant." She hopes for some form of religion that gives expression to an already existing faith. Church services with various immigrant maids fail to satisfy her. Somewhere there is a place for this questing child.

The Quaker Meetings at Swarthmore are a likely anchorage. But the price is enduring her father's anti-Quaker jokes. Another attempt at the Quakers, this time at the Buckingham Meeting, near Holicong, Pennsylvania, where the Meads now have a 107-acre farm. But the Meeting fails of itself: It seems to be composed of a few wealthy old people sitting in silence.

Then comes the final anchorage, one she will hold to her entire life. The rector of the Episcopal church, an Englishman named Mr. Bell, and his daughter Miss Lucia come to call on the Meads. Margaret attends a service at the church. "Almost at once I felt that the rituals of the Episcopal church were the form of religious expression for which I had been

A childhood watercolor by Margaret Mead's younger sister, Elizabeth, shows Grandma Martha Mead with Elizabeth (left) and Priscilla (right) at the gate to the family farm in Holicong, New Jersey.
Elizabeth became a teacher and part-time artist; she married the
noted cartoonist William Steig.

seeking," she is to state. "I had not been looking for something to believe in, for it seemed to me that a relationship to God should be based not on what you believed, but rather on what you felt."

The little church gives her not only a religious anchorage but a physical home, for she begins to haunt the rectory. She develops a deep friendship for Miss Lucia, "the most humanly sensitive person I had ever known." She takes on the problems of the church as her own. The other children in the congregation attend services only because they are told to by their parents, but Margaret is a willing member of the parish because she has made a free choice. "I enjoyed prayer. I enjoyed church. I worried over the small size of our congregation."

She begins to explore the world a little. One of her favorite trips is to New York; she stays in Brooklyn with her young godmother, Isabel Ely Lord, who had been her sponsor at baptism. Isabel teaches art at Pratt Institute. Margaret crosses to Manhattan by the DeKalb Avenue streetcar whenever she can. She falls in love with the city.

During this period—she is approaching her teens—Margaret is sent on a regular basis to the tiny Buckingham Friends School, an institution so small and hampered by the lack of funds that it has only one teacher for three grades, the eighth and the first two of high school. The school is so desperately poor that Margaret finds herself studying Latin from the same grammar texts that her grandmother has used two generations earlier.

After Buckingham comes one year in a public high school. When the family moves to Doylestown and Margaret transfers to a new school, she is forced to undergo a number of subjects she had already taken. She complains that she had to read Cicero for the second time, John Milton's *L'Allegro* and *Il Penseroso* for the third. But at Doylestown, no one has to study hard, and the students take time off whenever it pleases them.

Margaret is a child who likes challenges, who meets problems head on. A large amount of creativity is demanded, otherwise she will fall into the undemanding patterns of her classmates. She writes reviews for the local newspaper, helps launch a school magazine, puts on an amateur theatrical with friends; she begins to write seriously. Poetry, short plays, a diary demand her time.

"In school I always felt that I was special and different, set apart in a way that could not be attributed to any gift I had, but only to my background—to the education given me by my grandmother and to the explicit academic interests of my parents. . . . But at the same time I searched for a greater intensity than the world around me offered."

What career is she to pursue? A career is expected, for she is not going to drift into the regulated, restrictive life of a woman in a small Pennsylvania or New Jersey town. Alert, intelligent, talented, outspoken, Margaret cannot let herself moulder. A whole world is waiting for her to explore. With her mother and grandmother as role models, she expects to be both a professional woman and a wife and mother. She speculates about being a lawyer, a writer, a minister's wife with six children, even a nun.

The spring of 1917 has arrived. It is the year in which the United States enters World War I on the side of Britain and France against Germany and Austria-Hungary, a war that has been raging with frightful casualties since 1914. At a school prom Mead meets a young man named Luther Cressman, the young brother of one of her teachers at Doylestown. Margaret and Luther spend the night dancing. Luther is four years older than Margaret, a senior at Penn State. He is thinking of entering the ministry, his mother's idea. According to Mead's friends he is a good athlete, drives a car (automobiles were then not so common as they are now), and takes beautiful photographs. She thinks that Luther Cressman, with his slim build and engaging smile and wry sense of humor (but he can be serious, too), is handsome. The old snapshots show him as a typical young man of the period, fitting the pattern of male looks of his time, with a stiff high collar, neatly parted, brushed hair, a tie knotted tightly: It is the type of male look exemplified by the Arrow shirt ads of the age, a type so standardized that "Arrow shirt" became a term for conventional. Straight Arrow.

Margaret and Luther, in love (or is it mere infatuation?—from the distance one cannot tell her true feelings), do not see each other again until Christmas, when suddenly they become secretly engaged. Luther's plans to enter the ministry are now set and Mead looks forward to being a clergyman's wife in a big, old rectory with lots of children. First Luther must go fight the enemy: He has to attend officer's training camp.

Margaret takes over the job of running the Mead farm in Holicong; she cooks for the family and the hired hands, and works at the local Red Cross. Though she writes Luther a four-page letter every day, she still has not told her parents of the engagement.

The months move swiftly: The war ends on November 11, 1918. The Meads give up the Holicong farm and move to New Hope, a few miles away. Luther is demobilized and at last Margaret thinks it time to inform her parents of the coming marriage, a marriage that will take place not sooner but later, for she has not yet completed her education.

Ambiguities surround the couple, at least from Margaret's side. They will not marry for five years, until she finishes college and has done some postgraduate work. In all this time she seems to have loved Luther, yet there is a strange air of a lack of commitment, for sixty years later she can write:

> Father offered me a trip around the world and a very liberal allowance if I would give up my plan to get married. He was moved to do this by my grandmother's conviction that I was getting married because, in my mind, this was the expected thing for a girl to do after college. . . . In addition, he did not like my choice of a husband.

The crucial sentence I have reserved for special attention (it goes in the place of the ellipses above). Mead writes, "She [my grandmother] was right in this judgment." That is, this very unconventional young woman was, in the long run, being quite conventional, at least for the time. One senses a great lack of passion in young Margaret for her fiancé: She had more interest in the Samoans.

The Importance of Being a Woman

AND NOW COMES MEAD'S first great test of being a woman: She wants to go to college. She has her eye on Wellesley, for which she had been preparing by taking three years of French, for languages were one of that college's requirements. A crisis is precipitated: Her father opposes Margaret's going to college. The reason for his opposition is simple: "In the spring [of 1918] my father suffered a lot of losses in one of his private business ventures." Yet Mead is determined that she will go to Wellesley.

Tension mounts rapidly on both sides. But rather than face the issue squarely—we are getting her version—or perhaps as the result of his inability to convince his daughter that he has no money ("I had always been a match for Father," she has remarked), Professor Mead asks a doctor friend to try to dissuade Margaret.

The physician misjudges his audience. He offers a rambling and irrelevant argument: Margaret's hands are too small, she never has done a day's work in her life, she'll make a poor wife, she'd better study nursing. "Hearing this," she says, still vibrating with anger over the incident, "I exploded in one of the few fits of feminist rage I have ever had."

Somewhat chastened by the report he has received from

his friend, Professor Mead allows his wife to persuade him to let Margaret have her way. Somehow the money for tuition and expenses is available. But Margaret will not go to Wellesley. Emily Mead suggests that Margaret attend DePauw, her father's own alma mater, a well-known institution of moderate size located in Greencastle, Indiana. It is a kind of compromise: Her father has "won" by not sending his daughter to Wellesley; Margaret has really won by getting him to pay for college after all, despite "his financial uncertainties and worries."

Mead again has contradictory attitudes: In *Blackberry Winter* she can say both that "I greatly respected the way my father thought" and that "I was prepared to combat to the finish his conservative, money-bound judgments" and still preface this statement by admitting "his right to spend his money as he wished." DePauw is far away. Margaret knows only Philadelphia, south Jersey, a few towns in eastern Pennsylvania and New York, which she has visited often. In preparation for the coming year Margaret designs some dresses to wear at DePauw. They are run up by the family dressmaker. She has never been noted for style in clothing—she favors the shapeless—and her first designs are, to say the least, unusual. One is "an evening dress that was to represent a field of wheat with poppies against a blue sky with white clouds." Romantic but dreadful is her later verdict. But she soon has a wardrobe of clothing, which does not resemble anything the girls at DePauw, a rather snobbish, style-conscious midwestern college, actually wear.

Now seventeen, Margaret leaves the warmth of the family home for college, taking with her pictures of the Bengali nationalist poet Rabindranath Tagore and the Russian revolutionary Catherine Bushovka, the latter a special favorite of her mother, and letters to women in various sororities. DePauw is a place "to which students had come for fraternity

Margaret Mead, nineteen, spends a not very happy year at DePauw before transferring to Barnard in New York City to complete her education.

life, for football games, and for establishing the kind of rapport with other people that would make them good Rotarians in later life and their wives good members of the garden club."

For a moment DePauw seems friendly; Mead meets girls with whom she had corresponded over the summer, but quickly the awakening comes. The college is a far step from the idealistic, egalitarian principles of the Mead family, and she meets a snobbism she had not experienced previously. In her own home "no one suggested that we had any superiors, only people who had more money or were more interested in validating their special position." But in DePauw she is "confronted by the snobbery and cruelty of the sorority system at its worst." The social groups at the college are stratified and rigidly organized, and to her irrational. When she wears her unusual homemade dresses one of her previously friendly correspondents turns away, never to speak to her again.

She finds herself part of a minority, ostracized by the sororities, for along with her strange clothing, she has an eastern accent and is one of five people in the freshman class who do not belong to an evangelical church. As an Episcopalian, she cannot even belong to the local YWCA. Among the outcasts there are a Roman Catholic, a Greek Orthodox, a Lutheran and a Jew. To further compound her difficulties in this coeducational college, she realizes on the basis of one of her classes, which has two girls and a dozen boys, that when the girls get better marks than the boys, they suffer for their excellence. On the one hand, she does not want to do bad work in order to receive the approbation of the young men; on the other, neither does she want to overshadow them to the point where they dislike her.

The year at DePauw is her first and only experience with any kind of discrimination, though only a mild one, and, she speculates, it is virtually nothing compared to what people in actual minorities undergo.

> It is very difficult to know how to evaluate how essential it is to have one's soul seared by the great injustices of one's own time—being born a serf or slave, a woman believed to have no mind or no soul, a black man or woman in a white man's world, a Jew among Christians who make a virtue of anti-Semitism, a miner among those who thought it good sport to hire Pinkertons to shoot down miners on strike. Such experiences sear the soul. They make their victims ache with bitterness and rage, with compassion for fellow sufferers or with blind determination to escape even on the backs of fellow sufferers. . . . Injustice experienced in the flesh, in deeply wounded flesh, is the stuff out of which change explodes.

Mead feels like an exile. Because she does not belong to a sorority she has no dates. She makes one friend, a girl named Katherine Rothenberger, whom Mead gets elected to a class office by exploiting sorority rivalries. Unhappy at DePauw, she decides there is no choice but to transfer to an all-woman college. Another small-town college does not attract her, for she believes that such an atmosphere stifles the mind. It is New York that has the great call, so she persuades her father to let her transfer to Barnard College, part of Columbia University, in uptown Manhattan. New York has another attraction: Luther Cressman is there, and in the excitement of the big city she feels that she can have "a life that demonstrated in a more real and dramatic form that I was not among the rejected and unchosen."

Barnard brings her "the kind of student life that matched my earlier dreams," for here Mead is no longer an outsider but finds congenial friends, challenging courses and a stimulating intellectual environment. And Luther, studying at the General Theological Seminary, is not far away.

She immediately becomes friends with a group of intelligent, progressive, outspoken young women whose wide range of interests coincides with hers. American life is changing rapidly in the postwar period. American youth especially is asserting itself through rebellion, experimentation, questionings of elders, challenges to authority and institutions. She and her friends think of themselves as outcasts and radicals. (It is, of course, a romantic notion.) A sense of alienation is a key mood. But it is not the kind of alienation that she experienced in her year at DePauw, one of not fitting into a milieu because of clothing or accent or interests. This is far more widespread, for the women are aware of social problems, of sex in its various forms, of psychoanalysis and other new disciplines, and of radical politics.

As a means of challenging and confusing their elders, they take an amusing form of self-denigration: Each year Mead and her friends adopt a derogatory name for themselves. One year the group calls itself "a mental and moral muss," a term used by the head of one of the Barnard dormitories in frustration at being unable to control the lives of the students. The group thinks the term is apt. The second year, because of its liberal and radical attitudes, it is "Communist Morons," and the third, in a phrase it prefers to others, "Ash Can Cats," a name given it by one of its most popular teachers, Minor Latham, who was probably referring to a New York group of realist painters, the Ash Can School, who worked with vivid, contemporary material—life as it is lived in the great city. These nicknames are an innocuous kind of protest proudly borne, but puzzling to older generations more accustomed to quiet behavior on the part of young women.

They write poetry of fair competence. One of the group,

Léonie Adams, is to become a major American poet. They join picket lines, help with mailings for the clothing workers' union, invite liberal speakers to an organization known as the Sunday Night Club (Mead is the president). It is the time of the trial of Sacco and Vanzetti, two Italian-American anarchists accused of murder during a holdup. The case has become a symbol of the struggle between radicals and conservatives. The group holds a fund-raising meeting for the two men but can raise only $25.

The Broadway theater, in a creative, expansive, vibrant period, also gets their attention. One of the big hits of the time is *Rain*, a play based on a short story by the English writer Somerset Maugham. Jeanne Eagels is the star and the play runs a long time. The setting is Samoa; the story is about a tragic conflict between a reforming, harsh missionary and a prostitute trying to escape to a safer world.

When Calvin Coolidge (then vice president of the United States) asks rhetorically in a magazine article, "Are the 'Reds' Stalking Our College Women?" Léonie Adams replies in *The Barnard Bulletin*, "Cheer Up, Mr. Coolidge," for she thinks young American women have more political maturity than the vice president gives them credit for. "We belonged to a generation of young women who felt extraordinarily free," Mead says later. Though they are not conscious of it at the time, they are among the forerunners of the present women's movement. "We learned loyalty to women." The group believes that no woman need subordinate her friendship with other women in favor of men. They feel liberated from the ties and bonds that hampered their mothers and grandmothers. "[We were] free from the demand to marry unless we chose to do so, free to postpone marriage while we did other things, free from the need to bargain and hedge that had restricted women of earlier generations. . . . We did not bargain with men." They are forming their own identities, as

people, not subject to the prevailing attitudes that put
women in secondary roles.

In her teens Mead had wanted to be a creative writer. She
wrote numerous poems and prose pieces, along with reviews for the local newspaper. In her year at DePauw she
continued to write. In her first year at Barnard she expects
that she will write professionally. But at last she accepts
the fact that creative writing is not her true interest. "I
did not have the superlative talent . . . that was crucial for
success in the contemporary world," she admits.

She considers politics, too, but rejects it as a career, because
political success is too short-term and too demanding. Then,
in her junior year, she becomes interested in psychology and
begins to explore it. There are many new developments in
the field, a number of them due to the work of the Viennese
psychiatrist Sigmund Freud, then in his mid-sixties. Freud
had pioneered in probing various aspects of the subconscious
mind; his work already at that time has had a profound effect
upon the entire world, being applied to numerous other
scientific and cultural disciplines, from medicine to anthropology to art and literature. There is scarcely a field which in
some way or another does not react to the implications of
Freud's thinking about sex, the family, the role of the individual and each person's subconscious.

By her senior year Mead is fully committed to psychology
as a career. But two courses she takes this last year at Barnard
are to change her life irrevocably. One is a course in the
psychological aspects of culture given by William Fielding
Ogburn, a follower of Freud's theories; the other is a course
in anthropology given by Franz Boas, who is developing new
approaches in his own discipline.

Boas, a small, slight man, born in 1858, obtained his Ph.D.
in physics in Germany with a dissertation on the color of sea

water. He soon switched from physics to anthropology, a field which until late in the nineteenth century had been an unorganized and undisciplined science.

Much early anthropology was the work of Westerners in foreign lands who had gone abroad for other reasons. Many of them were originally missionaries or in the military, or were colonial administrators or businessmen who seized the unparalleled opportunities to study the strange societies among which they worked or travelled.

One of the most famous early anthropologists was the brilliant Englishman Sir Richard Francis Burton, who had gone to India as an eighteen-year-old officer serving under the East India Company and who went on to become a famous linguist and the explorer of exotic and primitive societies in India, Africa and the Middle East. His works such as *Sindh, the Unhappy Valley* and his three-volume account of his trip to Mecca (disguised as a Muslim from Afghanistan) contain material that can never be duplicated today. Burton was the founder of the organization which later became the Anthropological Institute of Great Britain. Still, he was an adventurer, and though an unsurpassed observer (and participant) he was not a theorist.

Another typical example of the nineteenth-century anthropologist was the British missionary H.R. Coddington, who lived in the South Pacific, then a very wild and primitive area, from 1863 to 1887 and was able to record island ways before they were destroyed by white encroachment; his *The Melanesians*, originally published in 1891, is still available and remains a classic work. Such men, by the dozens, if not the hundreds, laid the foundation for modern anthropology.

Though men like Burton and Coddington and their fellows, men of unusual courage, wit and sensitivity as well as curiosity, were able to record unusual and exotic cultures in detail and with insight, they gave little thought to theory. However,

nineteenth-century anthropology did gain some form from
the views of two men: the Englishman Edward Burnett Tylor
(1832–1917), and the American Lewis Henry Morgan (1818–
1881), both of whom were able to see a general shape to the
development of mankind.

Tylor is usually considered to be the first professional anthropologist, being the first person to teach it formally at a
university. Tylor disagreed with the view of previous
European writers (mainly French and English) that the
American Indians were examples of degenerated descendants of civilized man. In *Primitive Culture*, published in
1871, Tylor stated that culture evolved from the simple to
the complex, and that all societies passed through three
basic stages of development: savagery, barbarism, and civilization.

Morgan, an upstate New York lawyer, represented the Iro-
quois Indians in a land grant dispute and was adopted by the
tribe, thus gaining an unparalleled opportunity to study their
lives and culture. He gave up law to devote his time fully to
anthropology. In his best known work, *Ancient Society*
(1877), he developed Tylor's theory of the three stages into
a more complex structure, saying that the development of
mankind came from a "few primary germs of thought." He
believed that the family evolved through six different stages,
beginning with a "horde living in promiscuity" and passing
on to a stage where groups of brothers married groups
of sisters, to the highest stage, that of monogamy, with a
self-contained family unit possessing private, not communal
property. Later anthropologists could find no historical or
contemporary examples of Morgan's six stages, though the
German socialist Karl Marx was impressed by his analysis of
the development of the family and carried it a step further
to the stage where the monogamous family, private property

and the state would someday cease to exist and a form of "communism" analogous to Morgan's view of primitive society would develop.

When Boas appears to contest Morgan's assumptions and conceptions, it is a time when anthropology needs a second wind and some new insights and challenges to its hardening theories. Boas believes that the entire field must be reexamined. He has no use for any single theory of the origins, forms or development of the world's cultures, neither those proposed by Tylor and Morgan nor others that might posit that mankind came from a single source or a small number of archaic originating societies. Boas accuses his predecessors in the profession of working from inadequate data. Worse, many had not even gone into the field, basing their conclusions on the diaries, reports and travel books of merchants, missionaries and explorers, who, not being scientists, recorded only fragments of cultures, usually the odd and intriguing aspects. No wonder primitive people seem so "foreign."

Boas stresses the enormous importance of cultural variation, and he emphasizes the need to work in the field to collect vast amounts of material to be employed as the basis for interpretation and theory. An echo of Professor Mead's insistence on getting the facts before proposing theories is seen here. Boas's radical approach to anthropology, in which nothing is to be assumed and all is to be studied in each culture, sets a high standard for Mead to follow in her own work.

Boas is a challenging, engaging lecturer, formal, "somewhat frightening." His lectures are polished and clear, but he has the annoying habit of paying attention only to students who need help. Mead is ignored, but instead of taking it as a compliment, she has an understandable feeling of insecurity.

Perhaps she is too bad a student for Boas to aid, she worries. But at the end of the term he compliments her on her valuable contributions to classroom discussions.

In her own home Mead had grown up with many of the implied tenets of anthropology. "I was accustomed to regard all the races of man as equal and to look at all human cultures as comparable." By the spring of her final year at Barnard she seriously considers anthropology as a career, even though she is working on her paper for her master's degree in psychology. The subject, which is a suggestion of Boas's, for he has done some work on Italian-Americans, is a continuation of Emily Mead's work with the Hammonton immigrants.

Mead's thesis is entitled "Intelligence Tests of Italian and American Children." Boas had postulated that a new environment would produce changes in the immigrants' children. Measurements made by Emily Mead showed that the form of the children's heads had changed, confirming Boas's own work. It was, she said, an innovative study of the effect of environment on characteristics that previously had been considered unchangeable. Thus the work of the two Mead women supports Boas's supposition.

Boas's assistant is a woman named Ruth Benedict, who had entered anthropology three years earlier. She is a quiet, highly intelligent person, fifteen years older than Mead, and difficult to know. But young Margaret has a great liking for Benedict and relies on her judgment and opinions. They help each other with work, take on each other's responsibilities and share worries about their chosen discipline. "I began to know her not only as a teacher but also as a friend," she says of Benedict. "I continued to call her 'Mrs. Benedict' until I got my degree and then, almost imperceptibly, our relationship became one of colleagues and close friends."

Benedict is a slim, unpretentious woman, a great beauty who often feels ugly, wearing the same dress, hat and coat days, even weeks, on end. She has had a difficult marriage to a famous natural scientist, Stanley Benedict (her maiden name was Fulton), and after several attempts at finding some meaning to her life, including teaching and running day-care centers, settled on anthropology, entering the Columbia Graduate School in 1921 to study under Boas. In the future she will write two major works, *Patterns of Culture* (1934) and *The Chrysanthemum and the Sword: Patterns of Japanese Culture* (1946), plus an important, controversial pamphlet (with Gene Weltfish), *The Races of Mankind* (1942). Her first major field trip comes in the summer of 1924, when she visits the Zuñi; the next year she studies them again, along with their neighbors, the Cochiti. Living under primitive conditions, she writes home that her diet with the Cochiti consists of rice and raisins, enlivened by three cans of tomato soup found in the trading post—a statement made more in amazement than complaint.

Benedict, Mead remarks, humanized Boas's formal lectures, putting his general principles into specific terms and examples. Benedict, whose brilliance brought much jealousy from colleagues, thought that culture could be viewed as "personality writ large," each historical culture representing a many-generational process of paring, sifting, adapting and elaborating upon the life-style of a people. Each culture in turn shapes the ways of living, the choices and personality of the people born and living within it. "I feel about it [anthropological work] just as I do about a novelist's getting down his character with the correct motivations, etc. . . . What I'm fundamentally interested in is the character of the culture and the relation of that institutionalized character to the individual of that culture"—that is the underlying theme of Benedict's approach. She has a profound influence on Mead. Anthropology is what Mead now wants, but she is being wooed in other directions.

The problem is a frustrating one. A lunch with Benedict brings an amazing turn. Mead, a more voluble conversationalist than Benedict, is worrying aloud over her future: Should she continue with psychology, or go deeper into sociology? They are parallel, sometimes interrelated and interdependent fields, but one must adhere to one or the other. Benedict remarks in her shy, off-hand manner, "Professor Boas and I have nothing to offer but an opportunity to do work that matters." An unexpected solution! For Mead, anthropology is to be the direction of her life.

It is the spring of 1923. She graduates from Barnard with her B.A., with plans to go into graduate school under Boas and Benedict. Ogburn has offered her a job as an assistant in his department of economics and sociology. In the fall she marries Luther Cressman, an event that draws nationwide attention in small news boxes, for this modern young woman emerges from the ceremony in the tiny Episcopalian church in Buckingham, Pennsylvania, still Miss Mead. She refuses to become Mrs. Cressman, even with the marriage vows. "What is the world coming to?" is the observation of a number of people. The decision is not one of principle but of preference, says Mead, but the statement is on the ambiguous side, for she then adds that she is following her mother's belief that women should maintain their identities in all instances in preference to being submerged.

But all goes well, at least for the immediate present. Miss Mead and Mr. Cressman, now an ordained minister, find a small apartment in Manhattan. It is like many young couple's first apartment: two tiny rooms, a small vestibule, a two-burner stove atop the half-size refrigerator, secondhand

Luther Cressman, Margaret Mead's first husband, here seen at the General Theological Seminary in New York City. He was ordained a minister but soon shifted his vocation to that of anthropologist; later he became an archeologist, specializing in American Indian sites.

furniture, bookcases built as the result of Mead's childhood training in carpentry, hamburgers in various guises, numerous dinner parties for four, the most the apartment can accommodate. Luther has a graduate fellowship and is also an assistant pastor of a small church in an outlying Brooklyn community known as East New York. The church is an exhausting subway ride away, and Mead rarely makes the trip to see her husband in his pastoral role.

In the first bloom of their engagement, she had looked forward to the fulfillment of her childhood dream of being the wife of a minister and the mother of six in a drafty old rectory. But Luther's vocation is weakening, slipping away. He is considering abandoning the ministry, to take up sociology. The first year of the marriage, she will recall, is a time of "eminent peace." But is it too peaceful? There are none of the arguments and quarrels that test a marriage, that lead two people to come to a deeper understanding and knowledge of each other. Mead enjoys the absence of stress, for she carries memories of tensions between her parents, of her father's infidelities and her mother's rigidities.

This peace, however, seems to be on the surface. An undercurrent of unrest lies deeper, she can note on later reflection, and gives her poetry of the time as an indication. Analyzing her work afterward, she sees secret fears and worries. In one poem she compares herself to mercury but does not pursue the image: but—"My soul you cannot shatter/Ne'er hold in your hand." She is still an independent woman. In another poem she feels throttled by weeds. She wonders if she has not accepted marriage as an easy way in preference to a more adventurous, dangerous path, and in another poem speaks of tortured precious flesh but "You could not ease the pain."

One receives the impression that Mead had drifted into marriage because it was there. Has her relationship with Luther involved deep emotions? Probably not, for "peace" not "love" is the description she gives of the marriage. No problems to overcome, no pitting of one strength against another, of one personality against an equally strong-willed one. Blandness. So it seems a matter of course that by the fall of 1924 she and Cressman are agreed to go in separate directions for a year, to follow their individual interests.

So far as her marriage to Luther is concerned, this is the end, at least psychologically. Their marriage has been, as she is likely to remark from time to time in explanation of what happened, "a student marriage," one which she finally entered because it was the expected thing to do. The marriage has faded away rather rapidly, and seemingly without qualm or deep emotion. But still they will continue on what seems to be a superficial basis for almost another year.

Summer, 1924: The British Association for the Advancement of Science meets in Toronto. It is what is now called an "interdisciplinary" conference. As there are only a handful of anthropologists in the entire world, an even smaller handful can attend the Toronto talks. It is an exciting time: Jung's recently published theory of psychological types is argued over. Work among the Northwest Coast Bella Bella, work in the Arctic, work here and there, is presented. Mead feels a bit left out. Everyone has a special field. "My" people. "My Bella Bella." "My Eskimos." "My Italians at Hammonton" is not an impressive phrase. She, too, wants her own people, exotic people.

She must go into the field. But which field? She discusses the problem with Boas. Interesting new studies can be made in the way in which new customs in a new country, such as the United States, or new ways of life in an old country are related to older ones. It is the theme that guided her research in adaptation among the children in Hammonton.

Boas, however, has other ideas. He believes that sufficient work has already been done on the problems of cultural influence and borrowing. The questions he introduces are intriguing ones: Are the problems of adolescence shared by all cultures, or are they unique in certain ones? What in adolescence stems from the conditioning of a particular culture? What is inherent in the adolescent stage of psychobiological development with its various periods of growth, impulse and random discrepancies? He wants Mead to study the adolescent girl in a primitive society.

Now a struggle begins between the shrewd, experienced, elderly Boas and the shrewd, inexperienced, young Mead. Boas wants her to pursue this particular subject, but it must be pursued in a "safe" area. Mead, who is willing to compromise on the subject, wants to select her own area in which to work. That area is Polynesia, which was the subject of both a seminar report she had prepared and her doctoral dissertation. She is specifically interested in the Tuamotu Islands, a very remote group in French Polynesia, where life is primitive and the native culture is being rapidly destroyed by contact with the whites.

No, says Boas, with all the authority of his position and years. He is concerned that she would be too isolated in the Tuamotus, which are but infrequently served by ship. But where is he to send his most promising student?

There is no time to lose, for all over the globe "primitive," unaffected peoples—that is, those virtually untouched by the Western world—are disappearing. Languages and techniques of living, of hunting, fishing, farming, of arts, crafts and music, of government, marriage and death customs are rapidly vanishing. In the 1920's there is only a small number of anthropologists to carry on the vast work of studying disappearing and dying cultures, and few successors to count on: There are only four graduate students at Columbia and not many more at all the other universities. Boas could survey a map of the world with a sinking heart and see his smattering of troops facing insurmountable challenges. Siberia, sections of the Low Countries of Europe and parts of the Pacific will soon be lost to modernization. He can send Mead to any of these. But—for Siberia she needs Russian and Chinese, for the Low Countries French, Dutch, German and even medieval Latin, and for the Pacific "only" French and German. But the Pacific is dangerous, and Boas fears that Mead, so small and frail looking (she is five feet two and a half, and weighs ninety-eight pounds), will succumb to some illness or other. He suggests instead the American Indian, possibly the most studied subject of any in anthropology. But more work can still be done. His suggestion seems more like an order. Mead refuses.

The battle intensifies. She will not do fieldwork among the American Indians. She is determined on Polynesia. Too many people are already at work on the Indians, too little is being done in the Pacific. Boas is adamant. Impasse.

The struggle takes an interesting turn. Boas has power. Mead realizes she needs to change the battleground, to force Boas to fight on a different level. She approaches her father, not as her ally but as a rival to Boas. She tells him that Boas is attempting to force her to enter a field of study which has no interest for her. She wants to go to Polynesia, not an Indian reservation.

Professor Mead, in order to rescue his daughter from Boas's domination, offers her a trip around the world. She can work in Polynesia and then continue her voyage.

Victory for the young woman, but, she is to write later, the situation still bothers her, that her father has thus sacrificed his own long-planned trip to Europe. It is, she admits bluntly, an act of manipulation, pitting two men against each other in order to attain her own purposes. Whether or not there were alternate methods of breaking the impasse she did not consider at the time, nor consider half a century later.

In retrospect the "ethics of manipulation" concern her. The two older men have been used; as a young woman she seems not to have given much thought to what she did; but in her seventies she tries to come to terms with the situation: "When I seriously turned my attention to the whole question of manipulation, I began to understand that one should not use either a person's strength or his weaknesses against him." How is one to handle such a situation? "The only course that is ethically justified is an appeal to strength—not in order to throw one's opponent by means of his own strength, but on the grounds that reliance on strength will work for the good." People, she states, will operate not in the worst manner but constructively and honestly.

In the end Boas surrenders. His best student is going to Polynesia whether he agrees or not. But some minor compromises are now in order. In place of the remote Tuamotu Islands Margaret will select an area where there is a regular boat service of at least one boat every three weeks. Her choice is Samoa, where there is a United States naval base and a steamer from Honolulu on the stipulated three-week basis.

Samoa is still a fertile area for study, though it is hardly an unknown land. Foreign powers, missionaries, vagabonds, traders, writers, ethnologists and anthropologists have already been there. Much is known about the native people, though no one has yet found out what a Samoan girl experiences in growing up.

Robert Louis Stevenson had written many articles from the South Pacific, some about Samoa; he had spent his last years on the island of Upolu, across the strait from Pago Pago, where Mead will begin her work. *Rain* helped make the name of Samoa known, though the public had been more interested in the collapse of a missionary's moral code than Samoan life. At least the name Samoa is almost as well known as Honolulu or even Tahiti, where the bedeviled French painter Paul Gauguin had passed his last drunken, diseased years. So Mead prepares for Samoa.

Boas, now that the crisis is past, does his best for Mead. He obtains a grant for her from the National Research Council. He admits, "I myself am not pleased with this idea of her going to the tropics for a long stay," but obviously Samoa is better than the Tuamotus. He tells Benedict that he knows "Margaret is high-strung and emotional," but to prevent her from going now would create more problems than those posed by the trip.

She packs. She gets her shots. By today's standards of anthropological equipment what she takes is laughable, less even than what a well-prepared tourist would carry in jetting off for a world tour. She has a small strongbox for money and papers, a small folding Kodak, a portable typewriter, six large fat notebooks, typing paper and carbon sheets. She is warned not to take silk dresses, since silk "rots in the tropics." (In Samoa she finds that the American navy wives dress in silk.) She has no lamp. "When field workers were poor," she remarks of the past, the tendency was "to take along as little as possible and to make very few plans."

Margaret and Luther have a brief vacation together and then set off on their separate ways, the wife to Samoa, the husband to Europe. She is to meet Luther again, in Europe, but more as friends—one might say even as casual friends—than as spouses, keeping up for a short while the outward appearance of marriage.

The Quadrangle

SIX MONTHS AT THE NAVY medical post at Tau, on Samoa's remote Manu'a group, go by as if in a tropical dream. Tau, a mere eight by eleven miles, is "the only place where I can live in a white household and still be in the midst of these villages all the time," Mead writes home. (She writes long letters, often to Grandma Mead, which are copied and recopied by her family and sent to everyone interested.) Staying with the Holts provides her with the advantages of substantial American food (Samoan food is "too starchy," she tells her family) and a good American bed, while allowing her a free run of the villages on Tau (there are four clustered together) to study and talk, dance, bathe with the teenage girls, be treated as royalty (she is twice adopted into the families of chiefs). The Samoans call her Malekita, their version of Margaret; Malekita is also the name of the last queen of Manu'a. She also receives a ceremonial name, Fuailelagi, "Flower of Heaven."

The heat bothers her. "This is not an easy climate to work in," she writes Boas. She thinks her efficiency is diminished by 50 percent from the heat, and would be even less if she could not live in the navy post and had to stay with a Samoan family. But in the same letter she can boast, "I am quite well and standing the climate with commendable fortitude."

The heat intensifies. Millions of flies. Working in the Samoan houses, talking to people, listening, ears attuned for every detail, every nuance of Samoan life, she is bothered by the climate. The open houses are not so comfortable as one might imagine. Sitting cross-legged on the pebbled floors (on which Samoans walk with bare feet) brings endless aches. Sticky heat, heavy. Her skin feels as if it will peel off in layers. Strange buzzing in her head from continued concentration on what the girls are saying. The buzz of the flies, the buzz of voices. The Samoan meals she is forced to take. The ceremonies. A pig is sacrificed to celebrate a birth: Blood splatters on her cotton dress. The heat is broken when a hurricane strikes, leveling the village. Mead and the Holts with their babies take refuge in a concrete water tank. Only five houses are left standing.

Departure time comes too soon. Now she is nostalgic. Exchanges of gifts. For the Samoans from Malekita, sheets of writing paper, needles, cigarettes, ink, pencils, matches, onions, thread. From the Samoans, mats, flowers, a chicken. At last, among the swaying palms and rolling surf, the idyllic beaches and the round thatch-roofed houses, and the ordered, hierarchical life of the Samoans she has come to love so well, Mead, her work completed, farewells said, packs up her precious notes and rolls of Kodak film for the boat trip to the main island of Tutuila. Her six months in Manu'a among the teenage girls, so lacking in the stresses and strains that mark American adolescence, are to be known as one of the most famous field trips of anthropology.

At Pago Pago she packs for the continuation of her trip around the world, for she will return home via Europe. She makes a brief excursion to Vaitogi, where she had first been instructed in Samoan etiquette and customs. Only now does she realize that she is homesick after half a year in the field.

Loneliness and the lack of affection, occupational hazards of the anthropologist, have beset her. Letters from home have been rare—some arrive in Samoa after she has left—and she never receives the reply in time from Boas and Ruth Benedict about whether or not she has been following the proper field methods. Ahead lies a rendezvous not only with Benedict but with Luther and a Barnard friend, Louise Rosenblatt.

The steamer on which she travels from Pago Pago to Australia runs into one of the worst storms of the century. Many ships are lost, but her boat survives, and finally makes port safely in Sydney, where she changes to a large steamship.

In Australia Mead finds herself again in a familiar world: Here she can attend concerts, carry on conversations in her own language—a language she can speak without worrying about the niceties of rank and etiquette—and enjoy the benefits of an advanced society. Fate, which had sent her to Samoa instead of to an American Indian reservation or the remote islands of French Polynesia, now intervenes again. A dock strike holds up the ship. Most of the passengers take hotel rooms ashore, but Mead, with no extra money, stays aboard ship. The dining room steward puts her at the same table with a young man from New Zealand, who is also forced to remain aboard.

Her table companion is a psychology student on the way to England to take up a scholarship at Cambridge University, awarded to him for an essay about dreams. His name is Reo Fortune. She says, "It was like meeting a stranger from another planet, but a stranger with whom I had a great deal in common," for New Zealand was then a provincial backwater, outside the slow lines of communication from the rest of the world. Fortune has never seen a play performed professionally, nor seen a painting by a great artist, nor heard live symphonic music. But he has been reading omnivorously whatever comes to hand.

Fortune's most recent interest is psychoanalysis. He has read Sigmund Freud, whose work on dreams as spokesmen for the subconscious has been attracting much attention, but he is especially interested in the writings of a Cambridge don named W.H.R. Rivers, whose studies in physiology, psychoanalysis and ethnology are known among professionals all over the world. Evolution, the unconscious mind and its early origins in man's precursors were subjects of Rivers' work and he was critical of Freud's theories.

Fortune's essay takes Rivers as a basic theme. He tells Mead that without changing the basic premises, Rivers had stood Freud on his head, making fear, not sexual drives, the motivating force in man. Much of Fortune's work in dreams and sleep has been done upon himself. He is curious, for example, whether all the dreams dreamt in one night are the same dream, a question which had been raised by Freud.

On the voyage Mead begins to record her own dreams for Reo: She finds that one night she has eight dreams on a major theme and two on subsidiary themes—partial confirmation of Reo's inquiries. He will publish one of her dreams in his first book, *The Mind in Sleep.*

The two young people have much to talk about. Not only are they both the same age, but both are professional scientists.

The ship moves on slowly, casually, spending days in one port after another. The weeks drag on as it steams through the sultry seas. Margaret and Reo spend all their time together. Their conversations are intense, emotional. The bond becomes more than professional. "We were falling in love, with all the possibility of a relationship I felt was profoundly unsuitable," she writes in *Blackberry Winter.* "Reo was so young, so inexperienced, so fiercely ambitious, and so possessively jealous of any fleeting glance I gave another person."

Is he rebounding from an earlier affair? He tells her he had been passionately in love with a girl named Eileen in New Zealand, but she had eventually refused him.

They pass Ceylon, the Arabian peninsula, go through the Suez Canal, see Sicily in the distance. At last the ship arrives at Marseilles, where Margaret is to meet Luther. Should she continue to England with Reo, or go ashore to meet her husband? The ship docks. She and Reo are deep in intense conversation. Finally Mead is able to pull herself together: She sees Luther standing on the dock, wondering what has happened to her.

"That is one of the moments I would take back and live differently if I could," she writes.

She goes ashore to meet Luther, leaving Reo to continue alone.

In France Luther shows her the things he has discovered during his time there. They meet her college friend, Louise Rosenblatt. Mead is constantly preoccupied with memories of Reo. They meet briefly in Paris. At last she decides in favor of Luther. A firm decision. But there is much she withholds from us in *Blackberry Winter.* Clearly she is still in touch with Reo. Luther must go home early to a new job. She remains in Europe, meeting Ruth Benedict in Rome. She is to have a rendezvous with Reo in Paris. He crosses the Channel; her train from Italy is held up. Frustration. They can meet only at the last minute, when her ship sails for New York and her first job, which she has obtained through the help of Boas and Benedict. It is a post as Assistant Curator of Ethnology at the American Museum of Natural History, an affiliation she is to maintain, in various posts, her entire life.

The Museum will be her home. She is given a tiny attic room high up under its imposing roof. This niche under the eaves becomes her true home. "I felt secure," she says of her sanctuary, which had earlier been an apartment for the building's janitor and his family. "I would manage to stay there always." The room seems to be a lifelong refuge, a kind of Stone Age cave where she can escape from husbands and the public.

Now she finds she is a celebrity. Luther has been to Europe but Mead has lived among "savages."

At a dinner party the hostess asks her, "But do they have table manners?"

"They have finger bowls, Mrs. Ogburn."

At the Museum she rearranges the Maori collection, a task which does not demand too much time; her light schedule allows her to work on the manuscript of the book about Samoa. She also produces some shorter, more scientific papers for academic journals ("The Role of the Individual in Samoan Culture," "Social Organization of Manu'a" are examples). Luther, who has now left the ministry, is teaching anthropology, a subject in which he has no field experience. She remarks with what appears to be a touch of bitterness that she is a "resource" at breakfast, for Luther must draw her out about the subject for his courses.

In retrospect she labels the winter "odd." She is informed that she has a tipped uterus, and so cannot bear children. When she had married Luther she had thought of him as the future father of her children. Her dream of a life in a drafty old rectory with the Reverend Cressman and lots of children has fallen apart. She sees Luther as a failed minister, and seems to think little of him as a budding anthropologist. She can see no common goal with her husband, despite his shift in career. And her own life is obviously changed, for she cannot follow the role models of her grandmother and mother, of being wife and worker, slipping from one to another. A winter of unexpected demands and unpleasant surprises.

Mead is haunted by the question that arose when her ship docked at Marseilles, whether to stay with her husband, despite the lukewarm character of their marriage, or to throw in her life with Reo, brilliant and stormy as he is. She has taken the easy, the safe course. But the question remains with her. Coolly she tries to analyze the situation. Continuing with Luther as his wife could only be on the basis of "cooperation," a term she fails to explain over half a century later in discussing the dilemma in *Blackberry Winter.* But it is clear that to remain in her marriage would mean years and years of continued blandness. On the other hand, life with Reo offers challenges, excitement, opportunities to work together in the field.

As she mulls over the situation, following her career as an anthropologist but frustrated as a potential mother, as a woman, she comes to realize that she need not remain married to Luther. She faces a dilemma: Luther at home or the impetuous Reo, still at Cambridge, but only a few days away by ship. Luther or Reo? It looks to the faraway observer—and especially to her close friends and her relatives—as if she is making a coldhearted decision. With Luther a sense of shared purpose is being lost. With Reo she can have dreams of careers in common, even without children. She is nothing if not clearheaded throughout life.

But Reo, too, is having problems. He writes to Mead (they have kept up a running correspondence) that his teachers and he do not agree. They are respected men but he is having arguments with them. His ambition, as she had noted during the return from the Pacific, is pushing him hard. Reo wants to make his mark "immediately." He has changed fields from psychology to anthropology, but his work about dreams, *The Mind in Sleep*, has been published at his own cost. It does not receive a hearing in the scientific world.

Reo writes her again. He has received a grant from the

Australian National Research Council to do fieldwork and will go to Sydney later in the year. He will then continue on to New Guinea to study an obscure tribe called the Dobuans, a people much feared by their neighbors for their powers of black magic. Margaret and Reo set up a rendezvous in Europe.

Leaving Luther at home, she crosses the Atlantic by ship, ostensibly for a study of South Pacific materials in German museums, but actually to meet Reo. In *Blackberry Winter* she says little about the emotions involved in this secret tryst, whether she is anguished or guilty about the deception, or overjoyed at meeting the man who may become her second husband.

She sees that their relationship is still "tempestuous." Mead again faces the dilemma of her first meeting with Reo, but now it is condensed into unbearable tension, an unequal balance: One side of the scale is the almost plodding Luther, on the other an exciting, imaginative Reo, almost explosive with ideas for the future.

In recounting the event so many decades later, she seems cold, too analytical. One doesn't know the details of their intimate conversations—yet "when we parted I had agreed to marry him," she says in the fewest words possible. "I returned to New York to say good-bye to Luther."

Her head echoing with Reo's plans for the future, Mead puts the situation to Luther. He is agreeably pleasant. No stormy scenes are reported. No high emotion. In fact, he is almost too agreeable. It seems that he too has found someone else. The Margaret-Luther-Reo triangle quickly sorts itself out, the participants are realigning themselves, for now there are four people involved, and Luther will also remarry.

Everyone is understanding, so understanding that Mead and Luther can spend a quiet week together before he sails off to England to meet his future second wife. She will eventually bear him a child.

This is the end of Luther, though Mead can remark parenthetically in her autobiography that "he later became a first-rate archeologist, working in a discipline that brought into play all his skills with physical things as well as his human sensitivity. But that was later." One gets the impression that she is making an effort to be nice.

Family and friends are shocked by the quadrangle—Luther and his plans to remarry, Margaret and Reo and their plans. Divorce was still uncommon in the 1920's. "I found it difficult to bear the fact that most of my friends, when they had time to spare from their own complicated lives, were accusing me of heartlessness." She seems anguished by the accusations. But she has work to do, a manuscript to complete, a new marriage to enter into. She has to solve the details of getting together in a fortuitous place with Reo, who has now arrived among the Dobuans.

Reo's Dobuans—some forty souls in all—live on a primitive and remote island, Terewa. No one knows English, and from his second day Reo speaks no English whatever. "I had no interpreter," he remarks, "but acquired the language by contagion. At the end of three months nothing said passed over me, and nothing much in a quarrel with many shouting more or less simultaneously." It is dangerous work, and he is doing what few scientists have done (though traders and missionaries have often taken such chances), landing on an isolated cannibal island without a word of the native tongue and only a hearsay and inaccurate knowledge of what the people are like. Despite his high-strung emotions, Reo is also intelligent, courageous, intuitive and poetic, and he grasps the fearsome realities of Dobuan life, so enlivened by the frightening practices of sorcery. It is a trip untrammelled by aid, or even information, from any government official, and it is one of the few places untouched by missionaries. No outsider, black or white, has ever ventured to live among the Dobuans.

Terewa's high mountains, volcanic cones, bronzed rocks framed in the dense jungle overlooking bays and inlets of intensely clear blue water are picturesque scenes. But the mountains, though beautiful, are considered by the tribes on neighboring islands to be gloomy and treacherous—adjectives also applied to the Dobuans. A cloud of superstitious fear engulfs Terewa, for no outsider has dared approach its sandy shores. The Anglo-Polish anthropologist Bronislaw Malinowski, who had worked among the Trobriands, a few miles away across the strait, wrote that "the very name of Sewatupa [the main Terewan volcano] strikes terror into the heart" of all the other islanders.

The Dobuans eat both man and dog, and practice the most deadly witchcraft of all the islanders. They are mean and jealous, and dominate the entire area by their fearful raids: Entire canoe-loads of other islanders are known to have been captured and eaten by the Dobuans.

These frightening, mysterious people occupy five months of Reo's time on this, his first, expedition into the field. Yet he approaches them fearlessly. Immediately a strange myth springs up about the white stranger, though he is careful to dispose of it at once.

> I learned Dobuan quickly at the outset and made a journey across Fergusson Island [where the Dobuans obtained certain herbs for garden magic] speaking it, before rumour had gone across the Island announcing who I was or where I came from. One woman said I was the spirit of her dead brother come back from the dead. She prophesied, on this basis, a general resurrection of the dead shortly, and told everyone to kill all their pigs

and dogs. A wave of this superstition swept over the island and in several tribes the livestock, litters and all, were exterminated. The District Officer of the Administration tracked down the woman prophet who was partly responsible for the state of chaos that he found, livestock exterminated, no gardening being done, houses stored against a siege in fear of the coming resurrection of the spirits. He got her too late, after expectation had almost died and chaos was already changing back to normal routine.

A movement such as this, in which the indigenous people expected a savior of some kind, the expulsion of the whites, and the coming of many European goods for the islanders, was then known as a nativistic cult. These movements took dramatic turns, and at their height, immediately after World War II, they were called Cargo Cults.

Aside from whatever supernatural aspect the Dobuans find in Reo, they adopt him as a member of the Green Parrot clan, give him the personal name of a Green Parrot man of an earlier generation who died without any sister's children as heirs and provide him with land for a house. Reo thus joins the complicated kinship system, which is traced not from father to son, but from father's sister to the sister's son. Certain young people can now call him "my father," to which he replies, "my child."

Reo is also taught, grudgingly—but he is persistent—many charms and incantations employed in sorcery. Sorcery is the means par excellence of accomplishing virtually everything within Dobuan society. Gardens are planted according to charms and incantations, and other people's gardens destroyed also by charms and incantations. Men seduce women, and women seduce men, with the aid of magic (there can be no adult sexual relationship without sorcery). Charms, amulets, sacred stones, spittle, uneaten food, pieces of clothing, "personal leavings" (as Reo so delicately phrases it)—anything can be used against another person to gain one's own objectives. Nothing good or evil is attainable but through sorcery. Children begin to learn the charms and incantations at six or eight, and will grow up to be feared sorcerers.

Sorcery is "hot." The art requires, generates heat. When engaged in a magical rite, the sorcerer must keep his body hot and parched: He drinks salt water, abstains from food and chews ginger. Ginger is chewed to the accompaniment of many incantations, and is spat on the object of illness. It is chewed in all the incantations to ward off squalls at sea, and spat at the lowering winds. Ginger spat upon a canoe makes it seaworthy and speedy. The sight of a magician chewing ginger, spitting it at intervals on the object charmed and muttering his spell is a common one in Terewa. "Moreover," adds Reo, "there is believed to be virtue in ginger chewing alone—I saw men who were anxious to get a man who had just run amuck with a spear to chew ginger. I was engaged in deluging his body with cold water, while they were pressing ginger into his mouth—so there was some incompatibility between our theories."

It is lonely, dangerous work, but after five months Reo has accomplished a major task, the "functional" analysis of a difficult society—that is, how it functions, or works. Reo then visits the Basima, a neighboring tribe, staying a month with them. At last he returns to Australia to recuperate from the ordeals of jungle life. After three months at home, it is time for him to meet Mead, now on her way across the Pacific by ship.

The coming rendezvous has required much planning. It is not easy for two people in opposite sides of the world, in different hemispheres, to mesh marriage and career, especially in the light of jobs and other commitments. Mead, however, might be said to think on several levels at once. She has finished the manuscript of *Coming of Age in Samoa*—the book will appear while she is away, late in the fall of 1928—and she thus turns her attention to a field related to anthropology, one which she believes will enable her to meet Reo. She wants to do some research in psychology.

Under the influence of Sigmund Freud and his followers, especially the psychologists Lucien Lévy-Bruhl and Jean Piaget, many anthropologists have come to assume that "primitive" people and "civilized" children have much in common. It seems apparent to certain scientists that the adults in so-called backward societies are more or less on the level of children of advanced societies, being irrational, emotional, not particularly aware of logical deductions and conclusions, and that their unconscious minds function in similar ways. The mind of the "savage" and the mind of the child in the advanced culture, so the theory goes, are fairly close to each other in beliefs in nonsensical ideas: The savage's belief in myths and the supernatural roughly parallels the child's belief in fairy tales. But the child grows out of his "primitiveness." His mind develops and matures, while the savage's doesn't. Moreover, Freud had also said that both the child's mind and the savage's resemble that of the neurotic individual in certain ways.

The theory is interesting: On the surface it seems plausible, and some scientists have accepted it without careful analysis, and certainly without testing. Mead would like to test it. She is intrigued by Freud's three-part balance of savage, civilized child and neurotic, and she would like to carry the theory a step further. If primitive adults resemble the children of the Westernized, advanced nations in their mental processes and the unconscious (an assumption no one has proven, of course), what is the thinking of primitive children like?

Mead writes two articles dealing with Freud's hypothesis concerning the behavioral patterns of primitive people, "An Ethnologist's Footnote to Totem and Taboo" and "A Lapse of Animism among a Primitive People." She points out that the kind of experience that the Freudians postulate as common throughout the world—that all adolescents go through a period of "storm and stress"—does not appear among the Samoan girls she has studied. To her the issue seems to be an important one. Nothing has been done on it, and she wants to pursue it further by studying an even younger group, pre-adolescent children in an even more primitive society.

The research could be done almost anywhere, but since Reo is in the New Guinea area with the Dobuans, she leaves the choice of location up to him. He decides on the Admiralty Islands, an archipelago off the northeast coast of New Guinea. The complicated details are worked out between New York and New Zealand. Grants are obtained— Reo gets one from the Australian National Research Council, and Margaret the Social Science Research Council, a U.S. organization.

She travels alone across the Pacific by ship. At Auckland, New Zealand, Reo boards her boat. They have not seen each other for over a year, not since their secret rendezvous in Germany. Impetuous but not tempestuous, Reo demands that she marry him then, at that moment, instead of waiting until the ship docks at Sydney, as they had originally planned. Off to the registry office they rush, only at the last minute getting a ring small enough for her finger. But married they are and they return to the boat just in time for its sailing. Frustrating months of waiting have suddenly been dissolved. Ahead lies "a professional partnership in field work with Reo."

Growing Up with Reo

NOW JOINED IN MARRIAGE AND careers, Margaret and Reo, on shipboard, glide over placid seas, stopping at Sydney, where more passengers and freight are taken aboard. Then they steam northward toward New Guinea.

These are waters of unknown histories, for the peoples are primitive and have no written record, and tribal legends could be based on events a decade back or a thousand years before. But these deep blue waters have seen the migrations of unknown races on daring canoe trips, tiny groups of people brave enough to sail into the unknown. And, in far more recent times, Captain James Cook had sailed these same waters, discovering the New Hebrides chain to the distant east, and Australia and New Zealand, now to the south. After Cook had come the Dutch, French, Spaniards and Germans, claiming lands, founding colonies. Magellan had once gone through these waters, losing men and ships, but succeeding in making the first voyage around the world. Traders and beachcombers, missionaries, planters, slavers (the notorious blackbirders) had ravaged the islands in search of riches, coconut, sandalwood, cheap labor for the plantations of Australia and Peru, souls for the various churches. Ships had foundered and crews been lost; men and women had died of starvation, wounds, fevers, in cannibal feasts in these islands. It was a wild, savage area, picturesque as a postcard but often hostile, deadly.

Soon their ship rounds the southeast point of New Guinea, with its treacherous straits and reefs and mountainous jungled islands, and lands at Rabaul, on the adjoining island of New Britain.

All of the New Guinea Territory has been a favored field for anthropologists, for its many tribes show widely differing cultures and characteristics. The very wildness and isolation of the great island and its many offshore archipelagos and island clusters have produced hundreds of small tribal and clan groups, with unrelated languages, customs, myths and legends and religions. Even with European colonization, the region, in the late 1920's when Mead and her husband arrive to study, is, except for certain areas, virtually untouched by white influence.

Margaret and Reo find Rabaul a charming little tropical town, lying under the shadow of three threatening volcanoes, the Mother, the North Daughter and the South Daughter. Rabaul had been founded only as recently as 1910 by the Germans. (Much of the New Guinea Territory had been first a German colony, and after World War I ended in 1918, the islands had been administered primarily by Australia.) Rabaul is neatly laid out, resembling a garden more than the administrative center of one of the most important of the Pacific colonies. It is a center for a small population of white officials, traders and planters, for it is the only town with any kind of Western amenities. Though in the heart of an area overwhelmingly native, it is a solidly European town, ruled by whites through a native police force, whose members are recruited from dozens of different tribes.

Shortly after Mead and Fortune pass through Rabaul the police—called "boys" by the whites—go on strike, paralyzing the administration. Many of the police have come from a northern island called Manus, one of the Admiralty chain of the territory, and these islanders are among the strike leaders.

The strike is crucial in white-native relations, for in place of the sporadic outbreaks by people in the bush which the local district administrators put down easily, the police strike takes place in the very heart of the government, and is well planned and well executed. The main issue is one of wages, along with the manner in which whites treat the natives (a strike on another island is called the Dog Movement, because the people believe that they are treated as dogs by the whites). Led by the boss-boys, many of whom are from Manus, the police lead the entire indigenous labor force out of Rabaul to the relative safety of the Catholic and Protestant missions. Eventually the strike is crushed by the government; the police and the workers do not receive any better wages, but the natives have learned that they can defy the white man.

The strike is at that time outside of Mead's own work, but one of the leaders, whom she does not meet at Rabaul, is a man named Paliau. He is to play a role in her work some twenty-five years later. Meanwhile the young couple make preparations for their field trip.

Reo has decided on the basis of advice given in Australia by anthropologists there that the Admiralty Islands would be a fertile area for study, because no modern ethnological research has been done in them. He has further narrowed down the area to Manus, home of some of the police-boys, after a talk with an officer in the New Guinea Service whom he had met in Sydney. The choice of village where they are to work, Peré (or Peri), comes about because a government official at Rabaul "lends" him a schoolboy from that village to teach him and Mead the language. The boy, Bonyalo, is not happy about leaving this poinsettia- and orchid-filled tropical metropolis, with its many attractions, to return to his primitive village, but he has to acquiesce to orders.

The inter-island steamer brings them first to Lorengau, the government station on the Admiralties. Mead writes home that "There are some two dozen white people" at the post. "Everyone speaks to everyone else and hate is rampant. It was really better at Pago Pago where they didn't speak to each other." She describes the few officials, the missionaries, the traders and planters, some of whom are Chinese or Japanese, and adds: "Such flimsy structures of a hundred or so white men govern and exploit this vast country—find gold, plant great plantations, trade for shell, hide their failures in other lands, drink inordinately, run into debt, steal each other's wives, go broke and commit suicide or get rich—if they know how."

After ten days at Lorengau getting ready for the final leg of their voyage, Margaret and Reo, with their guides Manuwai and Bonyalo, sail off in a seagoing canoe to the distant village of Peré, where they will spend six months in fieldwork. It is midnight when they arrive in the village's moonlit lagoon, hungry and tired. The next morning they immediately go to work photographing the people.

The Great Admiralty Archipelago (as it is formally called) is about sixty miles long; it is made up of some forty islands in all, but the land mass totals only sixty square miles. The sea, rather than the land, is the prime source of livelihood for many of the people, especially the Manus, the most compact of the three major tribes inhabiting the islands. Of the other two, the Mantankor are also a canoe people, while the Usiai have a way of life that depends more on the land than the water. When Margaret and Reo land, the estimated population is about 13,000 people.

Reo Fortune

In Peré, Margaret Mead wears a costume worn by widows on Manus. The beadwork is obtained before death by the husband and the woman's male relatives after extended bargaining. Many factors—the hard life, dangers at sea, even sorcery—contribute to the early death of men and women alike in Manus and other South Pacific cultures.

The entire area is wildly primitive and barely out of the Stone Age cannibalism that the Germans had encountered when they had taken the Admiralties over as a colony. Until 1926 no white had ever entered the densely wooded interior of the main island. The people had not taken easily to white rule, and the whites had responded with punitive measures, in some cases killing off rebelling islanders.

Mead finds that the Manus (the people have the same name as their island) have only a superficial resemblance to the Samoans she had studied. The Manus, unlike the Samoans, live over the water, building their thatch-roofed houses on stilts along the shallows of the lagoon. Also, the Manus are not Polynesians, like the Samoans, but Melanesians, a dark-skinned people related to the vast family of Negro and Negroid groups of the tropical belt. Mead notes that until 1912, when they were pacified by the German administration, war had been one of their major, enjoyable preoccupations. She has come at a time when the Manus have shifted to another kind of economy: With war denied them as a means of gathering wealth, the Manus have, for the past few years, concentrated on voyaging and trading, practices that have become passions, ways of life and pastimes. The Manus are people of the shrewdest type, and their entire lives are centered around the accumulation of wealth, its display and its conspicuous consumption.

Mead finds Peré an idyllic setting: a great lagoon, waving palms, distant mountains, the roar of the open sea beyond the reefs, the canoes gliding gracefully about, children playing, people fishing. But, she says, despite the tropical beauty which so appeals to the visitor, "we shared in the local attitudes." To the Manus the reef is a constant threat, the mountains foreboding, haunted with spirits and ghosts. There is no dancing at night, as with the Samoans. Moralistic and avenging spirits will strike down evildoers. "The whole society is run by the spirits of the immediate ancestors, who preserve exceedingly human characteristics—easily angered, easily solaced. Each house has a special guardian spirit of the owner's father or uncle and this spirit both punishes and protects," she writes home.

At first Mead thinks the Manus are "a gay and open-hearted people . . . friendly in feeling, though unmannerly," but she later revises her opinion of the villagers, for the society seems rather oppressive. The young women are kept indoors, and the young men paddle aimlessly about the lagoon, with little to occupy their thoughts and time. For the two anthropologists there is little chance for play and relaxation in this ambiguous atmosphere; they concentrate on their research. "It's as delightful a place as we could have found in New Guinea," she says at first, only to correct this impression by saying later, it is "a hard-working life with almost no pleasures."

Margaret and Reo set about learning the language, which is but one of twenty in the Admiralties. It is enormously difficult, with sounds hard to pronounce, and a great amount of individual variation, but soon they can carry on simple conversations, and within a short time are able to do their research entirely in Manus, even making their notes in it.

For a few days Margaret and Reo live in a small house kept by the Australian government for its officials on tour, but then they have a house of their own constructed on the edge of the village. They have a host of child servants, a cook-boy and some teenage girls who are supposed to do the laundry but, since they must not be seen by certain males in Peré because of tribal taboos, are often hiding. After an initial enthusiasm for the food ("Food had turned out to be much better than we had dared to hope"), the diet is soon reduced to smoked fish and taro, a tasteless root, and occasionally a wild duck or pigeon shot by Reo.

Peré village is small—210 people in sixty-three households—but there are, for Mead's work, eighty-seven children under the age of puberty, or right at it. The small size of the village and the simplicity of Manus society make study easy for her. She goes about her work methodically, observing each child in detail in its play and home life, recording not only what the child itself does but all the details of family relationships, the number of children in a marriage and their whereabouts, how the marriage was financed and by whom (for fathers and uncles finance the weddings of younger men and spend much wealth in doing so). Both the men and the women in the household are questioned about their relationship with the guardian spirits—does the man have powers of divination (that is, can he talk to the spirits)? and is the woman a medium? The children, of course, are growing up very differently from children in Western households, and Mead wants to know when they were weaned, if they chew betel nut (a kind of narcotic) or pepper leaves, or if they smoke, if they wear clothing, urinate in public, can dance, can paddle a canoe, who are their companions and what games are played.

All the Manus children, no matter what age, are inveterate smokers and beg constantly for tobacco. To preserve their supplies, Reo smokes his pipe only late at night, and Margaret risks an occasional cigarette. Both the young anthropologists suffer from malaria—Mead estimates later that she was ill a third of the time at Manus. But the work goes on.

She wants the children to draw, seemingly a universal custom. It is, one would think, a part of a child's life in every culture. Drawing is a useful tool not only for the teacher but for the ethnologist, for it shows how the child views the world. Drawings also reflect what the child is learning and absorbing from peers, older children, parents and other models, as well as from teachers. But the Manus children have never drawn. "I found, contrary to all expectations, that these 'primitive

Margaret Mead's second husband, Reo Fortune, the brilliant but controversial anthropologist, accompanies her on the lengthy field trip to Manus. Reo is seated on the edge of the lagoon where Peré village is, with one of the ever-present children who follow Reo and Mead wherever they go.

children' showed not a trace of the easy animism of our own children, who draw men in the moon and houses with faces."

So Mead patiently teaches the Manus children, starting with those at puberty, and working down to the youngest, the use of colors and surfaces. Normally a hundred drawings will give an anthropologist basic clues to a culture, but she must collect 35,000 from the children before she is satisfied that she has understood the situation correctly. She finds that the children depict only the most literal representations of what she points out to them as possible subjects. There is no free play of the imagination. So her research convinces her that there is no natural animism among the Manus youngsters.

Nor does animism enter into the adults' religious life. Unlike many cultures, that of the Manus has a very simple religious system, one based on household spirits, each family being supervised by the spirit of a recently deceased male member. This spirit—"Sir Ghost" is the term Mead is to use later in her *New Lives for Old*—stimulates and chastises, protects and defends. Sexual standards, especially for the women, are extremely strict, and the Manus believe that all sickness is a punishment by the household spirit for either sexual or economic sins. Margaret and Reo learn to greet the news of an islander's illness not with a question about the nature of the disease but with what spirit is involved.

Manus life, the anthropologists realize, is strict, puritanical and not very creative. The children have shown there is little instinctive religious feeling, and no natural art. There is, in fact, no art at all in Manus culture, no artifacts, none of the great wooden statues and masks and carvings on houses and boats that so distinguish other Pacific tribes. The Manus are culturally barren, though neighboring tribes are superlative artists and create numerous articles of great beauty—war clubs, ceramics and bark cloth among them. Whatever art the

Manus possess comes from trading with other groups. They have much wealth as the result of constantly exchanging with inland tribes, always to their own advantage, trading artifacts back and forth to increase their economic and social standing. Their houses are filled with wooden objects, large slit gongs, carved platform beds, dagger handles, wooden bowls and scoops, human figures of all sizes, and numbers of beautifully made pots obtained from neighboring peoples. Why waste time on something you can get easily in trade? is the Manus attitude. Their food comes from daily fishing and periodic expeditions to onshore villages to get carbohydrate foods.

In the 1920's the traditional currencies of dogs' teeth and shell money, along with pigs as an item of barter on specialized occasions, are still in use; shillings obtained in work for foreigners are valued mostly as a means of getting more dogs' teeth. Dogs' teeth exhibit the same characteristics in the South Pacific islands as gold or silver currency in the rest of the world. The scarcity of dogs (as of gold) gives the currency more value.

The former German administration of New Guinea and the Bismarck Archipelago had come close to destroying the local economies at Manus and elsewhere; the Kaiser's officials had imported dogs' teeth from China and Turkey (where they had had no value at all), causing a rate of inflation of 800 to 1,000 percent. The price for a bride, Mead notes, is now 10,000 dogs' teeth, where 1,000 had been standard before German rule. The Germans had further devalued the dogs' teeth by introducing artificial—counterfeit—teeth made of synthetics, thus causing even more inflation. After this disastrous depression of currency in the German-administered areas, World War I had brought an end to the importation of fake dogs' teeth (and incidentally a crippling inflation in paper money in Germany, which one might have attributed to avenging South Pacific spirits). The

artificial teeth now developed into a valued commodity since
the supply had ceased. A simple lesson in elementary economics.

In the long run, however, all such currency as dogs' teeth,
shells and beads are to lose all value except ceremonially, as
Western monies come to predominate in the area. Many islanders become indentured laborers in order to earn the
hard currency with which to buy the European goods they
are soon persuaded to desire, such as steel knives, saws, mirrors, watches, lanterns, lockboxes, clothing, flashlights, beer,
alcohol, cigarettes and all kinds of trinkets.

The Manus of the 1920's have no strong political system.
There are no chiefs or headmen as in most primitive cultures,
though there is a rough semblance of rank. The men in control are the financial leaders, each of whom is a nucleus for
several lesser men who merely fish and feed their families.
Village political life is based on a complex system of exchanges on an "affinal" (or marriage-related) basis, imperish-
able valuables obtained in other trades being traded again for
food, ceramics, grass skirts and other items of daily use. The
shrewd men among the Manus are able to increase their
wealth in the constant bartering; the less businesslike fail to
advance.

The Manus are a simple, primitive example of the laws
of supply and demand, of the accumulation of property, of
the power of wealth. Every Manus man is constantly
stimulated to increase his holdings; a few succeed but others remain "middle-income" or poor, as in many societies
not only in the West but in more complex parts of Asia
and Africa.

There is much pressure on individuals and their families in
the endless struggle for more wealth. Consequently everyone
is active, and family and business ties are strong. But this
activity, and the power that wealth brings, works best for the

older, successful men. The young men are often quite dependent upon wealthy seniors who underwrite their marriages—always costly—and thus become dominant over the helpless juniors and entangle them in protracted economic exchanges. Only by becoming a ruthless trader himself can a man escape such involvement.

Many younger men leave the islands to work for Europeans, or join the police-boys. An Australian report summed up the precariousness of the situation of the Manus by remarking:

> Never have I met a people so individualistic. . . . Every man is jealous of his property rights and privileges however great or small. [Differences of] wealth and poverty . . . are seldom so apparent as in Manus. It is for this reason that one meets so many Manus men who leave their homes to work for non-natives and who never wish to return. They are the poor, and poverty means no standing in the community and no wife.

Margaret and Reo do not react to the Manus in the same manner. Still carrying memories of his recent stay among the Dobuans, so hostile and dour and involved in their sorcery, suspicious of each other and of neighbors and strangers alike, Reo finds the Manus by comparison open and friendly, though at first he suspects they are holding back information as the Dobuans had. But, in fact, the Manus have no information to keep secret. Mead, after her stay with the easygoing Samoans, sees the Manus as puritanical, materialistic, driven people who are prey to unseen forces eager to punish them for the least transgression or misdemeanor. But their varying views of the people create no problems between them. Instead they have a good-natured rivalry, which the Manus enjoy, in amassing specimens of artifacts, Mead for the Museum of Natural History, Reo for the Sydney Museum.

The work among the Manus takes six months, a short period for a field trip. Mead has often been accused of hasty research by some of her colleagues, but she makes the point in *Growing Up in New Guinea* that in a simple society such as the Manus, the trained investigator can do the necessary work quickly. "The cultural tradition is simple enough to be almost entirely contained within the memory of an average adult member of society. . . . With the immense superiority over the native of being able to record in writing each aspect of the culture as it is learned, the anthropologist is in an excellent position for research within a comparatively short time." She adds that an equally isolated village in a Western land is far more difficult to study than a primitive one, for it would be affected by "echoes and fragments from a hundred different kinds of cultural elaboration." A primitive village of the types she has been studying in the Pacific would have a few basic patterns, but an American town, drawing upon half the world, with numerous types of family structure, religions, ways of bringing up children, of viewing life, of marriage and work, of daily interests, is far more complex, and in effect can offer an infinite field of study for the anthropologist, one that can never be fully completed, for Western life is endlessly changing.

Decades later, Mead, more mature and more experienced, retracts this rather boastful view of her ability to grasp an entire culture, even a simple one, in so short a period. By 1953 she "calculated that it would take some thirty years of continuous observation to document the whole Manus repertoire, and Manus is not a very complex culture."

But the Manus study has been done, wonderfully complete, she believes, in a very short time, the precious notebooks and rolls of film carefully wrapped, the last exchange of tobacco and presents made with the villagers. The Manus consider their departure an act for mourning. The death drums are taken out and their deep mournful rumbling begins. The canoe is loaded, and Margaret and Reo wade through the edge of the surf and climb aboard. Pokanau, who has been Reo's chief informant, makes a farewell speech. The drums beat on.

Off the canoe goes, the drums dying away in the roar of the surf. The Manus have no way of knowing Mead's world; their horizons are limited: Rabaul, the most they know of the outside world, beyond the edge of the sea, and Sydney, a rare dream entered upon by but a few daring men. Mead knows the Manus will never see her book, view her photographs. They are completely illiterate, and they believe that she will be swallowed by the ocean. For her part, she assumes that they are a dying society, to be engulfed by the encroaching shapeless mass of Westernization, to become just another Pacific proletariat, rootless, without power, forgetting the slim culture that sustained them over the unrecorded centuries.

The two anthropologists are soon in civilized Rabaul, their six months of Manus life fading away into a collection of notes and photographic images. At Rabaul Reo leaves his wife to return to the Dobuans for a short period to take pictures for his projected book.

Mead stays in Rabaul with a woman named Phebe Parkinson, the wife of a now-deceased German adventurer named Richard Parkinson, a famous character of the South Pacific. Phebe Parkinson is half-American, half-Samoan, and is a mine of information about local customs and history, as well as current gossip. Phebe tells Mead about the problems of an English anthropologist named Gregory Bateson, who is living alone in the New Guinea jungle making a study of the Baining, an isolated tribe in eastern New Britain.

"Poor Mr. Bateson," says Phebe Parkinson, "didn't eat right and got those terrible tropical ulcers."

Reo returns from the Dobuans, his photographic work completed. Now a conflict arises between Mead and her husband. Even though he has been granted a fellowship at Columbia University, Reo would prefer for both of them to go to New Zealand to live. But since he has no prospects of a job in his own country, he believes that he would have to work as a laborer. Giving up a fellowship in favor of manual work might be romantic, but, Mead writes, it was an idea "that I had enough sense not to undertake."

On the other hand, she worries that life in a land—her own country—where Reo would be a stranger and where she would be well known because of the success of *Coming of Age in Samoa* (which she has learned is doing well) would be uncomfortable for him. Her common sense wins out: It will be New York rather than New Zealand. They board the ship for the long trip to the States.

At San Francisco Mead is operated on for an undisclosed problem—"something [during the operation] went wrong and I almost died," she remarks. She is weak, and the train trip across America is something of a nightmare for her. But in New York her friends tell her what she has learned by letter, that she is a celebrity because of *Coming of Age in Samoa.* The famous author and her unfamous husband take a brownstone on 102nd Street off Broadway in Manhattan, halfway between Columbia, where Reo is to study, and the Museum of Natural History, where Mead is to resume her job.

Coming of Age in Samoa has become a best-seller. With the kind of fortuitous good luck that marks most of her life, young Mead has selected an area and a community where her special talents might go to work. Her own background—the intelligent, academic family, her Grandma Mead's special tu-

toring, her education, strange as it has been, her self-posses-
sion, her ability to adapt to a totally unfamiliar world, one
with strange customs, food, language and housing, with remarkable ease—has helped in the task. If she had selected the
declining native culture of the Tuamotu archipelago, her first
choice, one must doubt that she would have produced so
successful a book, for the exotic background and the frank
reporting of sexual freedom of Samoan teenagers (though her
language is quite proper by today's standards), helped popu-
larize *Coming of Age.* Secondly, because others had already
thoroughly explored the more technical aspects of Samoan
culture, such as language, clan structure and mythology, she
was free to explore the completely overlooked area of the
maturing Samoan woman.

The book is unlike anything published before by a trained
anthropologist. As some reviewers pointed out (and some
academics objected), she brought a novelist's skill and insights
to bear upon her subjects. She was uncommonly gifted in the
art of expressing her observations and ideas in clear and
graphic English, simply and descriptively, with a maximum
of information in a minimum number of words.

Mead remarks later that it is the first such work written by
a serious professional for the educated layman in which no
effort was made to impress one's colleagues in the academic
world. She was not trying to score "theoretical points" over
her fellow professionals, but was arguing for "the future of
young people, who in the United States were becoming less
than they might be because we understood so little about
what a difference a culture can make, in terms of stress and
strains, in individual fulfillment or defeat." The important
people to reach, she says, are not the academics but "teenagers and those just escaped from adolescence, who would
soon be parents determining the shape of the world for their
children."

Coming of Age in Samoa is soon accepted as standard read-ing in the human or "behavioral" sciences, as well as a best-seller, as Americans become more and more conscious of the stresses of modern living upon the young.

Mead's father, who had a book about agricultural econom-ics appear at the same time ("a stimulating contribution" and "a sensible discussion" were typical reviewers' comments), told her she would never again write a book as good as *Com-ing of Age in Samoa*, because "as I grew older and wiser, I would 'know too much,' and the books would inevitably be harder to read. I believed this for a while, until a European psychoanalyst told me that when he read the book he be-lieved it to have been written by a very old lady."

The reviews were mixed, the popular and general publica-tions tending to accept it uncritically, and the academics finding things to complain about, however, without challeng-ing the core of the book itself. "A fascinating view of pagan girlhood . . . keen insight and a thorough knowledge of her subject" were key phrases in the review by H.F.M. in the *Boston Transcript.* "An extraordinarily subtle performance," said an unsigned review in *Bookmaster.* "Frank, with the clean, clear frankness of the scientist, unbiased in its judg-ment, richly readable in its style," said *The New York Times.* Mead's friend Ruth Benedict was unusually busy with re-views, for in *The New Republic* she stated that *Coming of Age in Samoa* was challenging not only to the educator and to the parent of growing children but also to the anthropological student of psychological problems among primitive people, and that "It is a book for which we have been waiting." In the *Journal of Philosophy* Dr. Benedict thought it was an "excel-lent ethnological picture of an alien culture."

The academics were harder. In the *American Anthropolo-gist*, R.H. Lowrie said, "On some points made by Dr. Mead I must frankly avow skepticism. It is hard to believe that all but the youngest boys and girls should fail to use ordinary kinship terms correctly; or, in an absolute way, that Samoan children do not learn to work through learning to play." Even so, Lowrie liked her methods of working and thought other people would soon copy them. The noted anthropologist Robert Redfield was more critical. "For all the intimate association with Samoans the book is somehow disappointing. There are exceedingly interesting pages," he said, "but Miss Mead is interested, one feels, in problems and cases, not in human nature. There is no warmth in her account." Nels Anderson in *Survey* was also critical. "If this is intended to be a work of art, then the 'gay spirit' and Dr. Mead's impressionistic style are in place. If it is science, the book is somewhat of a disappointment. It lacks documental base." And so Mead learns the pleasures of a best-seller and the hazards of having it reviewed by academics.

Whatever the critical reaction, her six months in Polynesia are to have a profound effect upon the thinking of many Americans for much of the twentieth century. She writes some long, specialist scientific articles for the professional journals, but it is the popular version of her experiences that affects the public's thinking, not only about so-called primitive peoples and their cultures, but even certain aspects of American life, for Mead has added two chapters dealing with parallel problems in America to her graphic details of Samoa. The subtitle (not repeated in some of the many editions) is "A Psychological Study of Primitive Youth for Western Civilization." In the library journals it is categorized as "Samoa—Social life and customs. Adolescence. Sex (psychology)."

So far as Samoa is concerned, Mead can answer the question posed by Boas, who sent her on her trip: that of the inevitable storms and stresses of adolescence. They aren't universal but are culturally caused.

What makes growing up in Samoa so easy, so lacking in

stress? Is it the general casualness of Samoan life, despite the formalities of etiquette and custom? No one aims too high (nor too low)—no one shoots a little farther as Mead the Sagittarian does.

Mead notes the lack of deep feeling, of the high emotion that can stand out so strongly in the more highly motivated Americans. A median level is the standard for Samoan culture; the gifted being is held back until the mediocre can catch up, for the Samoans see their lives in terms of all the people rather than of the individual, as is the American ideal.

Mead can also find factors in Samoan society that ensure "nervous stability" among people. From the earliest ages Samoans are firsthand witnesses to birth, sex, pregnancy, death and the decay of the body. No Samoan child feels guilty about witnessing events commonplace in themselves, which are so often kept from the sight of the growing American. In fact, these events are so much a part of daily life that their calm acceptance allows an absence of neurosis, she believes. And adjustment in marriage is rarely difficult because of the intimacies of teenagers when growing up. But it is not merely a free expression in sex that produces the easygoing patterns of Samoan life, but the entire process, which makes no heavy demands on individuals except for those of the royal families, pushes no one to "achieve" whether or not he or she is capable of better effort. There is none of the adolescent storm and stress in Samoa that is so obvious in America.

But why does it happen in America? Her chapters about her own country tackle the very point that Boas had raised. Mead wants to make the difference clear, and draws simple parallels between the two societies; since *Coming of Age in Samoa* there have been many analyses of what has gone wrong with the American psyche, but what is interesting is that Mead put the problem into perspective so graphically in 1928, in terms that read as if written today.

In America, with its numerous standards and choices, adults strive desperately to bind their own children to courses which they themselves have chosen. The child may often resort to "devious and non-reputable means" to escape beliefs, practices, courses of action that have been pressed upon him or her.

In our ideal picture of the freedom of the individual and the dignity of human relations, it is not pleasant to realise that we have developed a form of family organisation which often cripples the emotional life, and warps and confuses the growth of many individuals' power to consciously live their own lives.

America, she admits, is in a period of transition. Nevertheless

we pay heavily for our heterogeneous, rapidly changing civilisation; we pay in high proportions of crime and delinquency, we pay in the conflicts of youth, we pay in an ever-increasing number of neuroses, we pay in the lack of a coherent tradition without which the development of art is sadly handicapped.

In the end, what Mead asks for, in the light of the many gains we have made, and can make, is freedom for individual choice and universal toleration which a heterogeneous culture, not a single, simple society like Samoa, alone can attain. Since America has the knowledge of many ways, she asks, why not leave our children free to choose among them?

It was this openness in talking to American adults, as much as her descriptions of the amatory intrigues of Samoan adolescents, that made *Coming of Age in Samoa* such a popular, controversial work, and gave it the long life it has enjoyed. New editions, in hardcover and paperback, continue to appear. It has been translated into many languages, studied in thousands of classrooms and read by many hundreds of thousands of people, including the children and grandchildren of her Samoans, curious about the ways in which their mothers and aunts and grandparents grew up on Tau.

While *Coming of Age in Samoa* is gaining fame and sales, Mead immerses herself in her other projects. Always a person of endless energy, she handles a full-time job at the American Museum of Natural History as Assistant Curator for Ethnology, and finishes the manuscript of her book about the Manus, working very quickly and easily. The entire process of publication, from writing to typesetting and production, requires barely more than a year from the time she and Reo return to New York, and the book appears in the fall of 1930. As a concession to popular ignorance, she calls the work *Growing Up in New Guinea*, for she suspects that few people would be knowledgeable enough to be attracted to a title that included the obscure name of Manus or of the Admiralty Islands. Reo, however, does not work so fiercely as his wife. He is still struggling with his book about the sorcerers of Dobu, and has not yet touched his massive pile of notes about the Manus.

Mead is almost compulsive about getting her fieldwork into print quickly. She complains how often anthropologists, including the most famous, let their material accumulate, eventually reaching the point where they are overwhelmed by notes that never get transcribed, much less published. She has realized from the beginning of her studies that fieldwork is useless unless the results can be placed before some kind of an audience.

The Manus book, effortlessly written, and like *Coming of Age in Samoa* almost novelistic in approach, is one of her better works. (Isidor Schneider, writing in *The New Republic*, commented that it is "an even more interesting book than Miss Mead's widely and deservedly praised *Coming of Age in Samoa*.") Mead is quite conscious of the work's narrative qualities and the fact that it avoided academic jargon. In an appendix, she stated that it seemed "advisable to couch . . . the language . . . outside the realm of controversy—in the field of the novelist—in order that it may be intelligible when some of the present dialectic points and their terminology have been outmoded. Such a course has the additional advantage of making the material more accessible to students from other fields."

Her Manus are not the easygoing, uncomplicated islanders that the Samoans are, but people very much like Americans, hard-driving, success-oriented, somewhat puritanical in their outlook, especially in sexual matters, and conscious of wealth and its uses. In contrast to many cultures in which peoples work and live cooperatively as clans or tribes, among the Manus it is the individual who is important, whose aggrandizement of wealth and power takes precedence to loyalty and the social well-being of the village or tribal group.

Throughout the book she can connect the Manus to Americans. It might be argued that not all Americans are as she sees them, but her strictures do have a broad relevance. She finds that both Manus and American children grow up untrammelled, with little respect for elders, custom and the niceties of life, spoiled beyond measure and at times even feared by their parents. Both grow up without responsibilities, thanks to the labor of those who make these long years of play possible, but who receive abuse rather than thanks from their children. In both cultures the business of making a living is more important than the conduct of life as an art. The ideal Manus man has no time for play; he is always up early doubling his strings of shell beads and dogs' teeth.

Today her comparison of Manus and Americans seems as if she had written it recently instead of half a century ago. The narrow-minded parents of the 1920's and the somewhat rebellious young she describes in her summary chapters that deal primarily with America are still with us, except that yesterday's rebels are now today's narrow-minded grandparents. The generation gap is wide, she feels, and children and parents are worlds apart. Manus children, she says, and American children are as a rule very lightly disciplined and taught very little respect for their elders. Neither society instills respect for age or knowledge, courtesy or kindness for elders. Neither teaches the children to work (as the Samoans do).

Our children are given years of cultural non-participation in which they are permitted to live in a world of their own. They are allowed to say what they like, when they like, how they like, to ignore many of the conventions of their adults.

The American emphasis on the latest fads, the newest gadgets and most of all upon money as the basic standard produce

a society very much like the Manus, an efficient, well-equipped, active society in which wealth is the only goal, and what a man has is substituted for what he is.

People are pigeonholed by what they have, and the pigeonholes are "very dull ones, houses, automobiles, clothes, all turned out wholesale." The individual himself, as a person, is not considered.

> Wealth is separable from age, from sex, from wit or beauty, from manners or morals. Once it becomes valued as a way of life, there is no respect for those things which must be learned, must be experienced to be understood. . . . In Manus as in America, life is not viewed as an art which is learned, but in terms of things which can be acquired. Those who have acquired them can command those who have not.

The indictment continues in detail. Mead wants Americans (she offers no cure for the Manus) to shift their values from having to being. The core of the problem lies with the elders, who of course have been conditioned by their elders; the youth will perpetuate the problem; "they [will] take over the adult life sullenly, with dull resentment." She is not optimistic in this book, though she becomes so in others, particularly when she is one of the elders. But now

> To treat our children as the Manus do, permit them to grow up as the lords of an empty creation, despising the adults who slave for them so devotedly, and then apply the whip of shame to make them fall in line with a course of life which they have never been taught to see as noble or dignified—this is giving a stone to those who have a right to good bread.

Her discoveries about the similarities between Manus and America receive a mixed reception. Isidor Schneider (of *The New Republic*) remarks that "If the book had appeared as a modern *Gulliver's Travels*, the description of Manus society would have sounded like a bitter satire on American life." In the *New York World* Harry Hansen writes, "Some of Miss Mead's criticism is superficial, but much of it goes deep. Miss Mead senses the holes in our culture, the deficiencies in our individual life." Ruth Benedict, writing for *Books*, gives an uncritical summary, perhaps because she was disappointed yet did not want to hurt her close friend. "The book is non-technical and easy to read," she says, and points out that the research was done mostly in the native language.

The academic views are far more critical. A typical one is by Nels Anderson, in the little-known *Survey*, who prefers her facts to her opinions.

> Dr. Mead is strongest in this study when she is presenting her anthropological data. To me she is most interesting and informing when she stays with the concrete materials, with what they do and say in Manus. Just so, she is least convincing when she essays her educational comparisons. The final three chapters put her in the position of the man who tells a story and then bores us with explaining the point which was obvious all the while. These many references to the American father, what he does do and what he does not do, are neither wholly true nor wholly false.

But in the end, Mead's perceptions carry the book. In style and content, *Growing Up in New Guinea* stands on a level with *Coming of Age in Samoa*. Both books have helped her state her views on America. One feels in reading both, and thinking about her analyses of American life and culture, that she is not quite sure what she wants for her own country, for she is comparing the most highly evolved, technological society ever developed with two extremely simple, primitive, almost archaic, worlds. She can admire the informality and freedom of the Samoan teenager, with untrammelled sexual expression and the lack of guilt, though the adults conform to a strict hierarchy of social values, and lament the chaotic, materialistic Manus village so guilt-ridden because of its dependence on unseen ghosts and spirits. One senses that she would like to get America pinned down to a six-month study that can be neatly and deftly summarized in a third work. But this can never happen, because throughout her analyses of what is wrong with her country is the realization that it encompasses the complexity of ten thousand, a hundred thousand primitive societies and this very complexity almost defies definition.

While Mead is finishing her book on the Manus, the success of her *Coming of Age in Samoa* brings conflicts in her relations with Reo, still wrestling with the Dobuan magicians. They read each other's works at night—Mead is also involved in articles about the Manus—and each appreciates and criticizes what the other has done, but aside from this regular exhibition of professionalism, their household is "rather tempestuous." Each day with Reo seems like a battle.

At first the couple have no money, and only Mead has a job, a mere $2,500 a year, which is soon reduced because of the depression the nation is experiencing. Reo, with his fellowship at Columbia, earns nothing at all, and this adds to the tension. Then, the difficulties of a cross-national marriage—between a New Zealander, accustomed to a society where men usually have the say, and an American woman, accustomed to speaking out—increase the strain. "In addition," she says, "Reo did not like to see me doing the housework, which he did not intend to help me with"—because that was something New Zealand men did not do—"yet he felt it was a reproach to him that I had to do it at all"—because as head of the household he should have earned enough money for a servant. Despite their apparent community of interests, Margaret and Reo are still cultures and worlds apart.

The difference in cultures is a fact that Mead can observe scientifically as an anthropologist, though as a woman and working wife this insight does little to spare the pains. Reo carries with him the British-influenced background in which the man is dominant in most things and makes the major decisions. But she has grown up in the freer American world where the woman (above all in the Mead household) has a greater part than that and stands on an equal footing, especially intellectually. But she is attuned to the situation and Reo is not. In 1973, in *Blackberry Winter*, she writes:

I fully realized that it was essential to respect the sensitivities of men reared in other social settings and other cultures, and that their sense of masculinity could be impaired by being asked to behave in ways they had been taught to regard as feminine. I also had a great respect for temperament, and I was resigned to having my friends display varying degrees of neuroticism which I felt was compensated for by their unusual gifts.

But I thought then—as I do now—that if we are to have a world in which women work beside men, a world in which both men and women can contribute their best, women must learn to give up pandering to male sensitivities, something at which they succeeded so well as long as it was a woman's primary role, as a wife, to keep her family intact or, as a mistress, to comfort her lover. Because of their age-long training in human relations— for that is what feminine intuition really is—women have a special contribution to make to any group enterprise, and I feel it is up to them to contribute the kinds of awareness that relatively few men—except, for example, child analysts or men who have been intimately reared by women—have incorporated through their education. And so, when Reo thought or spoke or wrote well, I was perhaps his most appreciative audience, but I did not applaud where I felt applause was not due; I criticized in situations in which I thought improvement was possible, and I was silent when I believed nothing could be done.

What seems sensible to Mead becomes a slight to Fortune. She suggests that he take a small but sunny room in the back of the apartment in which to write. He sees this as an effort to shut him out of the living room. She must not only put in a full day at the office but shop for food, cook and clean. When she returns home every evening, her arms full of bundles, to find the living room covered with Reo's papers day after day, "and without a place to rest the eye," it is, she says, "one more penalty for being a female than I could bear."

To increase the tension, *Coming of Age in Samoa* is now earning considerable royalties. Reo, deeply involved in his *Sorcerers of Dobu* (the book does not appear until 1932), has yet to see anything published. Mead puts her money safely in a small-town bank in Doylestown, Pennsylvania, while Reo loses his in a New York bank that fails.

The depression gets worse. Breadlines are everywhere, the land is blowing away (it is the time of the Dust Bowl), dispossessing farmers—the Okies wander about the southwest in search of new land—and there is much social unrest everywhere. Mead's father, basing his predictions on the falling price of gold, in the past an infallible guide, states that within ten years a world war will break out.

The tensions at home are broken by an unexpected field

trip. In the spring of 1930 they are offered the opportunity to make a short expedition within the United States to study an Indian culture. The Museum will give Mead $750—a pitifully small grant—if she will study American Indian women: Men in all the Indian tribes from the Pacific to the Atlantic have been thoroughly researched, but women have been ignored.

Mead is not interested.

Ruth Benedict says that if she and Reo will agree to go to Nebraska to visit the Omaha reservation, where the remnants of a once-great tribe are languishing in poverty and illness, Columbia will give him a grant as well.

Nervously, in a Ford car, Margaret and Reo set out across the country. She will study the changing role of the Indian reservation woman; he will try to determine the role of tribal lore in the visions young Indians are expected to experience. It is a subject about which some broad generalizations have been made by other investigators. In general, anthropologists have assumed, not realizing the Omaha do not fit the pattern, that every Plains Indian male is free to seek a vision and claim the power it gives him; this vision gives the man his full standing in the tribe and is his right. But this practice is not actually followed by the Omaha. From the start Reo feels that he is expected to confirm assumptions by no means proved, and that if he finds otherwise he will be considered a failure. He is certain that American scholars, interested in nothing but their own "primitive" peoples, force their research to fit preconceived theories and will not accept variant results.

With this psychological block hanging over him, Reo, with Margaret, arrives at the Omaha reservation.

Heat, frightful heat.

They settle down in a frame house. The nights are so hot they can barely get to sleep before two in the morning.

Mead hires an Indian girl as a servant; the girl is from one of the more traditional families. It is an unusual situation, for such girls do not ordinarily work as servants, but, because Mead is considered by the girl's parents to be a kind of chaperone and is trusted, she is able to gain valuable insights into Indian family life and to make friends with Indian women of various backgrounds, who serve as informants, and give her much information in the way of gossip and chatter.

Margaret has an easier time of it than Reo, who works with the men. Writing to Ruth Benedict at home, she explains the situation.

> This is a very discouraging job, ethnologically speaking. You find a man whose father or uncle had a vision. You go see him four times, driving eight or ten miles with an interpreter. The first time he isn't home, the second time he's drunk, the next time his wife's sick, and the fourth time, on the advice of the interpreter, you start the interview with a $5 bill, for which he offers thanks to Wakanda, prays Wakanda to give *him* a long life, and proceeds to lie steadily for four hours.

And, she adds, "There is a belief that death follows divulging sacred things."

Other problems Margaret and Reo face are even more discouraging. The reservation is demoralized. Once one of the great tribes of the Mississippi valley, the Omaha, a branch of the southern Sioux, have seen their lands shrink to a fraction of their former size, their hunting grounds taken by whites, the wild creatures of the forest—their food—destroyed by the advance of the settlers, their tribal structures crushed. The Omaha are in a despondent state. Their religion, once centered on visions, has become pessimistic, focused on illness and death. It is, Reo notes, a society in a "deep, very real, emotional maelstrom," due to the impact of white influence. "Feeling and thinking are still curiously of the old [tribal] quality, and action only has suffered a very considerable transmutation from the influence of White contact." The Omaha, he says, show "distinctly as dissociated personalities"—in effect their personalities were being split between two unrelated, contradictory cultures, their minds and emotions moulded by their own culture, while "their hands and feet are compelled to . . . keep their bodies [free] from hunger and privation not exactly moulded, but hewn and battered into some apology of shape by a radically differing culture."

Broken homes, neglected children and general social disorganization are evident everywhere; Mead adds: "Drunkenness was rife."

Beside the conflict of cultural forces, the tribe is traditionally formed of two distinct sections, the members of secret societies and those who are not members. The societies include the Buffalo, the Ghost, the Grizzly Bear, the Rattlesnake, the Water Monster, and the Midewiwin. Also there are the Thunder Bird, and Night Blessed or Potlatch societies.

The most powerful men in the tribe are those known as doctors, who are especially feared by other Omaha. Doctors possess a quality called batho^n, which is translated as "odor," a form of influence. Batho^n could be called good or bad: It might cause disease, or it might cure it. In general, one stays upwind from a doctor because one might be affected by his batho^n.

The doctors practice shamanistic tricks to prove their power and prestige. The uninitiated regard the tricks as miraculous. Still, there is a strong element of belief even among the doctors. Each doctor carries hidden in his clothing a sacred amulet, called an "arrow," which is seen in the form of its symbol or representative, a terrapin, worm, lizard, snake or insect. The arrow is passed from one generation to another.

Without the arrow the doctor dies; to dispose of it is to commit suicide.

Reo, in his graphic but twisted sentences, gives a clear instance of both the power of the arrow, and of the tragedy of drunkenness, when he describes how a drunken medicine man takes his arrow—the symbol of his secret powers, of his very life forces—from its place of concealment.

The Omaha, when sober, often regard a drunken Omaha with an evident feeling of sheer physical repulsion almost akin to horror; quite evidently a more vivid feeling than I have, as I found when I put a drunken Indian beside sober Indians in the back seat of a car. At no time is this generalised horror raised to a greater height than where a rolling drunk leader of the Water Monster Society does what his companions regard as a possibly suicidal action. I never saw it, as it is very rare, but I heard two or three stories told me by initiates, of a leading doctor's taking his sacred arrow from his body when he was dead drunk; and the feeling about the sight of the action was still evident.

The work is more difficult for Reo than for Margaret, who gathers a great amount of material—gossip is the way in which it comes out—from the women. Reo must struggle for his material.

The actual facts are not easily drawn from any Omaha. A similar difficulty is encountered if one attempts to discover whether an Omaha ever obtains a subsequent return present for any gift that he gives away. He does very often, far more often than not. But no Omaha will admit the bare possibility, except perhaps under the rack. Fortunately for my work on the secret societies I had some informants literally under the rack of extreme privation and want, so I was able to penetrate into secrets that are not usually admitted.

Obtaining information under pressure from men who are on the edge of starvation may not seem a fair way of following one's profession, but Reo can show that among the Omaha, in contrast to other tribes—as far as what is known or surmised about them at any rate—membership in the secret religious societies stems from hereditary right only, membership being passed down from one generation to another, from father to son, uncle to nephew, even from grandmother to grandson. The solitary vision alone can not lead to membership. Only those with hereditary privileges can profit by a vision, normally encountered while a youth, under specific, trying, isolated conditions. The man outside secret societal structures, no matter how great his vision, can never participate in the societies. Nonmembers who claim visions were told they were liars. This discovery, so important in the comprehension of a vanishing style of life, is to be ignored by Reo's colleagues.

The task is finished at last. Work that should have taken years, perhaps even a lifetime, has been skimped into three frantic months. Both Margaret and Reo feel a sense of failure, though they have done outstanding work within the allotted time. Each will do a book about the work. Mead's is entitled *The Changing Culture of an Indian Tribe,* Reo's is called *Omaha Secret Societies.* Without the precedent of Samoa and New Guinea towering over her other work, Mead's book about Indian women would, alone, have helped make her career; now, overshadowed by her better Samoan and Manus works, it is virtually ignored.

Because of their distinctive personalities and their individual methods of working and of viewing the subject, the anthropologists' books seem like reports of two separate, unrelated tribes. Reo speaks specifically about the Omaha, and gives a clear portrayal of a society with definite characteristics. Mead calls them the Antler tribe, and, as she often does, also disguises the names and some of the case histories; her "Antler" women seem to be floating in space: They could be Mohawks or Navaho, or, as one critic remarked, even suburban white housewives.

Reo's book, *Omaha Secret Societies,* brooding, wry, joking, apologetic, by a mind that seems at home in its field but alienated in its career, is one of those oddities one might encounter in any discipline, a work so strange, moving and unusual that it cannot be categorized, and thus is set aside by the more formalistic members of the field. "I have not been excessively tender in my handling of the previous authorities," Reo remarks of the anthropological establishment, and they take the same attitude toward him. Mead can add sadly, to the account of his troubles, "This situation was so unusual, as Ruth [Benedict] had sensed, that Reo's analysis did go unrewarded. Americanists did not appreciate the detective skill, developed in his work with the Melanesian sorcerers, with which Reo had unraveled an unfamiliar fabric. . . . He is given very little [credit] for *Omaha Secret Societies*, the book in which he published the work he had the greatest difficulty in doing."

Omaha Secret Societies appears in 1932—both Reo and Margaret were again in New Guinea at the time—and the same year sees the publication of his *Sorcerers of Dobu.* Again, he does not make concessions to the public, whether the ordinary reader or the academic. His works are difficult to read at times, and express complicated theories that challenge established conceptions, or misconceptions. As with the Omaha Indians, Reo has worked with a people who do not fit the accepted anthropological patterns, and the experts are puzzled. The Dobuan forms of magic are different from those of other tribes. Their family structure, their gardens (which are planted with the aid of magic, and prosper by magic, or falter from black magic practiced by enemies), their kinship system, nomenclature, cross-cousin relationships (a favorite subject among anthropologists, who like to know who is considered a member of the complex clan structures and who is an outsider)—virtually everything is at variance with what others have found or assumed.

So *Sorcerers of Dobu* is famous but unread, and even ignored. The public finds its subject interesting on the surface—for magic and sorcery are popular topics—but difficult to understand because of the depth of its anthropological research; the professionals find that it goes against the grain of accepted knowledge about primitive peoples, and the reviewers either are puzzled or take a neutral stand. Only Ruth Benedict can be overwhelmingly positive about it. Her review points out that though *Sorcerers of Dobu* is "no travel book . . . for strangeness and intimacy, it surpasses any travel book." And she confirms that it is "a piece of serious ethnological research." In England, the London *Times* finds it "a very clever piece of work," and J.H. Driberg, in the *Spectator*, calls the narrative "lucid, nervous and dramatic," believing it should have a wider audience than mere academics. A former teacher of Reo's, A.C. Haddon, praises the book but is curiously unable to explain its merits, which seem to be beyond him. The anthropologist Hortense Powdermaker tempers her review by pointing out how short a time Reo was with the Dobu.

After the praise heaped upon his wife's books, Reo must feel like a real second fiddle.

There is a minor consolation, if Reo ever enjoys such ironies: Despite his wife's determination to remain "Miss Mead," the reviewers, the journals and the cataloguers of his books list her as "Mrs. Reo F. Fortune."

Small reward.

Whether Miss Mead or Mrs. Fortune, Mead has long been aware that she probably cannot have children. The doctors have told her on several occasions that she has a tipped uterus, and conceiving and bearing a child is not likely, yet she can continually hope for one. However, she should plan her life differently from what it would be if she were a mother, or might easily become one. Her youthful fantasy of being the mother of six in the Reverend Cressman's drafty rectory had long ago vanished. Nevertheless her initial reluctance to marry Reo Fortune came, she says in *Blackberry Winter*, because she thought that he would "not make the kind of a father I wanted for my children," and again, "I did not think Reo . . . would make an ideal father"—if she should ever conceive. Her reason was, simply, "He was too demanding and jealous of my attention." But now she suspects that her future life with Reo will be only one of shared fieldwork and intellectual collaboration.

Her long preoccupation with the human personality and the effects a culture has upon its development is to be her primary subject. She wants to concentrate on the ways in which cultures pattern the behavior of males and females. If a boy and a girl develop different personalities by maturity, she wonders, is it because of their cultural background, or because of their biological differences, or both? Are there broad universal norms that apply to all males, to all females? These interesting and important questions have not yet been fully investigated. Mead wants to develop data in the field upon which basic theories may be projected. But where can the work be done?

Margaret and Reo consider the Navaho as a field subject, for unlike the Omaha, their culture is still alive and intact and not destroyed by the disappearance of hunting grounds. But the Navaho "belong" to Gladys Reichard and Pliny Goddard. One does not intrude upon another anthropologist's subject, no matter how great the temptation. It is a question of professional courtesy. How Reichard's and Goddard's Navaho feel is an unasked question: They probably do not know that they are "owned." So Margaret and Reo must abandon the idea of working among the Navaho, though she complains that she can do better work among them than her colleagues can.

With the Navaho ruled out, Margaret and Reo turn to an area in which they have already had some experience. It is New Guinea, with its hundreds of small and widely differing societies. Financed by royalties from *Coming of Age in Samoa* and grants from both Columbia and the American Museum of Natural History, they will study somewhere on the main island of New Guinea.

They narrow down their choice to a people known as the Arapesh who live on the New Guinea plains, about a two days' walk inland from the northeast coast of the island. The term Arapesh is the tribe's own name for human being.

In the late fall of 1931, Mead and her husband go by ship through the Panama Canal and across to New Zealand, and then to Sydney, and on to New Guinea. After a series of small, difficult journeys from one small port in New Guinea to another, they go partly up the Sepik, the main river in the area, and one on which dozens of different tribes are located. While Mead stays with a local planter, Reo goes inland to scout about and to try to round up carriers for their tons of supplies, for now, instead of the suitcase with the five dresses, the Kodak, the typewriter and the notebooks of her first trip, Mead (and Reo) will work on such a grand scale that 250 carriers are needed.

The local people have enough trade goods—knives, blankets, kettles—and are difficult to persuade to work. "They don't like carrying," she notes. She writes home, about her husband's first efforts to get porters, "Reo was pretty hopeless at first." However, Reo has his own methods of getting unruly natives to do what they do not want to do. "He went about from one village to another, unearthed their darkest secrets which they wished kept from the government, and then ordered them to come and carry."

Eventually the necessary 250 carriers are found and bullied. It requires three days to get the supplies and equipment from the tiny port town of Wewak on the coast to the plantation where Mead is resting, and two more days to carry everything from there halfway up the mountain to a hamlet called Alitoa, the site of a small, rather dreary tribe Mead labels the Mountain Arapesh, for want of a better name. The people on the coast, also an Arapesh tribe, had been noted as a gay, sophisticated group, the source of trade items and gadgets as well as of information. The Plains Arapesh are famed for a high material culture and their practice of sorcery, which makes them much feared. The Mountain Arapesh, however, are a much despised group and live in fear of the sorcerers on the plains above.

Having brought the supplies halfway up the mountainside, Reo returns for his wife, who, having sprained an ankle, must be carried in a litter along difficult, rain-soaked trails. Mead arrives safely at Alitoa. Now trouble strikes. The bearers refuse to go farther, fearing the sorcerers above, and run away. Men from other mountain tribes will not carry either. Margaret and Reo can neither continue to the plains, nor can they return to the coast. It is a desperate situation. The only choice is to make the most of it. They will work among the Mountain Arapesh, a group, Reo says, who "haven't any culture worth speaking of." He soon adds to this negative view by saying that the Moun-

An Arapesh plains sorcerer. The plains sorcerers blackmail Arapesh on the mountainsides and the coast with threats of death by sorcery (a very real threat in primitive New Guinea, where people can die for inexplicable reasons), demanding pigs, knives, rings, axes, and other trade goods. A sorcerer will not wash when practicing his magic.

tain Arapesh—the people and the culture alike—are "form-less, unattractive and thoroughly uncongenial."

They live in a native house for a week while the Arapesh build them one of their own, a huge building with a central room, bedroom, storage room, wide verandah and separate cookhouse. Reo had promised the Arapesh that they would have all the matches and salt they wanted. (Salt is the chief form of currency.) The house has cost the equivalent of $10 and is run by six young boys, called "monkeys," who do all the jobs; one of them is the shoot-boy, whose main task is to keep the kitchen supplied with pigeons.

The language is difficult to learn; the Arapesh are dispirited and have a habit of disappearing from the village, so there are long hours with nothing to do, and few ceremonies to observe and record. The culture, Mead remarks, "taxed all my now well-developed field skills to make anything of it." Unlike the relaxed life of the Coastal Arapesh, with their sixty-foot-long houses, their well-tended gardens and their extensive fishing grounds in the swamps, the Mountain Arapesh live precari-ously: Their houses are but huts, the clusters of people small, the land barren; the tribe must fish in streams. Their gardens hug the mountainsides, and this year the yam crop, one of the chief staples, is smaller than usual; the pigs, a basis of food and wealth alike, are mean and savage. The people are aware of their inferiority to the other Arapesh, and rely on them for crafts and arts. They are overseen by certain spirits, the *mar-salais*, spirits of rain, living in sanctified spots in the company of the ghosts of the dead.

Reo is driven to fury by the Arapesh, and on several occa-sions Mead must prevent him from striking one of them. Her relationship with Reo, she remarks, is again "tempestuous." But she is able to make her notes and to observe cultural differences between men and women. Yet in the end she has to conclude, "Among the Arapesh there was so little difference in the culturally expected character of men and women that I felt nothing new had been discovered." The rough edges of the culture have been rounded off—it has "soft, uncertain outlines."

However, the Arapesh do exhibit one very unusual cultural variation. An aggressor in the Arapesh culture, unlike an aggressor in virtually all other cultures, is not punished but rather his victim is blamed for having moved him to anger and violence. Unlike many primitive and advanced societies, Arapesh society does not approve of aggressive behavior in whatever form. The small, ineffectual Arapesh group is concerned primarily with the harmonious growth of living things, whether human or plant. Men are as wholly committed to this cherishing adventure as are women. She writes of the Arapesh aim for the good growth of children and of the food upon which they depend, "It may be said that the rôle of men, like the rôle of women, is maternal."

Getting even the basic material is difficult work. Mead and her husband must share a single, knowledgeable informant. When they question the people, the Arapesh complain they get headaches from having to concentrate for more than ten minutes. Still, the work is more valuable than she believes at the time.

Frustrations pile up. "I felt somehow finished," she says. She falls into a depression. Reo is away much of the time on visits to other villages. She sits alone, in this strange hamlet where the men and women fear that each generation will be progressively smaller until there are no more Arapesh, and looks out from the mountainside. The mists hide the view, and she can see only a few great leaves of pawpaw trees in the engulfing clouds. "I felt that everything ahead looked pallid and uninviting." And: "I was thirty."

The depression vanishes. Carriers are found, and they descend to the coast, to spend six weeks in recuperation. While they rest, they recall a report in *Oceania* by Gregory Bateson about the Iatmul, a tribe on the Sepik River. The Iatmul seem exciting, creative, alive. A challenge. Margaret and Reo decide that the Sepik will be the next area for study, where Bateson is now on his third trip among the Iatmul.

Immediately they have second thoughts. Much as they would like to study the Iatmul, Bateson "owns" them: They are "his." "In those days the ethics of field work were very strict," Mead laments. Another tribe must be chosen, and so they turn to the Mundugumor, neighbors of the Iatmul but culturally different.

Like the Mountain Arapesh, the Mundugumor prove to be a "disappointing choice." They are fierce cannibals who live on the high ground of a tributary of the Sepik. They have recently been put down—crushed—by the Australian administration; their ties with the past having been destroyed, the Mundugumor are now in a kind of cultural paralysis. Ceremonial life, one of the central objects of ethnological study, has ended.

The mosquitoes are frightful. In fact, mosquitoes are a constant theme in Mundugumor legend and myth, knowledge easy to enjoy at a distance but impossible to endure in the flesh. Hard and unrewarding work is Mead's verdict about this cruel, harsh people, who themselves know that their culture has been lost.

She soon loathes the tribe, for its people have endless numbers of aggressive rivalries. There is no warmth among the Mundugumor. The preferred cultural type, whether male or female, is not a warm and cherishing person but a fiercely possessive individual. Children are exploited and rejected. Unwanted babies are thrown into the river. Anger and aggressive acts are the standard, and suicide is common, often taking an odd form: A person bent on self-destruction would get into a temper tantrum and drift downriver in a canoe, to be captured and eaten by another tribe.

"I felt completely stalemated," she writes. To make matters worse, her tempestuous relationship with Reo takes a bad turn professionally. In his work on the kinship system—a basic part of anthropological research—Reo "had missed a clue." Mead points out her husband's error. It is a tense situation. She can now equate Reo to the Mundugumor. "They struck some note in him that was thoroughly alien to me, and working with them emphasized aspects of his personality with which I could not empathize."

She complains of her husband's harsh treatment of her during illnesses. She has had many bouts of fever. He has treated his own fevers by climbing a mountain to force the illness out of his system. "He turned on me the same fierceness with which he treated his own fevers." She gets no sympathy due to his unrelenting attitudes.

"A very unpleasant three months" is her summing up. They finish their work shortly before Christmastime, 1932. A government launch picks them up and they chug downstream along the Yuat to the swift-flowing Sepik, where they go upriver toward the government station at Ambunti where they will celebrate the holiday. The Iatmul, Mead soon notes, as she and Reo pass by the magnificent villages with their great dwelling houses decorated with rattan faces woven into the gables and the immense double-peaked men's houses in the central plazas, are "a culture we would have liked to study." On the way they are to pass Kankanamun, one of the Iatmul villages where Bateson is working. The chance meeting with the rangy young Englishman will affect her as much as any of the chance visits to remote villages in her fieldwork.

The Bateson Era

GREGORY BATESON HAS BEEN WORKING in New Guinea since 1927; in 1929 he had made a brief visit to the Sepik River area and become interested in the Iatmul, one of the more outstanding tribes; the following year he returned to spend six months at a major Iatmul village called Mindimbit, where he studied a ceremonial custom called *naven.* The naven ceremony is performed by kinsmen to celebrate various accomplishments of a child. The child—usually male, and usually initiated in groups—may be very young; there is much cruelty involved—scarring the skin with knives, and forcing the drinking of putrid water, and so on, along with attempts to frighten the subject with ghostly sounds and strange noises at night or in the depths of the initiation house. Though the rites can be performed in several ways, the principal form usually involves transvestism, the men dressing as women and the women as men. Bateson sees naven as the core of Iatmul life, and he has returned to the Sepik in 1932, to continue his work at one of the largest of Iatmul villages, Kankananum, about two hundred miles from the seacoast.

Bateson is living in a ramshackle house, in which, despite the mosquitoes and other predatory insects, he has left an opening in the roof for his cat and for a tree. It has been a

117

lonely and depressing time for him. He is not sure of his work.
Many of his observations are quite tentative, for he is aware
that he cannot see everything among these active, creative,
aggressive people. He is not certain that basing an interpretation of Iatmul society on naven is correct. He is to say: "My
field work was scrappy and disconnected—perhaps more so
than other anthropologists'." He believes his work is hampered not by a lack of training but by "an excess of skepticism."

The Iatmul, one of the most powerful tribes of the Sepik,
are warriors and artists. The naven ceremony is an important
stage in an individual's attaining maturity. A major example
of the kind of event that leads to a naven celebration is a
killing, or helping others in a killing. No man is respected
unless he has killed someone—a woman is as satisfactory a
victim as another man. Lesser examples worthy of naven are
the slaying of a crocodile or a wild pig, spearing a giant eel,
even killing a small animal, or planting yams, tobacco, taro,
and so on, or making certain objects, like spear-throwers or
digging sticks. Naven, Bateson learns, is not only a serious rite
in a person's life but it can also offer comic relief in satire and
jokes, the mocking of ritual acts or of sexual intercourse.
Whatever happens is due to sorcery, and much takes place
under the shadow of an intangible factor called *ngglambi*,
which Bateson explains as follows:

> It is thought of as a dark cloud which envelops a man's
> house when he has committed some outrage. This cloud
> can be seen by certain specialists who, when they are
> consulted as to the cause of some illness or disaster, rub
> their eyes with the white undersides of the leaves of a
> tree, and are then able to see the dark cloud hovering
> over the house of the person whose guilt is responsible
> for the sickness. Other specialists are able to smell

ngglambi and say that it has a "smell of death—like a dead snake."

But at the same time the Iatmul, when it suits them, can take a lighter view of sorcery, even though it causes death, for they do not share the almost paranoid view of it so characteristic of many primitive peoples, such as the Dobuans or the Mountain Arapesh.

Bateson's grand opus dealing with the Iatmul (published in 1936) shows his worrisome approach by its title. It is called *Naven: A Survey of the Problems Suggested by a Composite Picture of a New Guinea Tribe Drawn from Three Points of View*, as if he could not surmount the material he had uncovered but had to "survey" it without coming to grips with its meaning and implications. He assembles all sorts of odd facts, trying to fit them into a grand jigsaw puzzle of what naven signifies.

His reference to the significance of the nose among the Iatmul illustrates his predicament. He is attracted by the emphasis placed upon this otherwise minor characteristic. The long nose is especially admired; it is a sign of beauty in both men and women. The discovery of the nose emerges slowly, for in his tentativeness in probing the ways of the Iatmul, Bateson is not sure of its importance. "When an informant told me that Woli-ndambwi had a big nose, I wrote his statement down, but with no idea that this detail of the culture might be of any particular interest."

As artists as well as warriors, the Iatmul are famous for their ceremonial houses, some as long as 120 feet. "Magnificent buildings," remarks Bateson. The houses resemble churches superficially, but there is no true parallel, because

Where we think of a church as sacred and cool, they think of a ceremonial house as "hot", imbued with heat by the violence and killing which were necessary for its building and consecration.

"Hot" is the general characteristic of Bateson's Iatmul as for Reo's Dobuans.

[In the initiation ceremonies] a boy is disciplined so that he may be able to wield authority, so on the Sepik he is subjected to irresponsible bullying and ignominy so that he becomes what we should describe as an over-compensating, harsh man—whom the natives describe as a "hot" man.

The Iatmul fall into two general personality types, according to sex: the harsh, egocentric, bullying males, tense in virtually all situations, and the lighthearted, relaxed and self-confident women, who, though subservient to the more powerful men, are still fully developed individuals, leading lives of psychic joys and pleasures the men resent. Often the men are fearful in dealing with the women, for the women will mock them when the men have made a mistake in a chant or a ritual. The children, whether boys or girls, are brought up alike by the women, without any special attention to their sexual differences, until at puberty the males are taken into the ceremonial houses for initiation. The men seem like outsiders, visiting their wives a little uneasily, waiting for the chance to bring their sons into the men's houses for the blood-filled rites which mark the passage from childhood into manhood.

The launch bearing Margaret and Reo to Ambunti stops at Kankananum, where Bateson is working. They go ashore, happy to have the opportunity of meeting Bateson, about whom they have heard so much. Bateson is tall, lank and wan, and towers well over a foot above Mead.

"You're tired," says Bateson to her. "The first cherishing words I had heard from anyone in all the Mundugumor months," she comments. She feels that she has been released from prison, a feeling that must be shared by the others, for during the past year, none of the anthropologists has met other persons with whom to discuss the work in which each has been engaged. The three of them talk all day and most of the time during the days that follow. They go to another village upstream, Ambunti, to celebrate Christmas with a group of government agents and traders, who are engaged in a continual, very drunken party. Mead makes an ethnologist's observation of the Australians: They prefer beer to champagne, and drink the latter only when the beer runs out.

Mead is becoming aware that she is drawn to Bateson, and that Reo is being left out of conversations. "By then Gregory and I had already established a kind of communication in which Reo did not share." She further defines the alienation Reo was undergoing by stating "it was always hard for him to cope with rivalry at any level."

The trio discuss future work. Bateson takes Margaret and Reo up a tributary of the Sepik, through blackwater canals dank with decaying vegetation, to Lake Tchambuli (now called Chambri). The lake is smooth as glass, with purple lotus, and pink and white water lilies, which the village women entwine in their armbands. Osprey and blue heron skim the waters. An idyllic scene. Margaret and Reo decide they will work in a village of people called, like the lake, Tchambuli, while Bateson works on the opposite shore with another group related to the Iatmul.

The Tchambuli number only 600 people; they had fled the area to escape the Iatmul, but now that the Australians have established peace, they have returned to the lake. They are more interested in art than in warfare, so their head-hunting

victims are either bought or are criminals from nearby ham-
lets. Most of the victims are criminals who have stolen food,
or infants and young children purchased from other tribes.
The Tchambuli consider it necessary that every young boy
kill someone; the boy's spear hand is guided by his mother's
brother in this first bloodletting. The victims' skulls are covered with clay and painted and hung in the men's houses. But
such head-hunting is sinking into a secondary role among the
Tchambuli. With warfare ended, they are more interested in
developing their artistic talents, and Tchambuli life is undergoing a renaissance.

Bateson comes regularly from across the lake to visit Mead
and Fortune, or they send messages back and forth. They
have endless discussions about what they are finding. Mead
is uncovering material among the Tchambuli that, fitted in
with what she has learned among the Arapesh and Mundugumor, makes a pattern. She is developing theories that she will
express in one of her most complex works, *Sex and Temperament in Three Primitive Societies.*

The three anthropologists spend endless hours in an eight-
foot-square mosquito-proof room discussing, analyzing, arguing. Each one has made important theoretical discoveries,
Mead in the realm of sexual temperaments, Fortune in kinship systems (which he will state in an article entitled "A Note
on Cross-Cousin Marriage," a work which, like his other
works, receives little recognition), and Bateson on the emotional "tone" or quality of a society.

Mead sees that among the Tchambuli the differences between men and women are markedly reversed according to
Western standards. Here the women, brisk, unadorned,
managing and industrious, fish, garden and trade. The men
are the artists and, decorated and adorned, spend their lives
in dancing, carving and painting. War is no longer a sport and
they fulfill their ritualized head-hunting with what seems like

reluctance. If men are the moody, creative, artistic individuals, a woman is measured by how well she performs her "masculine" role; if a birth is difficult for a woman, it is because she has not worked hard enough.

The theories that the anthropologists have been working out among primitive societies now seem to apply also to themselves. Here are three people from English-speaking cultures—American, New Zealand and British. It occurs to Mead that what she had posited about primitive cultures might also apply to the three foreigners.

> What if human beings, innately different at birth, could be shown to fit into systematically defined temperamental types, and what if there are male and female versions of each of these temperamental types?

She suspects that she and Bateson are the same types, that Reo is the outsider. She begins to question the traditional suppositions about male-female relationships. And she wonders if the expectations about male-female differences so characteristic of European-American cultures, the men aggressive and domineering, the women passive and "feminine," may not be reversed in societies like those of the Tchambuli, where

> women were brisk and cooperative, whereas men were responsive, subject to the choices of women, and characterized by the kinds of cattiness, jealousy, and moodiness that feminists had claimed were the outcome of women's subservient and dependent role?

Looking about the mosquito-room, she sees that "Gregory and I were close together in temperament—represented, in fact, a male and female version of a temperamental type that was in strong contrast with the one represented by Reo." She quickly adds that it would make no sense to define the traits she and Bateson shared as "feminine," any more than it would to call the behavior of Arapesh men "maternal" for being as nurturing and loving to children as the women.

But theory is one thing. Something deeper, more radical, is taking place. A marriage has now become a triangle. "Gregory and I were falling in love." They try to keep the relationship on a professional level. Coolness is the key word.

Eighteen months of work among primitive peoples are finished. It is now early 1933. Off they go, not together but following different paths. What Fortune has been thinking all along is something we can only guess at. Mead returns to the American Museum of Natural History to resume her job; she now has the apartment on 102nd Street alone. Bateson takes a freighter to England, and again assumes his post at Cambridge ("It was many weeks before I heard from him," Mead remarks). Fortune returns to New Zealand briefly, again meeting Eileen, the girl with whom he had once been so passionately in love, and then goes on to England.

Much work lies ahead for all of them, for they have not only manuscripts—articles and books—to work on but personal relations to solve. Mead finishes *Sex and Temperament in Three Primitive Societies*, Fortune some articles about the Arapesh, and Bateson his famous *Naven.* In the spring of 1935 Bateson visits the United States, where he and Mead, working with A.R. Radcliffe-Brown, tackle the problem of society, culture and character. No conclusions are reached.

By now Mead and Fortune are quietly separated, and he leaves England to go to China to teach. A marriage that had started out with high emotion, amid controversy, is ending on a subdued note. Mead's relationships with her various husbands (she will have three in all) seem to exist, to some outsid-

Lanky Gregory Bateson and Margaret Mead, newly married, discuss their work among the Iatmul at Tambunam in the Sepik River area of New Guinea. Mead wears pajamas under her skirts as protection against the overwhelming and ferocious New Guinea mosquitoes.

ers, in a kind of unreal world; the men are not listed in the various "official" biographies or fact sheets about her, and one wonders if they may not be merely some kind of drone to her worker bee.

Mead works out another faraway rendezvous, this time with Bateson. They will meet in Java, the principal island of the Dutch East Indies, marry there, and then go to neighboring Bali for an immense project that will consume several years of their time. But upon arriving in Java they find that complications prevent their marrying. They must fly over to Singapore for the ceremony.

Bateson is thirty-one, Mead thirty-four. She remarks that both look younger than they are. He is more than a head taller than she. Photographs of them look like two unrelated pictures in different scales pasted together into a composite. Mead can remark that she grew up at eleven, while Gregory still looked "asthenic"—slightly built—and that his silhouette was adolescent.

They go by ship back to the East Indies, first to Java and then to Bali. By now it is March 1936.

The Balinese are a sharp contrast to Mead's other cultures. In Bali, instead of a handful of Stone Age people, she and Bateson are to study one of the most complex of all the nontechnological societies, one she can equate in many aspects to medieval Europe.

Balinese society is both feudal and communal. Even the most ordinary act in daily life may bear a religious significance. The Balinese follow a diluted, relaxed form of Hinduism, with traces of Buddhism, the result of religious, economic and cultural colonization by Indians some ten to twelve centuries earlier. The rulers are descendants of the Indian *kshatriya* or warrior caste (in Bali known as *kasatria*), who dominate a Brahmin priesthood and a large number of now-casteless people.

Bali is to present a new height in fieldwork for Mead, and new challenges. The Balinese culture has a dreamlike character, and indeed trances, divination and numerous rites and ceremonies of esoteric origins form the core of everyday life; witches are common and are feared. The arts and crafts are highly developed, and the air is filled with music. Numerous plays entertain the people. Balinese society, already much studied, possesses written records, a long cultural history, reliable informants and much ceremony to observe and record. In Bali, Mead is no longer at the mercy of bearers afraid of sorcerers or at the whim of informants who are likely to disappear for unknown reasons.

After much discussion, she and Bateson move to a mountain village, where life is simpler than on the crowded plain. Here they have a house built for the two years they will be on the island. Mead and Bateson, who are collaborating instead of working as friendly rivals, as had been the experience with Reo, have a team of anthropologists and assistants to aid them, among them Jane Belo, who records ceremonies (Belo is particularly interested in the births of twins, to the Balinese a most unfortunate event), Colin McPhee, a musicologist, Walter Spies, who annotates music and works on the arts, and Katherine Mershon, a specialist in dance and religious behavior. There are also skilled secretaries and interpreters. And instead of the primitive equipment she had carried to Samoa—half a dozen notebooks and a folding Kodak—she and Bateson not only have the most advanced photographic equipment but even a movie camera.

Bali, Mead states, is "sheer heaven for the anthropologist."

We feasted on riches, day after day, and found each temple, each theatrical performance, and each shadow play more delightful and more intelligible than the last. . . . Bali was a high culture. . . .

But even life in the primitive mountain village, which they chose because they wanted a simple, uncomplicated society, is for an anthropologist highly complex. Bateson and Mead originally planned on taking some 2,000 photographic negatives, but will finish with 25,000. They must send home for bulk film, and improvise ways of loading cassettes. At night they develop each day's shooting. She finds she must now make ten times as many notes because of the tremendous number of photographs they are taking.

All is overwhelming in this feast of riches. They must study not one birth celebration but twenty; they watch and photograph young girls going into trances on fifteen different occasions, and must compare six hundred small carved kitchen gods from one village with five hundred from another; forty paintings a man did of his dreams are compared with the dream paintings of another hundred men. The opportunity for such work, Mead notes, is "dazzling," "so rich" is the material, and the progress in method and theory "exhilarating."

The very complexity of Balinese life inevitably results in a diffusion of her perceptions and her results. In place of the concise to-the-point focus of her work in Samoa, Manus and New Guinea, her researches among the Balinese are to serve more as a counterpoint for her analysis of men, women and children in the other societies. Her one general work is the magnificent photographic study she does with Bateson. Their *Balinese Character* is their only joint effort. It is based upon the 25,000 photographs that Bateson shoots, edited down to less than 800. (It is not published until 1942.)

Unfortunately for Mead's collaborative efforts, Bateson loses interest in this kind of study later and turns to other projects covering an amazing scope—he interviews schizo-phrenics and studies octopuses, otters and dolphins on the way to developing theories that lie outside Mead's own fields. But for her the work among the Balinese is not wasted. They form one of the seven societies in *Male and Female* (published in 1949) and get written up in technical papers she is to do upon her return from her second trip to Bali in 1939.

The two allotted years pass as if in a Balinese trance. Suddenly Mead and Bateson awaken to the fact that their work has run its course. They have completed their project. It is time to go. The war that Professor Mead had once predicted is ominously close: Hitler has occupied Austria and will soon invade Czechoslovakia. On the way back home to New York Mead and Bateson decide to spend a few months with the Iatmul to fill out some unfinished studies.

It is a difficult time. Bateson is often ill, and the Iatmul have been disrupted by an extended dry spell. Obtaining the necessary material—on the ways in which the Iatmul and the Balinese contrast in such things as raising children—requires extended work. Another six months pass.

Before they return home, they go back to Bali again in an effort to do some last-minute research before Europe's coming war prevents international travel. At home in New York again Mead and Bateson turn to their great masses of material, trying to assemble it into coherent form. And then, she writes, "The war engulfed us."

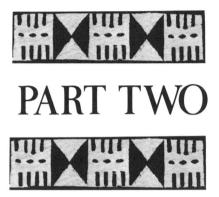

PART TWO

Immigrants and Natives

MARGARET MEAD DIVIDES HER WORLD—and all worlds—into two sections. The turning point is World War II, which ends the many thousands of years of past history and contains the seeds of all events to come, present and future. She points out that when the first atom bomb exploded at the end of World War II, only a few people understood that all mankind was entering a new age. Of those born before the war, now adults, she says, they are *all* "today immigrants in a changing world." The changing world belongs to the young generations, the people of tape recorders, atomic energy, Beatles: They share a common culture, while the adults are separated from each other by culture, language, customs, birth. The adults' world is a "foreign" world. They are strangers even in their own country. But "all children, in whatever part of the world in which they are growing up, are native to the kind of world in which they take for granted the thinking toward which their parents can only grope." Further:

In 1957, when Sputnik was launched, American and Russian children were fully able to visualize our new relationship to space as a reality; a few years later, among the Manus of the Admiralty Islands, school children expressed almost identical ideas about space exploration. The young are able to adapt because they are not burdened or confused by out-of-date information.

It is technology that has transformed the present world, and it is technology that can help now in the creation of a shared future for all the peoples of the earth. We cannot share in the past of peoples whose traditions are very different from ours, nor can others share easily in our past. But now . . . the whole world, through technology, experiences events simultaneously.

The problem for the prewar generations, Mead states—a theme she repeats often, in articles and speeches—is how to become citizens of the community—a Global Village, less and less restricted except superficially by boundaries, language and race—of which our children are the true natives.

This insight, which is so basic to her later thinking, and one which she has tried to convey to parents anxious and worried over the generation gap, is one that developed gradually. Two major events might be found to lie in the background, one the birth of her daughter, the other the unexpected emergence of the Manus as a twentieth-century people.

Mead had been told many times by doctors that she would never have children; she suffered many miscarriages with all her husbands. When she and Bateson made their brief return to Bali in 1939, she was sure she was pregnant. She was carried through the mountain roads in a bamboo chair. But one night the chair collapsed as she was being carried, and she again had a miscarriage. On the return home to New York, she was sure she was pregnant again, and this time she took even greater precautions against an accident. She cancelled a planned trip to England with Bateson, and stayed at home in the utmost quiet.

The year was a difficult one. In September Germany invaded Poland, and Great Britain and France declared war against Hitler. Bateson returned to his homeland for whatever wartime duties he might be asked to perform. Meanwhile Mead had met a young physician named Benjamin Spock, and talked to him about the problems of her pregnancy. Spock introduced her to an obstetrician, Claude Heaton, who was interested in American Indian medicine; he agreed with her that she could avoid taking an anesthetic during childbirth unless it became absolutely necessary, and that she should be allowed to nurse her baby, a practice then contrary to most medical thinking.

So Mead could prepare herself for natural childbirth, an idea that was then rare. Instead of worrying about the pains of labor, she could learn and think about the task of having the baby. "The male invention of natural childbirth has had a magnificent emancipating effect on women, who for generations had been muffled in male myths instead of learning about a carefully observed actuality," she says in *Blackberry Winter.*

But she still has apprehensions about the coming baby. What will it look like? She realizes that there were "members of my family whom I did not find attractive or endearing, and I knew that my child might take after them. Distinguished forebears were no guarantee of normality. But what I dreaded most, I think, was dullness." But she can also worry about other traits in the family tree, deafness, mongolism and one child with cerebral palsy.

On December 8, 1939, Mary Catherine Bateson is born, her birth being well photographed by a woman named Myrtle McGraw. Mead, who has spent so much time studying children in other lands, will now have the opportunity to keep extensive records in both photographs and text of her daughter's growth and development. Mead had planned on bringing up the baby in Cambridge, England, where Bateson was affiliated, but the outbreak of the war prevents that, and so she remains in New York. Although Bateson had gone home to see about his military service, after the invasion of Poland and its occupation by the Germans, the hostilities have abated, and there is very little fighting at the time, so Bateson is told to finish his work in America, and he returns to New York to his wife and baby.

"We called her Cathy," she writes. "She was fair-haired, her head was unmarred by a hard birth or the use of instruments, and her expression was already her own. I was completely happy." Mead goes to stay with her parents in Philadelphia. "Bringing up Cathy was an intellectual as well as an emotionally exciting adventure."

> I believed that the early days of infancy were very important—that it made a difference how a child was born, whether it was kept close to its mother, whether it was breast-fed, and how the breast feeding was carried out.

Cathy is "an early-responsive child" and Mead—and Bateson—are at her side to record every moment, awake and asleep. The baby is probably one of the most studied children in history: Certainly few children have had so expert an anthropologist to chart their growth. From the beginning Mead takes notes, following both her family's custom and her own training, about everything relating to Catherine; notes about breast-feeding, about when she cries or smiles, when she sleeps and speaks.

While Bateson had been in England, Mead had hired a young girl from Appalachia as a nurse for the baby. But Bateson is afraid the woman, with her backcountry accent, will give Catherine bad speech habits, and so he finds an English nanny whose language he approves.

Bateson, immersed in the Bali project, cannot draw ade-

Gregory Bateson with baby Catherine. Cathy, the daughter of two of this century's most famous anthropologists, is probably one of the most photographed and most studied children ever born.

quate funds from England because of wartime currency restrictions, so Mead goes back to work, teaching anthropology part-time at New York University and working part-time at the American Museum of Natural History, and caring for the baby during her free moments.

In December 1941, with the bombing of Pearl Harbor by the Japanese, the United States, too, is brought into the war. Bateson is already working in New York on a wartime project for England, and now Ruth Benedict enlists Mead in a series of jobs for the United States government.

The war years are an especially busy period for Mead. In the year before America's entry she had begun a study of the existing psychiatric literature on psychosomatic medicine, to search for links between illnesses and social patterns. This work is interrupted by her wartime duties. She is appointed Executive Secretary and Director of Research of the Committee on Food Habits of the National Research Council, a post she holds, despite many interruptions, until the end of the war in 1945. This job entails much travelling about the country to talk to people setting up food programs.

In 1943 she makes a trip to Britain, where many young American GIs are preparing for the coming invasion of German-occupied Europe, as a lecturer and "interpreter" of American-British relations, for both governments had discovered that there were vast cultural differences between their people.

Mead is often aided by a young anthropologist, Rhoda Métraux, a pupil of Malinowski and Benedict who joins her in studies of American attitudes toward nutrition, rationing and the problems of feeding Europe after the fighting ended. Mead and Métraux will continue over the years to study American culture together, and, at a distance, the cultures of France, Russia, China and Germany, and eventually, collaborate in fieldwork in New Guinea.

An energetic and inveterate proselytizer for her "Global Village," Margaret Mead never misses a chance to make her views known to the world. Here she addresses peoples of all races, cultures and nations on a United Nations broadcast. Mead can and does speak on virtually any topic, from the minutiae of daily living to the great problems of mankind.

Part of the time Mead and Bateson share a household with another couple, Larry and Mary Frank; the two families also vacation in New Hampshire, where they take in some refugee children from England. The war years are hectic: Mead, Bateson and Larry Frank are constantly moving about, from New York to Washington to Europe, and by the time the war ends, Bateson and Mead seem to spend more time apart than together.

By 1950 they are formally divorced, leaving Mead alone with her daughter. Bateson goes to California to begin a career of teaching and research; he accepts a post at Stanford University as Visiting Professor of Anthropology, and also teaches anthropology, cybernetics and psychiatry at the veterans' hospital at Palo Alto. Bateson, like the other husbands, seems to have played a role as a "collaborator"; he is the man who successfully impregnated her. Personal relationships are far removed. In fact, one of the reviewers of *Blackberry Winter*, Jane Howard, writing in *The New York Times*, points out that "Although none of her three marriages endured, she takes enormous pride in having finally become a mother . . . and in time a grandmother." Miss Howard adds that "What one misses most in this lucid, witty record . . . is more candor about the author's three husbands. . . . We are offered few marital vignettes of the sort that lend charm to Dr. Mead's sketches of her forebears."

Mead's constant travels bring her to Australia in 1952 on a lecture tour, and here she is told a strange story. She had been looking for new possibilities of study; her Australian colleagues convince her "that the most useful thing I could do was a restudy of Manus, where, it was reported, the most extraordinary things were going on."

The Manus, who had never expected to see Mead again—nor she them—were undergoing a series of drastic changes that, as she noted much later, took them five thousand years in half a century. When she and Reo left them, she thought they would deteriorate into one more abject version of the New Guinea work-boy, not fully native, not properly Western, but an unhappy mixture of both. Instead, on their own initiative, after exposure to both Japanese and Allied forces during World War II, they had begun to redesign their own culture, and moved as a group—grandparents, parents and children—into their own version of Western, and specifically American, culture.

What happened to the Manus was partly due to chance, partly due, at first, to events over which they had no control, and then to their own very skillful and intelligent insights into what it meant to be a member of the new world. In a sense, they were less "immigrants" from the past than "natives" of the new generation. Until the end of the war they were like a canoe smashed in a storm, they drifted with the course of history. Only when the war ended were they able to take matters into their own hands, to rescue themselves.

The change was so dramatic, so incomprehensible to the Australians who administered New Guinea and the Bismarck Archipelago, that they felt that Mead, the only person except for Reo who had thoroughly studied the Manus as a primitive culture, could understand what was happening. How, the Australians wanted to know, could she explain the strange events that had turned these seagoing ex-cannibal traders into adaptable members of the mid-twentieth century?

It is a challenging question, and she draws up a request for a grant from the Rockefeller Foundation, to be channelled through the American Museum of Natural History, for a restudy of the Manus. It is awarded to her, and she goes about making preparations for a return to Manus.

Field trips are becoming progressively more complicated, though now anthropologists can travel by plane in a day or so instead of by a boat trip of several months. But because the scope of study expands with each trip, more and more people are involved and the means of making the study require more and more technology. It takes Mead a year to plan the trip, and to find the right assistant. She queries departments of anthropology—now a popular subject—for "a graduate student who was well qualified in linguistics, theoretical and applied electronics and photography and who was interested in culture and personality studies." Only one person fits her demanding qualifications, a young man named Ted Schwartz, whose wife, Lenora, also wants to do fieldwork.

In June 1953 Mead and the Schwartzes fly down to the Admiralties. She settles down in Peré, and the Schwartzes in Bunai, some forty-five minutes away by boat, where they can carry on independent studies but easily keep in touch with her when necessary. This is not the Manus she and Reo had studied, but another world entirely. And as the Australians had said, strange events had occurred.

The Manus, Mead soon finds out, unlike so many other primitive societies, had not stood alone and isolated, slowly dying out while the rest of the world rushed into the nuclear, electronic age. The island's slim contacts with the West had not brought illness, death, the rupture of soul force, the end of a simple culture, but a radical change in life. Like Cathy, the Manus were "born" into the new world, the world of which they, and she, are the "natives" and in which Mead, anthropologist and mother, is an "immigrant." In both the Stone Age primitives and the tiny, attuned, intellectual daughter one can find sources of Mead's insights into generation gaps and new societal structures. The Manus, analyzing their own situation in the light of what they could view of the more powerful industrial West, would escape the fate of other peoples, not only in the South Pacific but in Asia, Africa and the Americas.

The tribe was shrewd and businesslike. The leaders understood that the religion of the West, Christianity, was a far more powerful force than their own cults of spirits and ancestral dead. They realized that if they adopted Christianity, many of their own religious customs and beliefs must perish, notably the cult of Sir Ghost, that noisy, demanding supernatural being who inhabited the households, scolding, punishing, berating people for their sexual and economic sins. There had been much discussion in Peré over what course to take, and after careful consideration, the Manus, for purely practical reasons, adopted Roman Catholicism. The Protestants had the disadvantage of collecting tithes, taught in the local languages, and did not practice confession. The Catholics did not tithe, taught the widely spoken Pidgin (otherwise formally called neo-Melanesian) and practiced the rite of confession, a rite the Manus also practiced. The Catholics had the additional advantage of secret confessions, in contrast to the public confessions the tribe enjoyed.

So the Manus threw out Sir Ghost and other spirits, and with them the amulets and charms that had been so necessary a part of their lives. They told Mead, who documented the many steps in the Manus entry into the modern world in her *New Lives for Old*, that in looking back upon the ghost cult they could feel that the spirits were like childhood fears.

The 1929 police-boy strike that had happened after Mead and Fortune passed through New Guinea had taught the Manus that the whites were not infallible or invincible. Throughout the entire New Guinea area, from the tiny offshore islands and the strings of archipelagos to the sandy shores and the remote mountains, the people were restless. Everywhere there were hints of a new world to come, a millennium, when the black peoples would replace the whites, when the foreigners would give up their ill-gotten spoils and return the land to the native people. However, except for the movement led by Paliau, the Manus police-boy who had been one of the strike leaders, little active rebellion took place until after World War II.

After his police service had been completed, Paliau returned home to Manus. Mead learned that he had come back to a culture in ferment. Various reforms were being talked about, she established, as people tried to grapple with what were evident abuses in Manus society. Attempts were being made to stop the constant bickering among people, especially that which resulted from the remnants of the ghost cults. Another police-boy attacked the traditional marriage system, which lay at the foundation of the cruel form of bondage of young men to older men who had financed their weddings. This man wanted the Manus to try a modern way of life, including "working for a living [instead of trading], buying European goods, and dressing up like Europeans." Paliau joined in the call for reform.

But events moved slowly on Manus. The war which Mead and Fortune had feared broke out, and the Admiralty Archipelago was occupied by the Japanese, who ruled with much repression and some torture to keep the people in line. It was with joy that the Manus told Mead of the American attack and counter-occupation. Allied armies, primarily American, landed in force and set up bases. One million Americans were to pass through this tiny, isolated territory with its population of 13,000; in comparison, Great Britain, with its forty million people, saw but two million American troops over a longer period.

Mead could understand the profound effect that the Americans had. For primitive tribes whose currency was shells, dogs' teeth, sometimes pigs and a few silver shillings, the effects were overwhelming. Not only did the

Americans have everything on a grand, virtually unimaginable scale, including much the Manus never dreamed existed, but they were also very generous with whatever they possessed. Americans shared food, drinks, movies, medical care, transportation with the Manus, Usiai and Mantankor. For the first time the people—and this is something that happened all over the Pacific—experienced racial equality. They also saw American black troops, though in segregated units, being treated pretty much as the white soldiers were treated.

Mead charted the Manus change of attitudes carefully. Another impressive factor for the people was that the Americans had machines to do the heavy work. Arduous physical labor, which would have required weeks, even months, for native laborers, would be quickly performed by giant machines. Jungles were cleared, airstrips leveled, garbage pits dug, all by bulldozers. Also the Americans took care of their sick with medicines that worked, instead of exposing them to the mysteries of witch doctors and incantations. More, the Americans were not at the mercy of Sir Ghost, with his mysterious penances for some economic or sexual sin inflicted in the form of illness. Illness was something the Americans treated immediately and efficiently. The Americans put the highest value on good health, and they shared their medical treatment with the Manus.

Other Pacific societies were found to have undergone somewhat similar experiences, but Mead could see in 1953 that few but the Manus were able to take a practical and positive view of events. American generosity and democracy had a profound effect upon Manus thinking, and led them to action. Under the Germans and Australians the native was an outcast in his own land; he could not enter the white man's house nor eat from his dishes nor receive his medicine. But now a Manus could enter an American's tent, join him on the chow line, sit next to him at the outdoor movies, lie in an adjoining bed in the infirmary, get equal treatment from white doctors and nurses.

Suddenly the Americans were gone, to other islands, to Japan, to their homes. The war had moved on, was over, peace ruled throughout the Pacific islands. On Manus the people were open to the return of the police-boy Paliau, and to his message of a new world, a world that would be the Manus version of what the Americans came from.

Paliau is a natural, straightforward orator, with a disarming frankness, a quality that impresses Mead. In writing home, she describes him thus:

Paliau is a man of about 45, possibly a little less, slight, pleasant, with the quiet assurance of a man who has always been able to think about what he wanted to think about and a manner which can only be described as quietly vice-regal. I have come to the conclusion that the essence of his genius is the completeness of his conception. All the people of the South Coast—and ultimately of the whole of the Admiralties—were to be welded into one unit and all the changes which would make it possible for them to belong to the modern world were to be made at once. A new kind of house, new clothes, a new calendar, a new social organization, a new form of church, a new ethic, and all the institutions necessary to support these things—a treasury, taxes, customs, a school, a hospital—all these were to be set up at once. He worked out the necessary negotiations to find space for the Manus villages on shore and supplied the design within which their entire life was rebuilt—on shore—while the Usiai (the bush people of the big island) came down to the sea coast and learned to live with the Manus and use boats.

Many people saw, as did Mead, an inner reserve which could never be broached. Paliau did not confide in others, and to the end he stood as a leader alone, ahead of and above the others. In the beginning, his message was in part mystical, based on visions, dreams and inspiration: The Garden of Eden would reappear if only sin were abolished (he was especially concerned with people's antisocial behavior such as stealing, quarreling and lying). Paliau also preached that a new world would come, the dead would rise, gifts would come to the people and they would gain their freedom from the whites. This kind of messianic expectation is known as a Cargo Cult, or Cargo movement, and Paliau's message was in the mainstream of the movement.

Cargo was a long-smouldering tradition, known throughout the world. Loosely defined, Cargo is the belief that someday the people of this or that place (the locale is most often the South Pacific) will receive certain material goods now possessed by whites and denied black and brown peoples by white selfishness. Belief in Cargo first arose in the nineteenth century when Europeans began to appear in numbers in the Pacific, as well as in Africa and parts of Asia. Cargo-type movements were noticed among the Maori of New Zealand, the Hawaiians and the Fijians, and also among the American Indians, Siberians, Africans and Chinese (the Ghost Dance movement and the Boxer Rebellion are famous examples) where the white presence was widespread and forceful.

South Pacific Cargo received its greatest impetus during World War II, after the arrival of American troops, who appeared suddenly and without notice on dozens of islands with unlimited quantities of strange Western goods, from war materiel to washing machines, movie theaters, Nissen huts, eating utensils, canned foods, candy bars and chewing gum, beer and whiskey and other luxuries undreamed of by people scarcely out of the Stone Age. Few of the islanders had any contact in the past with whites, and they made the natural assumption that such goods were the product of magic and if the white man could make such wonders appear by magic— for there seemed to be no other explanation, the islanders having no conception of the factory and the assembly line— could not the black, brown, red and yellow man also make things appear by his own magic?

Various messiahs arose everywhere, promising both the coming of Cargo by ship or plane and an end to white domination. Few of these messiahs lasted more than a short time: Cargo did not come as promised. Followers of the messiahs lost faith, turned to other leaders, or gave up the idea of Cargo, disillusioned and bitter. Some tribes reverted to their original subservient role as colonial subjects, passive and inward-turning. Others, maturing from the experience, saw the solution in political action, or in labor organizations, cooperatives and national parties.

The Manus were among the people to go through the Cargo experience and emerge more mature and independent, thanks to Paliau's own spiritual, psychological and political development. Where many other Cargo leaders remained on the level of the medicine man or witch doctor, Paliau developed into a true leader of charismatic qualities.

Paliau's impact was so powerful that Mead found that the Manus marked his arrival as the beginning of a new era and dated their calendar on it. He began to acquire a kind of supernatural aura. But shortly he abandoned his otherworldly themes and advocated more practical courses based upon his experiences in the outside world. He now emphasized a break with the past: Throw out the costly customs that have been such a burden to us, he told the

Manus. Stop wasting money on dowries and burial feasts. Use a currency more practical than dogs' teeth. Get rid of customs whereby a woman has several husbands, or a man several wives.

Not only must the wasteful practices of the past be discarded, but the people should cooperate for a better world. The sea people and the land people must work together, must share their resources. "The most remarkable aspect of the movement," an Australian government report issued in 1950 said, was "the achievement of Paliau in getting traditionally hostile seafaring and land-dwelling Manus native population groups to work together." The Manus had learned that if they cooperated wisely with each other they would soon have enough of the white man's goods to be able to live like white men, a premise whose worth was not challenged then, though it was to be a quarter of a century later. It seemed like a sensible proposition, and the practical and energetic Manus saw the reasons behind it.

Paliau demanded effort from his followers. He saw that the good life would not come without work. He insisted on peacefulness and good neighborliness, elementary methods of hygiene and sanitary improvements, and especially better housing and schools, viewing the latter as the places where the doctrines of a new world could be taught.

Mead could see that Paliau was not doing a mere patching up here and there. His reforms went to the core of Manus life. His insights into the problems of tribal structure were broad and advanced. He noted the low position of women and called for the end of traditional marriage practices, which would not only free the women but make marriage easier for the young men who lacked the necessary wealth for the bride price. Consequently, a number of young women, moved by his ideas, ran away from their husbands. Paliau gave them shelter, bringing the charge against him in Australian newspapers (which were not particularly sympathetic to the independent attitudes of their government's wards) that he was "the harem-keeping mogul of a 'Cargo cult.' "

Two brief imprisonments of Paliau a few years before Mead's arrival did not stop the movement, and the Australians released him. The last major step Paliau took was to move Peré. He convinced the Manus that they should have a new, "modern" village, on land instead of over the edge of the lagoon. A new town was carefully planned, houses were built on a magnificent piece of land along a beach, with a central plaza as the core of the new Peré. The sweep of the plaza was soon truncated for a school, which was so popular that the children of the neighboring villages were also sent to it.

Problems arose. The step into the new world, the Manus found, was also accompanied by modern headaches. Overcrowding, pollution and juvenile delinquency came to plague the village. Still, the people, who Mead had thought would soon fade away as a tribal proletariat, subject to the conflicting forces of a faraway government, the fluctuating demands of the copra planters on other islands and the stultifying traditional social structure, were now, by their own efforts, a dynamic, progressive little nation.

The Australians' suggestion to revisit the Manus was, Mead realized, a unique and unusual opportunity, for although anthropologists sometimes returned to societies they had studied, it was primarily to reexamine aspects they had slighted previously or to search out material to refute criticism from other anthropologists. Few ever returned a full generation later to see what had happened to a culture, especially one which had experienced radical, self-sought changes for the better.

Now Mead is back after half a lifetime to learn what has happened to the children of her own youth, the children she had so carefully studied for *Growing Up in New Guinea.*

So in the new Peré she gets her own house, not on the edge of a lagoon as previously, but one on the village's new ceremonial square. She has a magnificent view of the mountains and but a two-minute walk to look at the ocean. Because open land is at a premium, the houses, ringed around the square on three sides, are close together: Her neighbors are within six feet of her, so that she can look directly from her windows into theirs—"excellent for field work," she remarks.

Mead seems more mellow, more at ease in the new Peré. "Although the houses lack the style of the old village, on the whole it seems more beautiful," she can note. And of the new Peré inspired by Paliau she writes, "The astonishing thing about all this is that it seems to work." Instead of the harsh battles of the past, when "the air used to be blue with fury," she hears not one quarrelling voice.

Modernization seems to appeal to the Manus, for they are doing it according to their own desires, not according to plans drawn up by some faraway U.N. mission or the Australian government. On the broad view, they are looking forward to a federation of all the diverse tribes of the great island, united in brotherhood and a truly modern society. Paliau had hoped to eliminate the traditional tribal jealousies, to build a kind of utopia—a perfect state—not only based upon an adaptation of European law but one which would also stress good-humored friendliness instead of feuds, supernatural curses, sorcery and unbridled anger. The ancestral spirits that still inflicted so much psychic and even physical damage upon people would be replaced with the One God. Education would replace the ancient initiatory trials that the young men were forced to undergo, and there would be an end to local warfare and head-hunting.

The world is changing rapidly, Mead realizes. Even in the West, the transformations from the prewar period to the present are immense. Europeans and Americans have been jolted from a dying feudal economy into the nuclear, electronic age, and the Manus have decided wholeheartedly to step with the West into the same world.

In 1928 the young married women, Mead remembers, were still "primitives." Their heads had been shaved to show their state; their earlobes were weighed down with ornaments of dogs' teeth and shells, and their clothing was but two small aprons, one in front, one in back, made of pandanus grass. But even then they were in the process of abandoning such traditional dress for the shapeless cloth clothing introduced by the missionaries throughout the Pacific. In 1953 Mead found the women, especially the young ones, in contemporary cotton dresses, their earlobes bare, and the use of tatoos fading away. Along with their children and grandchildren, these women had entered into the new world as a group—there was no generation gap, but the movement of an entire people into the contemporary world.

Now all the children went to school. The idea had come from a Peré man, who during the war had been given two years of schooling by an itinerant chaplain. When the people of Peré decided to modernize their village, this young man had insisted on the village's having a school. A kind of "shadow" school was built for the real school of the future. The children were sorted by size, and the young man taught them numbers and letters. Later they not only had a real schoolhouse but a real teacher from outside, an Australian.

Even the peoples' names had been Westernized. Loponiu now called himself Johanis Lokus, Kapeli was Stefan Posangat, and so on. Pokanau, one of Mead's informants in 1928, now wore a khaki shirt and shorts like those of an Australian, and because of his great knowledge of traditional ceremonies and rites, he was called the "lawyer man."

The Manus, Mead reports, were perhaps the most successful model of adjustment she had ever recorded. The people were practical, enterprising, interested in the manner in which things worked, open to taking chances with their children and confident of their own ability to cope with the new world. They were making a good adjustment to the demands of the larger system of the twentieth century.

An entire system was transformed, releasing extraordinary amounts of energy. The exploitative kinship patterns of the past, in which the young men, as well as the women, were at the mercy of their elders, and feared the illnesses caused by avenging spirits, had disappeared in favor of the group achievement, cooperative actions and pride in mastering the demanding and superior institutions of the West. "It seemed," Mead states, "that self-initiated, complete change was better and more efficient than piece-meal change in which people partly adjusted to partial change, as a man might limp on a sprained ankle, exacerbating the inflammation."

She thinks that the Manus might be a pattern for the millions of other primitive and colonial people caught between old and new worlds, and that their example might make the transition for others smoother than had been expected.

She stays with the Manus at New Peré for six months, recording the ways in which change has taken place. The Schwartzes stay another six, and then visit an expedition in New Britain before coming home. The night Mead leaves, she is given a feast, as she had been given one twenty-five years earlier. And again the Manus do not expect her to return, for everyone is getting old. Many Manus do not—or did not then, due to inadequate medical care—live long enough to see their grandchildren, and Mead is almost fifty-three. Pokanau, perhaps closer to her than any other Manus, says formally to her, "Now, like an old turtle you are going out into the sea to die, and we will never see you again." The image is one that seems to intrigue her, and both she and the Manus think that this *is* the last time they will see each other.

Her work on the Manus seems to have brought the tribe up to date. They have joined the modern world, their new lives are amply documented and whether or not she will return again is not a pressing question. She has several other jobs to engage her, and a daughter to raise. Catherine is now fifteen.

Catherine seems to be a duplicate of her mother, and of her grandmother and great-grandmother: self-sufficient, intelligent, seeing life as a system and rather aware that there was no one like Catherine. One of her classmates remembers that when they were very young Catherine always had the most interesting items to display at Show and Tell—primitive masks, flutes, drums, grass skirts and other artifacts that no other child could even dream of bringing to kindergarten. Catherine knew she was far ahead of the others.

But Catherine is only one of Mead's activities. She has proved that she can be a working mother, and work she does, with an energy and a fury that leave others behind. Articles, books, reports roll out with regularity. Her main base, her home, her cave, her Stone Age retreat, is always her niche under the Museum's eaves. When she joined the Museum in 1926 it was as an assistant curator. She has not seemed overly ambitious on the job; her successes lie outside her cave. She did not become an associate in her department until 1942, at a time when she had a handful of other things to balance: her work for the government, committees to run—whatever the war effort required—a book or two to turn out.

When the war ended—and Bateson was on his way to other fields—she began to branch out, and from here on it is hard to follow her tracks. One can see the major roads she pursued, but some of the byways disappear in the blur of her speed, and the chronology overlaps. One of her first major outside posts is at Columbia University, where she becomes Director of Research in Contemporary Cultures, and then a professor of anthropology at the university and a special lecturer there; she also takes a post at Fordham as chairman of the Social Science Department and professor of anthropology, in the late 1960's.

But these posts, which would be enough for the ordinary individual, are only a beginning. She becomes Visiting Professor in the Department of Psychiatry at the University of Cincinnati, the Sloan Professor at the Menninger Foundation, the Alumni Association Distinguished Professor at the University of Rhode Island, the Fogarty Scholar in Residence for the National Institute of Mental Health, a member of the American Anthropological Association (becoming its president in 1960), and so on, with membership in such organizations as the American Ethnological Society, the Society for Women Geographers, the World Federation for Mental Health, the World Society for Ekistics. After a while one gives up the listing and wonders how she can fill so many chairs, participate in so many conferences, within the finite time of the ordinary day.

Her books appear almost annually. Some are in collaboration with associates or former students, some are mere collections of past work, some are collections of papers by others, with her name as editor, a few are original works. But now she is becoming diffuse, verbose, repeating herself, sounding like a wise, old grandmother who knows the world all too well and wants her children to do as she says—and does (no one

With United Nations members Arthur Lewis (left) and C.V. Nara-simhan (right), Margaret Mead speaks before U.N. TV cameras on the organization's Technical Assistance Program's tenth anniversary of aid to underdeveloped nations in 1959. Mead has firm ideas of the ways in which the poorer lands are intimately linked to the richer nations, believing all nations are joined by modern communications and technology.

can complain that she has not done incredible things)—but she always speaks with authority.

Her *Rap on Race*, a dialogue with the black writer James Baldwin, seems like a book with great possibilities, but the reviewers complain that it was ill-prepared and not very deep. The two had never met before. They spent an hour getting acquainted, and then the next day, in two sessions, talked about race and society. The "book seems like an urbane conversation of a Swarthmore liberal and a literary young Philadelphia black, both trying for admission to the Junior League," said J.J. Conlin in *Best Sellers*. His conclusion was that "Mead and Baldwin solve nothing and perhaps clarify nothing."

Rap on Race comes off as a noble try, but E.K. Welsh *(Library Journal)* complains of "the idle conversation that takes up too many pages in the book."

Blackberry Winter, more personal, warmer and with some touching passages about her parents and paternal grandmother, is a much more likable work, though to some it sounded as if she dictated it into a tape recorder while waiting for planes in airports throughout the world. The poignant moments are offset by much tangled chronology and unfulfilled descriptions. E.G. Detlefsen *(Library Journal)* typifies the general reaction by liking her behind-the-scenes material about her early expeditions and her attempts to relate her own childhood to present-day problems. But— "Mead has a tendency to be a bit 'preachy' in her chapter on childraising."

One of her lesser-known works, *Twentieth Century Faith*, in which she puts forward her religious beliefs (she remains a practicing Episcopalian), is attacked because she had merely brought together a lot of old articles and essays without revising them—"papers of highly uneven quality," says the noted Protestant theologian Martin Marty in *The Critic*;

he also complains about her "clichés about global culture." Her tribute to Ruth Benedict, *An Anthropologist at Work*, receives something of a similar complaint—it is a "paste-up memorial." The reviewers think she used her essay about her old friend to fight long-forgotten academic battles, and has also not selected the best of Dr. Benedict's works for reprinting.

One gets the idea that Mead is by now not writing books but merely issuing compilations to satisfy a public already attracted by her early works. Surely none of her recent works, it seems, is done with the style and intensity and skill of her first two books.

She seems to do better with her *Redbook* columns, which begin in 1961. It is in these columns that one gets an idea of the themes that run through her mind. Someone asked me about her "philosophy." I could think of none except grandmotherliness, a concern that the world run rightly (according to her own ideas), and that everyone work toward the great Global Village. It is in *Redbook*, in which she speaks to women directly, her calm, rather rambling exhortations to understanding and future cooperation sandwiched amid articles about the new women's sexuality, crash diets and gourmet dinners, shortcuts to redecorating and going it alone, that one finds Mead at her most natural.

Her mind spans all subjects, and she is concerned about everything. Nothing seems to be beyond fixing, at least for her. She is above all an optimist. "Certainly there seem to be grounds for pessimism," she admits about the world, but another column puts down this idea with a firm foot, for, as she constantly emphasizes, "We are in the process of creating a new civilization." There will be problems along the way, especially since others do not think with her clarity, but we will reach this almost heavenly vision, just as certainly as the primitive tribes of the South Pacific thought that someday their islands would flip over, drop the whites into the sea and right themselves, with a golden age for the Melanesians.

Or she may ask rhetorically, "Someday will the whole world be a city?" We know she thinks yes. And for the future Global Village we need a new language, she states firmly. But it won't be English, now so widely spoken; for our shared civilization the secondary tongue should be "the natural language of a small, politically unimportant non-European literate people." This is a tall order, and she avoids giving specific suggestions.

The present world and the coming one share problems, Mead points out, not only that of communication but especially of population, which must be controlled. But we can succeed, she decides, after a sobering analysis of the baby boom, by "free access to information"—that is, to birth control—and "a new shared ethic."

Yet not all is presented on a broad scale. She can speak directly, as if at a coffee klatch, to American women about what it is like to be a guest in a primitive culture, saying in effect, "You can do it too, despite the problems." She says to her readers that "the Arapesh, for instance, were reluctant hosts and guests," and in the Sepik River villages not only an outsider like a trader but even a clan member "used to go in fear of his life." Even in the Manus village today (this is written after a third trip to the Admiralties) "there is no comfortable place for a stranger to stay." On the other hand, "the visitor to Samoa is always welcomed and feasted." And she can pointedly remind her audience that "even the escapists among us, the ones who feel that civilization is dull and confining, are likely to choose a primitive people whose way of life includes the use of soap, cloth, starch, scissors, sewing machines, razors and modern cosmetics." She can talk about the peoples of the South Seas as if everyone now knows about them, and to some extent, everyone does, due to her own travels and books.

Nothing, no matter how seemingly insignificant, escapes her notice and avoids being used to make some kind of point. She can talk of what snapshots mean to a family to recall pleasant times, or how Christmas and the Western New Year have become universal holidays. She can connect the fourteenth-century Portuguese explorer Prince Henry the Navigator to the American astronauts as equally brave and daring men adventuring into the unknown. Everything fits into her grand view of the world, of the cosmos, as one vast global society coming into being, made up of parts and pieces of thousands of smaller societies whose children all, almost as one child, have leaped through the invisible but very real time zone demarcated by the first atomic bombs exploded in 1945.

The 1960's are a time of special importance for her, because it is in this period, troubled by the Vietnamese War, campus riots, the growing use of drugs and the flaring independence of the young, that she comes out squarely in support of the new generations, without alienating too many of the older generations; her streams of consciousness imprisoned in *Redbook*'s pages surely helped quiet some of the fears of parents and grandparents.

In one of her earliest columns she points out that "today's children are the first generation to grow up in a world that has the power to destroy itself." Three years later, in 1965, she emphasizes that the youth riots that are sweeping the world are not the youthful pranks of the past but something else entirely, caused by many new factors, and that adults must share a large part of the blame.

"Large-scale youthful rioting cannot succeed without adult provocation and connivance." Adults have made frightful conditions in the world, she says. "Present-day youthful rioting is essentially a drama, a dramatic expression of the tensions within the individual who, wherever he may be, feels hemmed in and powerless to move or get his hand on the reins. . . . With one voice we urge young people to assert themselves, however meaninglessly, while with another voice we tell them—and ourselves—that the performance is carried out in vain." But in another column she can express the idea that youth ought to shape up: that one of the best things for all of them would be a period of national service, good for the nation and the individual alike.

So she goes on, to talk about city planning, gypsies, trial marriages—she thinks a temporary marriage ought to be attempted before a formal marriage is agreed upon, but reader reaction makes her revise her opinions—birth control, the American family, the nature of the policeman (whether he seems fearful or friendly), small-town neighborliness, the space program, nudism (she seems to be in favor of some nudity but is actually ambiguous about it), aggressive behavior, and so on, all in an easy, informative, conversational manner. She is rarely caustic or sarcastic, but from time to time she can take a swipe at the American family. Its plastic, artificial qualities bother Mead, after her experiences in the South Pacific. One of her favorite targets is the American male, and her views of this unfortunate creature deserve a direct quotation.

What does the American man expect in a wife? Probably more than has been expected by any other husband in history. If the American wife fulfills his hopes, however, her rewards are supposed to be great. . . . Her husband will try to come home every evening and never go out on the town with his friends. He will spend his nights in strange cities telephoning to her. He will try never to accept an invitation or take a vacation that doesn't include her. He will carry the biggest life-insurance policy he can afford. He will help every evening and on weekends, even with a newborn baby. He will carry all her heavy packages. He will try to remember to bring her flowers and small presents and never to give her cause for serious jealousy. . . . He will, in short, be one of the most devoted husbands the world has ever seen—mass-produced by the thousands and safely indistinguishable from every other husband.

That was written in 1962, a period of relative quiet—a few articles, a few seminars, no books. But a year later she is involved in another great project, grander than any she had ever attempted before. Theodore Schwartz, her assistant on the second trip to Manus, proposes a return to the Admiralties, his object being a survey of the twenty different languages spoken in the group. She plans an extended expedition. Even by the painstaking standards of current fieldwork, it is a detailed, ambitious program.

Mead, who is now sixty-two, an age when many elderly Americans are taking early Social Security benefits, lays out a three-year program, during which she will make three visits to the South Pacific. The field trip will culminate in a TV program shot by a National Educational Television crew, filming the ways in which this tiny Melanesian world on Manus has rejected its past to become a part of her Global Village.

"I live neck deep in the past," Mead announces when she arrives at Peré in 1964. Again she has a house to herself; Schwartz, with his new wife Lola, is next door in another house. She finds that one of the children who had worked for her as a houseboy in 1928 has come to reminisce about the past. He is Lokus (formerly Loponiu), and he is about thirteen years younger than she, but "I feel him as frail and old and his hearing and eyesight are going."

In 1964, in the great central square of the new Peré on Manus, Margaret Mead, accompanied by the inevitable crowd of inquisitive children, stops to make notes. By the time of this trip to Manus, Mead's third, she is accepted as a member of the village and is treated like one of the respected elders.

The entire Manus society is still changing together. It has not been merely a breaking away by one generation, the young, as happened in the West, but an entire people, young, old, middle-aged, men and women, who as a tribe decided to modernize. People who before the war would never have dared sail too far from the sight of land or from the known currents and wave swells, or at night, are now flying in jets.

Dozens of the young people are abroad studying or teaching or holding government posts. Paliau, who was responsible for the new Manus, is now a respected figure at Port Moresby, the new capital of the New Guinea territories. More people are taking Western names, and a new word—"worried"—has crept into the language.

The village itself is open to the outside world. Some houses have rooms set aside with a table, chairs, a bed (the Manus sleep on the floor). Pictures of rock stars hang on the walls: The Beatles, Dylan, the Stones and Baez are no more foreign to the young Manus than they are to young Americans. But there are also changes people don't like to see. Pokanau is growing old, though he is still known as the wise man of the village. He is the one who remembers the warring past, and today he is anxious that his knowledge be taken down on tape so that the Manus of the future will know their history. His sight is failing, but he can still see faraway stars. All his contemporaries have died. In the distant past it was a rare individual who saw the birth of a son's children. Now Pokanau has witnessed the birth of twin great-granddaughters.

The drama of independence, enacted all over the world, from Indonesia to India and Pakistan to Africa and the Pacific islands, is being symbolized in Manus. What was once rebellious and subversive is now legalized, honored.

Mead can now note that Manus is a model for what is happening in the great Global Village, for good and bad. She approves of searching for new knowledge, education and foreign experience, of the desire to participate in world affairs, for the Manus have a strong sense of their own worth. But she can also worry over some of the effects of participation in the world outside.

Paliau, like some others, suffers from "modernization." She notes that he is a member of the New Guinea Parliament, which is working toward statehood, and in 1966 during her stay he is elected president of the Manus Council. Though Paliau might be a political genius, and largely responsible for the progress at Manus, his role is being undermined by lesser men and women. His progress is compromised by his poor English, and the world is being run with English as the lingua franca. Other, younger New Guineans, better educated, fluent in English, challenge him, threaten his leadership. Without English a man cannot communicate with the tribe on the adjoining islands or on the other side of the mountain. Mead sees that Paliau is handicapped even though his integration of the Admiralty Archipelago stands as a monument to his organizing ability.

Still Mead is pleased at the progress she sees. In the council halls at Peré and Port Moresby young people trained as teachers, nurses, clerks, interpreters, accountants and government workers are taking their places in the new government. As happens in virtually every society where there has been a revolution, violent or peaceful, there comes a time, a generation or two later, when the young take over from the Old Guard.

If the Manus were capable of such major changes, what might have happened to the Iatmul? It is a question that interests Mead. Her fellow anthropologist Rhoda Métraux spends a year in planning a trip to the Sepik to investigate the Iatmul at Tambunam, where Bateson and Mead had worked in 1938. What had been heard about Tambunam was not encourag-

ing. During World War II the men's ceremonial house had
been bombed. In early 1967 floods temporarily wiped out
many gardens and destroyed innumerable coconut trees.
Curio hunters were looting the people of their ancient heritage of sacred objects, the masks, drums and carvings that
were the sanctified tools of their worship. Moreover, how did
the younger people, now being educated in the newly
founded schools, react to their head-hunting, war-loving elders, with their endless ceremonies and obscure rituals? Was
there anything left to honor? Or had all been swept away by
the war and the subsequent leveling of primitive culture by
the West?

"I felt rather as if I were hurrying to a deathbed," Mead
writes, "to record the death pangs of the Tambunams, once
the fiercest, the proudest and most flamboyant people on the
Sepik."

The motor launch winds its way up the gently flowing,
muddy river to Tambunam. "But I need not have been fearful," Mead reports shortly after her arrival in June 1967. The
great houses, with their tremendous carved posts, high
pitched roofs, gables and statued eaves are still standing. No
longer able to engage in war and head-hunting—the white
administration was quite firm about stamping out such practices—the men have experienced a tremendous outburst of
creative carving. They have retained what they needed of
the past, what was important artistically, and at the same time
have selected what is useful in the present, the outboard
motors, transistor radios on which they could hear broadcasts
from all over New Guinea—especially of music—cigarette
lighters, watches and clothing. The school children are
dressed in European clothing.

These changes mean a radical transformation in the economic system. Now a European form of currency has replaced shells and dogs' teeth in exchanges. And money means

Back in Tambunam among the Iatmul in 1967, Margaret Mead confers with her principle informants, Mbaan (left) and Peter Mbetnda (right). Mbaan is an authority on tradition and language; Mbetnda, Mead's table boy on her first trip in 1938, is years later a respected and knowledgeable leader in the village.

that men either have to work as laborers or must produce objects which will bring cash rather than barter.

Rhoda Métraux, Mead's long-time collaborator and close friend, has worked with her on many other projects over the years. Métraux is an expert on Haiti and Montserrat in the West Indies. Now she is following up Gregory Bateson's 1930's work with three trips among the "new" Iatmul.

The culture is now a mixed one. The scene has changed little, however. The brown water of the Sepik flows gently or swiftly, according to the season. Across from the great houses, on the opposite bank, are the gardens, and beyond them, stretching to the horizon, are the endless marshes. The people still paddle about in their slender dugout canoes with carved crocodile prows. The newly constructed houses are exactly like the ones built sixty years earlier, when the white man was but a shadow in far-off jungles. Tambunam is still known as the handsomest village on the Sepik.

But changes are noticeable, too. As always, the little children run about naked, but now the older ones wear nylon shirts or blouses, and trousers or dirndl skirts. Many have watches and transistor radios. But like their mothers and grandmothers, the teenage girls still smoke pipes and chew the red-staining betel nut. There is a further, significant change: The Sepik is at peace. No longer is Tambunam, or any of the other villages, threatened by raiding parties from neighboring tribes. Head-hunting is a distant memory, and women are no longer captured and taken off as booty.

There is a joyful reunion, Mead and the villagers, the recollections of each other, of who is dead and who alive, of gossip and memories. Almost immediately Mead and Métraux are asked an unexpected question: Do they have a tape recorder? The Iatmul want their heritage taken down for posterity. So every evening the people come to sing, to chant the old, old war songs and ceremonial rituals and to play their bamboo instruments and drums, listening to what they have just recorded, praising, analyzing and criticizing. The Iatmul have a new stage for their beloved expression of the dramatic.

A man who remembers the past in vivid terms announces, "I will now sing the song we used to sing when the heads of the slain were lined up in the men's house." And after the last soft, haunting notes have died away, enshrined in the plastic tape that makes no judgments, he remarks casually, "Yes, my youngest son is away at school. He is studying to be a doctor."

The Tambunam see not only the old ways within themselves, but the new as well. They can encompass both, without destroying their heritage. They see before them a larger world, of which they and their past are a part, but a world in which they hope their children's future will be different from their own. The older generation lacks the skills for the world beyond the Sepik. But their children, now learning to read and write, will have other opportunities. A villager who spans both generations, the man who brought the first of the Tambunam to their new school, talks to Métraux of the day when "all men, black men and white men, will walk along one road together, sit down together and eat together like brothers."

Despite the continuity of the past that she can see in the Manus and Iatmul, Mead dares not hope for a continuity in her own life. She fears that her inability to bear children easily will be repeated in her daughter, Cathy. In 1960 Cathy marries a young engineer, Barkev Kassarjian, of Armenian ancestry. Like her mother, Cathy wants to combine a career with motherhood.

Mead is concerned about the marriage—perhaps even about marriage as an institution, with three abortive ones behind her. She says, perhaps with Reo in mind, that she rather carefully tried not to "think too much about the kind of father my son-in-law would be." Yet because of her own

Margaret Mead's granddaughter, Sevanne Margaret (called Vanni), with her father, Barkev Kasserjian, and her mother Catherine Bateson. Mead is proud to note that "through no act of my own I had become biologically related to a new human being."

experiences with Grandma Mead she wants to be a "re-source," though she believes that Cathy should be able to lead her life independently. In 1947, in the last poem she ever published, Mead had told Cathy, then eight:

> That I be not a restless ghost
> Who haunts your footsteps as they pass
>
> . . .
>
> You must be free to take a path
> Whose end I feel no need to know . . .

But clearly Mead does feel a need to know. She is concerned about Cathy's choice of husband, but she accepts the fact that Barkev is Cathy's mate, not hers, and forces her mind to thinking of what this man with the long Armenian heritage means to her fair-haired daughter of English and American parents, the latter also of English ancestry. Mead seems to be revealing an unsuspected bias here, but she states, "It was an added delight, then, to discover that I enjoyed him very much." She can appreciate "his analytical mind, his keen enjoyment of all the concrete details of life, his sensitive regard for persons and lively respect for the nature of things."

Dark-haired, dark-eyed Barkev Kassarjian meets Mead's approval and becomes—in 1960—a member of her family. The Kassarjians' first child, Martin, born while the couple are living in the Philippines, lives only a few hours. At last, however, in 1969, Cathy successfully bears another child, a daughter named Sevanne Margaret, called Vanni. Now Mead can see the continuity of the future. "I suddenly realized that through no act of my own I had become biologically related to a new human being."

The term "biologically related" might seem too coldly scientific to many people but Mead experiences its human joys, too. "As a new grandmother, I began both to relive my own daughter's infancy and to observe the manifestations of temperament in the tiny creature." As with her mother and grandmother, dual roles are still in operation, those of mother and worker. As a grandmother Mead is extra conscientious: She states she experiences none of the freedom from responsibility that grandmothers are supposed to have. It appears that her obligation to be a resource but not an interference is every bit as demanding now as when Cathy was a baby. In summing up, it is both as a scientist and as a woman who has experienced all three of the major roles—child, mother and grandmother—that she can say—plead—that "everyone needs to have access to both grandparents and grandchildren in order to be a full human being." She adds, "Seeing a child as one's grandchild, one can visualize that same child as a grandparent, and with the eyes of another generation one can see other children. . . ."

She is thinking of her own world, with its generation gaps, its hostilities between parents and children, between parents and grandparents, when she says this. But at the same time it applies to what is happening in Manus, for again that microcosm of change is experiencing another upheaval, like the earlier ones, unexpected. Here grandparents and children are being resources to each other, in ways that charm Mead as a human being and thrill her as a scientist. Life in Manus, one sees, is both linear and cyclical: One goes straight in order to return.

The year is now 1975. Mead has made two quick trips to the South Pacific since her extended expeditions of the 1960's, minor jaunts in 1971 and 1973. Another checking-up seems to be in order, requiring some major work. She arrives in the village of Peré in mid-1975. There seems to be a great psychic reward in her repeated visits, something that satisfies her sense of history and confirms her need for "continuity." In a letter home written shortly after her arrival she says:

> I am most conscious of the enormous sense of continuity as I look at old men whom I knew as children and see the grandfathers' faces reflected in their descendents. The shared memories, the shared experiences bind them together in a web that is stronger than the ancestral ghosts they fear if they do not send money and gifts home to parents who put in hard work to rear them.

Nearly half a century has passed since Mead and Reo Fortune visited Manus. Of all the adults living there half a century ago, only the two foreigners, the tiny American and the tempestuous New Zealander, are still alive. Pokanau, the "lawyer man," their best informant and the repository of the tribe's traditions, has recently died, the last Manus to have witnessed the arrival of the strange white couple on the beach at Peré.

A curious turn of events has taken place at Peré, Mead notes. Just as in America many children or grandchildren of immigrants have taken a new interest in the lands their parents left and the culture they so often rejected in an effort to be truly American (even to the extent of anglicizing their names and abandoning customs, religion and foods), so too have the young Manus begun to wonder about their past. No longer are there elders to tell the people how things "were always done," to keep alive the heritage of music, ritual and custom. But, unlike many small societies (and even larger ones) that have made a transition from a primitive world to a modern world, the Manus have a thorough record of the old days. Their past life is excellently described in the popular, still-in-print book, *Growing Up in New Guinea*, and in a number of technical papers (Mead's "Kinship, in the Admiralty

Islands," "An Investigation of the Thought of Primitive Children with Special Reference to Animism," and Fortune's "Manus Religion"), the literature from the 1953 trip (Mead's *New Lives for Old*, Theodore Schwartz's *The Paliau Movement*), and the thousands of photographs, the documentary films, even the drawings done by the children under Mead's persuasion. And then others have also studied the Manus, so there is no lack of information about their past and their recent history.

However, the Manus now have some basic questions they want answered. Have they thrown out too much? Have they gone too far into the modern world? Mead, in her trip to Peré in 1975, is to find a new Manus, one she had expected no more than the one she had found in 1953.

Continued observation of a single culture over an extended period is rare in anthropology. Mead's first return to Manus in 1953 was itself unusual, and her subsequent trips back to the island produced ethnological research unlike anything else ever done. Each voyage since the very beginning has been one of discovery. In 1975 she notes changes that no one could ever have anticipated. For the Manus, having deliberately rejected much of their own culture and systematically accepted Western civilization on a very pragmatic basis, picking and choosing what they thought would work—in a Manus context—now reject parts of the new world and deliberately seek to reintegrate elements of the old Manus culture.

In 1975 the entire area, not only Manus but all the islands within the New Guinea archipelago, has become an independent state, Papua New Guinea. The new nation has been self-governing since September. When Mead stops at Port Moresby, the capital of the new nation, she encounters a number of people from Manus, who, like other members of once-primitive tribal groups, are now holding important positions. One man from Manus is the new chancellor of the University of Papua New Guinea; another Manus man is the minister of housing for the nation; she meets another young Manus who is on his way to the United States to study comparative literature.

On Manus itself, at the new provincial capital of Lorengau, she meets a young poet, the first from Manus; he is teaching creative writing at the local high school. Another young man, who had gone to Chicago to study for the priesthood, has returned home to put his energies into more secular work; he is in charge of dredging a polluted channel.

In the villages there is a practical alliance of old and new. Plywood is being used alongside traditional planks and palm thatch. Such Westernization in daily life is to be expected. What is significant is the return to prewhite traditions.

Ancient Manus customs have resurfaced. The old practice of validating marriages by the exchanges of goods through "the side of the man" and "the side of the woman" has been restored, except that in 1975, in place of sago, fish, pigs, oil and goods traded from other tribes, the exchanges are effected through European goods and gambling winnings in European currency. And where dogs' teeth and shells had been basic to family exchanges at a wedding, now cash alone could be the basis of validation.

Old ceremonies are again being practiced; dances, songs and oratory in the old style have become popular. And the drums, which during the postwar period had been made of cast-off torpedo casings, are again being carved in the ancient slit wooden gong style. And while a woman might wear a Western brassiere but no blouse, she has returned to the traditional multicolored grass skirt, having abandoned the famous Mother Hubbard imposed by missionaries.

Deeper reforms can be observed too. In the late 1920's, when Mead and her husband had first visited the Manus, the young men expressed their new rebelliousness against the control of their elders by going off to work on plantations and refusing to send their wages home. Now the young men, like their fathers and grandfathers, still go away to work but insist that if they send their earnings back to the villages, the money must be wisely invested. And some of the young men who had aspirations to an entirely different way of life and had gone away for education, to the main island of New Guinea or to a foreign country, are now returning home to resume the hereditary ways of trading and fishing, ways which some young people had even despised for a while as being too "native."

A new consciousness has developed in Manus. It is still an integrated society, and just as it has moved into the twentieth century as a unit, it is now moving into its new "true" self as a unit. After she returns home, Mead can remark that she has been fortunate in witnessing a primitive people's emergence out of the bleak, limited milieu of the Stone Age into an almost total absorption in Western ways, and then a final balancing between the best of both. Mead remarks in *Natural History* magazine:

> The extreme emphasis on modernization and rejection of the characteristics of an earlier period were now gone. The society was still distinctively Manus, but with a new sense of identity, ready to combine the old and the new. I realized how little we had been able to learn when we used to study a people only once, and how illuminating and unique was this opportunity to follow the same population—a microcosm of the world—for forty-seven years, as they

fanned out into the wider world, but retained the core of their culture at home.

The Manus are a kind of touchstone for Mead. But she does not limit herself to them, though they are the core of her work, of her deepest thoughts. Planes have made anthropological work easier, and Mead travels constantly, and whatever she sees is with an anthropologist's eye.

A visit to Rhoda Métraux in Montserrat in the West Indies in 1966 gives her a quick study of a Caribbean village; a trip to see the Schwartzes, at work in a Mexican village, not only enables her to view Latin American village life in capsule form but to see displaced villagers in Mexico City's slums with the help of Oscar Lewis, who has specialized in that aspect of anthropology. On other trips here and there she can stop off at a desert settlement in Saudi Arabia to note the ways in which nomadic Arabs adapt to their environment, and then spend two weeks at a kibbutz in Israel, make a trip to a reserve for aboriginals in Australia, visit Iran where she observes nomads on a market day. Even when she is forced to make stopovers on long trips she does not waste idle hours in hotels or in shopping: In South Africa, with a few hours to spare, she rushes off to a native village, and in Japan a day in a traditional Japanese village with a Japanese anthropologist gives her more insights into the nature of people and their ways of living. Whatever exists, whatever is, goes into her head, to be stored and retrieved when the proper time comes. Not a moment is wasted: Waiting out a rainy day in Montserrat she reads *Encounter, Counterpart* and *Transaction* magazines, Kenneth Read's *The High Valley* (a book about the highlands of New Guinea), Chow's *Social Mobility in China* and Goveia's *Slave Society in the British Leeward Islands at the End of the Eighteenth Century.*

Mead has an intense memory: She can recall sights,

scents, sounds from her childhood, so she can speak knowingly of what it is like to be a child. She has been in love
and has married men of promise and talent and has been
three times divorced. She suffered the tragedies of miscarriages but had a child, and after her, a grandchild. She has
seen savage lands as well as American suburbs and city
life. She can speak knowingly to people of all ages. Her
immense knowledge and experience, her compassion and
understanding, make it possible for her to talk of what is
shared in common by jungle tribes, highly civilized Balinese, and twentieth-century Westerners. Her interest is
what is held in common, but she is also as aware of what is
diverse and different, and of everyone's right to a very
personal independent life.

All experience seems to fall within her grasp. The cry of a
jungle baby heard in 1930 is as vivid to her as the nighttime
cries of her daughter and granddaughter. The death of old
informants in Samoa is as close as the more recent deaths of
her own parents. All life is awake to her, throbbing to be
heard, and she listens, records, writes, photographs and
speaks. She is absorbed with life, absorbed with the continuity
of life, and absorbed in the ways in which each person works
out his or her life. Certain elements are passed down from
one generation to another, but they also repeat, return, in
order to lend depth to human growth. Patterns, traits, customs, traditions surface again and again to give strength to
life.

Her memory can go back to her grandparents, and beyond
that to what she has been told of *their* grandparents. And now
she is projecting into the future, wondering about granddaughter Vanni's grandchildren. It is a tremendous span of
life and Mead is in the center of it, with her fingers on every
throb of humanity's pulse, her notebooks and tape recorders
and cameras ready to analyze, imprint and remember what

her vast slice of humanity has done and said.

Old age interests her along with birth. Approaching a biblical span of years, she can look at her own lifetime with scientific curiosity and objectivity. She can recall her own angers at her father, her impatience with her mother. But all of these adolescent attitudes are tempered by her recollection of both parents in their last years, as she sees them—almost like a speeded-up film—progress from the active, exciting, involved young couple of her childhood into middle age with its slowing down and the final, almost static years of old age. By the late 1940's she had become aware that they had indeed grown old and that the end was near. "The way in which one's parents grow old matters a great deal," she believes. Her mother, who had a stroke, fought to recover. Her father's personality remained intact and his mind stayed keen and fresh, alert to whatever was new and interesting. Then, in a surprising reassessment of the influences upon her early life, she decides that it was her father, more than her mother or even Grandma Mead, who had been most important, "who defined for me my place in the world."

"Watching a parent grow is one of the most reassuring experiences anyone can have," she says, "a privilege that comes only to those whose parents live beyond their children's early adulthood." Emily Mead died in 1950 but her husband survived her another six years. He continued to develop and mature until the end. Mead remarks that, when she gave a seminar shortly before his death, he, rather than the young people, asked the most searching questions. And she is proud to state that he gave up his earlier racial prejudices and also came to accept such new institutions as Social Security and other social programs which he had once opposed as government interference in private life.

She adds, "I have been fortunate in being able to look up

to my parents' minds well past my middle years." They, too, as well as Grandma Mead, were resources.

As a grandmotherly resource herself and as a scientist, her work goes on. Mead, having served the American Museum of Natural History as a curator of various kinds for forty-two years, is made Curator Emeritus in 1969. The books, articles, reviews continue in profusion. The United States Congress, the United Nations, public and private institutions and organizations and NASA, call on her for advice, seminars, speeches. She is a visiting professor here and there, a consultant in the social sciences, chairwoman and chairperson of numerous organizations and committees, each job or honor alone worth a lifetime of work.

The writer Gail Sheehy (in an article in *New York* magazine) asked how she could fit together so many lives. "You certainly had to make some sacrifices and compromises along the way," said Ms. Sheehy about Mead's combining career and motherhood and doing so much with each.

"Yes," Ms. Sheehy reports her as saying. "Because I have enough energy to do two jobs. For my generation, to have even one child and a career took a tremendous amount of energy. Which I had. . . . And I understand the culture well enough to study and, in a sense, to outwit it."

But Mead is being modest here. It takes a full-time "bibliographer" on her staff to get the facts of her life in order—the trips, the publications, the events, the titles, the positions, the honors—but sorting things out consumes years, and a final compilation is not ready until the winter of 1976, the time of her seventy-fifth birthday. An interviewer at the time calls Mead "an industrious conglomerate." Her assistants—four hard-working young women serving their apprenticeships as anthropologists—refer to her as "the General."

A doctoral candidate at the Massachusetts Institute of

Wherever she goes, Margaret Mead is surrounded by young people eager to hear her encouraging messages on "Growing Up" and "Coming of Age." Here she takes time out from a World Population Conference sponsored by the United Nations to talk to teenage questioners in Bucharest, Romania.

Technology, Rae Goddell, points out that Mead is one of a handful of "visible scientists" who play an extraordinary role in communicating their latest views on important issues, even though the subjects are often outside the scientists' chosen field. Circumventing traditional scientific channels of communication—the technical paper published (or buried) in an academic journal would be one—these scientists go straight to the public with their opinions on such subjects as environment, energy, race and I.Q., war and population. Miss Goddell had examined forty major figures, putting eight in the first rank, one of whom is Mead (the others are Isaac Asimov, Barry Commoner, Paul Ehrlich, Linus Pauling, Glenn Seaborg, William Shockley and B.F. Skinner). A controversial, colorful, issue-oriented figure is her opinion of Mead, as of the others. The public sees the scientists credibly, for they have long-established reputations, and can speak out in language the average person can understand. Thus Mead (as with the other "visible" scientists) is a "resource" for the public, for Americans and for the world, just as she is for Cathy and Vanni.

The Old Turtle

WHAT OF MEAD HERSELF, STILL active in her seventies, still hopping off on trips, after half a century in the Pacific and at home, in which she had combined the old and the new, had crossed rural frontiers into the nuclear, electronic age, had become a member of the Global Village? Now truly an "old turtle"—it is an image she referred to several times in her writings, for it pleased her—she could sum up her career on the celebration of her seventy-fifth birthday with humor and insight.

"Sooner or later I'm going to die," she told Laurie Johnston of *The New York Times,* sounding as if she didn't mean it, for she seemed a lot more durable than the brownstone mass of the Museum where she was speaking, "but I'm not going to retire." She appeared to be indestructible.

The Museum seemed to agree, for it established a Margaret Mead Fund for the Advancement of Anthropology. Some five million dollars are to be raised; she is the key figure in the activities. Five million dollars!—and she went on her first field trip funded by a mere $450 doled out piecemeal. The money will endow a Margaret Mead Chair of Anthropology at the Museum, finance research scholars and help preserve, reorganize and "edit" the Museum's collection, and will reopen the

Hall of the Pacific, which Mead long ago assembled. Almost enough to keep Mead busy, but not quite, for she had her seminars, trips here and there, appearances before august bodies of scientists, academics and legislators, as well as playing a role model—self-sufficient, understanding, noncriticizing, being open and helpful, a resource—for Vanni and thousands of other young people looking for someone in the older generations who knew what it was like to grow up, who could speak in calm terms about adolescence, drugs, education, sex, conflicts with parents, war, the environment, generation gaps, shared futures arising from the dichotomous past.

She maintained a busy schedule, spending less time in her Museum cave, and doing much office work from her apartment on Central Park West, a few blocks from the Museum. She would arise at five, no matter how late she had come home the night before from a trip or a lecture or a rare evening with friends, to go over stacks of mail that she would annotate for her secretaries, skim through magazines and books, sign letters and approve (but rarely reject) applications from students for grants. The entire pile would be stuffed into shopping bags and left outside her door, where one of the assistants would pick it up and take it to the "cave," returning at the end of the day with another pile. The process would be repeated five times a week.

During the day she might drop by the Museum for a short while, or take a plane to Washington, or some other city, for a lecture or a meeting; she liked to return home the same day if possible. Her personal interests seemed to have been reduced to Cathy and Vanni. Her lingering emotions about the three men she had married seemed faint; she was resentful of Reo Fortune, but tolerant of Bateson, with whom she might share a speaking engagement. More often she could be humorous and deprecating about all three. "All my marriages were interesting—they were all endogamous," she said to

Laurie Johnston, explaining for the uninitiated, "That means, 'within the group.' " She had an interesting view of what had happened. "It wasn't so much that they didn't work out—they got used up. They were like theatrical marriages, when the two play opposite each other on a stage."

An interesting view, which might have stood some examination in *Sex and Temperament,* her analysis of South Seas male and female roles.

Her views were always very positive. The world is an active, encouraging place. One sees it with enthusiasm. Growing Up. Coming of Age. A Way of Seeing. New Lives for Old. Growth and Culture.

Positive views. The world is becoming a unit. The Global Village. We have crossed a divide, a watershed in history marked by World War II. The parents, the grandparents came from isolated cultures, unrelated societies. Papa Franz Boas had long ago demolished the belief that society stems from a common origin. Before the watershed all is diverse, after, all is one. The new generations are linked together by music, political ideas, blue jeans, a yearning for freedom, by eight visible scientists. By Margaret Mead.

Often she was asked what she would choose to do if she had her life to live over again.

"About this there is no doubt in my mind. I would elect to be an anthropologist."

Up to the end of her life Mead worked and traveled, advised, wrote, lectured, planned for the future. More trips to the Pacific, always if possible with a stopover at Manus, to see what the people, collectively or alone, had done. No trip was too far, none too esoteric. She visited Cathy and Vanni and son-in-law Barkev in Iran, where they were teaching.

The trip was no more fatiguing than hopping off to Washington to testify before, or lecture to, a congressional committee.

For a long time she relied upon her staff to handle details, work out plans for her. She had seen so much, thought so much, observed so much, analyzed so much, written so much, that in her last years she threw out all but the essential. Her assistants plotted the minutiae of daily life for her, moved her about on her travels, gave her cards each day with schedules. Her mind was on other things. She might claim from time to time that her memory was failing, but she seemed to have total recall for every fall of a leaf in the jungle, every nuance of faces from Museum halls to Bali. The problem may have been that in her seventies she suffered from information overload, like an overworked computer that has been programmed with too many details of primitive, advanced and industrial societies, languages, ways of sitting, speaking, dancing, forms of etiquette in addressing tribal chiefs and heads of state. Too much to remember, perhaps.

She was one of the great figures on our horizon, tying the rites and rituals of Stone Age ex-cannibals to the rites and rituals of technological men and women, seeing the common humanity in all, envisioning a shared future for the slim brown-skinned children of Manus and the Sepik and the white-skinned children of the West, communicating not only through English (which they all seemed to be learning now) but through rock and funk, blue jeans and *Mad,* wall posters and transistors.

To the end, the old turtle, crossing the seas of the world by jet, by canoe, here and there, Manus, Iran, Bali, the Sepik, India, London, Africa, to wherever there was work to do, something to note, something to say, an observation to record. The death drums beat too early. When they sounded again, the deep rumble could only have been an echo.

"Sooner or later I'm going to die," Mead had said. Had she a forewarning of the terrible, sudden cancer that was to strike her down? She seemed indestructible, enduring, a rock. An institution. More permanent than the massive Museum walls that were her home. I wrote this book while Mead was still alive, travelling, lecturing, talking, speaking out, giving opinions and pronouncements, spanning generations and continents alike with formidable ease. The death of the great, as well as of relative and friend, often may come as a personal blow. I had lived with this biographical portrait a long time, from the moment that I had realized that Margaret Mead would be an interesting subject for a book—I had been doing research for a trip to the South Pacific, where I studied a Cargo Cult in the New Hebrides similar to the one that Paliau had initiated in Manus. I could see Mead's greatnesses, and some of her faults. The latter I often overlooked: This is a book not about her lapses but her successes. In retrospect I think she was not an easy person. She stood too far above the heads of others to bend. She had talents that most of us lack. She could see from a distance, a grand view with a 360° arc; at the same time she could discover microscopic significant details that linked cultures, civilizations, families, races, tribes, communities and nations. Close up with people she could be very difficult; some of her personal relationships ended in disaster. A few of her friends had remarked that she never, or rarely, had to suffer the private torments that many people experience, and that she was unable to understand that sometimes situations and circumstances overpower lesser mortals. Mead conquered where others succumbed. Moreover, she was blessed with good fortune and success: She always could draw upon the money and resources for her work; she was never denied funds for a project or an expedition, while other workers languished because they were unable to obtain financing in order to undertake valuable projects. Mead seemed to have little need of monetary rewards; her rewards came in the form of public recognition, though academic approval was never as great as might have been expected. Her formidable talents brought much opposition from her less gifted peers. Yet I am sure it was Margaret Mead, taking off from the foundations laid by Franz Boas and Ruth Benedict, who changed anthropology from a minor and neglected science into the popular subject it has become.

In writing the early chapters I felt that the role of her husbands in her success has been underplayed. She was married to two exceptional men during a crucial period in her career, in her twenties and thirties, an age when the basis for great reputations is founded. Both Reo Fortune and Gregory Bateson have never received as much recognition as I think they deserved for their part in Mead's life. Personally, I liked that eccentric, sometimes abrasive, character, Reo Fortune, and people who read the manuscript of the book have commented on it. Mead, carrying on age-old arguments, disliked my sympathies for him when she was shown the text before it went into production; Bateson, too, whose range and scope of interests surpassed Fortune's, is an amazing and talented figure who deserves wider credit and fame.

Mead was fortunate in the breadth of her life, which included a vanishing rural America and the technological space age, the most primitive of archaic societies and the most advanced of the modern. No one, I think, has been so articulate in binding such disparate cultures into one global view.

In the vast hall of her home base, The American Museum of Natural History, Margaret Mead poses for photographer Ken Heyman with her New Guinea forked stick, a symbol of authority. The stick, which she always carries in her later years, has come to be a kind of primitive magic for Mead.

Selected Bibliography

MARGARET MEAD HAS BEEN AN extremely prolific writer, but it was not until 1976 that a complete bibliography of her works was drawn up. Though she has some eighteen "popular" books to her credit, many of her writings are highly technical and beyond the scope of the average reader; most of her papers appeared in academic journals with extremely limited circulations, and are virtually impossible to locate outside a specialized library. However, most of her books written for the general public are kept in print in various hardcover and paperback editions, and can usually be found in good libraries and bookstores. Some works, like *Coming of Age in Samoa* and *Growing Up in New Guinea*, have been reprinted in so many editions that it is difficult to know which are in print at the moment. Others of her books are less widely reprinted.

Though Mead is a national, even international, figure, there is little writing about her, except for reviews of her books, critiques in academic journals, and a few popular articles. The primary sources for her life are her own works, especially *Blackberry Winter* and *Letters from the Field 1925–1975*. *Blackberry Winter* is available in both hardcover (Morrow) and paperback (Simon & Schuster) editions. The autobiography covers the years of her life up to World War II, with some afterthoughts about her daughter Cathy and granddaughter Vanni. There are many memorable passages about her parents and the continuity she sees in her own child and grandchild, but some of the material is hastily written, as if she were dictating on the run. *Letters from the Field*, also available in both hardcover and paperback (Harper & Row), fills out with much humor and detailed information and local color what is only sketched in the autobiographical accounts of the field trips.

Mead's first two books, *Coming of Age in Samoa* and *Growing Up in New Guinea*, are definitely her best and should be read. The first title is the one that made her famous and helped make the profession of the anthropologist both glamorous and respectable. *Growing Up in New Guinea* is her account of the Manus whom she visited in 1928 (and did not expect to see again). It should be read with *New Lives for Old*, the work in which she tells what happened to the tribe in the twenty-five years after her first field trip to their island. Unfortunately, the follow-up work lacks the conciseness and vividness of the initial work, though the material is far more dramatic, since it deals with a people who have rejected the past, survived a major war and deliberately moved into the modern world.

Two works deal with her favorite subject, the differences between male and female and what causes them. They are *Sex and Temperament in Three Primitive Societies* and *Male and Female: A Study of the Sexes in a Changing World*. The first title analyzes sexual types among men and women as she saw them among the Arapesh, the Mundugumor and the Tchambuli; the latter includes these tribes and a number of other societies, including American. Both works seem highly subjective, some points get lost and several conclusions are not clear.

A Way of Seeing is a collection of her wide-ranging columns from *Redbook* magazine. Here she is at her most grandmotherly, but she is also calm and often makes it seem that her viewpoint is the right one, which it may be at times. *A Rap on Race* is the famous dialogue with the black writer James Baldwin; many well-expressed personal viewpoints but also much irrelevant material that gets in the way of the discussion.

THE HUSBANDS' WORKS

Margaret Mead's second and third husbands, Reo F. Fortune and Gregory Bateson, are both superlative anthropologists, perceptive, concise, imaginative, but not so visible to the world as she was. The books they did on field trips shared with her, or on related subjects, are worth reading, though they are harder going than Mead's work. Fortune's *Sorcerers of Dobu*, about the very formidable and dour magicians of Dobu, should be read along with her *Growing Up in New Guinea*, though it is often difficult to understand, since Reo does not compromise either with himself or the reader. Mead's *The Changing Culture of an Indian Tribe*, about her field trip to the Omaha reservation, should be accompanied by Fortune's *Omaha Secret Societies*, for they are a good example of how two scientists can see the same situation in different terms.

Bateson's *Naven* forms a trilogy with *Growing Up in New Guinea* and *Sorcerers of Dobu* in its picture of primitive societies in the Southwest Pacific. It is, like Fortune's book, a complex work and not easily finished, making many demands upon the reader. Bateson gets the major credit for *Balinese*

Character, the photo study of Bali done with Mead. The photographs are interesting but not unusual, despite Mead's pride in developing a "new" technique of presenting ideas and themes visually.

This has been a rather personal bibliography. Many of Mead's other works are available but, to many readers, of limited interest. Among them are: *And Keep Your Powder Dry* (1942), *Soviet Attitudes Toward Authority* (1951), *The Small Conference* (1968), *Culture and Commitment* (1970), *Twentieth Century Faith* (1972) and *Ruth Benedict* (1974), to list a few. Then there is Mead's favorite work, *Continuities in Cultural Evolution.*

Few books are written in isolation. I owe great debts of gratitude to my editors, Edite Kroll and Robert O. Warren of Harper & Row; to Dina S. Guha of Bombay (where the manuscript was begun); to Christopher H. Rice for some basic anthropological texts; to the staff of the Hampton Library for finding certain rare works; to Amy Bard, a member of Dr. Mead's staff; and especially to Dr. Rhoda Métraux, who twice went over the text with much patience.

Index

Adams, Léonie, 43
Admiralty Islands, 71, 75, 76, 78, 144, 165
Adolescence, 3, 10–17, 54, 58–59, 91–92
Adulthood, 70, 133
Africa, 147
Aggression, 114–15
Ambunti, 121
American Anthropological Association, 155
American Anthropologist, 90
American culture, 92–98, 138, 160–62
American Ethnological Society, 155
American Indians, 46, 49, 55, 102–6, 110, 147
American Museum of Natural History (New York), 62, 86, 94, 138, 141
  grants to Mead, 102, 110
  Maori collection, 63
  Margaret Mead Chair of Anthropology, 183
  Margaret Mead Fund for the Advancement of Anthropology, 183
Ancient Society (Morgan), 46

And Keep Your Powder Dry (Mead), 194
Anderson, Nels, 91, 98
Animism, 82
Anthropological Institute of Great Britain, 45
Anthropologist at Work, An (Mead), 158
Anthropology
  defined, 3–4
  fieldwork, 11–13
  history of, 45–48
Arapesh, 110–14, 159
Art, 82–83, 121, 127, 128, 166
Asimov, Isaac, 182
Australia, 60, 149, 150
Australian National Research Council, 65, 71

Baining, 87
Baldwin, James, 157
Bali, 126–29
Balinese Character (Bateson & Mead), 128, 193
Barnard Bulletin, The, 43
Barnard College, 41–50 *passim*
Basima, 69
Bateson, Gregory, 87–88,

Designed by Kohar Alexanian
Set in 11 pt Gael
Composed by The Haddon Craftsmen, Inc.
Printed and bound by The Murray Printing Company
HARPER & ROW PUBLISHERS, INC.